THE BOY
IN TWO MINDS

Time travel to Ancient Olympia

by

J M Newsome

The Connection Trilogy
The Boy in Two Minds
The Girl in Two Worlds
An Ancient Connection

Birkby Books

Praise for 'The Boy in Two Minds'
(third edition of 'The Boy with Two Heads')
The Connection Trilogy Book 1

"A very clever concept for time travel. … I'm loving it …!" *Caroline Lawrence*, author of *The Roman Mysteries* series and the *Time Travel Diaries*, on Twitter.

"This book transported me effortlessly back to ancient Greece, vividly evoking its exotic sights, sounds and even smells. And it seems that young people's issues have hardly changed in 2,400 years!" *Marion Clarke*, fiction editor.

"A wonderful story which brings the ancient Olympics to vibrant life. You can almost smell Greece from its pages … I was so engrossed by the story and the dramatic climax that I did not realise how much I had learnt until it was all over." *Philippa Harrison*, former Managing Director of Macmillan and Little Brown UK.

"… extremely well written, highly believable and engaging … I would love to see this book used in schools, because the aspects of every day life in Ancient Greece are so cleverly and easily portrayed here." *Fiona Robson* on Goodreads.

"This was a very engaging read. Lovers of the Grecian era will find it interesting, and the blog is a good twist." *Prudence* on Amazon.

" … a story on different levels, from different points of view. It brings ancient Greece to life, … excellent … well-researched … well-written story." *Sally Katherine Bracher* on Amazon.

" … well written with plenty smells (*sic*), intrigue and pace to keep the reader wanting to turn the next page …" *Anne Bryson* on Goodreads.

" … enthralling read, I did not want to put the book down." *Bill* on Amazon Kindle.

Also by J M Newsome

Fiction:

Maria's Dilemma (Richmond Readers, level 1)
Saturday Storm (Richmond Readers, level 2)
Nelson's Dream (CUP, Cambridge English Readers, level 6)
Winner of 2009 Language Learner Literature Award
Dragons' Eggs (CUP, Cambridge English Readers, level 5)
Winner of 2011 Language Learner Literature Award
Better Late Than Never (CUP, Cambridge English Readers, level 5)
The Connection Trilogy (Birkby Books)
1. The Boy in Two Minds
2. The Girl in Two Worlds
3. An Ancient Connection

Translation:

Europa
(Ammos Editions, Athens)
(Modern Greek to English)
Vergina: Treasures, Myths and History of Ancient Macedonia
(Ammos Editions, Athens)
(Modern Greek to English)

Contents

Ancient Athens, 430s BCE

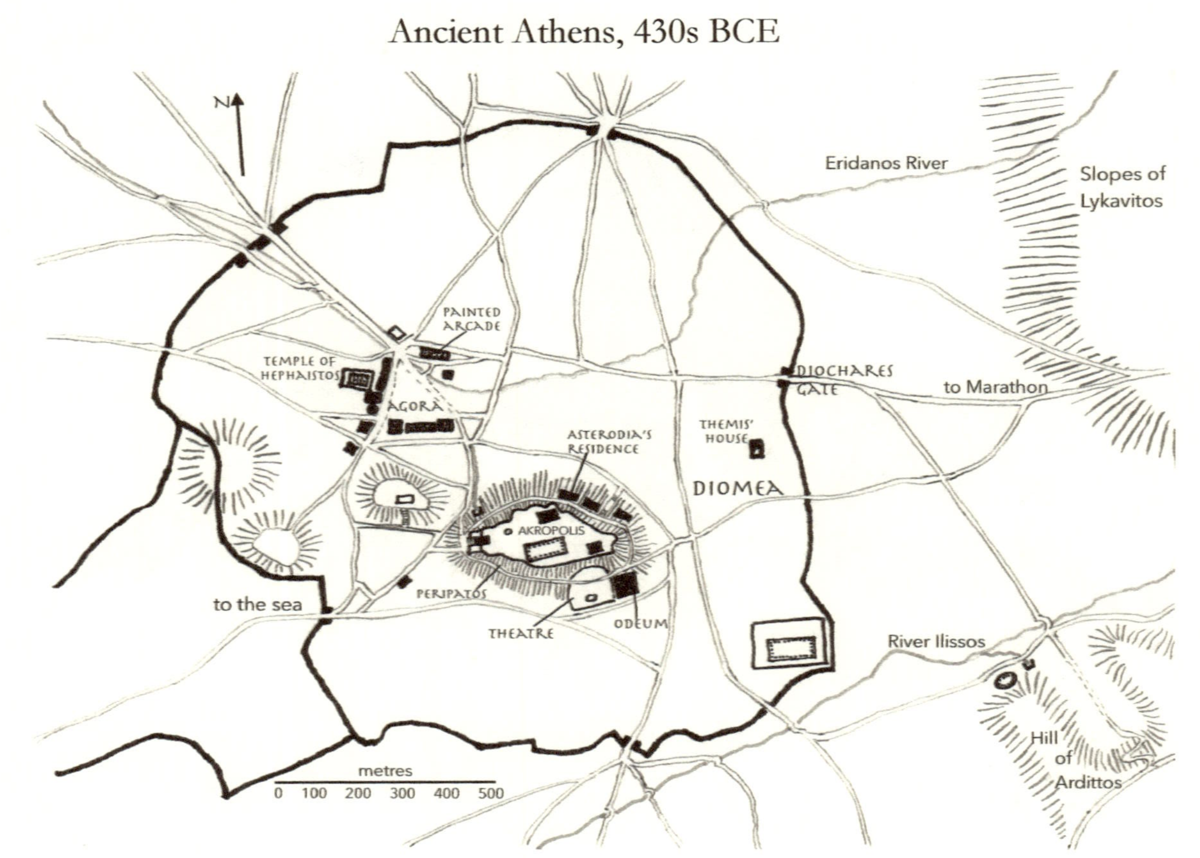

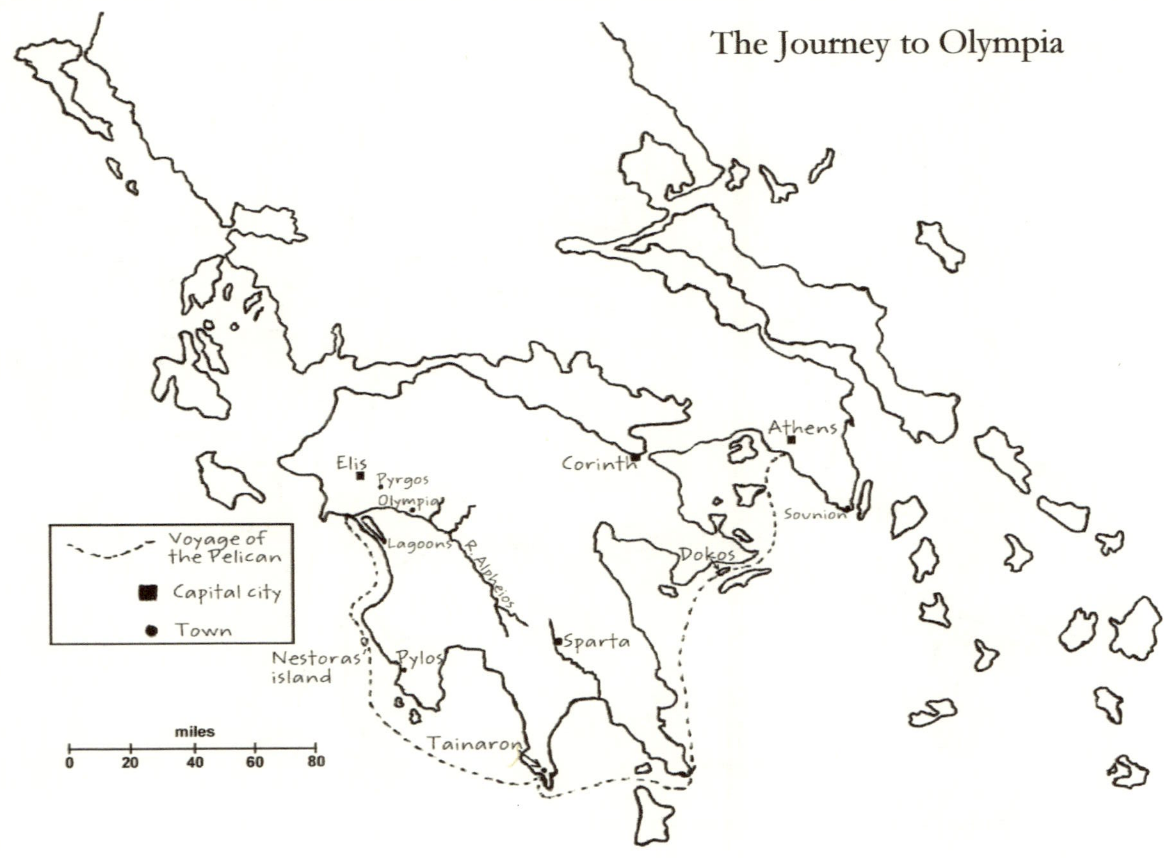

The Journey to Olympia
Athens
Corinth
Sounion
Dokos
Elis
Pyrgos
Olympia
Lagoons
R. Alpheios
Sparta
Nestoras' island
Pylos
Tainaron
Voyage of the Pelican
Capital city
Town
miles
0   20   40   60   80

The Holy Precinct (Altis) of Zeus and Hera and its surroundings at Ancient Olympia

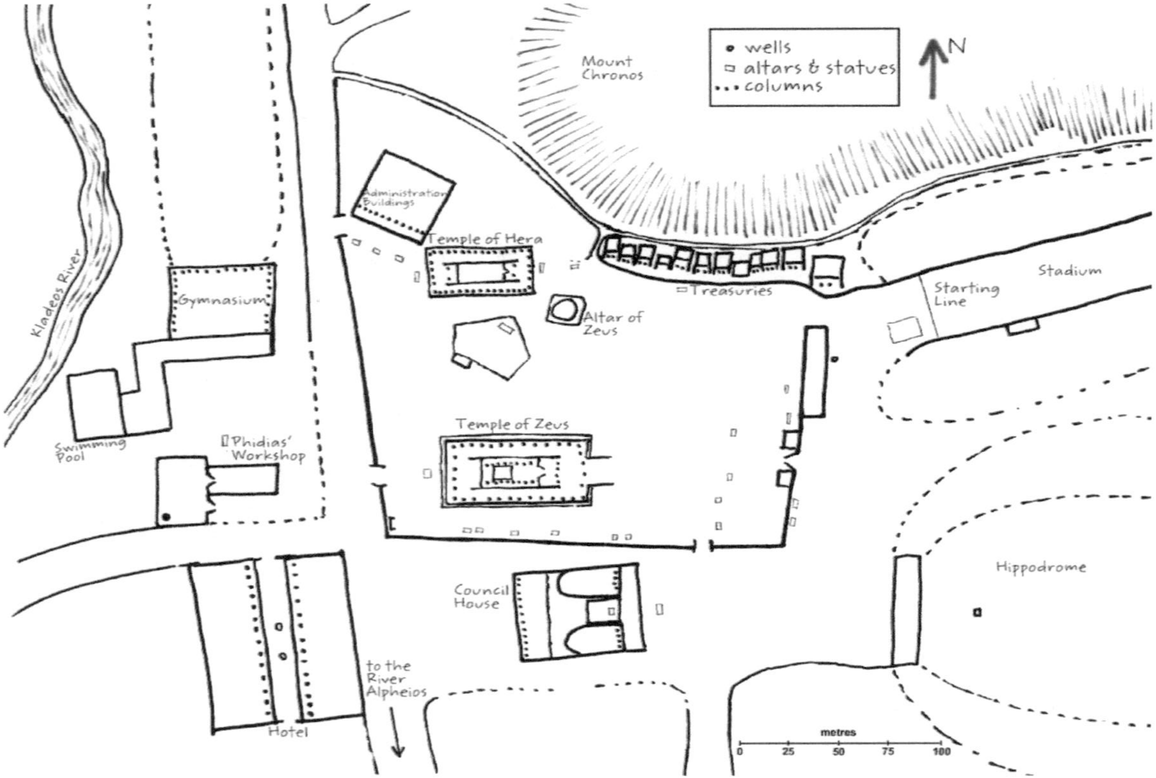

N

wells
altars & statues
columns

Mount Chronos

Stadium

Starting Line

Hippodrome

Treasuries

Altar of Zeus

Temple of Hera

Temple of Zeus

Administration Buildings

Council House

Gymnasium

'Phidias' Workshop

Swimming Pool

Kladeos River

Hotel

to the River Alpineios

metres
0   25   50   75   100

Characters

The spellings used here are almost all based on Modern, not Ancient, Greek pronunciation. The debate as to what the Ancients sounded like continues. So, rather than try to resolve a centuries' old academic controversy, I've used modern versions of the ancient names except for the few most well-known.

People who really existed are marked with an asterisk (*).

Ancient Greek gods and mythical figures are in a separate list after the mortals.

The name Themis can be either male or female, referring to someone called Themistokles (male), or to the goddess of natural law (female).

Athens 432 BCE

Arianos, physical training tutor

Asterodia, priestess of Demeter

Artemisia, Panainos' wife

Athamas, Themistokles' music tutor

Chloe, Themistokles' younger sister

Diodotos, Themistokles' older brother

Efsevios, Straton's older brother

Eirini, Themistokles' mother

Frog, Themisokles' personal slave and friend

Io, Phidias' elder daughter

Ismini, Eirini's friend, wife of Phidias

Kallistos of Diomea, Themistokles' father

Melanas, male slave in Themistokles' house

Menelaus, Myrto's husband, Themistokles' brother-in-law

Mika, female slave in Themistokles' house

Myrto, Themistokles' older sister

Nikanor, Themistokles' uncle, Kallistos' brother

*Panainos, Themistokles' uncle, Eirini's cousin, Phidias' brother, master painter

Panax, Diodotos' dog

*Perikles, the equivalent then of the Prime Minister of the Athenian State

*Phidias, Themistokles' uncle, Eirini's cousin, master sculptor, famous architect

Photios, Themistokles' classmate and friend

Polycasta, Phidias' younger daughter

Straton, son of Ypatos, classmate and sworn enemy of Themistokles

Themistokles, son of Kallistos, Themis to family and friends

Timodemus, Themistokles' nephew, Myrto's son

Tryfonos, wealthy young Athenian man, admirer of Xenovia

Xenovia, priestess of Athena, daughter of Asterodia

Cumbria 2010 CE

Bernie, year 10 student, Penrith, classmate and friend of Suzanne's

Cassie, athletics trainer

Donna, Dan Short's girlfriend

Eliot, Suzanne's younger half-brother

Gina, year 10 student, Penrith, classmate of Suzanne's

Gordon Keely, researcher in Edinburgh

Grandad, Suzanne's grandfather in Florida

Granola, Suzanne's stepfather's mother

Green, Mr, history teacher

Ian, Suzanne's ex-boyfriend

Jake, year 10 student, Penrith, classmate of Suzanne's

Jenkins, Mrs, Suzanne's mother

Jenkins, Steve, Suzanne's stepfather

Josh, Bernie's older brother

Kyle, friend of Bernie's

Laila, year 10 student, Penrith, classmate of Suzanne's

Mandy, Nurse, at Penrith Hospital

Nigel, a psychotherapist

Rallis, Miss, modern languages teacher

Miss Rawlings, teacher

Ron, year 12 student, Kendal

Robbie, Suzanne's youngest half-brother

Rolls, Bernie's mother's dog

Short, Mr, Dan, Suzanne's father

Suzanne Short, sometimes called Suzz, year 10 student, Penrith

Tom, classmate of Suzanne's and Bernie's

On The Pelican 432 BCE

Beast, Captain Stomio's dog

Molon son of Lykiskos, Straton's cousin, temple messenger

Nestoras, village headman

Stomio, captain of the Pelican

Olympia and Elis 432 BCE

*Agorakritos, sculptor, student/colleague of Phidias

*Alkamenes, sculptor, student/colleague of Phidias

Amintas, client at Kadmos' gymnasium

Anthoussa, daughter of Judge Iasos

Apollodoros of Korkyra, boy athlete

Ariphron, athlete, Photios' cousin

Commandant of the Guard

Efthimios, apprentice weaver, client at Kadmos' gymnasium

Esperos of Massalia, boy athlete

Glafkos, skilled worker with gold, gilder

Gulkishar, scribe to Phidias

High Priest of the Temple of Zeus

Herakles, temple cleaner

Jason, quarry overseer

Judge Iasos, one of two judges who organise the Olympic Games

Kadmos, Olympic trainer, gymnasium manager

Kleandros, senior bronze caster

Ligya, Themistokles' nanny

*Lykinos of Elis, boy athlete

Lysimachos, client at Kadmos' gymnasium

Mantius of Athens, young athlete

Master Caster, in bronze foundry

City Archon of Elis

Melpomeni, Mrs, stall holder

Nikitas, Themis' brother

Niris, Panainos' slave

*Pantarkes, Phidias' favourite boy companion

Perilaos, one of two judges who organise the Olympic Games

Pyrros, client at Kadmos' gymnasium

*Thukydides, political opponent of Perikles of Athens

Tilemachos, apprentice to Phidias, lent to Panainos

Timon of Plataea, boy athlete

Tindareos of Taras, boy athlete

Vion, archon of Olympic Tent City

Voithus of Sparta, boy athlete

Xenon, a guard

Yellow dog
Yron, guard from Elis
Zephus, relative of Thukydides

Ancient Greek gods and mythical figures

Apollo, god of the sun, the arts, living souls, son of Zeus
Arion, famous rich musician
Artemis, goddess of virginity, the hunt, the moon, twin of Apollo
Asklepios, god of healing
Athena, goddess of wisdom, guardian of Athens
Circe, mythological enchantress of great beauty
Demeter, the goddess of agriculture, harvest, the seasons, sister of Zeus
Dionysos, god of wine, madness and theatre
Hades, god of the dead and the Underworld, brother of Zeus
Hephaistos, god of crafts and metalworking, son of Zeus
Hera goddess of marriage, patroness of women, sister and wife of Zeus
Herakles, mythical hero, demi-god
Hermes, messenger of the gods, conductor of souls to Hades, son of Zeus
Homer, ancient poet
Odysseus, mythological King of Ithaca
Pan, god of the countryside and wild places
Poseidon, god of the sea, brother of Zeus
Nike, goddess of victory
Zeus, father of the gods

Greek words used in the story

Agora: open space in a city used for a market and other municipal functions.
Altis: the holy precinct at Olympia. The word *altis* is derived from the word *alsos*, which still means a wood or glade in modern Greek.
Amphora: large, earthenware storage jar, some were larger than a man.
Andron: room used only by men for eating and socializing and as a study.
Archon: municipal officer: a mayor, or a magistrate, or the head of a government department
Cella: main room of a temple
Chiton: pronounced 'kite-on', *hitona* in modern Greek. This is the main garment or tunic worn by men and women. It fell from the shoulders almost to the ground, hitched over a belt tied round the waist or hips. Slaves and children

and men working, fighting, hunting or riding, wore shorter versions.

Drachma: unit of currency, worth six obols which were originally bars of iron before coins were made. The word *drachma* comes from the Ancient Greek for hold or grab. An average man could hold six of the bar obols in his hand.

Hellas: The name for Greece in Ancient Greek. The modern Greek for Greece is Elladha, a different form of the same name. **Hellenic** is the adjective, and **Hellenes** are the people.

Helot: member of a lower 'caste' of people subjugated by the Spartans to work in agriculture and support occupations.

Hoplite: citizen foot-soldier, usually armed with a spear and shield.

Himation: cloak, heavier outer garment, often with a hood.

Hundred-foot temple: (in Greek *Ekatopedon*) later called the Parthenon, it was known by this name at the time it was built.

Kithara: stringed musical instrument similar to a lyre, not a guitar.

Megaron: large, high room, usually with a circular hearth in the middle.

Nike: Victory. The abstract quality, and the goddess believed to crown victors.

Paean: song or hymn of triumph or thanksgiving.

Peplos: similar to a chiton (see above), often of fine wool, worn by women.

Stade, stades: measure of length, 1 stade was approximately 200 yards or metres, the length of a stadium. It varied. Five stades were approximately equivalent to our kilometre, 8.8 to our mile.

Symposium: a drinking party for men, usually after an evening meal, often involving discussion of serious topics, at least in the early stages.

Ancient Greek place names
as they often appear, and as they appear here.

Acropolis	Akropolis
Aegina	Egina
Brauron	Vravron/Vravrona
Euboea	Evia
Hydra (island)	Ydra
Kerkyra/Corfu	Korkyra
Lacedaemonia	Lakonia
Lycabettus	Lykavitos

I DECLARE
THAT LATER ON,
EVEN IN AN AGE UNLIKE OUR OWN,
SOMEONE WILL REMEMBER WHO WE ARE.

Attributed to Sappho, Ancient Greek poet (630 – 570 BCE),

translation Aaron Poochigian

For
Alexandra and Andrew

PROLOGUE
Then and Now

Athens, Greece, February 432 BCE – outside the city wall

'Apologise!' demanded Themistokles.

'Make me!' challenged Straton, wheeling his pony. He galloped down the little valley to the bridge and the straight road beyond it to the city's eastern gate.

'Young masters, young masters!' bellowed Arianos the trainer. 'You'll get five lashes for this!'

But the boys were out of earshot, dashing towards the river.

The sun had disappeared behind a bar of cloud, thunder rumbled overhead, and the first drops of rain were falling.

Straton crossed the bridge at a gallop, his pony's hooves drumming on the wooden planks. Themistokles had almost caught him.

Lightning suddenly crackled through the air and a sizzling BOOM echoed from mountain to city wall.

As it died away, Themistokles' pony trotted off the bridge, riderless.

Athens, Greece, February 2010 CE – Panathenaic Stadium

At the top tier of stadium seats, Bernie finally catches up with Suzanne.

'Hey, Suzz!' She is panting. 'Did you see that statue?'

'Mmm,' says Suzanne, distracted.

'It's got a head looking each way, and lower down it's got a penis looking each way.' Bernie giggles breathlessly. 'Just a block of stone with two heads and two penises. Weird, eh?' She tucks damp red curls behind her ear. 'Look. Down there.' She waves a hand at the distant floor of the stadium.

'Sorry?' says Suzanne.

Bernie is suddenly still. 'What's up, Suzz?' she says.

Suzanne has her hands deep in her pockets. 'He's dumped me.'

'Dumped you? How d'you know?'

'Text,' says Suzanne.

'Today!?' squeals Bernie. 'Just now?'

Tears sparkle in Suzanne's lashes as she looks around and makes a face. 'You don't need to tell the whole world,' she says. 'I got it while you were crawling up the steps from the bottom.' She points with her chin down to the floor of the Panathenaic Stadium. Zappeion Park and the city of Athens are spread out in the sun beyond it.

'It's hot,' says Bernie. 'And I'm not a bloody gazelle like you.'

Half way down, Gina is standing on the walkway, taking a photograph. She throws a plump, zig-zaggy shadow across two tiers of white marble seats.

Suzanne and Bernie sit in shocked silence in the shade of the eucalyptus trees growing round the top of the stadium. The stone is cool through their jeans.

<<<

From the head of the little valley, looking towards Lykavitos Hill, the road to the city was clearly visible. It crossed the bridge over the Ilissos and headed for the Diochares Gate between farms and orchards.

A small procession had left the city and was approaching the bridge. The procession was led by a bright yellow cart pulled by two white oxen.

In the well of the cart, a boy lay on a soft mattress. He was covered in a rich, yellow blanket, his head hooded and protected from the lurching by a deep pillow. His skin was pale and the blue of his veins shone through. He showed no sign of life.

The day was unsettled, with a gusty wind and dark grey clouds, but the cart glowed like a splash of sunshine.

A small, colourful crowd followed it. Near the front, a tall woman in a long, dark blue peplos held the hand of a little girl in yellow. The child looked up apprehensively.

'What will happen, Mama?' she asked.

The woman turned sharply to her daughter. 'I don't know,' she said with a shudder. 'Maybe nothing.'

'Or maybe we'll see God Apollo,' insisted the little girl.

Her mother shrugged. The plumper, younger woman behind said, 'Let's hope so.' She was clearly also the tall one's daughter. She wore sky blue and walked beside a young man in a scarlet tunic and grey cloak.

The little girl skipped excitedly. A powerful-looking man in a simple brown garment took her other hand and put a finger to his lips.

>>>

Suzanne pulls her mobile out of her pocket and hands it to Bernie.

Bernie reads the message and says through gritted teeth, 'How could he make you give up your dream of competing in the Olympics, *and* make you fight with your dad, *and* make you cut your hair, and then DUMP you?' She hits her thigh, the phone clenched in her fist.

'He just did,' says Suzanne, looking straight ahead. 'Hey, look down there,' she goes on, her voice hardly wobbling. 'Gina's taking one of her arty farty photos.' They stand up and wave their arms with the huge Olympic Rings symbol behind them.

Gina signs she's got the photo, and turns to take a picture the other way. The rest of the group is trudging up the marble steps of the central aisle in the unexpected sunshine. No one else is bothering with photos. They'll all choose from Gina's later.

The girls sit down again.

'Did he say why?' asks Bernie.

'I'm … too bossy and don't respect him enough.' Suzanne sniffs. She zips open her backpack, looking for tissues.

'But Suzz, you're not bossy!' Bernie pauses. 'Was it because you wouldn't let him – '

'P'raps,' says Suzanne impatiently. 'But you know, Bernie, I'm not sure I know the difference between being bossy and … doing what I really feel, not what I'm expected to feel.' She blows her nose.

They watch as Gina is joined by Laila and the three boys from their class. Miss Rallis is chivvying them from behind and Mr Green is already nearing the top of the steps beside them.

'What will you do now?' Bernie whispers.

Suzanne breathes in, jumps up with a flourish, and turns to Bernie. 'Now? Now I'll flirt with that guy Ron from Kendal – '

Bernie exclaims, 'Don't you dare! He's mine.' They're both laughing now.

' – and when we get home, I'll start training again.'

Mr Green has reached their level and turns towards them. Bernie gets up.

'That'll please your dad. Pole vault again?' she says.

'Perhaps.' Suzanne cups her hands round her mouth. 'Come on!' she calls to their classmates. 'It's cooler up here.'

A pair of pigeons flies out of a tree behind them.

<<<

Behind the cart and in front of the family strode an old priestess, staff in hand. Her bones made angles in her green linen robe. Her wild white hair fanned out over her shoulders.

Beside her was a priest in orange and yellow, attended by two muscular slaves carrying gold-painted spears. The priest was leading a white bullock with yellow ribbons tied to its horns.

Four musicians, their bright tunics swaying, played a jaunty tune on two flutes, a lyre and a drum. A group of onlookers had joined the back of the little procession.

So this was not a funeral, and yet the boy in the cart was as still as death as they approached the crossroads at the bridge over the river.

The driver of the cart pulled up and turned to the priestess.

'Where now, Sacred Lady?' he asked quietly.

The priestess turned a questioning look on the man in brown. 'Arianos?' she said.

Arianos stepped forward. 'It happened here, at this end of the bridge.' His country accent was strong, his voice rough with grief. 'We'd finished training over there, between the two hills. The boys dashed off, racing their ponies. Themistokles was galloping over the bridge when the lightning struck there, at the foot of the Hill of Ardittos. The pony reared up here.' He gestured at his feet, where he stood on the end of the wooden bridge. 'Themistokles fell down the bank to the edge of the water, there. He must have hit his head on this.' He slapped the stone abutment.

A flock of pigeons in a nearby tree flew off with a clatter of wings.

>>>

Suzanne stands watching the pigeons fly down the perfect white arc of the marble stadium, into the blue sky over the tall, dense trees in the park beyond. Her jaw is set in anger. 'Maybe I'll try kick-boxing,' she whispers to herself. 'He wouldn't know what hit him.'

'We'll have lunch here,' says Mr Green loudly.

They all crowd into the narrow band of shade and sit on the long curve of the top seat. Suzanne doesn't move, her eyes on the birds.

'I bet it's hard-boiled eggs and cherry tomatoes again,' says Gina, wriggling her ample bottom from side to side.

'Stop it,' squeaks Laila. 'You'll push me off!'

The hair on Suzanne's arms stands up. She turns to Bernie.

'Have we been here before?'

'Of course not!' says Bernie, sitting down and getting out her lunch box. 'You said that on the Akropolis, too. We've only been here one day. You've seen photos, that's all.'

'Where *is* the Akropolis?' Suzanne murmurs. 'It should be behind that hill.'

'Who cares?' says Bernie. 'Come on. Sit down and eat.'

'Just a sec.' Suzanne strides off to their right, round the top of the stadium. She walks until the Akropolis comes into sight beyond the trees on the slope above the stadium to the left. She stops and takes a deep breath, her hand shading her eyes. 'Must have dreamed it,' she says to herself. She looks around her, aware suddenly of where she is. '*I knew this stadium would be fantastic,*' she thinks. '*Brilliant to compete in. Wish I'd been around in 1896.*' She turns back towards the group. '*No women in the Olympics then. But still …*'

<<<

The priest motioned to the two blond slaves. They stood with their spears crossed, blocking the bridge and holding back a small crowd of athletes returning from training in the deep little valley between the hills.

The young man in red and Arianos lifted the mattress and the motionless boy from the cart, lowering them carefully to the ground by the abutment. The rest of the party made a respectful circle around the boy and the priestess. Passers-by stopped and stared.

The music changed to a lilting, yearning melody. The priestess began to sing. 'Golden Apollo, do you see us? We are begging you to hear us.'

The little girl let go of her mother's hand and began to twirl slowly to the music. The woman tried to catch her back, but the priestess shook her head to show it didn't matter. Other voices began to sing.

'What is your daughter's name?' asked the priestess above the song.

'She is called Chloe, Sacred Lady,' answered the woman.

'Come and stand with me, Chloe,' said the priestess. 'Sing with me beside your brother.'

Chloe stood by the priestess. She sang in her child's voice, clear above the rest, repeating again and again, 'Golden Apollo, do you see us? We are begging you to hear us.'

As she chanted, Chloe looked along the road towards the city. High above the walls, the cliffs of the Akropolis rose, sheer and pale against the threatening sky. Behind the wall on top of the cliff, she could see the smooth roof of the new temple with the golden helmet and spear of the statue of Athena beyond.

As Chloe looked, a flock of doves circled, white against that dark grey sky, tumbling in the wind.

A bright beam of sunlight slipped between the seething clouds. Was this Apollo coming? Chloe looked up at the priestess as they sang.

The old lady's eyes were wide open, fixed on the sunbeam. The lines on her face had disappeared. She was standing as straight as a spear. The sunbeam was still at first, flooding the Akropolis with light and igniting Athena's gold. Then it began to move towards them.

>>>

'We need to start back,' says Miss Rallis, brushing crumbs off her lap as she stands up. 'We're meeting the bus at Zappeion in fifteen minutes.'

'Where's that, Miss?' asks Jake.

'Down there, among those trees, in the park across the road.' Miss Rallis points down the length of the stadium.

Suzanne is at the top of the steps. 'Beat you down, Jake,' she challenges.

'Ooh, Suzanne,' Gina sneers. 'Never let the chance of doing something with the boys pass you by.'

'Oh shut it, Gina,' drawls Bernie.

'It's not that,' says Suzanne. 'Just imagine competing in here!' and she sets off down on her own.

'Not my thing!' says Gina to Suzanne's back, grining as she heaves her bulk upright so that even Miss Rallis laughs.

Their guide counts them out at the railings and locks up behind them. They straggle across the dazzling white paving towards the main road and the park beyond. Mr Green collects them together at the curb.

While they wait for the green man, Suzanne gets her camera out.

Mr Green says, 'Sixty years or so ago, they covered up the Ilissos, the river that ran across here, and built this road over its bed.'

Suzanne has turned back and is taking her own photo of the stadium with its tiers of seats shining white against the bright blue sky. The five rings of the Olympic symbol at the far end are tiny now. The lights change and the others walk across. The red man suddenly comes back. Suzanne has missed it. The traffic revs up and roars past. She waves at the others and turns to take another picture. She tries to imagine the river running under the road, under her feet.

<<<

As the sunbeam approached, the priestess began to thump her staff down on the wood of the bridge in time to the music. The rhythm grew louder and faster.

'Golden Apollo, do you see us?

'We are begging you to hear us.

'Please bring your light and strength to help us.'

The priest led the bullock forward. He had a curved knife in his hand.

Chloe clutched the priestess' hand. Would God Apollo arrive on a chariot, or just flying through the clouds?

The priestess was shaking and swaying from side to side. Suddenly she let go of Chloe and laid a wizened hand on the priest's arm. 'There must be no death! No other spirit must enter the ether here.'

The Priest of Apollo was resentful. 'A bullock has no spirit!' he declared. 'And it has been paid for. The family have paid.'

'Apollo commands!' The priestess looked straight into the eyes of Chloe's mother. 'I will call the spirit of Themistokles, son of Kallistos, to return to his body. If the bullock has just died, the wrong spirit may enter.'

Chloe's mother turned to the priest. 'We'll leave the sacrifice until later,' she said.

The priest stepped back, his face dark with anger. He dragged the bullock with him. The crowd sighed with disappointment.

The music and the echoing thump of the priestess' staff rose to a crescendo and stopped.

There was silence.

Even the birds were quiet as the priestess laid down her staff and knelt behind the boy's head, trembling slightly. She put her hands on his shoulders and rocked backwards and forwards.

Her eyes turned inwards and went white. Chloe ran to her mother with a squeal. No one else stirred.

The patch of sunlight moved steadily towards them. Chloe grasped her mother's hand in both hers.

The priestess croaked, 'We beg you, God Apollo. Give Themistokles back his life.' As she rocked her voice rose. 'Come home, Themistokles, son of Kallistos. You are sorely missed and longed for. Enter your body again. Live and thrive, and bring joy and honour to your family.'

The sunbeam reached the bridge. The river suddenly sparkled and shadows sprang from nowhere.

'Apollo! Lord of Delphi!' cried the priestess. 'God of light and beauty, guardian of living souls!' A spasm shook her whole body as her blank white eyes searched the sky. 'Bring him back! We beg you!'

She was forcing her voice between chattering teeth, straining upwards. Her hands still clasped the unconscious boy's shoulders.

The noise of the traffic almost drowns Mr Green's voice when he calls, 'Come on Suzanne!' as the lights change again. Suzanne steps off the curb and crosses the road thinking, *'Is the river still running under here now?'*
She's almost on the opposite side when the red man comes back. A motorcycle is hurtling towards her, between the revving cars and the curb.
It hits her left side hard.
She feels herself fly through the air and hears a loud roaring sound, then a crack. She is sucked into a searing white void.

<<<

A sound from deep in the priestess' chest, a roaring note, rose and became a wild, bitten-off scream. She fell sideways, her head making a hollow crack as it hit the wooden bridge. Her fingers still grasped the boy's shoulders like claws, the connection unbroken.
The boy took a long, deep breath and made a low moan.
The sun went in.

PART ONE
Together

Chapter 1: void

From Bernie's Blog. Feb 15th 2010, Monday

Athens, Hotel Artemis

THIS HAS BEEN THE WORST DAY OF MY LIFE!!!!!!!!

Where do I start?

Poor poor Suzanne. Will she be OK? Why did this happen? And in a country where I don't understand anything!

So… Concentrate! Start at the beginning …

This morning we all got our backpacks together with packed lunches from the hotel, and water bottles, and questionnaires, and all the usual tourist stuff. And Suzanne seemed a bit quiet. Yesterday she was leaping around and like 'We're gonna see where it all began.' Meaning the Olympics, of course. She's obviously still obsessed, even though she gave up the idea of competing because of bloody Ian.

But today she was really quiet. Then she told me that Ian had dumped her. Up at the top of the Stadium! By text! Right in the place she'd been so excited to see. 'Where it all began'. And now, maybe where it all ends.

OMG!

Pause for tears. Oh help …

Right. Trying to get it together now.

We were all crossing the road along the open end of the stadium. We'd all got across except Suzanne. She missed the light to take a last photo. I was just teasing Gina about there being no cake in the packed lunch, when I heard a screaming noise from an engine and a load of shouting. I turned round and saw that Suzanne was lying on the tarmac near the pedestrian crossing. The traffic was stopped dead. A motorbike was on its side in the middle of the road and Mr Green had his arm round a man's neck. I couldn't move, but Laila ran over and checked Suzanne was breathing. Miss Rallis was standing still, phoning for an ambulance. We all just stood where we were, like idiots. There was a load of shouting, which we couldn't understand, of course.

The ambulance came along the pavement on the other side of the road with its siren shrieking. They put Suzanne in it and screamed off. The hospital wasn't far, they said. Miss Rallis went with her.

We were left with Mr Green and the police. One of them spoke English. They took the man from the motorbike away – he was bleeding – and they wrote down all our names and addresses and those of the drivers in some of the cars.

When they'd finally finished, we went and sat on seats in the park while Mr Green called for reinforcements. After a bit, Miss Rawlings appeared. The others were all texting and phoning and stuff. I don't remember what I was doing. Mainly wishing it was all a dream, I think.

Then they took us to meet up with Kendal School as if nothing had happened. And we all got on the bus and were taken round the Museum! You are joking! You think I can remember anything I saw?

Then the bus came and took us back to the hotel. I sat on our balcony and called Miss Rallis. She didn't answer, so I texted and then she called me back. She said Suzanne was unconscious and had bad bruising on her side where the bike hit her, a big mess on the side of her head, and maybe a broken collarbone. The doctors said she'd have to stay – maybe for a couple of weeks!!

I went down to the lounge by Reception and ran into Mr Green. I asked him about the motorbike rider and he said that yes, he'd been arrested, but he needed some medical treatment himself. I hope he dies!

And now they're saying we'll leave tomorrow as planned!

HOW CAN THEY DO THAT!!! How can I leave Suzanne there, unconscious and possibly DYING?

Has anyone told her parents? Can I get a taxi to the hospital? I don't even know where it is!!

Later – night

I managed to talk to Miss Rallis again and she says Suzanne's mum is on her way to Athens. I asked if I could stay, but she said no, I should go on with the trip. But she said she'd text me often to tell me what's going on.

Can't sleep, can't think. Going to see what Laila's doing.

<<<

The first thing the boy was aware of was a moaning sound. He opened his eyes. A sharp pain sliced through his head. He shut them again, squeezing them tight.

He could hear a lot of people around him, and running water nearby. He could feel a breeze on his face. So he was outside. He risked another slit of light. A dark presence was leaning over him. Voices chattered quietly. He shut his eyes tight again. The moaning had stopped.

Someone took his hand and held it to a wet … what was it called? 'Head' came into his mind. 'Face? … No, cheek.' He opened his eyes. Yes, the woman in the dark dress was holding his hand against her wet cheek.

'How are you feeling, my child?' she asked. Her voice was rich with wonder and she was smiling through her tears.

'Feeling?' The boy considered this word. He could feel his breath going in and out of his … what? Chest? Chest, yes. He could feel the rest of his body. He moved his fingers. He took another deep breath. That felt good. He felt good – except for the lurking pain in his head. He opened his mouth to speak but found he didn't know which word to use. He shut his mouth and groaned. 'Mmmm.' It was the same sound as he had heard a few moments ago.

A child's voice said 'He knows you, Mama. He's trying to say Mama.'

'No!' he said, shocking himself into opening his eyes. The pain was less this time. He blinked carefully. The dark woman was a blurred shape between him and a grey sky that was far too bright. He caught a glimpse of the tops of trees against it before he shut his eyes against the pain.

'Who..?' That was the word he wanted. 'Who?' he said. It sounded right. He took a breath and said it again. 'Who? Who? Who?' The child's voice laughed and he felt a weight crawl onto his … what? his what!?

'Who?' said the child. 'Who?' answered the boy. They made a song of it. 'Who?' 'Who?' 'Who?' 'Who?'

The dark woman sobbed and he felt drops fall on his face. He opened his eyes again and focused on her. He saw tears running down her … cheeks. 'Cheeks,' he said out loud. 'Cheeks, who, cheeks, who,' he sang with his eyes shut, and the invisible child sang with him. He tried to move his head to see the child, but the burning pain shot through him and he lay still.

He thought, *'I am in a bed. That's what it's called. A bed. But why am I in a bed outside? And … who am I?'* He squashed rising panic, and tried to breathe smoothly. He was warm and comfortable, with soft stuff touching his skin all over. He wriggled his toes. It felt good. He heard himself saying 'Mmmmm mmmmm', while another part of his mind was still asking questions. 'What is all this? Where am I? What's my name?'

The dark woman, who may have been his mother, dropped his hand. He felt the wind of her garments as she whirled away from his bed. Even with his eyes open he couldn't see her now. But he could hear her.

'Oh, Apollo! Devious Lord of Delphi! What have you done?' Her voice was swollen with pain. The boy reached a hand towards the weight of the child. It was taken between two smaller hands.

His mother went on. 'Other gods have taken so many from me – one son, one daughter, two husbands. And now you too have failed me! You have given me back half a son, his body but not his mind!'

So he was her son – a boy. 'No,' he said, quite quietly this time, but with his eyes shut. All the other voices stopped. 'No. I have a mind. But I don't know … who I am … or where I am, and I don't …' He searched for the word, '… re … remember anything.'

An old, calm voice said, 'He'll need time to reach back and find himself.' And the boy felt two hands on his shoulders. He winced. There were bruises there. 'You must have patience. Apollo does not make mistakes.' Warmth was spreading through him from those hands. He felt as if all the fibres of his body were being smoothed out. He sighed deeply. The gurgle of running water was comforting, and he felt sleep wrapping him in peace.

'Let's take him home,' said a man's hoarse voice. 'He'll get better now.'

Chapter 2: name

The next time the boy woke, he was fighting for his life. He couldn't breath and it was completely dark.

He tried to lash out. Something was holding his left arm down, but his other fist hit something that gave way. Suddenly he could take a breath. There was a faint lightening of the dark. Someone nearby was choking but trying not to make a noise. He pushed himself to sit up. A shadow immediately leant over him. His left arm was free now and he lashed out again. This time he hit something hard. There was a crack and muffled cry. Footsteps ran off. He lay back panting, holding his splitting head together with aching hands. Male voices all around him began asking questions. He took a breath to answer, but slipped away into a pale green mist …

Drops fell on his face. 'Rain?' he said, opening his eyes.

'He's awake!' said a female voice.

He was breathing. Nothing stopped him. It was easy. Lots of people sighed. They were all in a brighter room. Had he been here before? 'It's working …' said the voice in a whisper.

A smell of sweet herbs filled his head. He tried to move, but there were weights all over him. He lay still.

Music was playing far away. It came nearer and voices in the room began to chant in time to it. He was floating in a scented cloud. The rhythm of the chant rippled through his body.

More people were near his bed now. They seemed to be wearing … clothes? … cloaks? yes, maybe cloaks… over their heads. Someone wiped his face and chest with a cool cloth. A softer cloth dried him. Hands stroked his forehead, touched his breast-bone. The music was loud now. A drum rumbled and growled. Lamps were appearing like … stars.

Suddenly all was still and silent. Then one voice called out, 'Asklepius! We beg you to guide our hands and our minds and our hearts as we care for this young man.'

Then the music began again and all the weights that were on his body became hands that lifted and turned him over in one huge, sickening wave of movement and pain. His stomach heaved and his head filled with roaring blackness.

>>>

From Bernie's Blog. Feb 19th 2010, Friday

Home

Mrs Jenkins texts me every day. Suzanne is just the same but yesterday she stopped breathing, it seems!!! Gave Mrs J a terrible fright. But they got her back again with CPR and oxygen. Not dead, but not alive either. I asked for a photo and she's just lying there with tubes and wires and drips everywhere, tucked in tight in a bed with railings all round it. I feel sick like my stomach is being pulled out through my throat whenever I think of her – which is most of the time.

Dad asked me today what was wrong. I didn't answer cos I just wanted to scream. Josh said, 'She's worried about Suzanne, Dad. What d'you think?'

<<<

It was dark again, but he was in a different room and there was moonlight. Not far away, he could hear someone … snoring. And there were trees … swishing? yes! swishing in the wind nearby. It felt familiar, safe. But he had no memory of why.

He moved his arms and legs. They seemed to work, but his hands ached. He opened and closed them. The left hand was quite sore.

He sat up slowly, expecting more pain. His head swam a bit, but it passed. He swung his legs off the bed. There was a cup of water on the floor. His foot knocked it over and he watched a small pool spread out, shining in reflected moonlight.

The floor was cold to his bare feet, but he found he could stand.

'*I must be really ill, otherwise I'd know my name,*' he thought. Then, '*Is that the word? Ill?*' It seemed to have no meaning when he focused on it.

He took three wobbly steps to the window. The moon shone diagonally into the room. He looked down into a courtyard. The side to the right had a low roof, supported by columns. Opposite, a wooden staircase climbed to a walkway on the same level as he was. A vine grew up the columns onto the roof.

'*I'm sure I should remember this place,*' he thought. He pulled a stool to the window, making a loud sound on the wooden floor.

'What are you doing!?' came a voice, shrill with alarm. He turned. The woman who seemed to be his mother was there, on a bed in the darkest corner. She sat up, her long hair over her shoulders. Another woman appeared with a light in the open doorway.

'Where is this?' he asked.

'Oh, dear gods!' said the mother woman crossly, getting off the bed. 'This is our house in Athens, near the Diochares Gate. You are Themistokles, son of Kallistos of Diomea. I am your mother, Eirini. Don't tell me you don't know all this already!'

The boy felt her impatience as though she'd slapped him. He sat down carefully on the stool. 'No, I don't,' he said. 'I don't know who I am, or where I am, or … anything. The first thing I can remember is waking up under the sky near a river. Then flying with some strange … companions? (is that right?), and then waking up trying to breathe …'

'You remember that?' asked his mother.

'I hit someone, or maybe something …' He rubbed his painful hand while Eirini looked at the other woman with alarm.

The woman at the door asked, 'Are you hungry, Master Themis?'

'Hun…gree. What an odd word…' He suddenly understood. 'Yes!'

he said. 'I'm hungry,' and he laughed at the discovery.

Eirini pointed at the water on the floor. 'What's that?' she asked.

The boy looked down. 'It's what was in the cup,' he said. 'I … kicked it by mistake.'

'You take this, Mika,' said Eirini, handing the upset cup to the other woman. 'Come on, Themis. Back to bed.' Mika disappeared.

He tried to stand, but he was dizzy now. He let his mother help him back to bed. She said, 'You know if you need to pee there's a pot under your bed.' It was embarrassing, because he didn't recognise her as his mother and she seemed to be so angry. But he did notice that he was nearly as tall as she was – and he seemed to have a name. Themis. It didn't sound familiar.

'How's your head?' she asked.

'Full of … flies? or bees? – and questions … Oh-oh. I'm very dizzy …,' he said as he lay down. He touched his head where there was some pain, and found that he had almost no hair! Instead, there was a domed lump dotted with thick scabs.

His mother took his hand away from it, put it on the blanket and patted it. 'No need to touch it. It's far better than it was,' she said. 'Now, it's a long time till dawn. You rest and I'll find you some bread and milk. Just don't touch the wound or we'll have to bandage it.'

'Milk?' said Themis, closing his eyes, trying to remember. His hunger growled and he put a hand to his stomach as the two women left with the light.

But the bed was rocking on a choppy sea … No, not the sea. It was being pushed this way and that by a herd of giant sheep. They were pressing in on him from all sides, warm and soft, pressing irresistibly, harder and harder …

A deep, masculine cough brought him back. He opened his eyes but he couldn't see anyone in the moonlight. Was it a god, angry that he hadn't recognised his mother? Or was it his father? Did he have a father?

The cough came again. It didn't sound angry.

'Who's there?' said Themis loudly, trying to sit up.

'Stay still, young master,' said a deep voice near the bed. 'I am Melanas, your father's personal slave.'

'Why can't I see you?'

'I am black and it is night. Can you not see my eyes?'

Themis became aware of two round, white eyes looking down on him.

'Are you a … an owl?' he asked with interest.

He heard a deep chuckle and white teeth appeared below the eyes. 'Not normally, though some say I can see in the dark. I guessed you had woken. The women are keeping you hidden away while you are ill.'

'Say your name again,' Themis said.

'You should call me Melanas,' came the answer with a flash of white.

'Melanas,' repeated Themis. 'Melanas, Melanas. And am I Themis? Or Themistokles?'

'You are both. Themis to your friends, Themistokles, son of Kallistos and Eirini to the outside world.'

'Eirini. My mother. She went to get me something to eat.'

'I heard. But I thought you might feel confused because this is not your usual sleeping room. You share that with your brother, Diodotos. You are here alone … '

'No. It's not that … Melanas,' said Themis thoughtfully. 'I am confused because I don't remember … ' Themis had a sudden vision of the vast empty space of his memory. His mind slammed a door on it. 'How old am I, Melanas?' His voice was loud, defying the panic.

'Quietly, young master. People are sleeping. It's something over twelve years since you were born.'

'And where is my father?'

'He is … dead. He was killed 51 days ago.'

At that moment Eirini came back, a tiny light and a tray in her hands.

'Shall I light the lamp, madam?' asked Melanas.

Eirini froze a moment, then said, 'That's a good idea, Melanas.'

The rich yellow lamplight chased out the black shadows. Themis tried to sit up, but needed help this time. Melanas lifted him, and his mother packed pillows behind him. Then she placed a bowl of bread soaked in warm milk on his lap. The smell made Themis' mouth fill with saliva. His mother bent to wipe up the water he'd spilled earlier.

'Shall I stay with him, madam? He has many questions.' Melanas' deep voice was almost a whisper.

Eirini stood up. 'That might be best, Melanas. You know which ones to answer.'

Themis picked up the spoon with his left hand, but it hurt, so he changed to his right and began spooning the food into his mouth. It was warm and slightly … salty? Yes, salty.

Themis watched Melanas nod to his mother as she left the room, then sit on the stool near the bed. He asked Themis, 'What else would you like to know?'

'Everything!' Themis waved his hands, spoon and all. 'There is nothing in my memory at all. How did my father die? Who is the child I've seen once or twice? Where is my brother? Do I have other … siblings? Why can't I find the words I want? What happened that made me lose my memory? What did I hit when I woke up trying to breathe?'

Melanas chuckled. 'Enough, young master. I'll start with those. You eat, but slowly! Here, take a drink now,' and he handed him a beaker.

Themis drank the water and then ate some more of the mush in the bowl while Melanas talked.

'Your father died in an ambush on the border with Megara. His detail was sent there on a special mission to protect the sanctuaries of Athena and Demeter in the hills. I went with him but I did not see him die. I brought back his armour for your brother. He spoke to me often of his love for you children and your mother.'

Themis looked at Melanas' sad face. He was sorry that he couldn't remember this loving father, and he felt none of the pain he could see in Melanas' eyes.

After a few moments, Melanas went on. 'As for the child, that is your sister, Chloe. She is six. Your older brother Diodotos had to go to manage the farm when your father died. He is nearly eighteen and will join the army with the next intake. You have one other sister, Myrto. She is sixteen and married, with a baby boy. Her husband is called Menelaus. He has a farm on the other side of Lykavitos Hill.'

Themis lay back on the pillows. His stomach was satisfied, but the dizziness was back. 'Are we rich?' he murmured.

'You are of the voting class,' said Melanas. 'Let me take these away…'

Melanas took the bowl as Themis slid down in the bed, already asleep.

>>>

Chapter 3: home

From Bernie's private diary. Sunday Feb 21st 2010

Home

I can't deal with this. I can keep it together most of the time when I'm awake, but if I sleep I dream about Suzanne. I went out to Laser Wars last night with Laila and the gang, but kept being reminded of her and so I came home early. I did eventually go to sleep, but I dreamed of her dangling on a rope over the middle of a boiling volcano. I was in a helicopter, trying to pull Suzanne up. The pilot was a skinny old woman with long white hair and a long dress. She left the controls so she could help me, but she had oil on her hands and it made the rope slippery and I couldn't get a grip. Woke up shouting, with Mum sitting on my bed. It wasn't the first time.

Food tastes like sawdust and my new jeans are too big.

Somehow I have to go to Suzz. Supposing she dies when I'm not there! Dad won't let me go back on my own and says he can't afford to send someone with me. But tickets are less than a hundred pounds return and hotels are really cheap at this time of year. So so angry and scared …

<<<

Themis was lying in long grass. A chestnut pony lay beside him. It rolled over to whisper in his ear. 'It must stay a secret,' it said.

'What must stay a secret?' Themis asked. The pony snickered and rolled away.

'He mustn't know,' said Eirini's urgent voice.

'Never, madam?' said a man. He sounded shocked.

'Yes. If possible, never. They say it could kill him and anger the gods.'

'As you wish, madam.'

Themis opened his eyes. The sun was shining into the window. Where was the pony? Kill whom? Did they mean him?

He was alone in the same room, and he could hear someone coming up the stairs.

'Oh, please. Come on.' It was the child's voice. 'You just need to help him down to the back yard. He'll love it there in the sun. Please, please!'

Melanas' deep chuckle sounded. 'See if you can wake him up then, Miss Chloe. See if he agrees with you.'

Themis said, 'Outside! I'd love to go outside,' and began to sit up. 'I can walk by myself.'

Chloe said, 'You've been asleep for nearly two days this time.'

They sat him on a warm stone bench in the sun. His eyes watered and sometimes didn't focus clearly, but it felt wonderful. The walls were white and plants grew in painted pots. Leaves and flowers glowed in the evening light. Their fragrance was stronger than the faint but fetid smells of the house. Birds sang busily. A breeze swayed the trees and bushes in a constant dance.

'What colours!' Themis exclaimed as a butterfly opened red and orange wings and flew from one plant to another. '*And what patterns,*' he thought. A dove settled ontop of the wall with a throaty, bubbling call.

Chloe was dancing on the paving stones round a tree in a huge pot near the middle of the yard. She had wound a long piece of faded red cloth round herself.

She approached him in her dance, with two yellow apples in her hands. 'After your many days in Hades, Mighty Herakles, I thought this garden would please you,' she sang.

Themis laughed. He had no memory of Hades or Herakles and no idea why she called him that, but the light and the warmth were feeding his bones. Whoever he was, he could feel he was getting better.

'Who are you? What do you have for me?' he asked.

'I am Asterodia, priestess of Demeter. I have fruits from the mountain for you. Eat and you will be well.' She did a final twirl and deposited the apples in his hand.

Themis sniffed deeply at an apple.

'They're not bad, silly,' said his sister impatiently. 'I had one earlier. They're wrinkled but they're sweet.' She stood still and watched as Themis ate. 'Good?' she asked.

'Perfect,' he answered with his mouth full.

'You've always liked apples best,' she said, prancing away on her toes into another twirling dance.

'What else do I like?' asked Themis.

'Oh, you love meat, especially beef,' called Chloe. 'And especially when you're training hard.' She was on the other side of the tree, whirling round and round.

Melanas cleared his throat. Chloe stopped dead and looked at him. Then she twirled round again. 'Do you like my new word? Especially. Especially. Especially,' she sang.

Themis also looked at Melanas, who said with a wide grin 'She's such a little … performer, isn't she?'

'What do I train for?' asked Themis.

'Just with the twelve-year-olds at the gymnasium,' said Melanas. 'You all have a programme for athletics and a bit of combat with a man called Arianos. You were with him when your horse threw you.'

'So he could tell me about that?'

'He's already told your mother, but yes, he could …'

Themis stood up carefully. 'Then I must go and see him.'

'Young master, you only have to ask and he will come and see you. He is employed by your parents … your mother, as your combat tutor.'

'Then please ask him to come as soon as he can,' said Themis, taking a step away from the bench. He thought, '*How odd to be able to tell a grown man what to do.*'

As they walked he said, 'Do I go to … ?' then couldn't remember the word. He tried a different way. 'Do I have lessons?'

'Yes. You have tutors for music and recitation, arithmetic, and writing, as well as the … gymnasium and so on.'

'And am I any good at these lessons?' Themis asked.

'Not the world's strongest student of music and poetry, I hear,' smiled Melanas. 'But quite good with numbers, and with your hands – drawing, modelling, and so on. Better to ask your tutors. I was only here when your father was on home-leave.'

They had come back to the bench in the sun. Themis found he was already tired and sat down. Chloe had laid flowers and leaves in a ring on the end of the bench.

'Don't sit on the magic circle,' she called across the yard.

Suddenly Eirini's voice shouted something in her salon. Melanas took a step towards the closed door.

Eirini was saying, '… No! No! I cannot agree to that!'

A man's voice grumbled and Eirini's rose shrill above it. 'Please just leave me alone. I have no intention of – the very thought makes my skin crawl.'

Chloe whispered to Melanas, 'What does Uncle Nikanor want?'

'That is for your mother to explain,' growled Melanas.

The street door slammed, echoing through the house. They could hear Eirini return to her salon, talking angrily. Then she cried out, 'It's full of myrrh! Myrrh is for dead bodies! What does he think I am?' and there was a crash.

Eirini burst out of the door into the yard and saw them.

'Where's Mika?' she shouted.

'I'll fetch her,' said Melanas quietly, and set off towards the kitchens.

'I … dropped something,' said Eirini.

'It smells,' said Chloe.

'Mika will clear it up,' said her mother.

'Did you fight with Uncle Nikanor?' asked Chloe.

'He made me angry,' said Eirini, turning back into her salon. 'He's gone now,' and she went in and closed the door.

'That means we can't talk about him,' said Chloe to Themis, rearranging her magic circle.

'Let's get you back to bed, young master,' said Melanas returning.

>>>

From Bernie's Blog. Feb 22nd 2010, Monday

Home

Everyone at school is getting more and more depressed about Suzanne. We keep remembering her in the middle of lessons and when we're talking about other things. Miss Rallis said I could move to sit with someone else, but I decided not to.

I texted Ian that he's a shitty twat. He's avoiding me now. I asked Josh to beat him up but Josh just said I should deal with my own conflicts. Don't know what to do with all these horrible feelings. Never felt so sick or been so angry and sad and hurt and – oh, just *frightened* before.

<<<

Chapter 4: friend

Every morning, two girls would arrive and climb the stairs to the workroom along the landing from Themis' room. They spent the day weaving, whispering and teasing except when Eirini joined them. Their muffled voices reminded Themis of his dreams.

Later that day, Themis was downstairs, pacing the floor slowly in Eirini's salon that opened onto the garden yard, waiting for Arianos, the trainer. The smell of the broken jar of myrrh lingered. He could hear a regular note like a heart beat and quiet voices. Were they the girls upstairs, or was he dreaming even though he was awake?

Arianos arrived at last. He was a tough looking man in a short tunic with brown legs knotted like olive-trees. Eirini brought him to sit with Themis in her salon. Arianos seemed uncomfortable there.

'Excuse me a moment, Arianos,' said Eirini. 'I have to help one of the girls replace some loom weights. I won't be long.' She looked hard at the trainer.

He bent his neck slightly and said, 'As you wish, madam.'

Something stirred in Themis' memory at the sound of his voice, but it was gone before he could grasp it.

As Arianos sat down he muttered, 'Hmm. Not much hair left, have you?'

'Have you known me all my life?' Themis asked.

'Nope. Met you when you were eight.'

'Do you know what happened to make my hand hurt? I remember hitting something or someone. It must have been hard. Look at the bruise.'

'I heard someone tried to smother you as you slept. They didn't catch him. It was dark.'

'Someone tried to kill me?' The hair all over Themis' body stood up. 'But why?'

'No one knows, and your mother thinks whoever it was made a mistake and attacked the wrong patient.' Arianos looked like he wished Mrs Eirini would come back.

'Patient?'

'You were at the new Asklepion. They were preparing another "waking ceremony" for you as you didn't seem to want to wake up again. Mrs Eirini was getting worried.'

Themis guessed the Asklepion was a place for sick people. He must have been there when they turned him over and it hurt so much. He would ask his mother. Then a sudden thought struck him. 'Do you think Zeus wanted me dead? Was it he who tried to stop me breathing?'

Arianos was horrorstruck. 'No, young master. Of course not. If the Great God Zeus had wanted you dead, you wouldn't be here now. What makes you think that?'

'Everything is so strange,' said Themis. 'There are moments when I just can't believe that I belong here.'

'There's no question that you belong. Whether you remember or not, you have been here since you were born.'

Arianos seemed more uncomfortable than ever. 'So you've known me since I was eight?' Themis said.

'Yes. That's when your dad started his boys with weapons. Not like Sparta ...' Arianos' voice was gruff, but he looked relieved.

'Do you come from Sparta?' Themis asked.

'No. But we're going to have a war with them pretty soon, so it's good to know how they train.'

'How do you know there'll be a war?'

'Just the way Perikles is being stubborn with the Megarans,' answered Arianos, his chin out. 'He should – '

'Can I ask you about the accident?' Themis interrupted, his skin crawling with apprehension. 'How it happened? Was it another attack? Or did I do something stupid?'

'No, Master Themis, no one attacked you and you did *not* do anything stupid. The "something" was done by the Great God Zeus, and it is not up to us to say whether it was stupid or not.' The worry lines in Arianos' face softened. 'There was a storm. You were racing your pony against Straton, heading for the crossroads at the other end of the bridge.'

'Is that the bridge I woke up beside?'

'Yes, over the Ilissos River. Just then Zeus decided to throw a lightning bolt. It frightened your pony. He reared. You fell onto the bridge abutment. When I got there you were down the bank, all mud and blood.'

'You brought me home?'

'Yup.'

'Thank you.' Themis didn't know what gesture to make to show his thanks, so he said it again. 'Thank you.' Arianos looked embarrassed.

'Can't go losing students,' he grunted. 'Might be seen as careless.'

'So it wasn't an attack,' said Themis thoughtfully. 'And the … smothering was a mistake … If only I could remember … ' He looked at the trainer's worried face and smiled to lessen the tension. 'So, Arianos, tell me what lessons we do together.'

Arianos took a breath and looked at the olive tree in the yard. 'Well, we do sparring with wooden swords, shields, blunt spears. Running with weighted belts, general strengthening exercises. We're just beginning with bows and arrows. That's about it.'

'Where do we do all this?' Themis was longing to see the world beyond the house.

'Mainly in the gymnasium.'

'Where's that?' asked Themis.

'Just outside the City walls. Or we go up the little valley – where we were that day. We'd ridden up there. '

'Tell me about the other boys I train with.'

'Usually you are five. Your closest friend seems to be Photios. He's a bit of a dreamer, though, not like you.'

'What *am* I like, Arianos? Am I a good student, a strong fighter?'

Eirini came in at that moment, followed by Mika with a tray. Eirini was flustered and looked hard at Arianos, not at Themis as she spoke.

'Of course you're a good student, Themis. But you're not really a fighter. More of a strategist.'

Arianos cleared his throat. 'That's about it, Master Themis. You're a thinker rather than a doer.'

Eirini poured water and wine for Arianos, and a cordial for Themis which smelled heavy with honey.

'To Themis' recovery,' said Eirini as they each poured a few drops into the libation dish. 'May the gods see fit to aid it.'

Themis was thinking, '*Or are they out to get me? And what's the problem my mother has with Arianos?*' But he said, 'I'd like to see my classmates, Mama. Could they come here for a visit?'

'One at a time, maybe,' said Eirini.

'Perhaps Photios first, and see how they get on?' suggested Arianos.

'Why wouldn't we get on?' asked Themis. 'Is there something more wrong with me than just losing my memory?'

'No, my child,' said Eirini with a smile, 'of course not. But as you don't remember anything, it's as though you are … another person. So you might not like the boys who were your friends before. And also you get tired very easily. So one boy at a time is enough.'

'Have I changed a lot then?'

Eirini looked at Arianos. He said, 'It's just you're a bit quieter than you were. Which is natural,' he added hastily, his eyes on Eirini's face, 'as you're not well. And the other boys might expect … ' He shrugged.

'Me to be noisier?' asked Themis.

'More … boisterous,' said Eirini. 'But it is important that you stay calm while you are recovering.'

She stood up. 'Let's ask Photios to come over tomorrow afternoon, shall we? Can you join us, Arianos? I think that would be best.'

'Of course,' said Arianos, standing up to leave.

>>>

From Bernie's Blog. Feb 23rd 2010, Tuesday

Athens, Hotel Artemis

I made it back! Josh came with me. He is ABSOLUTELY THE BEST BROTHER IN THE WORLD! I'll have to wash his crappy car every weekend till I'm 30, but he persuaded Dad, and we're here!

The flight was better cos it was daylight and we could see all the snow on the Alps and the boats crossing the Adriatic. The hotel remembers us of course cos of Suzanne's accident and they're being very nice to us. I texted Mum the minute we landed and we caught a bus in from the airport. No sweat. All the signs are in English as well as Greek – at least at the airport. How come I didn't notice that before?

I'm going to the hospital by metro this afternoon. Josh was going to come with me, but he wants to see Avatar at the cinema. He didn't believe I can get around on my own. I told him I've been here before!

Just wanted to let everyone know that I've arrived safely. And to thank Dad again for the money.

Later

Saw Suzanne. Horrific. She's still in the bed with bars round it. She's thin and pale and they've cut off her lovely hair. How could they do that?! It's like she's growing some kind of brown moss on her skull now, except where the bulge is green and yellow and yucky. There are various pipes and wires going into or out of her – as well as a drip.

When I got there I held her hand for a bit. She groaned once, but she's not with us at all. Her mum sits by the bed all the time and said that was the first time she'd groaned. There's a machine that measures her 'vital signs'. It beeps every time her heart beats. Mrs J said that's how they knew she'd stopped breathing the other night. It made one long beep. Now it sometimes goes a tiny bit faster for a few seconds, but nothing else seems to change.

The room is nice, with sunshine and a view of a sort of park. There's two other patients in there, but they're not in comas, so they just carry on as normal round Suzanne. Lots of noise and Greek arguments.

Josh will be back in a few minutes. Maybe he'll come to the hospital with me for a while. At least now I've seen Suzanne perhaps I won't have bad dreams. Mrs Jenkins says the doctors say she won't die now, but this could go on for another few days, or months – or even for years. Poor woman. Poor Suzanne!

<<<

Themis' friend Photios was shorter, blonder and smaller all over than Themis. The day was blustery and chilly and Eirini had suggested that the 'men' should meet in Kallistos' sitting room, the andron. The boys were dwarfed by couches along the sides, dark murals of warships and olive groves, and the gleaming armour hung in one corner. There were scrolls and tablets stacked on shelves on one wall and a table under the window onto the courtyard.

Photios came in with Arianos. 'Hello,' he said shyly, and stood looking round for a moment. Then he looked more carefully at Themis.

'Oh!' he said, his eyes wide with surprise, 'what happened to your hair?'

'They cut it off,' said Themis 'because of the wound. Look.'

Photios came over to see in the light from the window. 'That's disgusting!' he said with a delighted smile. 'Can I touch it?'

'Better not,' grinned Themis, stepping back. 'It itches and I'm not allowed to scratch.'

'I was there, did they tell you?' said Photios. 'I watched you thrown up in the air and fall onto the bridge post. I couldn't believe it.'

'Believe what?' asked Themis. 'That I was dead?'

'No, that you were alive! Arianos brought you back up the bank and laid you on the road. We could see you were bleeding and then the rain got heavier and spread the blood out all over the road.' Photios smiled. 'Anyway, we could see you breathing, so I knew we hadn't got rid of you after all.'

'You poor things, saddled with me for ever.' Themis sat down on the edge of a couch. 'So it really was just an accident.'

Photios sat beside him. 'Yes. What d'you mean?'

'No one attacked me?'

'No. You fell off your horse all by yourself. Why?'

'I just wondered, because it looks as though someone tried to smother me when I was unconscious – '

Arianos broke in, 'You mother explained that to you,' he said. 'The smotherer was trying to kill the boy with epilepsy on the next couch.' He sat on a stool. 'It was a mistake.'

On a low table there were some cups and a jug of something hot that smelled delicious. He poured some of it out for the boys.

Photios took his cup and raised it towards Themis. 'Your health,' he said formally.

'Thanks,' said Themis as he took his own cup. The drink was warm, fruity and sweet.

'How *are* you feeling? I mean really *feeling*?' asked Photios, his face tight with concern.

Themis took a breath. 'My body feels fine. Can't wait to get out of the house and see what goes on at the gymnasium. But there are things going on in my mind, … dreams and stuff. Some of it's harmless, just weird places … and animals. But sometimes there are really scary things, like flying into huge fires and not being able to stop.'

'Yuch! Does it hurt?'

'Not in the dream. But I wake up sweating and they tell me I scream sometimes.'

'Perhaps seeing me and the other guys will help your mind get rid of that stuff.' Photios reached up and touched Themis' forehead.

'Maybe,' Themis said, leaning away. Then he shrugged and smiled. 'But there *is* a problem.'

'What sort of problem?' asked Photios suspiciously.

'I really, truly, don't remember you.'

'But I thought that was why Mrs Eirini wanted me to come. If you remembered, there'd be no point.'

'Right!' Themis laughed with relief. 'Well, start reminding, then. I don't remember you, but you seem alright.'

'Well, thanks a lot!' Photios took a deep breath. 'I've been thinking about where to start since yesterday. I think I should tell you about – '

Arianos cleared his throat, stood up and offered the jug to fill up the cups. Photios looked up at him and went on deliberately, ' – about how good you are at drawing. Or maybe you're not any more, but you were.'

Themis' mind was full of questions he wanted to ask Photios alone. Did people blame Arianos for the accident? Why had he just interrupted again? But instead he asked, 'What d'you mean – drawing?'

'You used to paint pictures of us on bits of pottery.' Photios spoke fast, as though expecting more interruptions. 'Your lesson tablet always had doodles on. And you painted a fabulous bed-cover for your sister when she got married, full of portraits of all the people at her wedding. Some of them were a bit … unfriendly.' The boys burst out laughing. 'Ask her to show it to you when you visit.'

Arianos said, one eyebrow raised, 'You were severely punished for drawing your Uncle Nikanor as Hades and your father as Zeus.'

Photios looked serious. 'Well, that was sacrilege, of course, but then we didn't know that at the time.'

Themis turned to Photios. 'What did I use to paint with?'

'Brushes and stuff. You kept them with your lesson tablets under your bed.'

'In the room I shared with my brother?' Themis said.

'Yes,' said Photios. 'Let's look.'

Themis wondered why no one had told him this before. They went across the courtyard and into a large room. There were two beds at right angles and a series of shelves on a third wall. Here, too, a table stood under the window into the courtyard. Themis pulled a chest out from under his bed and threw open the lid. He and Photios sat on the floor and took things out: tablets, styluses, a catapult, toys from when he was small, and yes, some worn brushes and a flat wooden box with three coloured paints: red, black and white.

'You see?' said Photios. 'And these are some of your victims.' He stood up and indicated a row of ceramic tiles on a low shelf. Each tile showed a person exercising or playing music or working at something. And all of them had exaggerated features: a nose too pointed, or teeth too prominent, or muscles bulging too much.

A boy slave came in with the tray from the andron and set it down.

'I painted these?' said Themis in wonder. 'Are there any more?'

The slave boy went silently to a low cupboard and opened the doors. Themis saw a large box. He pulled it out. It was full of terracotta tiles, curved bits from broken pots, wooden tablets and rolled-up pieces of rag and papyrus. On all of them were drawings in red, white and black of people, animals and buildings.

'Wow!' said Photios. 'You've been busy!'

'Not that I remember,' said Themis, staring at the box and shaking his head. 'Who are they all? How did I ..?'

Photios sat down by the box. 'Come on, let's get them out.'

The two boys pulled out the paintings, one by one. There were pictures of the house slaves, people in the street, boys at exercise, all doing something, like weaving, or cooking, or dancing. Photios named any that he knew.

'And this one is Straton being beaten at running by me!' laughed Photios. 'You made his hair much wilder than it is. Straton is your rival in everything. Of course, he's not as strong as you when it comes to –' Arianos dropped his cup and it rolled under the bench.

'Sorry,' he grunted.

'Yes,' Photios went on. 'Straton's a bit of a bully, but you usually keep him in line.'

'Come along, Photios,' said Arianos. 'He's beginning to look pale again. We've tired him out.'

As they left, Themis was thinking, *'I'm not tired. I just want to know if I'll get better and remember who I am. And what will happen to me if I don't …'*

>>>

Chapter 5: enemy

From Bernie's Blog. Feb 24th 2010, Wednesday

Athens, Hotel Artemis

There's a cold wind and it looks like it will rain, not like when we were here with the school. I spent a while with Suzanne last night. Held her hand and told her stuff about friends and things. It's easier to talk to her when I know the other people in the room probably don't understand what I'm saying. They just seem to think Mrs Jenkins and I are nuts, talking to someone who can't hear us, but the doctors say it's good.

But it seems Suzanne had a bad night. Mrs J said she had been groaning and thrashing around. I stayed for ages this afternoon so that Mrs J could get some sleep at the hotel. Josh and I are having a meal tonight with some Americans he met. Then I'll go back to the hospital and stay there till morning. Must tell Suzz about the sexy messages Josh's girlfriend texts him. Shouldn't mention that in a blog, I suppose …

<<<

Themis stood at the window of his sick room looking down on the courtyard. Melanas was walking through it, carrying a huge bundle. He put it down near the street door. As he straightened up, a man rushed out of the house into the courtyard.

'In the name of all the gods, Nikanor!' shouted Eirini. 'Just get out of my house! Leave me and my family in peace! You created your problems alone. You must solve them alone.' She turned and rushed inside.

'You'll be sorry!' Nikanor called after her, shaking his fist. 'I'll make you sorry you didn't support your husband's brother in his hour of need. May the gods curse you and all that is yours!'

Themis stood up in alarm at the curse and Melanas looked up at him. Nikanor followed his glance and spat on the ground when he saw his nephew, then turned and stormed out of the courtyard into the street, slamming the door.

'Nothing to worry about, young master,' said Melanas. 'It's not the first time Mr Nikanor has come trying to borrow money.'

'He seems to really hate us. What will happen?' asked Themis.

'Nothing,' said Melanas. 'He's a bear without claws.' He disappeared into the kitchens.

Themis sat on by the window. There had been so much hate in Nikanor's eyes that he felt sick. Had he perhaps done something bad to his uncle in the past? Was that what everyone was hiding? *'I wish I could ask my dad or my brother,'* he thought. *'Or just anyone I could trust to answer my questions truthfully … Perhaps I have a tutor who could help. I'll ask Mama if I can go back to lessons.'* He sighed. *'But she'll probably say no.'*

And yet, when Eirini and the slave woman Mika came in and he asked her, she said, 'Good,' as she threw back the covers on his bed. Mika rolled them up. 'We'll just get your bedding into the sun and then I'll send a messenger to your music tutor.'

'Oh, right,' said Themis, pleased at how easy that had been. 'Photios says I used to play the flute,'

Eirini laughed. 'Very badly,' she said. 'But only because you wouldn't practise. All your tutors say you are perfectly capable at your lessons but you rarely do the homework!' And she swept out.

Themis followed her. They found the boy slave in the courtyard. 'Please go to Athamas' house,' Eirini said to him, 'and ask if he can give Themis a lesson tomorrow. Bring his answer back.'

The boy lowered his head in acknowledgment, looked at Themis with a conspiratorial smile, and left.

'Who is that?' asked Themis, as they went into Eirini's salon. The slightly musty smell was overlaid now by floral perfume.

'Athamas is your music teacher,' said Eirini, picking up her sewing.

'No, the slave boy,' said Themis.

'Oh. He's known as Frog. Your father found him in a pond on one of the campaigns in Evia. The orders were that all the people in the area be killed, but your father somehow couldn't kill a baby. Why?'

'Just the way he smiled at me as he left.'

'Well, you did use to go hunting for hares with him before your accident. I'm sure he thinks of you as his special master. You're almost the same age.'

Themis was thinking, *'He'll know.'* But he just said, 'I've only seen him once that I remember.'

'I haven't allowed him into the women's rooms since he was seven or so.' Eirini stood up and took her sewing to the window.

A hubbub at the door to the street drew them both back through the salon into the courtyard. Two women had arrived together.

'Good morning, Ismini!' called Eirini to the first one. She put her work on a bench and approached the second, much older woman. 'I salute you, Asterodia, sacred lady,' and she bowed her head. 'Thank you for coming.'

'I am interested to see how the summoned spirit is getting on,' said the old lady, and looked directly at Themis as she spoke. The force of her gaze made him take a step back. Then, as she came towards him and reached out for his hands, he held his ground. Her eyes were intense, with green and golden flecks and a bright green line around the iris. She was the same height as he was.

She took his hands in her warm, dry grasp and turned him gently so that his back was to his mother. Her face was calm, lovely even, though the skin was finely wrinkled all over. He felt energy flooding into him through their hands.

But suddenly, visions of wounded, screaming goats and horses filled his mind, immediately replaced by a black sky shot with light from whirling suns over a river of fire lapping at his feet. His heart raced, he broke into a sweat, and he could hardly breathe.

The old priestess let go of his hands and the visions disappeared. Themis was panting and shaking. 'What..?' he muttered in bewilderment.

Asterodia had gone very pale, but she took a slow breath and massaged her hands together. 'Are these your dreams?' she asked.

'Yes,' Themis nodded, wiping sweating hands down his tunic. 'How ..?'

'These dreams – when you think you are going to die – they are the echoes of your accident.' She reached again for his hands, but he held back. 'We won't go there again,' she said reassuringly. 'I promise.'

He gave her his unsteady hands and felt again the tingle of her energy. 'Do you have other dreams?' she asked.

'Lots,' he said. 'Sometimes they're frightening, like that one, or when I'm falling off a cliff, or into a whirlpool, but sometimes the animals I see are wild and free, not wounded or dead. And I hear human voices. I can't understand them and I can't see them – but they sound kind. And sometimes, even when I'm awake, I hear a single note, like a lyre-string plucked, repeating again and again, very quietly.' He looked into those searching eyes. 'Sacred Lady, what does it all mean? Will I ever remember? Is this ever going to stop? And what will happen to me if it doesn't?'

Asterodia looked down at their hands and touched the fading bruise. 'Ah … ' she said, and released him. 'Yes, I believe it will pass.' She looked back at his face. 'Eventually. Perhaps the gods are being kind in hiding some of your past from you. You must be patient – and brave. Having some unhappy things in life wiped away for a while can be a boon.' She was keeping her voice very low.

'But what things?' murmured Themis as she stepped away.

The street door flew open again and a young woman rushed in with a child in her arms, followed by a slave girl. Asterodia turned to greet her.

'Hello, everyone!' the young woman sang merrily. 'Mama! Mrs Ismini!' She put the toddler down and he stumbled off towards the kitchen. 'Sacred Lady,' she said as she approached Themis and Asterodia. 'Our saviour – or rather Themis' saviour.' She kissed Asterodia's right hand. 'I hear he's not himself yet, but I hope he's thanking you properly.'

'I … I didn't know…' stammered Themis with an apologetic smile.

'No one told him, Mrs Myrto, that it was I who officiated at his "return",' said Asterodia briskly. 'And he'll be himself again soon enough.'

'Oh, no!' laughed Myrto in exaggerated protest. 'Not himself! Not the never-sits-still old Themis. Please don't say we've got *him* back!'

Themis looked a question at his mother. Eirini laughed and said, 'Don't you recognise Myrto, your sister?'

'I wasn't sure,' he said. 'Hello, sister.' But Myrto saw her baby tottering back towards the water trough by the well in the courtyard and ran to catch him up into her arms. Themis went over to them. 'And hello to sister's son. Shall I hold him? What's his name?'

Myrto looked amazed for a moment and then handed the boy to Themis. 'He's Timodemus. You really don't remember, do you?'

'Not a thing,' Themis said with a grin. 'So whatever you did to me before the accident is now a total secret!'

The women went into the salon, talking and laughing. Myrto sang as she laid out hairdressing implements. Chloe came walking carefully to join them from the kitchen with a plate of misshapen sweetmeats.

Themis carried Timodemus out through the salon to the open yard. 'What a din they make, don't they, Timo,' he said to the little boy as he put him down on the paving. 'Come and see this.' He led the toddler by the hand to a large thick bush. There was a dead bird on the earth under the bush.

The toddler made a grab at the bird with his little fist. 'Do you want to have a look?' Themis asked him. He picked the bird up, carried it to a bench and laid it down on its back. He sat beside it and stroked the soft feathers on its breast. 'Nice,' said Timo, his clumsy movements rocking the stiff little corpse.

Asterodia stepped into the garden from the salon. 'What have you found?' she asked. When she saw the bird she stood completely still, as though listening. 'It was a song thrush,' she said at last.

Myrto sang out from in the salon, 'Come back, dear Sacred Lady. Come back and see our work. I was only joking about Xenovia. She's a wonderful priestess. She just didn't understand that I was teasing her.' She came out and saw her son playing with the dead bird. 'Oh, Themis! You didn't let him touch that dead thing, did you?'

'It's a song thrush,' said Asterodia. 'Are you staying today, Myrto?'

'My plan is to take Themis back with us to the farm this afternoon,' said Myrto, picking Timodemus up. 'Themis, please bury that, or throw it out or something.'

'But look,' said Themis. 'See how light it is. And how soft its feathers are.' He threatened to put it down the back of Myrto's chiton.

'Yuch!' she said as she skipped out of his way and back to the salon, carrying Timodemus on her hip.

Asterodia held out her hands for the bird. Themis suddenly felt stupid. He laid it gently between her lined palms. Her lips moved as she walked away with it to a collection of pots in the corner.

Themis followed Myrto into the salon. The three women and Chloe were laughing as he sat down.

Eirini was saying, 'When Asterodia comes back you must all apologise for being rude about her daughter. Xenovia is a beautiful and intelligent woman, and a talented administrator and singer. You really should not have teased her yesterday, Myrto. She may later have the "power" like her mother. It may show itself when she's older. You can never be sure.'

'Not with priestesses!' said Ismini, laughing wryly. 'They know how to keep everyone guessing.'

'They have an academy where they are taught exactly that!' declared Myrto with a giggle. She was unplaiting her mother's hair and had a tray of pins and ribbons beside her ready for the new style.

'That's enough!' said Eirini. 'Themis, Frog tells me that your tutor can fit you in tomorrow morning, so go and find your old music lessons. The flute you played is in the andron, on the top shelf.'

Yes, the flute was there, and yes there was some kind of notation on the tablets beside it that Themis was pretty sure was music, but he couldn't work out what it meant.

As he puzzled over it, Asterodia came in. 'The bird is buried and I must leave,' she said. 'But I just wanted to ask you something.'

Themis stood up. 'Of course,' he said. 'And I haven't thanked you properly for all you did to help me recover. Thank you, Sacred Lady.'

'Your recovery has only just begun,' said the old lady.

She sat down on the couch opposite Themis as she spoke. He had an uneasy feeling that women were not supposed to sit in this room. But he sat down too, where he could see her face. She said, 'I wanted to ask you something more about your dreams. Is there some kind of pattern to them? An image that recurs – after you've eaten meat, for example?'

Themis was at a loss. 'Not that I've noticed,' he said. 'I'm just so glad to wake up …'

'And have you told anyone else about them?'

'I mentioned them to a friend and Mama knows they happen, because she's woken me to stop me shouting more than once. But she hasn't asked what I see.'

'Your mother is a good woman. Since your father was killed, she's been trying to make plans. She has just applied to become a "mother" at the sanctuary of Artemis Vravron.'

'What …' Themis was bewildered. 'What is … Artemis Vravron?'

'It's a place on the east coast of Attica, about two days' walk away. Apart from a festival every four years for younger girls, there is now a school for young women, to prepare them for marriage. They go in groups and stay for forty days or so. They take lessons and sing and dance and pray to Artemis and Hera. They are taught by priestesses and cared for by "mothers".'

'Do you teach there?'

'No, I don't,' Asterodia said. 'No. My work is here in Athens, mainly in the temples of the Akropolis and of Demeter in the city.'

'So … is Mama going to leave?' Themis covered his mouth with his hand. He felt dizzy and sick. Would this 'new' world ever stay the same long enough for him to feel he understood it?

Asterodia's sternly beautiful face softened into a smile. 'She has to be accepted first,' she said kindly, 'and that will take a while. I'm sure she won't leave until you are completely well and your brother Diodotos is in the army. You should tell her more about what you dream.'

'I'll … mention it to her,' said Themis, but he was thinking, '*What good will that do if she's intent on deserting us? And what will happen to me – and to Chloe?*'

Asterodia stood up. 'Good. I am reassured now that you are under the protection of a god, or possibly more than one.'

'Is that good?' Themis asked, standing up, too.

'Usually. Though the gods are known for demanding something in return for their special attention.'

'How will I know which god – or gods? Or what they want me to do?'

'They will make it clear – and I'm sure they'll tell you if there's a price to pay.' She looked for a long moment into his eyes. He felt calmer. 'And now, I must go' she was brisk again. 'Your recovery will be slow, but I believe that it will be complete.'

Themis bowed slightly to her, but found he couldn't speak.

At the door the old priestess turned and said, 'Oh, and please, Themistokles, persuade Myrto that she – and you – should not go to her home today.' Then she was gone.

Chapter 6: sister

Eirini made it quite clear that Themis would *not* be going to Myrto's farm after the midday meal, but Myrto insisted she had to go home anyway. So she set off in her husband's farm wagon with her son, her slave girl, and the driver.

Themis stood by the street door watching them leave, thinking how soon he might be completely alone. His mother was on her way up the stairs when he said to her, 'Can I ask you something, Mama?'

'Not now, my son,' she said. 'I have to sort something out on a loom. You get some rest.'

He went through to the kitchens to see if he could find Frog to answer some questions, but Frog had been sent to one of Eirini's customers with a message.

Themis climbed the stairs and flopped down on the bed in the sick room in a state of shock. Who would explain things and where would he live when his mother left? Was there in fact someone out to harm him even though everyone said there wasn't? And if it wasn't that, what was it that everyone seemed to be hiding? Why couldn't he remember anything? He started to go through everything he did remember …

He must have slept, because suddenly there was a man with a loud voice in the courtyard. Themis got up, straightened his chiton and looked down from the window. Eirini was greeting a man with a stomach so large that Themis couldn't see his feet.

'Come in and sit with us in the salon,' she was saying. They moved off. She looked up and signalled to Themis to join them.

As he entered, Eirini said, 'Themis, this is your uncle Panainos, my cousin.' Themis sat where his mother indicated. 'He's interested in how you are feeling.'

'Uncle Panainos.' Themis greeted him with a respectful nod.

'Themistokles, my boy!' boomed his uncle. 'How are you getting on?'

'I'm getting much better in my body, thank you …' Panainos opened his eyes wide and looked at Eirini as if to say, 'How right you are.' Themis went on, '… but I have no memory of my life before the pony threw me. I am very confused … and I dream a lot.'

'In your sleep, I hope, young man,' laughed Panainos. He had stained and broken teeth. 'Not day dreams of how you are going to conquer the world.'

Eirini made a tutting sound and shook her head at her cousin.

Themis smiled hesitantly. 'Not that kind of dream at all.' He was thinking, '*Is this who I'll be going to live with?*'

'Themis is beginning lessons again tomorrow,' said Eirini. 'But I think we will postpone the gymnasium for a while.'

'You wouldn't have allowed your mother to do that in the old days,' said Panainos with a wry smile. 'Always dashing around doing something foolhardy, you were.'

'Well, he doesn't do that now. He is still recovering,' said Eirini with a hard look at her cousin. 'Have you tried painting anything since you found your paints?' she asked her son. 'Perhaps you don't remember, but Panainos is a famous painter.'

'*He must know the secret*,' thought Themis. '*I wonder if* he'll *tell me*.' He began to answer, 'No, I – '

But Panainos interrupted. 'Do you really not remember coming with me to see my Battle of Marathon in the Agora? You asked me if I'd been there!' He laughed with his head thrown back. The sound echoed off the walls of the salon, while his stomach danced under his tunic.

'No, I'm sorry, uncle, but I don't remember anything. Why is that funny?' Themis found himself smiling in spite of his worries as he watched the stomach bouncing with what seemed like a life of its own.

'The joke,' chuckled Panainos, 'is that the Battle of Marathon was sixty years ago, and even I am not that old.'

'Ah. Then I ap … apologise, is that the word?' said Themis. 'Was I being rude, or did I just not know?'

'Yes. Apologise is a good word here,' said Panainos with an appreciative nod. 'Oh, you knew, all right. You were just playing to the crowd.'

'Crowd?' asked Themis.

'Yes. We were in the Painted Arcade, in the market place, where my painting is. There were lots of men around. Some had recognised me and followed us to see what we were up to.' Panainos became more serious. '*Do* you still paint?'

A loud battering on the street door interrupted them. 'That'll be my wife,' laughed Panainos.

But Eirini had jumped up. 'Where's Melanas?' she called, and walked briskly into the courtyard. Themis followed her. Melanas was already at the door. On a nod from Eirini he opened it.

A man in a rough woollen tunic almost fell through it. He could hardly speak he was so breathless. 'Disaster! Hermes deserted us!'

'What are you talking about?' Eirini shouted in alarm. 'What's happened?'

'It's Mrs Myrto, Madam,' he sobbed. 'She is hurt. The wagon turned on its side and she is trapped under it. I ran …'

'Melanas, take the master's horse and go,' ordered Eirini as she pulled the messenger to a bench in the courtyard. 'Take a rope!' she called as Melanas ran to the stables.

'What about the little boy?' she asked, shaking the man's shoulder as he sat.

'I don't know. I didn't see him after the wagon went over into the ditch.'

'You are the driver?'

'Yes, madam.'

'So what did you do to tip the wagon into the ditch?' Eirini had raised a hand to hit the man, but Panainos was beside her and caught her arm. She snatched it from his hand. The sound of a horse galloping away came to them from the street.

The driver explained. 'A rider on a horse came straight at us, madam. I tried to make my oxen move over. They pulled hard to get away from the galloping horse and stepped too far to the side. The wagon slid off the road into the ditch and suddenly turned over.'

'How is it that *you* were saved? Why weren't *you* hurt as well?' Themis wasn't surprised that Eirini was raising her voice, but he hadn't seen her shaking with anger and fear before. He was suddenly dizzy, and sat down abruptly on the ground.

'I jumped off towards the road as the wagon went over. There was a strange sound, madam. Like a crack of something breaking, but Mrs Myrto shouted at me to get help, so I didn't stay to see what it was.'

Eirini had raised her hand again and hit the man on the head with her fist before Panainos could grab her. 'You stupid idiot,' she screamed. 'You should have checked she was all right!' Panainos put both his arms around Eirini and held her tight. She began to sob. 'What have you done to my daughter, to my grandson … ' They stood like that for a few moments. Panainos looked at the driver and motioned with his head that he should go to the kitchen. The driver limped off.

Eirini suddenly took a deep breath and pushed away from Panainos. 'We must prepare a bed for Myrto. Melanas will bring her back here if the gods are willing.' She looked down at Themis. 'The weavers must go home and you'll have to move down to your own room. Mika!' She called for the slave woman and ran up the stairs to the women's rooms.

Panainos said to Themis, 'I'll be off. I'll only be in the way.' He was gone and the street door had closed before Themis had even stood up to say goodbye. The two girls who wove for Eirini in the upstairs workroom came clattering down the stairs and followed him out.

A while later, Themis heard a horse coming at a fast walk down the street and the voices of a child and a woman in great pain. He pulled open the door and the horse came in. Melanas was riding, with Myrto in front of him. She was screaming and sobbing. She held Timodemus away from her chest. Themis reached up and took the boy from his mother. He was covered in mud, crying at the top of his lungs. Myrto's slave girl limped behind.

Melanas dismounted and Myrto slid off into his arms with a cry. She was in a terrible state. Her breathing was ragged, her clothes were torn and covered in blood. One leg was hanging useless, and her face was deathly pale. She was calling on all the gods to help her.

Eirini appeared and she and Melanas carried Myrto up the stairs while she screamed and cried and prayed. The slave girl took Timodemus from Themis and carried him up after them.

A few moments later Eirini came to the window and called down to Themis over the cries from inside the sick room. 'Go and find Ismini, Themis. Tell her to bring a healer from the Asklepion. Someone who knows about bones. Go! Go!'

Themis called 'On my way!' before he realised he had no idea where to go. He ran into the kitchen and asked the driver who was having his foot bathed by Mika. 'Turn left out of the door, next left, second right, on the right with a green door and a new Herm,' were the instructions.

'What's a herm?' Themis asked.

'The statue by the door,' said the driver, shaking his head in disbelief.

Themis ran out into the street. It was the first time he had been outside the house. He noticed the statue of Hermes outside their own door as he set off at a run. It was about chest high, just a stone column with the head of a man with lots of hair and a curly beard on the top, and a worn and chipped phallus lower down. When he got to Ismini's house he saw that their Herm had a much more realistic head and a more flamboyant phallus. He banged on the street door.

A small window in the door opened. 'What do you want, young master?' asked a man's voice with a strange accent.

'My mother, Mrs Eirini, needs Mrs Ismini's help immediately. There's been an accident and my sister has been hurt.'

'What is it?' came another man's voice from inside. The door flew open and a large courtyard appeared. A tall, muscular man with no hair at all stood in the entrance. He was wearing a magnificent chiton of dark red with a silver border. 'How are you, Themistokles?' he asked. 'Is it Myrto or Chloe who is hurt?' His voice was surprisingly melodic for such a powerful man.

Themis had no idea who this was, but he answered, 'Myrto'. At that moment he saw Mrs Ismini come hurrying through the courtyard. She was carrying a bag. She swept past the tall man with a rueful smile and grabbed Themis' arm, propelling him back along the street the way he had come.

'My mother said to ask you to bring a healer who knows about bones,' said Themis breathlessly.

'Right,' said Ismini, stopping in the middle of the street, causing passers by to bump into her. 'In that case, take my bag and go home. Say I'll be there immediately. I'll have to go this way,' and she pointed towards the Akropolis.

She rushed off and Themis ran home. He delivered Ismini's bag to his mother. He was feeling breathless and giddy, so he sat on the bench in the yard. The sun was dipping into gold and grey clouds as evening came on. Myrto's cries were muffled now.

After a while, Melanas came and sat beside him. 'Her left leg is broken and some of her ribs. She can hardly breathe,' he said in a worried voice. Chloe crept up to them. She lay along the bench with her head in Themis' lap.

He stroked her hair, but couldn't speak. He was remembering the last words that Asterodia had said to him: ' … persuade Myrto that she … should not go to her home today.'

Chapter 7: sabotage

From Bernie's Blog. Feb 25th 2010, Thursday

Athens, Hotel Artemis

It was a good evening, last night. I actually forgot to worry for a couple of hours. The American girl said she loved my hair and that she'd always wanted to be a redhead, like Christina Hendricks, whoever that is. The guy just called me Little Miss Sunset everytime he spoke to me! They're here studying European politics in the 1960s. The food was great! Stuffed cabbage leaves in lemony sauce and really tender pork chops. And the chips – a different thing altogether! The taverna was in a basement – very cosy!

This morning, Josh wanted to walk to where Suzanne got hit. When we got there I took a photo – I'll post it later. The traffic was horrendous.

Two doctors came to see Suzanne today. They didn't tell us much, but they say she is definitely not going to die. They changed the medication in the drip and checked the collarbone. Her body's still ok, they say, and there are small signs that she will come round one day.

One day! What does that mean?! They say her being restless and even unhappy is good. It means something is repairing itself in her brain. The MRI they did before I got back shows improvement because the blood clots are smaller.

I held her hand all the time I was there today. Sometimes I gave it a
squeeze and asked her to come back and sometimes I just read to her
from 'Twilight'. She didn't move at all. How long can this go on?

'Melanas!' whispered Eirini as she came down from the sickroom.
'Madam?'
'Sleep here by the stairs in case I need you. The healers are leaving
now.'

After much screaming and wailing, Myrto was quiet. Eirini went on.
'The healer says Myrto's leg will be straight if she uses crutches for
sixty days or so. Her ribs will be painful for a month at least.' Her
voice broke. 'But it seems she was pregnant – perhaps seventy days
…'

The healers came quietly down the stairs with their bags and left.

Myrto was in Themis' sickroom, so he went to the room he shared
with his absent brother and lay down. He didn't feel at all sleepy, but
suddenly woke to find it was morning.

Eirini was at the door. Perhaps she had been awake all night, but she
had tidied her hair and seemed as alert as ever. 'Do you remember that
we let your guardian slave go when your father died?' Themis shook
his head with a frown. Eirini went on, 'Never mind. You didn't like
him anyway, and wanted to go to your lessons on your own. But I've
asked Frog to go with you to Athamas for your lesson today.'

'Thank you,' Themis said, sitting up in bed. 'How is Myrto?'

'She bled a lot and has a lot of pain, but she is managing to eat
breakfast.' Eirini smiled a strange smile. 'They didn't get her this time!'

'They?' asked Themis.

'Whoever caused that wagon to turn over.'

'What do you mean?' The note of the lyre, regular, faint, was back
in Themis' head. He ignored it as usual.

Eirini came and sat on the foot of his bed. 'The driver and Melanas
went back to the wagon at dawn to take it home. But the axles had
both been cut almost through from underneath. So when it tipped
over yesterday, the wheels broke off.'

'You mean it was … what's it called?'

'Sabotaged. Yes. I've asked my cousin to have the guards investigate,
because someone wanted Myrto or her husband, or both, to get hurt.'

'But why?' Themis' frustration at his empty memory was loud.

His mother answered, 'Hush now. I know. And I can't think who, either. But it seems Myrto forgot to make any offerings to Hermes before she set off to come here. Perhaps the god gave the idea to a slave to work on those axles, or made another young woman jealous of Myrto because she has a child, or found someone with a grudge against Menelaus, or – '

'I've forgotten who Menelaus is,' Themis interrupted.

'Myrto's husband.' Eirini, deep in thought, spoke from a long way away. 'However, I have my suspicions …'

Themis had a sudden horrible thought. 'What about Timodemos?'

Eirini shuddered slightly and jumped up. 'It seems he's fine. He'd rolled into the ditch and got very dirty, but no injuries. He's playing with Chloe,' she said. 'You'd better get a move on if you want something to eat before you go to your music lesson.'

Frog said that Athamas' house was near the road up to the Great Gates to the Akropolis.

Frog walked a little behind Themis, carrying his tablet bundle and the flute. At one point, he said quietly, 'Turn right here, young master.' They took the turn and he added, 'Bad night.'

Themis nodded but didn't reply. He wasn't sure of his relationship with this boy, so he just walked on as though he was thinking deeply. Which in fact he was. He was confused by the idea that a god would want to hurt a mother and a baby for not praying to him. He thought it was much more likely that the 'clawless' Nikanos had arranged for the accident.

But he didn't want to think about that, or his coming lesson. So he looked around as they passed a large open-air theatre and then a small temple beside the road. The streets were full of busy people and lumbering wagons. The music teacher's house was quite small, and near enough to the Akropolis to hear the hammering and creaking of builders and their machinery.

'The Great Gates are only half-finished,' Frog told him. As they got closer, the screeching sounds of a lute under torture came to them.

Themis was shown into a small room to wait. Frog said, 'Your mother wants you to have a short lesson today, so I'm to stay until you're finished. I'll be ready any time you've had enough.' He winked and left for the slaves' room.

The painful practice stopped and the door opened. Athamas was short and thin with a neat black beard and curly hair. He wore a long straw-coloured chiton which he swirled as he showed a young boy out. The boy smiled at Themis with false brightness as he called for his slave.

'Ah, Themistokles. Come in, come in, do,' said Athamas with a sigh. 'It's good to see you well enough to be here, but I was sorry to hear about Myrto's accident. Your family is having a lot of bad luck lately.'

Themis followed Athamas into the music room. There was a large window onto a small yard, in front of which two stools and a stand for tablets were set.

'So, take your usual stool and let's see what you remember,' said Athamas, trying to sound enthusiastic.

Themis didn't sit. 'That is my problem, Mr Athamas. I don't remember anything.'

'Oh come on.' Athamas sat on his stool. His voice was tired and had a hard edge. 'You always have excuses for not doing your practice. But I've never heard that one before.'

'Perhaps I am wasting your time altogether, sir, but I really do not remember anything from my life before my injury.' Themis saw that Athamas was speechless, so he went on. 'I've looked at the tablets that my mother says are from our lessons, but I do not understand them.'

Athamas stood and took Themis' arm. He pulled him gently towards the window.

'May I see the injury?' he asked more kindly.

Themis tilted his head to the light.

Athamas put both his hands round Themis' head very gently and moved it slowly back and forth. He took a deep breath. 'And you have lost your memory completely?' he asked.

'Yes,' answered Themis. Athamas smelt slightly of something that made Themis think of maggots. 'I am well in other ways, but ...' Athamas began stroking Themis' remaining hair, so he stepped back, kicking his stool.

'In that case,' said Athamas, suddenly professional, 'we should start at the beginning. Do you have your flute?'

Themis found the lesson interesting, to his own and Athamas' surprise. But his teacher looked at him oddly from time to time. And he soon found it hard to focus his mind. When Athamas came and stood behind him to show him a fingering sequence, Themis decided he should go.

'I'm feeling dizzy,' he said. 'I think that'll do for today, Mr Athamas.'

Athamas nodded. 'You've certainly changed your attitude,

Themistokles,' he said, with a smile. 'I'm sure we can make a great deal of progress together if you carry on like this.' He took Themis' elbow and gave it a little squeeze. Themis looked into his eyes and saw a sly glint there. He hurried out of the door.

'Why does he keep wanting to touch me?' he asked Frog.

They were walking back along the busy street.

'Ah,' answered Frog. 'Did that bother you? You told him not to do that in … very strong terms just after your father died, I heard.'

'Why didn't I just stop going?'

'You didn't want to upset your mother.'

'Hmm … Frog, did you and I used to hunt hares together?'

'That's right,' answered Frog.

'So you knew … er … know me quite well?'

'Only from the hunting. Oh, and when you used to run for training.'

'Have I changed a lot, would you say?' Both boys were looking ahead, negotiating their way between pedestrians and laden donkeys.

'You didn't use to be so polite,' said Frog. 'You made out you didn't care what people thought of you. You were quite pushy and stopped people criticizing you by criticizing them first.'

'What did I use to say to you?'

'To me?' Frog laughed. 'Apart from the usual … er, vulgarities, you mean? In company, you'd call me a crippled donkey when I couldn't keep up with you, and a blindworm when I missed with my catapult. But then you didn't seem to mind when I called *you* reckless or butterfingers.'

'That's not allowed?'

'Not from a slave, no.' They were both quiet for a while, then Frog said, 'You really have changed. You want to be careful. People could see your politeness as weakness, and make things difficult for you.'

'Like Athamas?'

'Maybe. If you don't stop him bothering you. His attention is the not the kind you want from older men.'

'And it sounds as though the boys I do training with are not all as decent as Photios.'

'You going to start training again, then?'

'I don't think Mama will allow it yet. But I feel I need something to get me away from the house. With Myrto so sick, I'm in the way.'

'We could go hunting, then,' suggested Frog. 'We needn't do anything too active, just walking and running and a bit of target practice.'

'That would be great!' The cloud that Athamas had created in Themis' mind disappeared. 'How about this afternoon?'

'I have duties this afternoon, but tomorrow morning should be good.'

'Beat you back to the house,' said Themis and set off at a jog.

>>>

From Bernie's Blog. Feb 26th 2010, Friday

Athens, Hotel Artemis

Just had a huge fight with Josh. He's booked for us to go home on Sunday. Of course he has to go to work and I should be at school. But leaving Suzanne in this place, so foreign and uncomfortable and unhome-like is more than I can bear.

Ran out in the street cos I was so upset. Walked all the way to the hospital. No change, but I squeezed her hand and told her in my head how I feel about leaving her – purple panic!!

<<<

When Themis' stone hit the hare on the flank, Frog whispered, 'You've been practising!'

Themis laughed quietly. 'All afternoon yesterday! Your turn next.'

Frog insisted that they were completely quiet while they hunted. But when they stopped, Themis took the opportunity to ask him, 'Frog, do you know why everyone is lying to me? What are they hiding?'

Frog shook his head and shrugged. He said, 'I don't know what you mean. I don't know anyone who is hiding things from you.'

He was very convincing. Themis felt stupid again and they walked back in silence with a hare and a rabbit for the kitchen, and a huge appetite. They ate in the kitchen with Mika and Frog teasing each other over Themis' head, while he tried not to fall asleep at the table.

In his room, he curled up on his bed, pulling his pillow over his head to shut out the whimpers of Myrto in her pain and sadness, and the bustle of life in the house. He'd enjoyed the mountain but there were times when he'd heard that recurring note and felt his skin crawl with more than the morning chill. '*It's all so weird,*' he thought …

Between the trees, Themis could see two hares, huge and black, with their paws raised to box. One said, 'Nikanor hunts the white hart. He thinks he's a lion.' The other replied, 'Lions maul and crunch. I box.' When they attacked each other, Themis left them and walked with some purple trees along a wide valley, but he could still hear the hares' voices, quiet and concerned now.

'Are the other bones sound?' the first one said.

'No further damage. Just the one break,' the other answered.

Themis carried on walking beside the trees. They seemed to be talking to him, telling him a story, taking turns, calm and loving.

>>>

Chapter 8: dreams

From Bernie's Blog. Feb 27th 2010, Saturday

Athens, Hotel Artemis

Went to the hospital tonight to say goodbye. Was feeling awful. Mrs Jenkins and I sat quietly for a while, holding Suzanne's good hand. Other patients had visitors with loud voices, though they did quieten down later.

I asked Mrs J whether the doctors had said anything about paralysis and whether her other bones were sound. She said there was no further damage, just the one break – in the collarbone.

And then Suzanne moaned and I jumped out of my skin.

Mrs Jenkins looked at me and said 'This is what she does sometimes, especially at night.'

I hadn't heard it like that before. 'She could be conscious, couldn't she?' I was so excited I forgot to whisper and the woman in the next bed made a really loud shhhhhsh noise, like she hadn't been the reason for all that noise earlier!

'That's what the doctors say,' whispered Mrs J. 'So we have to go on holding her hand and talking to her. And they say it's even more important now she's giving these kind of signs.'

Suzanne muttered something. So I picked up her hand and held it and told her who was in the room. Her mum smiled and stroked her knee and told her about her brothers at home. Then I said what it was like outside and that we were trying to be quiet not to disturb the other patients – anything I could think of. When I ran out of things to say, her mum began remembering when she was little and they'd gone on holiday to the sea.

So we were taking it in turns and I'm sure Suzz squeezed my hand a bit, though her mum said she doubted it. Anyway, she didn't make any more sounds.

Then Mrs Jenkins got a call on her mobile from Suzanne's father. She looked all flustered and had to go out to the kind of dayroom place to take it. When she came back she told me that they'd decided that Suzanne had to be taken back to England, to a hospital in Newcastle! Fantastic! Pity I'm going back tomorrow, but at least I'll be able to visit her soon.

Suzanne's dad, Mr Short, had arranged this without asking Suzanne's mum, but I could see that she was grateful. Her present husband has not been very supportive, always calling and asking when she's coming back. Doesn't he get it? She can't exactly leave her daughter in a coma in a foreign country, can she?

So Mr Short is making the arrangements and they'll probably be ready to leave in a couple of days. High fives, everyone!

Midnight

Can't believe it! Suzanne's dad has been reading my blog and he's arranged for me to fly back with S and her mum. He's been in touch with my Dad, and Josh goes back tomorrow as planned.

Awesome! Stunning! Thank you, Mr Short. You're just wicked! And yes, I'll keep this blog up to date every chance I get. I'll be at the hospital at eight in the morning and post more by lunchtime.

<<<

That night, as he was going to bed in the boys' room, Eirini whispered, 'Sleep well, Themis. Thank the gods for this better day.'

'Good night, Mama,' said Themis. He lay down on his bed, and looked out at the small piece of sky he could see, trying to remember the names of the stars, so as not to think and not to remember his dreams.

At last he felt sleepy and turned over. But he found he could not feel his arm. When he looked down, it was missing. He could see a young man carrying it away. He followed the young man, walking between pale linen walls, following the sound of a fountain. People passed behind the walls, talking quietly, and the lyre-note beat its rhythm.

He woke in the courtyard, his feet in the water trough.

His heart gave a lurch when he realised where he was and that the sounds he had been listening to were only a dream. He was shivering. As he stepped out of the trough he slipped and fell to his knees, but at least he had two working arms.

'Are you all right, young master?' came Melanas' growl from the dark.

'I was trying to find my ... something in my dream,' Themis answered, his teeth chattering and his heart hammering. 'I seem to have walked in my sleep.'

Melanas put an arm round Themis' waist and almost picked him up as he helped him back to his room. Once he was back in bed, Melanas said quietly, 'Perhaps someone should sleep in this room with you, or next door in your father's room?'

Themis nodded. 'The dreams seem to be getting stronger, not weaker,' he murmured.

'I'll be next door from now on,' said Melanas. 'Lie down now. I'll light a lamp and bring you linden tea with honey.'

>>>

From Bernie's Blog. Feb 28th 2010, Sunday

Athens, Hotel Artemis

Josh left on the bus to the airport about midday. He texted later to say he'd arrived in London and was on the train to Penrith.

Not much happening at the hospital today except that it's Sunday and the little church in the grounds was very busy. I sat reading to Suzanne most of the day, but walked up Lykavitos Hill this afternoon to look at the view. I wish I'd known about it earlier. It was fantastic! One of the other patients had a woman visitor who spoke English and she told me about it. She said it was more than three hundred steps on the path going up. I was puffed out, but it was worth the effort. You can see for a hundred kilometres, she said, and I could see all round, mountains to the north and sea full of islands to the south-west. Athens is huge.

Suzanne didn't move. Mrs J had lots of phone calls and we'll have to spend tomorrow and Tuesday getting things organised for the trip. I'm to 'Suzanne-sit' while she does the legwork. It seems that there will be no bill for this hospitalisation as the UK is still part of the EU. Mrs J is relieved! The plane home is going to be expensive enough.

<<<

'What should I do, Frog?' Themis asked. On a piece of broken tile, he was painting a picture of a dead butterfly he'd found in the yard. 'I really don't want to go back to Mr Athamas. Aren't there any other music teachers?'

'I was hoping you'd say that,' laughed Frog. 'You'd better ask your mother.'

'Shall I tell her why?'

'Why not? This is just the beginning. You'll have plenty of invitations from older men soon. You'll be quite pretty when your hair grows back.'

Themis stopped painting, looked sharply at Frog and said 'I'll be what?'

'Not *my* fault, young master,' said Frog, spreading his hands. 'It's a truth that no one is telling you. You have good skin, a nice voice, and a new … graceful way of moving. Also you're from a good family – and have a good education.'

'Which I don't remember at all!' said Themis. He was thinking, '*Is this THE truth that no one is telling me? It doesn't seem important enough.*'

'That won't bother them. You are attractive. And they know that you are your father's son and that's a big advantage in this city. He was very well-thought of, unlike his brother.'

Frog turned to go. Themis said, 'Those older men – what do they want?'

'Beautiful boys,' said Frog. 'Some of them want to have sex with them. Others want to remember being young. I hear they like to pass on what they've learned in their lives.' He shrugged. 'They think the boys are themselves when they were fifteen. They give them presents, send them poems – '

'I don't think I'd like that much,' Themis said.

'I doubt you'll escape it,' said Frog. 'Most boys are flattered. But it *is* more usual for boys two or three years older than you. Melanas might be more help. He knows your father's friends.'

But when Themis asked him about Athamas, Melanas was dismissive. 'Perhaps it's time you got away from him,' he said. 'Don't bother your mother with why. You can arrange to change your music teacher because he lives too far away. Photios has a good teacher. He lives nearby.'

'How do you know that?' asked Themis.

Melanas laughed. 'Photios likes the music of my country. We sing and play together sometimes. You don't remember?'

Themis shook his head sadly. 'Thank you, Melanas,' he said thoughtfully. 'I'll see what Mama says.'

He found Eirini coming out of Myrto's room. She put a finger to her lips and they crept downstairs.

In the salon she wrote something on a wax tablet, put it on a shelf, then turned to him.

'Is anyone doing anything about Myrto's sabotage?' Themis asked, gesturing at the room above where his sister lay.

'Myrto's husband and his parents are working on it. And Phidias and

Panainos. But they don't have much to go on.'

'Do you think whoever fixed that axel is the same as whoever tried to smother me? I want to try and find out about that but – '

'They can't be connected, my son,' Eirini interrupted kindly. 'That was a mistake. The family of the boy next to you had all but decided to do away with him as his epilepsy was so bad.'

Themis shrugged, unconvinced. 'It still gives me nightmares.'

'Of course, but they'll pass. Is that why you came to find me?'

'No. No. I just … It's not working with Athamas being so far away,' Themis said. 'Would you mind if I arranged to have Photios' music tutor? He lives nearer.'

'I'll need to talk to him first. Can *you* arrange that?'

Themis was once again surprised at how amenable his mother was being. 'Of course,' he said. 'And what about my other lessons?'

Eirini suddenly lifted her head as though listening. Then she relaxed and looked back at her son. 'The other boys have moved on, so you'll need some extra arithmetic and logic lessons to catch up.'

'Fine,' Themis said, 'as long as … do they cost a lot?'

Eirini laughed. 'You have changed so much, my son, that I sometimes wonder if you really are the same person. In the old days you would never have considered what something cost, and you would certainly have tried to get out of the extra lessons.'

'I just thought … '

'But you are making me very happy!'

'I am?'

'Yes! And it's fine about the money. The ritual at the bridge cost a good sum. But with all Diodotos' hard work at the farm and my weaving workshop doing well … yes, you can start your lessons.'

'And the gymnasium?'

'The healers said to give it a month before you start, so we'll see about that in ten days or so.'

'And … there's something else that's worrying me, Mama.'

'What sort of something?' Eirini's attention was on small sounds from above again.

'Please tell me what it is that no one is allowed to say to me.'

Eirini's attention snapped back to Themis' face. 'What on earth do you mean?' she said with a slight frown.

'It's just that I have this feeling that something or someone is trying to destroy me, and yet everyone is being so … evasive …'

'Don't be ridiculous, Themis,' said his mother. 'We're all trying to protect you and help you recover completely.'

'But it's obvious everyone is hiding something from me. If I knew what it was, maybe I could do something about it ...'

Eirini's face softened. 'There's nothing like that at all,' she said. She put her arms out to her son and he allowed her to hug him for a moment. 'It's just as I said, you are pleasantly different from before. You've been very ill, close to death, my little one. But you are growing into a man I am going to be proud of.'

Themis stepped back, still sure his mother was lying, still feeling sick. But all he said was, 'I hope so, Mama.'

'Why don't you ask Melanas to buy you some blank shards or even some papyrus when he goes shopping next?' Eirini suggested. 'So you can do more drawings.'

Themis looked at her for a moment. 'I could draw my dreams,' he said. 'Then maybe they wouldn't seem so ... so strange,' he said, stopping himself saying 'terrifying'.

'Tell me about them,' said his mother.

'Well, er ... I lost my arm in one of them and had to go searching for it. And last night I watched a man cutting various pieces off my body and putting them into a pot to boil.' Eirini looked shocked. Themis went on hurriedly. 'It didn't hurt, but it did make me ... well, afraid.'

'I'm not surprised, my son. But this sounds like the old you is being pared away so that the new you can flourish. Don't be afraid of mere dreams. They should fade away soon,' she said, her attention again on the room above. 'But if they don't, you can go to the professionals at the Asklepion again. Tell me if you want to do that.' Fast footsteps sounded upstairs. 'I'd better go and see,' she said and hurried out.

'Can I visit Myrto yet?' he called after her.

'Not now. Soon,' she called back.

Themis went to look for Melanas. He was in the stables with Themis' chestnut pony and the great black gelding with a white blaze on its nose.

Themis breathed in the scent of fresh hay. He'd been told to stay out of the stables in case he got kicked. 'Melanas?' he called quietly.

'Yes, young master.' Melanas appeared from behind the gelding, grooming brush in hand. The chestnut snickered, wanting Themis' attention. He went over and rubbed its cheek and nose while they talked.

'My mother says that when you are next in the agora, you can get me some plain pot shards and some papyrus for my painting.'

'I shall do that, young master. It is good to see you working on your pictures again.'

'And I wanted to ask you … is anyone else here?'

'Not at the moment. You look … Are you not feeling well?' Melanas stopped his work and looked down into Themis' face.

'I'm … I feel a kind of … of sickness … or dread, all the time these last two days. My mind is clouded, my skin feels too tight, and my stomach sinks in me all the time. Sometimes I shake. I don't know if I'm ill, or cursed, or what. I didn't tell Mama, but I thought I might go and see Asterodia – or is that not allowed?'

'I'm sure she would be very pleased to see you. I'll ask your mother for permission to accompany you. May I tell her about your waking up in the water trough?'

'No. No. Just say Asterodia asked me to keep her informed about how I feel – which is almost true.'

Chapter 9: rupture

From Bernie's Blog. March 2nd 2010, Tuesday

Athens, Hotel Artemis

This will have to be short! We're leaving on a flight at 10.30 pm tonight to Heathrow. That way we can get a flight in the morning to Newcastle and be in the hospital there by lunch time tomorrow and the specialist can see Suzanne straight away.

Yesterday I went with Mrs J to the embassy to get some papers stamped and then she used my laptop to pay for something. She also spent a lot of time on the phone, so I stayed with Suzanne.

Mrs J told me she didn't know how she'd have managed without me, which was kind. Mind you, she's right. You need at least two people to look after a sick person here. The nurses don't have time to do all the right things at the right times, so someone has to keep an eye on the drips and the catheter bottle, and call a nurse when they need changing.

But mostly I just sit holding Suzz's hand. It's usually cold when I pick it up, but it warms up fast.

She groaned again today, and twitched, too. Mrs J and I were both there at the time. We almost danced round the ward! Once we get her home I'm sure she'll get better really fast.

Next news from Newcastle. Yeah!

<<<

'The offices and residence of the Temple of Demeter's priestesses is entered from the Peripatos,' Melanas said as they threaded their way between the hurrying crowds in the narrow streets.

'What's the Peripatos?' asked Themis.

'It's the road all round the bottom of the Akropolis rock,' said Melanas. 'There are many shrines and caves on the upper side of it, under the cliffs. Some of them have … strange reputations.'

'Like what?' asked Themis.

Melanas chuckled as he danced out of the way of a fat slave with a pair of huge baskets smelling of fresh bread. 'Some good, some bad, especially the caves,' he said over his shoulder. 'Your father didn't let the family use the Peripatos except with him. He would say "The gods might suck your soul into one of those caves – or worse still, your money!" '

A man who was passing with a stack of tablets under his arm, laughed out loud at this. Another, who was pushing his way past Melanas, turned away in a crouch and, muttering, slipped down an alleyway.

'Are you being sa … sacrilegious, Melanas?' asked Themis with mock severity.

'Not *my* words, young master,' said Melanas, his grin flashing above the heads of the crowd.

They climbed the last few steps up a narrow street and came to the wide, paved Peripatos stretching out to left and right. Ahead was a steep slope of grass and rocks and small trees at the foot of the sheer cliff. Far above, along its top and pale against the vivid blue of the sky, was the Akropolis wall made up of stones of varyious shapes and sizes.

They turned right and Melanas stopped at a gate on their right.

'Here we are, young master,' said Melanas. 'You must go in alone.' There were stone benches along the high white wall on both sides of the gateway. 'I'll wait here for you. If you are going to be long, please ask someone to let me know.'

Themis knocked on the dark wood. The gate opened almost immediately onto a courtyard and closed quietly behind him. A veiled woman hurried away into the doorway opposite without a word. Themis stood still, irresolute.

An olive tree shaded the wide expanse of raked white pebbles. A line of great pots by the wall contained clipped bushes with dark green leaves. In a corner was a waterspout in the shape of a lion's head. The scent of herbs and the trickling water were soothing.

Asterodia came out of the doorway. 'You are troubled,' she said as she took Themis' hands. 'You will wash and drink from our spring and then you can explain.' Her silver hair was caught into a plain snood, her gown was pale green, and her hands were hard and cool.

Themis washed at the spout and drank from the shallow cup on the shelf by the basin. Asterodia handed him a towel. Then she led him over to a bench between two of the huge pots. They sat in the last of the sunshine. Themis caught the crisp scent of mint.

'Tell me,' she said, then looked straight ahead.

Themis took a breath. 'There's something no one will tell me,' he said. 'It makes me angry when they lie – and it … frightens me.'

Asterodia looked at him for a moment, then said calmly, 'Go on.'

'And now my dreams are getting more frightening, too. Sometimes pieces of my body are missing. I feel a … dread in my stomach, like a stone, even during the day,' he said. 'I think I'm ill.'

Asterodia was quiet for a moment. Then she turned to him and said, 'May I suggest that you stay here tonight?'

'You mean, sleep here?' Themis was surprised.

'Yes. There is a room you could use with a good bed. I will give you food and drink and you will sleep. If you dream, I will be nearby and you can call me. We will face this "dread" together.'

'Are you sure this is …? Is this something known to be …?'

'Appropriate? Helpful in cases like yours?' finished Asterodia. 'Each case of an illness varies. Each human being is different. But some things are common to most of us, and one of those things is the effect of fear.'

Themis looked down at his hands.

She went on. 'Fear needs to be named, given a shape and taken control of. Just now, you cannot do that on your own. Later you may find that your god will agree to take on your fears. But for now, will you allow me to help?'

'I must tell Melanas, but yes, I would like that,' said Themis, looking into her face.

>>>

56

From Bernie's Blog. March 3ʳᵈ 2010, Wednesday

Newcastle

Well, we're back in England. Suzanne is in a ward with only one other patient, also in a coma, at the Freeman Hospital in Newcastle. The specialist was waiting for her when we finally arrived. So was her dad. The neurosurgeon says she will be able to tell us more in two or three days, but anyway she does not foresee operating. So Suzanne will stay a few days 'for observation'. After that, they may send her to the hospital down the road from home, in Penrith.

She has even more tubes and wires attached to her now and the doctors have all her notes. The nurses are super-efficient and visiting times are rigid, so I can only stay with her for a couple of hours at a time. In Greece we could stay all the time.

I'll have to write up the journey tomorrow. I'm so tired now I'm dizzy. At least we made it this far. We're staying in a B&B just down the road from the Freeman. I suppose I'll have to go back to Penrith tomorrow. I'm missing too much school. Maybe I can come back at the weekend.

<<<

Themis' family were behind him. They were in danger and they needed him, but the ground was moving, carrying him forwards, away from them, towards a great cave ahead. He tried to step backwards but the ground kept moving him on.

A roaring sound was coming from inside the cave mouth. He tried to call for help but his voice was drowned by the roar. The blackness of the opening was coming closer and loomed above him. The roar grew louder and louder and a reek of rotten meat reached him. His mother's voice shrieked from behind him. 'Help me! Help us! Themis, help us!'

Now he could see teeth in the arch high above him. He was standing on a monster's tongue and it was pulling him into its mouth as it roared. He slipped and slid as he backed away in panic. Saliva dripped on him as he was dragged under the arching row of teeth. The monster's hot breath blew his mother's screams away.

Themis shouted, 'I can't leave them! I can't leave them!!' Then he too screamed as the roar echoed louder and louder and the great mouth closed over him …

Asterodia's dry, cool hands rustled as they stroked his forehead. Themis opened his eyes. A lamp was burning by the bed and the old priestess was bending over him. She was muttering something very quietly to herself, perhaps a prayer.

Themis' whole body was rigid with fear and when he closed his eyes he could still see and hear the gaping, dripping maw enveloping him in roaring blackness.

So he opened his eyes and kept them open. He looked up at Asterodia's concerned face and focused on the calming rhythm of her strokes.

'Be still,' she said. 'Be still now.'

'I - I think I'm going to be sick,' said Themis suddenly, in a different kind of panic.

Asterodia smiled and all the lines in her face danced into a new pattern. 'I have a bowl,' she said. 'Sit up.'

Themis sat up, swung his legs off the bed and took the bowl onto his lap. He vomited a surprising amount of unidentifiable stuff. Had he really eaten all that? He took a couple of breaths and then he vomited again. He felt he was bringing up his very stomach. It went on a long time.

Asterodia held his forehead and sang a quiet hymn of thanks, patting him on the back as a reward each time he brought something up.

At last it was done. There were no more spasms.

She took the bowl from him and handed it to someone he hadn't noticed in the shadows. She wiped his face and hands with a damp cloth and gave him a cup of water to drink.

'Tell me, Themistokles,' she said as she helped him to lie down again. 'Do you know a young woman with clouds of hair the colour of sunset?'

'No, Sacred Lady,' murmured Themis. 'Red hair? … No. Why?'

'She appeared in my mind as I was holding you just now. She seemed to be calling out, saying "suss" or "sazz", or something similar. What could she mean by that?'

'Nothing I can think of,' said Themis, trying to stop his eyes closing.

'No matter,' said Asterodia with a gentle shake of her head. 'Sleep now. You won't dream again.'

>>>

From Bernie's Blog. March 4th 2010, Thursday

Home

I was too tired to think yesterday, and feeling like a zombie. Dispirited, Miss Rallis would call it, but it feels more like being in a black hole in outer space. We had such hopes that Suzanne would pick up and show more signs of recovery, but what happened on the plane seems to make that unlikely after all.

All the business of getting her to the airport in an ambulance and getting onto the plane before all the other passengers went ok. It was late at night, and Mrs J and I were both tired already, so every little hold-up annoyed me, but at last they got Suzanne on her stretcher onto the special bed in a section curtained off from everyone else.

Then, when we were sitting in our seats with our seat belts on and the engines beginning to warm up, Suzanne began to struggle.

She had a couple of straps over her but nothing like the railings on her bed in hospital. She moved in sudden jerks, not like she was having a fit, but like she was trying to push herself backwards into the mattress. And as she obviously couldn't, especially with one arm strapped to her chest, she started to thrash about and the drip tube went all over the place. Mrs J undid her own seat belt and got up to hold Suzanne down. She talked to her, but I couldn't hear what she was saying because the plane was finally taking off and the engines were very loud.

Suddenly I heard Suzanne's voice shout 'I can't leave! I can't leave!' and she made a really awful sound like she was in terrible pain. I leapt up and grabbed her good hand. I stroked and stroked it and called her name again and again. Mrs J was holding her head so she couldn't thrash it about. In the end, one of the cabin staff came and asked me to sit down. By then Suzanne was totally still. AND SHE HASN'T MOVED SINCE.

It took ages to get her off the plane at three am. And then we had to wait for the one to Newcastle. The staff on that one were brilliant, but the ambulance to take us to the hospital wasn't at the airport so we had to wait. Mrs Jenkins was amazing. She kept calm and was polite to everyone, even when she was furious.

Suzanne's vital signs are still there, though her heartbeat is slow and her blood pressure low. She hardly moves her chest at all to breathe. But the nurses at the hospital are upbeat. They said she must have been upset by the journey and she'll soon get back on her recovery curve.

I had to leave her with her mum at the Freeman and come home by train. I'm so depressed I can hardly write this. I feel like someone stole my will to live, like I've been switched off. How can I do anything to help now?

Later

If I can afford it, I'll go again on Saturday. P'raps Laila or someone will come with me.

<<<

Chapter 10: mother

Themis' arrow hit the small white ring on the tree trunk with a thud. He jumped in the air with triumph.

'Good shot,' growled Arianos.

'Fantastic!' shouted Photios. 'Three in a row from fifty paces. Best any of us has ever done.'

The other boys came and slapped Themis on the shoulder, congratulating him. Even Straton came up to him and put an arm round his waist.

'That was good,' he said loudly. Then he went on in a whisper, 'But not good enough to save you.' His face was so close that his breath stirred Themis' short hair.

'Save me?' Themis said, pulling back from the embrace. 'Save me from what?'

'From what you deserve for that picture you drew,' whispered Straton through gritted teeth.

Themis laughed and stepped well back. He raised his voice. 'It's just a joke, Straton. If you hadn't left your love poem lying around I wouldn't have even thought of it.'

Straton shook his head from side to side, his hands clenched by his hips. 'Shut up!' he shouted. 'Just shut up!'

Photios laughed. 'Is he upset by your drawing, Themis?' he asked.

Arianos said, 'Enough, young masters. It's time we were getting back. It will be dark soon. Collect up your swords, bows, quivers, and shields!'

The five boys picked up their wooden weapons from under the trees. Above and behind them the cliff face of Lykavitos was reflecting the furnace glow of the setting sun.

Straton stepped up to Themis again. His sword was in his hand, his shield on his arm. 'Just because Arianos says you're not allowed to fight hand to hand yet, doesn't mean I won't find you on your own sometime. And when I do, you'll wish you were still in a coma!'

He stepped away and ran down the slope ahead of everyone else.

Photios shouted after him, 'Straton, beware of the wolves!'

One of the other boys howled mournfully and they all laughed as they strode down between the trees to the cultivated terraces. Arianos walked beside Themis.

'Straton's a bit older than you and the others,' he said quietly. 'You'll see in a year or two that you'll start writing love poems, too. It might be an idea to apologise to him.'

'I thought he'd find the picture funny,' said Themis.

Photios laughed and sang in the style of a bard, "*Not even the sight of fifty warships with sails full SET, Could draw my eyes from your dear face, so perfECT.*" It was crying out for someone to make fun of it.'

'I'm just warning you all,' growled Arianos with mock severity. 'The time will come when you'll all be writing worse stuff than that to girls – or men – who take your fancy.'

The boys laughed delightedly. Themis turned to Arianos. 'Will you let me join in all the exercises now? You see I can run and do the moves for sword and shield.'

'And shoot!' added Photios.

'So can I get down to real hand to hand stuff now?' pleaded Themis.

'Have you got your memory back?' asked Arianos.

'No, but I think I'm doing fine without it. And I don't have headaches any more.'

'Never?' asked Arianos.

Something in Themis' mind lit up. That had been the voice that said, 'Never, madam?' and Eirini had said 'Yes, if possible, never. They say it could kill him …'

'*I knew he'd know!*' thought Themis. But with the other boys around, he couldn't ask Arianos what it was he must never know. And Arianos was still speaking, 'You'd better talk to your mother. I can't judge something like this.' They jumped down a terrace onto the track to the city gate. 'See what she says,' added the trainer.

And what Eirini said was an emphatic no! 'You must not tempt the Fates with blows to your head of any kind!'

She put her sewing down and stood up to walk backwards and forwards in the salon. The breeze from her skirts made the lamp-flames flicker. 'You still have no memory from before, and your dreams seem to get more vivid rather than fade away. You must have patience. I really couldn't bear to lose any more of my children.'

Themis stood up too. 'But I'm well! I can outrun all the other boys in the training group. I can shoot, and spar with a sword better than most of them. My muscles are beginning to show, and I can chase hares and rabbits all day. I've even been riding with Melanas.'

'But that doesn't tell us what is happening inside your head and why that hasn't come straight,' insisted his mother, raising her voice. 'Supposing you hit it again and lost the power of speech, or the use of your legs. There is a big chance you could become as epileptic as that boy in the Asklepion and start having fits. If that happens your life will be ruined. You would be no better than a beggar then. The healers have said to avoid blows to the head, and that is what you must do!'

'Was it the healers who said it would kill me?'

'What would kill you?' snapped Eirini, staring at him in fury.

'Whatever it is that you won't say.' Themis' heart was beating too fast.

'Not that again!' said Eirini. 'Who is telling you such things?'

'I heard you and Arianos talking, when I was in the sick room.'

'You dreamed it, then!'

Themis looked at his mother. She was clenching her jaw and her fists as she stared back. She would tell him nothing in this mood.

He sighed as though he accepted what she said. 'Perhaps,' he murmured.

'Of course you dreamed it. Look at the other things you dream.' She picked up her work and sat down, breathing deeply.

'Mama, there *is* something else I want to ask you.'

'And what is that, my son?' She did not look up.

'More than once you have mentioned that you have lost a son and a daughter. They would have been my brother and sister. Will you tell me about them?'

Eirini sighed and gestured that he should sit on a stool. Her shoulders relaxed. 'Before I married your father, I was married to another man. We had a little girl, Phrynys. I wasn't well after the birth and went to make offerings to Hera at the temple near our farm. While I was away, there was a fire at the farm and everyone was killed except two slaves.'

Themis covered his mouth with his hand. After a moment he said, 'Have you told me this before?'

'No. You've never asked me such things before.'

'And the other boy?' Themis saw Eirini steel herself to speak. She began sewing and her voice was strange – distant and muffled.

'The boy was … about five when he died. He was … between you and Myrto. He caught a fever. No one else got it. He died quite quickly.'

'Would I remember him if … ?' Themis insisted.

Eirini looked up. 'I'm not sure, but I think yes. However,' her eyes focused on Themis again, 'he is gone. We don't speak of it any more. You are recovering, and I still have two strong sons to look after me in my old age!' She laughed with determined mirth. 'Did I tell you that

Diodotos is coming tomorrow for the festival?'

Themis stood up. 'Yes. And I am to go to the Agora in the morning – '

'That's right. With your Uncle Panainos. He will come and fetch you to "further your education".' Eirini looked up at Themis from under her eyelashes. 'He takes more interest in you than any of his other nephews and nieces because you can draw. So … '

'I should be polite to him at all times?' said Themis, wrinkling his nose.

'Of course,' said Eirini with irony. Then she was serious. 'No, I mustn't joke about him. He has been a great help to me lately. With my father dead, my brothers in Massalia, and Kallistos' brother … Well, Panainos and Phidias have been my closest male relatives since … your father was killed. They've been trying to get an answer concerning Myrto's accident. And they support my wish not to marry again.' She smiled. 'And anyway, Panainos always cheers me up!'

'And there's this big family gathering in the afternoon?' Themis asked.

'That's right. And we're going to decide what you and Chloe will do when I go and join the sanctuary at Vravrona.'

'You're really leaving?!' Themis' whole body tensed up.

'Not just yet.'

'But … '

'Don't look so worried, Themis. I won't desert you, however much you infuriate me!' laughed Eirini, standing up. 'Come and see Myrto.'

Eirini left Themis with Myrto, who was praying.

When she finished, Themis said, 'Mama says she's leaving, did you know?'

'She wants to get away from this house,' said Myrto. 'She … misses Father.'

'But what will happen to the house, and me, and Chloe?'

'Oh, it'll be ages yet.' Myrto waved a languid hand. 'You'll probably both go with her – or maybe she'll change her mind. She only started talking about it a day or two ago. Don't take it so seriously.'

'Has it anything to do with your accident – or mine?'

'I'm not sure. Have you heard any more about the wagon? No one tells me anything, least of all Menelaus.'

Themis shrugged. 'No. Nothing new. Your parents-in-law and our uncles Panainos and Phidias are having it investigated.' They were quiet for a moment. Then he asked, 'What's this celebration tomorrow? Do I need special clothes or anything?'

'It's the Diasia,' said Myrto with a tut and a roll of her eyes. 'To thank Zeus the Kind for … well, being Kind, I suppose. It's always been your favourite festival, because of the toys and presents.'

'Should I pray to Hades to look after Father?' asked Themis doubtfully.

'Say the prayers with me,' offered Myrto, and they intoned entreaties to Zeus and Hades, Demeter and Apollo to look after Myrto's husband and son and farm and their father in the Underworld. Themis had no memory of ever doing this before and found it difficult to believe in all these imaginary creatures directing everyone's fate.

But in the night, twisted and plaited with the strands of his dreams, he heard those strange, calm voices saying things like, '… will need time to rebuild social awareness' and '… some memories never come back.' Were they the voices of gods?

The next morning was windy but fine and Panainos was at the door early. As they stepped out to meet him, Melanas handed Themis his bag with a tablet and stylus for sketching. 'Enjoy the Agora,' he said.

'Aren't you coming with us?' asked Themis, apprehensive at the thought of being alone with his uncle.

Panainos reached up to clap Melanas on his gleaming black shoulder. 'No slaves today in the Agora!' he said loudly with a laugh. 'No, boy, you are on your own!'

Melanas looked pointedly at Themis, head on one side.

'That will be a … privilege, sir,' said Themis to Panainos.

With a twinkle in his eye, Melanas turned to Panainos. 'Please remember, sir, that you are invited to the meal here a little after midday.'

'We'll be back in plenty of time,' promised Panainos, squaring his shoulders so that his stomach wobbled and lifted. 'Never miss an invitation to eat Mika's bean and barley hotpot. Come on, young man. Let's see what this new you makes of my Marathon – and Polygnotus' Troy and all the other paintings.' He patted the old statue of Hermes on the head and strode off down the street at surprising speed, green cloak flapping, wiry greying beard thrust forward.

Themis slid the bag over his shoulder, and ran to catch him up.

Chapter 11: goddess

'We'll take the Peripatos,' called Panainos over his shoulder.

Themis caught up with him and asked, 'Is it safe?'

Panainos guffawed happily and put a heavy arm over Themis' shoulder. 'It's time you knew a bit more about what goes on in this world, bash on the head or not,' he said. He took his arm away as they turned into a street that was a series of steps up towards the looming eastern cliff of the Akropolis.

'In that case, can you tell me, uncle,' Themis began, looking sideways as they climbed, 'what it is that no one is mentioning about that "bash on the head"? Arianos won't. My mother won't. Frog won't. What have I done that everyone is hiding?'

Panainos stopped and turned to look at Themis. He said kindly and seriously, 'I believe it's just that you are much easier to deal with at present. Everyone wants to stop you going back to being such an unpredictable … pain in the arse.' And he exploded with laughter. 'Cheer up, nephew. You're going to be fine!'

Themis had to smile. Could that be true? What a relief, if it was. 'I hope you're right,' he said, as Panainos took him by the arm and they went on up the steps.

'Of course I am,' said his uncle.

Feeling more relaxed than he had for days, Themis hardly noticed the brightly painted houses on either side of the steep street. He concentrated on keeping perfect pace, step for step, with his uncle. That way he could watch the sway and check of the stomach under the stained tunic. No one he'd ever met (as far as he could remember) had such a stomach.

They arrived at a crossroads with the Peripatos. There was quite a crowd going in both directions, while a further set of rock-cut steps opposite led up to a built platform and cave entrance. Incense burned in shining cauldrons on tall stands and flowers garlanded railings and columns. Panainos led Themis away to the right, past Asterodia's residence.

'That's the shrine of Aglauros,' said Panainos, gesturing back to the cave. 'Your brother will be sworn in to the army of Athens there soon.'

To their right, the view over the city was immense, the horizon ringed with mountains. But Themis was still studying the stomach.

'Does it hurt?' he asked, realizing too late how rude this must sound.

'Does what hurt, young Themis?' countered Panainos, nodding to a man he knew coming the other way.

'Er...' Themis didn't quite know how to go on.

'If you mean my large and comfortable stomach, no, it does not hurt.' Panainos was looking straight ahead, but he was chuckling again. 'It gets in the way at times...' This made him laugh his huge laugh, so people turned to look at him. 'Yes, it can be a nuisance, but it doesn't hurt.'

Themis laughed too. His uncle was good fun, after all. 'You're an important artist, aren't you?' he said.

'Hmmm. Not as important as my brother Phidias, of course. But then he's not a painter really, more of a sculptor and architect. You and I are the painters, aren't we?' He was chuckling again.

'So did you see my drawings?' asked Themis.

'I did.'

'And ... what do you think of them?'

'My opinion is ... that you have talent and a smattering of technique but very little passion. And all three are needed in equally large quantities. Also,' and he became reproving, 'you have to move away from recognizable caricature into serious representation. Caricature can be ... er ... unhealthy for the artist in the end. Some special lessons would help.'

'Yeah!' shouted Themis enthusiastically. He skipped a couple of paces.

'You can say "thank you" without shouting,' Panainos said.

'Thank you,' said Themis, walking normally again but with a big grin. 'Thank you thank you thank you.'

They passed some other steps and entrances going up to shrines under the cliff to their left, then were held up by a large crowd at the way up to the platform of one of them.

'From here,' said Panainos, 'take my arm, Themis. I don't want to lose you in this chaos.'

They pushed and pardoned their way through the throng, Panainos using his stomach as a battering ram. Further on, the crowds were thinner and they walked comfortably again.

'That was the way up to the sacred grottos of Pan and Zeus and Apollo,' Panainos said. 'People leave their offerings there.'

A thought struck Themis. 'It was Apollo who brought me back to my body, they tell me,' he said. 'Should I write him a poem or something?'

'Don't worry yourself about that,' scoffed Panainos. 'If Apollo exists at all, he'll be too busy to read your poem, though a quiet prayer of gratitude for your recovery will never go amiss.'

'*If* he exists?'

'You and I used to discuss the existence of all the gods at great length, young Themis,' said Panainos. 'You were inclined to be an atheist, which pleased me, but infuriated Phidias, of course.'

'I really wish I remembered!' The vast emptiness of the past was suddenly unbearable. Themis shook himself and said, 'Have you learned anything about Myrto's accident?'

'My brother's working on it,' said Panainos, pausing to look down over the wide, open market place of the Agora laid out beyond the nearest buildings. On a rocky knoll to the left was a newly-finished temple.

Where they stood, under the cliffs of the Akropolis looking north, they were in the shade. But the sun was shining on that temple. It gilded the fluted yellow columns and made deep shadows among the red and blue painted figures sculpted under the shining new marble roof. Themis' heart lifted. He opened his satchel and got out a tablet and stylus.

'A true artist,' smiled Panainos, 'can keep an image in his mind.' He lifted his empty hands for emphasis. 'Try to remember this view of the temple of Hephaistos, and then draw it from memory when you get home. It's a good exercise.'

'But it's … glorious!' said Themis, transported with quiet wonder. 'The light, the colours, the shadows. I just want to suck it into myself and keep it inside me.'

'Well, now. Did I say something about lacking passion?' Panainos was turning towards his nephew when his eye strayed to look beyond Themis' head. His stomach, comfortably filling the gap between them, suddenly began to shrink. It halved in size in a couple of moments. Themis looked at Panainos in alarm and saw that his jaw was jutting and his lips were pursed.

Themis turned round to see what had caused this strange transformation, and found himself looking at … a goddess, a real living goddess!

She was taller than Panainos, in a fine dark blue tunic to the ground, under a deep red cloak that also covered her hair. Her eyes, wide open and beautiful, were staring at him. Her skin was smooth and the same pale golden brown all over her face and arms. The lines of her cheekbones, jaw, and dark eyebrows were crisp and straight. One lock of hair had come loose from under the cloak and spiralled over her shoulder, gleaming black against the blue. Themis thought, '*Not really a goddess, but the perfect model – for Athena perhaps?*' He sighed in awe.

In her hand, she held a large water jug covered in painted figures.

'Xenovia, Sacred Lady,' Panainos said in a new, deeper voice. 'May we draw some water for you from the spring?'

'Thank you, Panainos,' answered the goddess with a slight smile. 'And who is this?' Themis was fascinated by her eyes. They glowed with a colour somewhere between green and brown. And she continued to look at *him*, not at the famous artist behind him. Her gaze turned the bones in his legs to water and sent a tingle through his belly.

Panainos said, 'My nephew, Themistokles. He had an accident and has lost his memory. Otherwise, I am sure he would know you, even if you do not remember him.' Xenovia's eyebrow twitched and she smiled kindly at Themis.

Panainos turned to him. 'Themis, this is Xenovia, senior priestess of Athena at the Temple on the Akropolis. Please take Xenovia's jug and fill it at the spring over there.'

Themis held out his hands in a trance. Xenovia placed the jug carefully between them so that he could hold it securely. She looked into his face.

'I did hear something about your fall. But I think we may have met before, Themistokles,' she said. 'Perhaps with your father one day?'

'I … I don't remember anything, Sacred Lady. If we *have* met before, I don't remember it. Please forgive me if that is impolite.'

Xenovia threw back her head with a happy laugh. 'No matter, Themistokles. Be careful with the jug.'

Themis was reluctant to stop looking at her, but he took the jug and turned towards the sound of running water.

At the junction of the Peripatos and the wide, stepped road up from the Agora, was a tiled roof on pillars over five lion-headed waterspouts. These were at head height and gushed water that fell onto low blocks standing in a narrow channel. To collect water in the jug, Themis had to lean over this channel and steady the mouth of the jug on its block under a lion's mouth. His sandals got splashed, and the full jug was very heavy, so he had to use both hands to hold it. Carrying it in front of him, he returned to Xenovia and Panainos, who were standing very close together. They moved apart as he approached, and the goddess held out her hands for the jug. A sweet, heady fragrance hung around her.

'It's very heavy now,' Themis warned, as he handed it to her.

'But you kept it dry,' murmured the goddess. 'That makes it easier to hold.'

'I have a strict tutor in my sister,' said Themis.

'Your sister?' asked Xenovia.

Panainos said, 'Yes. Myrto, wife of Menelaus. You have met her, Sacred Lady, many times. And now she is ill at her mother's home.'

'Ah yes,' the goddess smiled. 'I remember. Eirini's daughter with the cutting sense of humour, and now a broken leg?' She looked at Themis. 'Thank you, Themistokles.' Light shone from her eyes as she smiled at him. Her cloak had fallen back from her face and more tendrils of her gleaming hair were visible, tumbling from the netted snood at the nape of her neck. Themis had never seen anything so attractive. He wanted to bury his face in those shining, scented curls.

A blond, muscular man in an elaborate tunic walked up to them.

'Xenovia,' he said. 'May I carry that for you? Are you going home, or to the school?'

Xenovia smiled slightly to Panainos and Themis, and handed the jug to the man. She said, 'To the school, thank you, Tryfonos.' She and the man turned and walked back the way Themis and Panainos had come.

Panainos sighed deeply as he let his stomach relax. 'Fuhhhhh. Such beauty, and she a virgin of the Goddess. What a waste.'

'Those eyes,' said Themis in wonder. 'Is she related to Asterodia?'

Panainos nodded as they set off. 'Her daughter.'

'*Ah,*' thought Themis, '*the one Myrto and Ismini don't like. Of course they don't! She is the most beautiful woman I've ever seen.*'

Panainos was striding down the steps now, and Themis had to run to keep up. They were soon on a wide road between lines of stalls selling carved and moulded votive figures, sparkling trinkets, garlands and ribbons. The awnings were brightly coloured and the voices of the vendors musical. Elusive perfumes made Themis want to stop and take deep breaths, in spite of the constant dust.

To the left, a rocky hill behind the municipal buildings was crowned with the temple to Hephaistos that had drawn his gaze from a distance. Smoke from charcoal fires would have given it an etherial air, but for the creaking of the cranes of builders and the loud hammering of metal nearby. Was this where the armour makers worked?

The stalls became more domestic, with fish and bread and cooking pots neatly laid out as they approached the other side of the Agora. The voices were more urgent, selling special foods for the day's festival. The sky was bluer and the shade trees taller as they neared the Eridanos stream. This flowed from right to left in front of them. Its fetid smell mingled with that of fresh bread and honey cakes and burning wood.

They were heading for a small bridge over the sluggish river, between two spreading plane trees.

A voice from their right called out to Panainos. 'Hey, Master Painter! Your order's arrived. Come and see!' The man stood behind a red and green stall. In front, large bags and boxes lolled in tottering heaps.

'I'll be back soon – before midday!' called Panainos as he passed.

They stepped onto the bridge and Themis stopped dead. Across the stream was a row of columns along the front of a gallery, roofed with translucent marble tiles. Inside, on the walls, huge paintings glowed with wonderful colours in the diffused light.

So this was the Painted Arcade. This was where the best artists were asked by the City to paint its history. Themis walked over the bridge in a dream.

Groups of men stood talking on the steps up to the columns. Panainos came back to take Themis' arm.

'Come on, fishface. Close your mouth and come and see something wonderful.' He led Themis up the steps and between the fluted columns, to look at the far end wall.

'My Marathon,' he said with pride, opening his arms wide. Everyone around them stopped talking and looked at Panainos. He turned and bowed. Some clapped, some called 'Long life to Panainos'. But they went back to their business when they saw that there would be no speech.

'There it is, my boy,' said Panainos, gesturing broadly. 'Marathon – the battle that stopped the Persian barbarians, and in which our forebears fought.'

The huge picture showed the battle from ground level, with phalanxes of Hellenic soldiers advancing against the Persians, whose ships were pulled up on the beach to the left. The Persians wore tight garments under their armour, which made them look as if they had patterned skin. The Hellenes were just in tunics and cuirasses. Some were even naked except for their helmets and shields. Crested helmets, shields, and spear tips shone gold and bronze in the melee of colour and movement. In the background, the gods Zeus and Poseidon looked on, with Pan of the forests and other spirits Themis didn't recognise. But to his eye, the painted goddess Athena had a familiar look, even though her face was turned away. The line of her jaw and the shape of her head were Xenovia's.

Themis stood staring upwards until his neck ached. Two eagles, painted in a fighting clinch, claws and beaks tearing at each other, tumbled in the hazy blue sky above even the gods.

'Will you teach me how to do that?' Themis asked his uncle.

Panainos laughed hugely. 'Perhaps one day,' he said, recovering his breath. 'But you'd better see the other paintings, too.' He led Themis to look at Polygnotus' painting of Troy. There, among less realistic gods and soldiers and citizens, Athena was painted full face, stern and warlike in her helmet and with the aegis over her chest. She was in no way as beautiful as Xenovia.

Chapter 12: uncles

Themis asked, 'But how can you paint such enormous pictures? They go up to the ceiling, and that's higher than a two storey house.'

'Scaffolding, dear boy,' answered Panainos.

'*You* climbed up scaffolding to paint up there?' Themis pointed at the Marathon picture.

A new voice spoke from behind them, before Panainos could answer.

'He was younger and slimmer then,' it said. 'And of course, we rigged up a hoist for when he ate more than usual.'

Themis turned and had to look up. Ismini's husband was smiling down at him.

'You lie about the hoist, dear brother,' laughed Panainos. 'I was thinner and more handsome than you in those days.'

'You certainly had more hair!' returned the bald man. His skin was brown from the sun and, although he must have been in his fifties, his shoulders were broad and powerful, his beard short and mainly dark. People stopped chatting to stare at him.

Panainos put an arm round Themis' shoulders and said, 'You see, my dear Phidias, how Themistokles is growing?'

'He'll be working the hoist for you soon,' laughed Phidias. His voice was light, musical. 'Has my brother been exhausting you with descriptions of the consistency of the yellow and the need for genuine squirrel-hair brushes?'

'No, sir. But I wish he would,' said Themis.

'Are you perhaps … interested?' Phidias' eyes danced with humour.

'In painting? You know I am, Uncle. But I had no idea there are so many colours available. I've only got three.'

'They may be available, but you need access to the treasury of Delos if you want to afford some of them,' said Panainos.

Quiet mutters ran round the listening crowd.

'I'm glad you're here, dear brother,' said Phidias, turning his dancing black eyes to Panainos. 'There's our little matter of some paintings you promised to do at Olympia.'

Themis' skin suddenly prickled all over. The single note sounded in his mind again, faster than usual but just as haunting.

Panainos glanced at the crowd. 'Let's go over to The Hungry Bear and sit down with a bit of breakfast,' he suggested.

Phidias took his brother's arm and they walked down the steps to the roadway. Themis followed. 'Sadly, I can't spare the time for another breakfast,' said Phidias. 'But it would be helpful to know when you think you can come to Elis and help me finish off the Zeus at Olympia.'

'*So Olympia is a place,*' thought Themis, '*not a god. But it seems Zeus is there.*'

'As you know, brother. I'm working on a commission here, given to me long before you remembered that I am the best painter in Hellas,' said Panainos with mock severity.

'Where did you suddenly find such a sense of fair play, Panainos? It doesn't suit you.'

'You mean it doesn't suit *you*,' Panainos replied cheerfully. 'Here, Themis. Sit and tell me what you will have for breakfast.'

'I need your Olympian work finished within a month,' Phidias said, standing over the bench where Panainos sat.

'I could help you!' Themis said suddenly, surprising himself.

'Ah. An apprentice, Panainos?' Phidias raised an eyebrow at his brother.

'Oh, I'm sorry,' said Themis, now confused and embarrassed. 'That just jumped out of my mouth. I'm not … I wouldn't be able … I shouldn't have said anything.'

Panainos gave Phidias a steady look. 'An apprentice to help me at Olympia? A tempting thought …'

'But would taking him to Olympia be a good idea?' Phidias asked quietly.

Panainos' face changed. He said, 'But no, that wouldn't … No. The City taxes are rising too fast. I can't afford an apprentice.' He smiled sadly at Themis.

'Then you'll have to find someone else to finish off your local job and bring your stomach with you to Olympia immediately,' said Phidias.

'All in good time,' chortled Panainos as his order of sweet bread and fig-and-walnut relish arrived. 'Talking of things that just jumped out of his mouth, d'you know what this young scalliwag asked me earlier?' Phidias sighed and shook his head. 'He asked whether my proud and noble stomach was painful?'

Phidias' face split into a wide grin. Wrinkles raced across his cheeks. 'The old Themistokles would never have even noticed the size of it,' Phidias confided in Themis. 'Unless he was drawing, of course.'

'That was something else that maybe I shouldn't have said,' said Themis, looking down.

'He's so much more polite than he was before he cracked his head open,' said Panainos. 'Do sit down Phidias. You're obviously not going to dash off to order a hundred Ionic columns before noon – or are you?'

'Not columns, in fact, but frieze blocks,' Phidias said with a wink at Themis. Panainos snorted into his buttermilk.

Phidias smiled. 'But I really do need you in Olympia very soon, brother. The Elians are hard taskmasters and won't pay unless everything is done on time. I have a hundred craftsmen waiting for their wages.'

'It'll take me six or seven days to get there.' Panainos was counting on his fingers. 'So … I'll be there in fifteen.'

'Then you'd better arrange to bring young Themis with you so he can help you do the work in half the time,' grinned Phidias as he stepped away from them. 'I'm off, but I'll see you later at the festival.'

Themis watched Phidias step nimbly aside to avoid a man with a huge bale of fabric on his head, and disappear into the crowd.

'Could you do that?' he asked.

'What?' said Panainos through a mouthful.

'Take me with you to Olympia?' Themis heart was beating twice as fast as the repeating plucked note and his voice cracked.

'Olympia! No. Certainly not.' Panainos seemed very put out. 'Not unless your mother asks me to. It would look odd if I asked *her*.'

'Why?'

'You're too young.' Panainos spoke fast and looked over Themis' head at the busy Agora. 'You still have lessons, and it would look as though I had designs on you. Your mother must do what she knows your father would have wanted, which is probably to keep you safe at home for another couple of years.'

'Did Father tell you that?'

'Not in so many words. But just look at how he brought up your brother. Diodotos hasn't left home even now.'

Themis was silent. Just the name of Olympia rang like a bell in his mind. And the idea of being apprenticed to draw and paint there – or anywhere – was almost too perfect to imagine. He would find a way somehow.

But Panainos had called over an acquaintance and was now discussing something about Spartan politics.

And Themis had forgotten to ask Phidias about Myrto's accident.

On the way back, they picked up Panainos' large parcel of paints and bought some honey crisps and newly baked bread as a gift for Eirini's house shrine.

To avoid the chaos where the new Great Gate to the Akropolis was being built, they walked past the spring where Themis had filled the jug for Xenovia. He looked around in case she was somewhere near, but of course she wasn't.

A beggar boy, sitting cross-legged by the road, his eyes rolling in his head, caught at the hem of Panainos' tunic. Themis couldn't help looking at him with pity.

Panainos extracted a small coin from somewhere. 'Here!' he said briskly, dropping it into the boy's dish. Then he took Themis' arm firmly and pulled him away. 'We're going to be late. Your family will already be by the river.'

'Is that boy sick? I think he was blind – ' Themis began.

'He's epileptic – he has fits. It's best to keep away. The gods know better than I do what he needs.'

'*You don't really believe in the gods though,*' thought Themis. '*Epileptic is what Mama thinks I might end up like.*' As they hurried on, he sent up a silent plea that he wouldn't, and a prayer of thanks that he hadn't, just in case there were gods listening.

The official gathering by the river was crowded and noisy. Men gesticulated at each other under the great trees, discussing the imminence of war with Sparta. Women met in groups comparing the price of linen and gossiping about their men. Chloe met three of her little friends at a stall full of terracotta dolls and toys. Themis joined Photios, who was telling the story of Themis' accident for the hundredth time to his father and brothers as they stood by the offending abutment.

Looking along the bridge, Themis saw Straton and his two elder brothers walking towards him. A determined voice in Themis' head said, 'Let's have a go at him,' while another ordered, 'Avoid! Avoid!'

And before he could decide which to obey, the three young men were standing in front of him.

'Hello, Themis,' said Efsevios, the eldest. 'Been bullying any more poets lately?'

'Not good ones,' replied Themis.

Efsevios and his brothers stepped up very close. Efsevios leaned towards Themis' ear. 'Drawing *insulting* pictures can get you into a lot of trouble,' he whispered.

'Only if they lie,' said Themis with a grin, stepping back. The crowd near the bridge was thick and some had turned to watch.

'Don't go out alone,' threatened Straton as they turned away.

Phidias approached Themis at that moment, with his wife Ismini and their two girls.

'Themistokles, these are your second cousins, Io and Polycasta,' he said formally. 'Io and Polycasta, this is your second cousin Themistokles.'

The elder, Io, laughed and said, 'We know Themis, Papa.'

'Ah, but does he know you?' said Phidias with a raised eyebrow.

The girls looked at Themis's head with interest, then at each other and burst out in giggles. He decided to ignore them. They were at least two years younger than him, anyway. Straton and his brothers had disappeared.

'Can I ask you something, Uncle,' Themis said to Phidias.

'Go ahead,' said the sculptor, looking over their heads at the Temple of Artemis among the trees by the river.

'Is there any news about Myrto's accident?'

Phidias looked back at Themis. 'I'll be reporting to the family later,' he said kindly. 'But nothing conclusive.'

Just then, Eirini's voice rang out. 'Time to go!'

She'd made her offering of bird-shaped rolls and honey, and now she was gathering everyone together to go home for the meal. They hurried back, laughing at the tricks of the children to persuade their parents to buy them toys from the colourful stalls by the road. Themis stopped briefly at one of them.

The house was full of delicious smells of baking bread and bubbling vegetable stew. At the shrine to Zeus-of-the-House everyone washed in the basin and picked up a garland.

A huge dog appeared from the kitchen and lay down in the sun beside the shrine. He was light brown with short, smooth hair and a pointed face.

Myrto had been carried down to the courtyard. 'Diodotos has finally arrived,' she called. 'He's in the andron. Did you buy me anything, Themis?'

Themis laid a small pottery pull-along cart he'd bought for Timodemus in her lap and walked towards the andron. The dog stood up and came to meet him. Themis was surprised and stood still. The dog seemed to expect a caress, its head on one side, looking at Themis with a lopsided smile. Themis reached out a tentative hand to the smooth head and patted it gently. The dog lifted its muzzle and sniffed at Themis' armpit. It seemed confused and looked up into his face with questioning eyes.

'Hey, Panax, what's the matter with Themistokles?' a voice asked.

Themis knew this must be his brother Diodotos. He also knew he had never seen him before. Diodotos was tall, very dark, and rather thin, with a soft moustache and sideburns, and a furrow between his straight brows.

'Hello, Puppy Dog,' he said to Themis, his hand on Panax's head. 'You've grown!'

'Hello,' said Themis, ducking away from Diodotos' other hand that came out to tousle his growing hair. 'Are you Diodotos?'

The furrow deepened. 'And are you Themistokles?' Diodotos replied, his dark eyes concerned and puzzled. 'You look the same, except for being a bit thinner and your hair's a bit short. But Panax obviously isn't sure.'

'I ... suppose I must be,' Themis replied with a shrug and a smile.

'Good!' Diodotos swooped down on Chloe, picked her up and threw her up in the air. She squeaked and giggled. 'You're getting too heavy!' he laughed as he placed her back on her feet. Panax gave her a quick nuzzle. His head was on a level with her neck.

Chloe shook him off and smoothed out her best chiton. 'Or maybe you're just not as strong as you were,' she said to Diodotos, tossing her head.

Her elder brother snorted with laughter and turned to Mika, who was carrying a large platter of bread rolls to the table that had been placed in the middle of the courtyard. He grabbed one and said, 'Any real food going?'

Over her shoulder Mika said, 'Only if you help bring out some dishes.'

A short time later, Eirini sat at the end of the long, laden table.

The thanks had been given, the libations made, everyone had started to eat and the chatter had subsided.

Themis was intrigued to see Panainos eating again so soon after his breakfast. His wife sat quietly next to him, but Themis hadn't been told her name. Her hair was in the most elaborate twisted and curled shapes and like everyone else she was garlanded with a wreath of young oak leaves, coloured ribbons and spring flowers. But her gown was a sad shade of mud.

Myrto was very pale and sat by her mother with her splinted and bandaged leg up on a cushioned stool. Her husband Menelaus hadn't arrived yet. Diodotos was at the other end of the table from Eirini, in what had once been his father's place. Themis found himself next to Chloe, halfway between them. Phidias' daughter, Polycaster, was opposite while Io took her turn to play with Timodemus in the shade of the portico.

The same evergreen leaves as decorated the shrine of Zeus-of-the-House were laid along the middle of the table. Themis picked up a sprig and sniffed it. It had a sharp, lively smell.

'What's this?' he asked Chloe.

'Rosemary,' she answered with her mouth full, 'from the bush in the yard. It's the one they burn for Zeus.'

'It's in the soup, too,' he said.

'Just a little,' said Chloe. 'But there's coriander and rue, too. I watched Mika making it.'

Eirini's chair scraped on the flagstones. She stood in her long, indigo robe with a sad smile on her face as she looked at the family gathered at her table. Her glance went to the shrine of Zeus-of-the-house for a moment, and she took a deep breath. Then she clapped her hands together three times and everyone was quiet.

'It's reassuring to see everyone together at this table again,' she said. 'With my brothers far away in Massalia and my husband in the world below, I have asked you to come and consider with me my next step.'

Everyone was looking at her, but they went on eating as she took a sip of water. 'As you may know, Kallistos' brother Nikanor mentioned marriage to me, ostensibly in the tradition of protecting the widows of soldiers. But it turns out he had other motives, so I have refused him. Since then, Myrto's cart was tampered with so that she had the accident that broke her leg, among other injuries. My cousins have been investigating as to whether Nikanor had anything to do with that.'

Eirini nodded at Phidias. He stayed seated and said calmly, 'It is clear that Nikanor himself did not sabotage Myrto's cart, and he swears by all the gods that he did not employ anyone to do so. He is famously a coward and we put that to the test, but he still did not admit to any such action or plan.' He looked at Diodotos. 'So, with reservations, Panainos and I have concluded that Nikanor was not behind the "accident".'

Diodotos smiled wryly at his uncle. 'Thanks,' he said quietly.

Eirini went on, 'So it seems we must keep in mind that someone wants to hurt Myrto, unless of course it was a case of mistaken identity, like the attempt to smother Themis when he was so ill. Meanwhile, after much prayer and many consultations, I have decided that I wish to join the sanctuary of Artemis Vravron as a house-mother for the young women who are learning there. With four living children and the memory of Kallistos still shining in my heart, I have no wish to marry again.'

Themis looked with dismay at Chloe. She didn't seem concerned and just gave a little shrug.

Eirini went on. 'Diodotos will be going into the army after the late spring harvest, and Chloe will come with me to Vravrona. The farm will be managed by Melanas. That leaves Myrto, who already has a husband and a home, … and Themistokles.'

Chapter 13: Zeus

Everyone turned to look at Themis. He was putting a piece of bread in his mouth. He looked round the table, but no one was giving anything away. Had anything already been decided about him? There had not been time to discuss Olympia as far as he knew.

Eirini walked round the table to him, so he put the bread down and turned on his stool to face her.

'Themis,' she said to him. 'There are various options for you. And that is why I wanted to decide this with the others here. My own idea is that you should stay here at the house for five days out of ten for your schooling. Then you would join Myrto on her farm for the other five days and learn about how that works. But Diodotos and Panainos have other ideas.'

Themis' mouth had gone dry. He stood up and turned to the table.

'Diodotos,' said Eirini, standing behind Themis with her hands on his shoulders. 'Tell us what you think.'

'I hear,' said Diodotos, 'that Themis is now a more thoughtful and careful person. So perhaps it would be a good idea if he were to spend his time on *our* farm. He could keep an eye on things and help Melanas. He could train better there as a cadet for the army, and ride and run and start taking on duties.'

'He's much too young for that!' said Panainos loudly. 'He doesn't have a head for figures and prices and – '

'I think you're wrong there, Uncle. He always could manage figures. But also he sees what people are up to – at least he used to,' said Diodotos. 'I must say,' he added thoughtfully, 'he has changed considerably since I last saw him.'

'Are you worried that Melanas is not the best choice to manage the farm, Diodotos?' asked Phidias.

'Frankly, yes. He has no experience.'

'But,' said Eirini, 'he has loyalty.'

'That's not much good, Mama, if you don't know how to prune the olive trees to get the most fruit from them, or who will pay top price for cheese,' objected Diodotos.

Eirini squeezed Themis' shoulders and said, 'There's time, Diodotos, for you to teach Melanas a lot before you leave. And I'll be coming to stay on the farm until I am accepted at the sanctuary. Melanas is very intelligent and will learn fast.'

Diodotos sent a patronizing glance at his mother. 'With both your cousins in Olympia for months, Father's brother unreliable to say the least, me in the army, and you at the sanctuary, who will make sure he does? The only member of the family left is Themistokles. He's growing fast and could easily – '

Myrto was waving her arm at the other end of the table. 'There's my Menelaus,' she said. 'You've forgotten about him!'

'And there's you, once your leg is strong,' said her mother.

'Unless whoever really did doctor your wagon succeeds in getting rid of you after all,' said Diodotos with a worried frown.

An uncomfortable silence fell.

'What did Menelaus learn at your end, Myrto?' asked Phidias, pushing back his chair and reaching for his cup.

Myrto's face was bitter. 'Menelaus had our two wagon-slaves tortured,' she said, 'but no one could get any names from them.'

Themis suddenly felt sick. 'Where are they now?' he asked.

'The slaves?' Diodotos said. 'If they can still work they'll have been "sold" to the silver mines, won't they, Myrto?'

'Yes. Even if they didn't do anything, they may have helped someone else do it,' said Myrto with an edge to her voice. 'I can't think of anyone who would do anything so bad to me.'

'Someone who used to have beautiful hair and let you loose on it?' suggested Diodotos wryly.

'Be serious, children,' said Panainos, 'and be vigilant. If in fact it was Nikanor, or someone else who really wants to hurt Myrto or Menelaus, they will try again. And the best time for that will be when we are all out of the city.'

'All the more reason for Themis to stay either at our farm or at Menelaus',' said Diodotos. 'We need all the eyes and ears we can find.'

Myrto said, 'Yes. He must stay with us as Mama suggests!'

Themis was horrified and looked at his sister pleadingly. 'Oh, Myrto,' he said, 'can't you –'

'I have a different suggestion,' said Panainos loudly.

Everyone turned to him. He cleared his throat. 'I think Themis should come and be my apprentice for a year.' Themis couldn't believe his ears. Hadn't his uncle completely denied that possibility earlier? Panainos went on, 'I will promise that he will do his basic lessons and keep on with gentle' (Panainos emphasised this word) 'physical training. He will pay me by making up my colours and doing backgrounds to my pictures. Meanwhile, if my dear wife agrees, she will relinquish some of her domestic duties to my eldest daughter and visit Melanas at the farm every ten days. As we all know, when she took over the management of her father's farm she was little older than Themis is now, and she showed herself, in the long run, to be an outstanding farmer!'

Everyone started to laugh and Eirini even looked relieved. Themis realised this was a family joke.

Phidias said, 'Let it be a lesson to you, my daughters. Your Aunt

Artemisia's first harvest was more thistle than barley and her first bargain was one hundred eggs for … a ball of string.'

Artemisia smiled. 'It was good string,' she murmured.

'But in the end you became a wonderful farmer,' said Phidias. 'And you could teach Diodotos a thing or two, I'm sure!' More laughter. Phidias glanced at his wife Ismini. She nodded and he stood up. 'But I have an even better suggestion than my dear brother, who may find it expensive to take on an apprentice. I will undertake to teach Themis to be a sculptor, engineer and architect if he would like to be my apprentice. I'm not sure how long this would take, but I can certainly offer two years, the first few months in Olympia working on my statue of Zeus for the temple there.'

Eirini knocked over her cup as she stood up again. 'Perhaps later in the year, Phidias!' she exclaimed, staring hard at him, her jaw set. 'In the autumn, maybe.'

'But it is now that I need another helper,' said Phidias quietly. He went round the table and put a reassuring hand on Eirini's shoulder. 'I would take care of him as if he were my own son,' he said looking into her worried eyes. 'You could be sure he would come to no harm, and we should be finished before the frenzy of the Games.'

Something painful was invading Themis' head. Gooseflesh was rising all over his body and he could hardly breathe. Phidias' and Eirini's voices seemed to come from the bottom of a well.

'I prefer Panainos' idea to that,' said Eirini loudly. 'Themis could continue at his present school and keep the same friends. He could – '

'But Panainos will be coming to Olympia himself in the next few days. He has a commission there,' said Phidias.

'This is true, but it will be over well before the … summer.' Panainos' voice was wheedling but his eyes were cold as he looked at his brother. 'So we'd be back in Athens, perhaps even before the Thargelia Festival.'

Themis' heartbeat was loud, and his head was full of muffled voices.

There was a knock on the street door and everyone turned to look at who came in.

It was Xenovia. She came into the courtyard in a swirl of rich brown drapery, her dark hair gleaming under its coloured garland. Themis' heart skipped a beat and the blur of sounds in his head receded.

'Eirini, dear Eirini,' called Xenovia as she approached the table, holding out both her hands to Themis' mother. 'Mother sends apologies. How wonderful that the whole family could make it on this first festival without Kallistos.'

Eirini signed to Mika to bring a chair and a cup for Xenovia. They were placed beside her, opposite Myrto.

Myrto said sweetly, 'We thought you were my husband. What brings you here? This must be such a busy day for you.'

Eirini looked a warning at Myrto and said, 'Welcome, Xenovia. Please, sit.' Xenovia sank gracefully onto the chair. 'We are honoured you should visit us. We were just talking about the situation you and I discussed the other day at the wool merchants'.'

'You mean what is to become of your brood while you are away in Vravrona?' smiled Xenovia as she surveyed the almost empty dishes.

'Exactly,' murmured Eirini.

Xenovia raised a hand and her slave brought a platter to the table. On it were small barley-and-honey buns in the shapes of rabbits, ducks and frogs. She bowed her head to everyone at the table, and most heads bowed respectfully. At her gesture, her slave girl began to move round the table, offering the platter to each in turn. Themis took a bun in the shape of a frog. It had currants for eyes and a smiling mouth. He would give it to Frog later.

Chloe refused a bun, but jumped up and ran round to stand beside Xenovia, gazing at the flowers and ornaments in her hair.

Then, still standing, Eirini gathered herself and said more loudly. 'As I told you, the girls are no problem and Diodotos will be in the army soon. Both he and I would prefer for Themis to stay in the city to carry on with his schooling, but my dear cousins have each offered to take him on as an apprentice. He is indeed talented as a painter and would benefit from the experience, but I feel he's too young to be apprenticed.' She sat down, leaning forward, her chin on her hands, looking intently at Phidias.

Themis was watching Xenovia. Apart from being the most beautiful woman he'd ever seen (and smelling of roses and sandalwood this time), she now seemed to have some say in what was going to be his future. He saw that her eyes kept turning to his brother Diodotos at the head of the table. Was she going to agree with Diodotos' plans for him? He felt light-headed with anxiety.

'Being an apprentice to a great artist is naturally an honour,' said Xenovia with a charming smile at Phidias and Panainos, 'but Themis is at a dangerous age and is growing more attractive with every day. No apprentice is protected as well as a son or brother would be.'

Phidias stood up. He moved his chair carefully away from the table. His voice was quiet but there was an edge Themis had not heard before. 'This apprentice is my cousin's son. He is part of my family and will always be cared for as such. Ismini agrees with me.'

Ismini nodded enthusiastically.

Xenovia also stood. Her eyes flashed green although her voice was as smooth as ever. 'But your lifestyle, Master Sculptor, is such that you are almost never at home. If you are at home, your visitors are exactly the kind of people Eirini is worried about influencing Themis for the worse. But you are often away, either on your magnificent ship, or to fulfil a commission, both paid for, of course, out of the public purse. How can you suggest that Themistokles would be better protected by you than if he were staying with his sister on her farm or with the family slaves on Eirini's own farm?'

Phidias took a deep breath and looked down his nose at Xenovia. 'And how can a woman without her own children who lives the er … *sheltered* life of a priestess of Athena, know so much about the life of a craftsman like me?'

Themis was now feeling very strange. His head throbbed with rising voices, both from the table in front of him and from behind what seemed like a door in his head. He stood up and blinked as he looked along the table to his mother. 'I think I would – ' he began.

Eirini stood up too. She raised her voice over Phidias' and Xenovia's argument. 'There are four possibilities for what happens to Themis,' she said. 'Two of them involve his staying in or near the city, the other two seem to involve at least a short time in Olympia – a daunting prospect and a long journey. Perhaps we should hear what he has to say himself?'

Xenovia turned her animated face sharply to Eirini. Then she remembered herself and inclined her head with a smile. 'Of course,' she said and sat down. Phidias shot a condescending look at her and also sat down.

'Themis?' Eirini said.

Themis had come out in a cold sweat. He took a deep breath to speak. But suddenly the scene spun away from him. His head filled with a rushing grey mist, then a silent black night.

>>>

From Bernie's private diary. Saturday March 6th 2010

I don't want to write this on my blog cos it's a bit too personal – at least for Suzanne, if she ever recovers and reads this stuff. And after today, I'm more hopeful that she will!

I visited her this afternoon. (No one wanted to come with me, and I'm staying at the B&B in Newcastle with Mrs Jenkins again tonight.) She looked just the same as on Thursday. Perhaps she's a bit thinner and a bit whiter. I talked with her mum about the trip back from Athens, and I held her hand for a while. It was like before, really cold at first but it soon warmed up.

The other two beds had different people in them this time and their monitoring machines made quiet sounds. Suzanne has a drip and a catheter now, and is still hooked up to a heart monitor, but the big tubes have gone. This monitor sounds more like 'ping' than 'beep'.

A bit later, Suzanne's father came in. I hadn't seen him for ages, like three or four years. He's gone quite grey. Anyway, he and Mrs Jenkins started talking. First he asked her how much time she could be there and she was like, 'I'm staying in Newcastle. I come whenever they have visiting hours.' Then he asked if Suzanne would be taken back to Penrith soon. Mrs Jenkins said yes and that she would probably stay at the hospital in Penrith until she came out of the coma.

Then Mr Short went off to see the nurses and came back to say Suzanne could be looked after at home if someone could be there 24/7. I could tell he was worried sick and wanted to be with Suzanne all the time, but also that he didn't want to have to see Mrs Jenkins much.

Mrs J stood up at that and said she could arrange to have nurses at home and so Suzanne could be in her own room. Then Suzanne's dad (whose name is *Dan* Short, I think) said it would be better if she came to his place. But I know he lives miles away, in the middle of Carlisle. He kept saying things like he could spend more time with her as he didn't have other young children to care for, and it would be quieter at his place, and he could afford constant care by professionals, with a much bigger hospital close by.

I started feeling a bit embarrassed. They were both whispering, but leaning over the bed, one on each side, hissing over Suzanne's face.

I left and they didn't even notice. I went and sat in the corridor to give them time to calm down. After about ten minutes, I went back and they were still at it! They each had both hands on the side of the bed and were nose to nose across Suzanne. And they weren't whispering any more.

As I came in I saw Suzanne's hands twitch! She took a sudden little breath. They hadn't noticed she'd moved. I grabbed her good hand and I'm sure she squeezed mine.

'Look!' I shouted, and they stepped back from the bed. 'Look, she's here! Stop your fighting and just look!'

So they did. Suzanne took a load of little breaths through her nose, as if she was sobbing or angry. But she didn't open her eyes. I held her hand tight and said, 'I'm with you Suzanne. And your mum and dad are here too.'

They both made a dive to stroke her face. I stood back and said something like, 'She needs you both to be on her side, not at each other's throats. Nothing can prove who loves her most.' They made me so sick I turned my back on them and went and looked at one of the other coma patients. I had tears dripping down my face so I got some blue paper towel from by the basin on the wall and wiped them off.

What is the matter with adults?! This was just about them, not about Suzanne. I wanted to swear at them and tell them to get out. But of course I was quiet and went to get my stuff from her bedside cabinet. As I turned away, her dad took my arm very gently and whispered, 'You're right, Bernie. We're idiots. Stay a bit, please. We'll work something out in the TV room.'

So they trooped out and I stayed with Suzanne. She was definitely trying to be with me. She held onto my hand slightly and made tiny sounds. She had a little frown and moved her head from side to side. She seemed in a lot of distress but when I called in a nurse she said this was all a good sign.

So I told Suzanne all about school and that we were just waiting for her to get well to start the history project on Greece. And I told her about the gig Gina went to last week when one of the guitarists stepped backwards off the stage and fell into the crowd. She stopped the headmoving after a while and the frown went away. She seemed to sleep rather than be unconscious. There was a kind of slight smile on her face. I stroked her hand and kept talking till her parents came back.

Her mother had been crying and her dad didn't seem to know what to do with his hands. Anyway, Mrs Jenkins said, 'If you need to go, Bernie ..?' so I got my bag. I looked at them both and shook my head at them in an 'I can't believe you're so stupid' way. Then I left her there with them. Did they even notice she was almost conscious?

I had to talk to someone, so I called Laila. We had a good time dissing certain parents! Then I texted Mrs J about what the nurse had said. I went out and got an Indian to eat in my room and watched 'Juno' on my laptop again. Why aren't I as tough as that!?

<<<

The black began to thin out. The voices had faded away as Themis drifted in the dark. A tinge of purple spread, and then a light ahead that shone more and more brightly within a golden haze. He allowed himself to float and feel dizzy. This was much more comfortable than most of his dreams.

The haze wrapped itself around him. Below, he could see earth and rocks. He floated down towards them in the golden cloud. There was no moment when he felt that he'd landed, but he found he was walking through clearing the mist towards the light.

Now, with a dark blue, starry sky above, there was a huge gold and black chair in front of him, tall as a temple. Facing him, on the corners of the footstool, were the golden faces of lions with black manes and white teeth. They snarled at him and stared with wild yellow eyes. As Themis lifted his gaze, he saw there was an immense man seated on the chair. His chest was bare, but from his waist to his sandalled feet he wore golden robes. He had a long curling beard and his hair brushed the stars. A garland of golden olive leaves shone on his head. Each of his hands was the size of a dining couch. His left hand held a staff with an eagle on top. His right hand was stretched out over his lap. Themis knew without doubt that this was Father Zeus. The god leaned forward.

Themis' whole body shuddered at each heartbeat. *'So this is what happens when you die,'* he thought.

He was lifted up without being touched and found he was sitting on the lap of Zeus. The golden fabric rustled as Themis turned round and looked up at the mighty face. Zeus had turned aside to lay down his staff. The dark curls in his beard gleamed and sparkled as if they were dusted with gold. Then Themis felt himself being gently pulled backwards to lean against the god's right hand. The left hand hovered over him for a long time.

He was expecting the final blow every moment, and he could feel his heart leaping around in his chest with fear. And yet his mind felt clearer than he ever remembered. A huge finger, as long as Themis' arm, came closer and closer to his face. It was joined by an even more massive thumb. Beyond them, the god's own face was frowning slightly as if he were trying to focus on something very small: perhaps a twig caught in Themis' hair, or an eyelash on Themis' cheek. Themis could feel warmth from the hand's shining skin as it approached. He suddenly relaxed, feeling that if this was dying, it was more comfortable than living. He thought, *'Perhaps in the underworld I'll get my memory back and meet my father.'*

There was a great, deep sigh as the forefinger actually touched Themis' right temple. It was warm, and smooth as polished marble that's been in the sun. Then a huge voice growled and echoed in the gleaming chest.

'You must come to me again. You are not ready.'

The vibrations of the voice ran right through Themis body. He felt himself picked up as the god leaned forward and he was lifted down and down, past the knees, the sandals, the lion footstool, and at last laid gently on the ground. 'Come again when you are ready,' said the voice from far above.

Chapter 14: drawing

The smell of burning herbs caught in Themis throat.

'It's rosemary,' he said, and opened his eyes. 'Rosemary for Zeus.'

'That's right,' said Chloe's voice. 'Are you back? Where have you been?'

Themis sat up. He was on one of the dining couches in his father's andron. His mother, Xenovia and Ismini were all standing over him. Phidias and the others stood up from the couches opposite.

'What happened?' asked Themis. His voice shook.

'You fainted,' said his mother.

'You were overcome,' said Xenovia. 'Did you have any dreams?'

Themis swung his legs to sit on the edge of the couch. He looked at his hands for a moment. 'Yes,' he said. 'I had a very strange dream.'

'Tell me what you saw,' said Xenovia, sitting down beside him, her perfume chasing away the scent of burning rosemary. 'Now, before you forget it.'

'I shall never forget it,' said Themis, alarmed at the truth of this. 'It's very clear. Something is going to happen but I'm not ready for it.'

'What sort of thing?' Xenovia was fascinated. 'Something painful or something nice?'

Themis wasn't sure what the reactions would be from his mother and uncles if he described his dream, but he felt Xenovia, because she was such a venerable person, might find it rather trivial, and he didn't want that. 'I think I had better draw something from it,' he decided at last.

Eirini took Themis' face between her hands and looked into his eyes. She seemed to be searching his soul. 'Are you feeling well now, my child?' she asked.

'Yes. I'm fine again, Mama. I'm sorry I frightened you. Everything just went black.'

She stepped back from him and everyone went back out into the courtyard. The food had been cleared from the table and now torches were being lit as the sky darkened.

'Let's have the second table,' called Eirini and they all took their seats again as the slaves brought in sesame cakes and all the sweetmeats the guests had brought to celebrate this festival of Zeus the Kind.

Xenovia followed Themis as he set off to his room to get his paints.

'I'll only be a moment,' he said.

She stayed close to him. 'Is this your room?' she asked as they approached the doorway.

'Yes. Diodotos and I share it.'

'May I see?' she asked and walked in ahead of Themis. She looked around in the gloom. 'It's … very masculine,' she said with a low laugh. 'Naturally!'

'Yes,' said Themis, feeling shy. 'I'll just get my paints.' He had to pass close to her to reach the bed. He pulled the box out from underneath it.

'It's quite dark in here,' said Xenovia.

'Yes. I'll draw in the yard while everyone's eating the sweets,' he said. He felt a tension in his belly as her perfume filled the room.

'Are these paintings by you?' She was looking at the row of ceramic tiles on the shelf. She picked up the one of Melanas preparing to mount the black gelding and took it to the window. 'Who is this?'

'My father's body-servant. He's from beyond Egypt, I think.' Themis was overawed that this wonderful woman should pay him so much attention. He stood frozen in the middle of the floor. Xenovia was weighing the tile in her hand.

A loud banging sounded at the street door. Xenovia hurriedly put the tile down, walked past Themis and through the door. She reached out her hand as she passed him and touched his chin, as lightly as a feather. A shudder ran through him right down to his toes.

It was Menelaus at last. He laid his offering among the leaves and loaves on the shrine, and placed a large platter of cakes on the table. Then he went up to Eirini and bowed his head low over her hands.

'My humble apologies for being so late,' he said. 'The sun has almost set, but we found some coins buried in the barn. It took a while to get any information about them. We thought they might have been payment to a slave for damaging the wagon that broke Myrto's leg.'

Themis couldn't take his eyes off Xenovia. He felt shaky but elated as he watched her glide round the table to her chair.

Menelaus stood and looked down at his wife for a moment. Then he took her hand and sat beside her. 'Where's Timodemus?' he asked.

Myrto looked around. 'Over there with Phidias' daughters.'

Eirini said over the hubbub, 'Tell us what you found, Menelaus.'

'Just a few silver coins. We were preparing to move some of the olive oil in there and had raked the floor.'

Phidias said 'Are you sure the coins haven't been there for a long time?'

'Can't be sure, of course,' answered Menelaus. 'But from the looks on the faces of my other slaves, I'd say they were blood money for something.'

'And no real clue as to who ordered the sabotage?' asked Xenovia of the table at large.

'Nothing from our investigations,' said Phidias.

'Nor from mine,' said Menelaus. 'But enough of that! I need a cup of wine and to find my son,' and he jumped up and left the table.

Themis had been sitting under a newly-lit wall torch, listening to this as he began to draw. He found his hand was quite steady as soon as he focused on the tile. He had no yellow and so could only suggest the gold by highlighting its shine. He drew the huge god, seated on his throne with the lions' heads on the footstool, and a tiny Themis in his right hand. He put stars in the sky behind. As he was drawing these, he heard someone come to look over his shoulder. He looked up and saw it was Phidias.

The look on Phidias' face made Themis' stomach cramp with fear.

'What's the matter, Uncle?' he said.

'Where did you see this?' asked his uncle urgently.

'In my dream.'

Phidias looked as though his eyes would never close again. 'You dreamed of this? Just now?'

'Yes,' replied Themis. 'It was quite like my other dreams until I was lifted up. It must have been Zeus. He took me onto his lap, and he spoke to me.'

'By all the gods! What did he say?' exclaimed Phidias.

'He ... seemed to want to pull something off my head, but he couldn't grasp it. And then he said, "You must come to me again. You are not ready".'

'So that's what you meant when you came round. Is that when you woke up?' Phidias' voice was harsh and urgent.

'N … not exactly, but soon afterwards.'

'Did he say anything else?' The black eyes burned in the tanned face.

'No. He just said the same thing again as he was putting me down on the ground.' Phidias' reaction was frightening. Did his uncle know what the god meant? It must be something terrifying.

'What, exactly?'

'I-I think it was, "Come again when you are ready".' Themis was shivering now.

Phidias looked up at the gathering. The adults had begun on the wine now and there was more laughter.

'Have you finished your drawing?' asked Phidias, less intently.

'Y-yes. It was far more beautiful, of course. His clothes were gold and his skin much warmer than I can make it here.'

'Write what he said to you as you were being put on the floor, and then give it to me for a moment.' Phidias face had gone almost grey. His hands were shaking when he took the tile.

He turned to the table and said loudly, 'I think you should all know what Themis saw in his dream when he fainted earlier.'

The chatter died down and chairs moved. A giggle or two came from Panainos and Artemisia.

'What is it, Phidias,' asked Eirini anxiously.

Phidias stood in the light from the torch with the tile facing his chest. He said, 'Themis has drawn a picture of what he saw, and he's written down what he heard. Before you see it, I have to ask him something.'

Themis stood up and looked at Phidias. His hands were sweating. 'What is it, Uncle?'

'Do you remember ever visiting any of the temples where I have made the statues?'

Themis was confused. 'I haven't visited any temples since my fall,' he said. 'I've only been to a few shrines, but not inside a temple.'

'So you have no idea what the statues inside them would look like?'

'Well, I've heard your gold and ivory Athena described. And I've seen a drawing I did before I lost my memory of the bronze Athena with the golden helmet outside on the Akropolis.'

'Have you heard about the one I'm making at Olympia?'

The back of Themis' neck prickled. 'Just that it's Mighty Zeus and it's nearly finished.'

'Shall I show you a drawing of it?' asked Phidias.

Themis couldn't breathe.

Phidias held up the tile for everyone to see. '*This* is a drawing of my statue of Zeus. It is the only one with lions' heads on the footstool. Themis says he doesn't have gold paint for the robes, but this is what he saw in his dream just now. He saw my statue in Olympia as it will be.'

Chapter 15: dread

And so, in a strangely hushed and reverent discussion, it was agreed that Themis had been summoned to Olympia by the highest authority. Even Xenovia agreed. But she and Eirini stood firm against the apprenticeship to Phidias because of his high-society connections and debauched reputation, deserved or not. It was finally arranged that Themis would be Panainos' apprentice while he painted the screens he had been commissioned to do. Then they would return together to Athens as soon as the screens were done. Everyone seemed to think that, within that time, Themis would be able to visit Zeus in his temple, and that by then Themis would be 'ready'.

No one even discussed what 'ready' might mean, though there were one or two remarks about the age of puberty and when 'a boy becomes a man'. Whatever it was, Themis was now more confused than ever.

His cheerfully ambivalent belief-disbelief in the twelve gods supposedly living on Mount Olympus and controlling every facet of life, had been completely undermined. He had seen and heard Zeus himself! Even Panainos had been shaken, exchanging looks of horrified doubt with Artemisia.

Now, as Themis listened to the adults talking about him and deciding his future, his heart sank. Everyone else seemed to think that Zeus would *give* him something. But from Phidias' response and the god's actions, Themis was sure that Zeus was waiting to *take* something from him. Would this be more of his mind, or something only he knew, or a promise to be a priest, or perhaps even his life? He couldn't know. And he felt sick.

The party was getting noisier, celebrating the visit of the god on the day of his festival, but Themis felt completely drained. When

Diodotos fetched his lyre and Eirini her flute and an argument arose as to which song they would start with, he slipped away to his bed, pulled a blanket over his head, and fell into merciful, dreamless sleep.

He gradually became conscious of quiet voices in the room. He knew he wasn't dreaming this time. It was almost completely dark, but through the blanket he could just see the faint glow of a tiny lamp. He recognised the voice of his brother and assumed, from the two partly-visible shadows, that he must be talking to their mother as he prepared for bed.

'This one is just a typical bent-wood lyre … ' Diodotos was saying.

'So, being a first class cadet is not your only strength?' whispered the female voice. 'You are an estate manager and a talented musician, too.'

Not Eirini, then. And that perfume was familiar.

Diodotos said more loudly, 'Not exactly talented. Now *this* is my grandfather's lyre, tortoiseshell and ivory. Its strings need replacing, but its tone is much sweeter.'

'It's lovely …' Themis' heart leapt. This was Xenovia. 'You'll be going to Elefsis soon,' she said, obviously making conversation. 'Have you started the initiation lessons yet with my colleagues?'

Themis concluded that she must have come into their room again to find him. She had been so concerned about him earlier.

Diodotos said, 'Of course,' and there was the sound of the table being pushed against the wall. Themis threw off his blanket. Xenovia was standing very close to Diodotos with the old lyre in one hand. With her other hand she was touching Diodotos' fluffy sideburn with her finger. When she heard Themis move, she jumped back.

'What's that!?' she exclaimed. 'Oh Themistokles! You gave me such a fright!'

'Are you looking for me?' said Themis as he stood up.

'Not … I really must go now,' said Xenovia, handing the lyre back to Diodotos. 'Thank you for showing this to me.' And she swept out of the room.

By the light of the little lamp, Themis looked up at Diodotos as he stood away from the table. 'She wasn't looking for me, then?' he said.

'No,' laughed Diodotos. He sat down on his bed with a sigh of relief. 'Phew! She certainly wasn't looking for you. She was *flirting* with *me*.'

Themis said, 'I don't believe it. And even if she was, you should be honoured.'

'You're joking!' said Diodotos. 'You've just got a crush on her. She's at least as old as Mama, though not as wrinkled, I'll give you that. She was really embarrassing me. Thanks for breaking it up, little brother. I wasn't sure how to get rid of her without being punished by Athena.'

'Don't you think she's beautiful?' asked Themis. 'And anyway, she's a virgin, so she can't have been flirting.'

'You're new to this, Puppy Dog. She's been making eyes at me all afternoon.'

'Don't call me Puppy Dog!' Themis said aggressively. 'It was Uncle Panainos who told me she's a virgin priestess.'

'Very unlikely, little brother.' Diodotos was unlacing his sandals. 'None of our gods demand eternal virginity, even Artemis, who is a virgin herself. Panainos was teasing you.'

Themis remembered Panainos' reaction to Xenovia near the spring, and how closely they'd been standing together. Had he misunderstood? Had his uncle been lying? To his shame, tears threatened and he ran out of the room into the courtyard – and bumped into Phidias.

'Themistokles, the visionary!' said his uncle in a slightly drunken voice. 'I am privileged to be your relative. And I am very glad that you are coming to Olympia. It would mean a lot to your father.'

Themis just looked at his feet in confusion.

Melanas, who was holding a torch to show Phidias out, said quietly 'This way, sir.'

They were at the street door now. Phidias called out, 'Good night to all and may the gods protect you till the dawn!'

Melanas saw him on his way and then closed and bolted the door.

Everything had been cleared away and Mika and Frog were sweeping up. Themis walked through his mother's salon into the yard and sat on the bench under the olive tree. The moon was rising above the pale wall.

Suddenly life had turned upside down. His brother was arrogant and hateful. Panainos, who had seemed such a good man, was a liar. His mother was indecisive and perfectly capable of changing her mind about Olympia in the morning. Phidias drank too much and could not be trusted as a pillar of strength. There really seemed be gods controlling everything and probably watching his every move. If he did go to Olympia, which would be astonishing and glorious, he would have no chance of seeing Xenovia again for months, which would be foul and awful.

And, most disturbing of all, the Zeus in his dream wanted to take something from him. This was made worse because the dream had felt so good, so perfect. But the dread that gripped him whenever he imagined Zeus declaring him 'ready' gave him a cold, hard feeling in his stomach, even though part of his mind still managed to doubt the god's existence. He began to tremble again and held his head in his hands to stop it.

Panax padded up to him and a paw appeared on his lap.

>>>

From Bernie's Facebook Wall. March 8th 2010, Monday

Hi, again everyone! Came back from Newscastle at lunch time yesterday. Suzanne had an MRI this morning and Mrs Jenkins just texted to say the results are better than expected. The blood clots are still getting smaller and no other horrors, but lots of normal-seeming brain activity.

So the docs are happy to move her and they're arranging for her to come to Penrith tomorrow! Anyone going to come with me to welcome her? I'll let you know what time.

<<<

'What's that you're drawing?' asked Diodotos.

Themis put a hand over his work. 'Nothing,' he said.

'Come on. Show me,' insisted Diodotos, grabbing Themis' wrist.

Themis gritted his teeth. 'Let go of my hand and I'll show you.'

'Alright, alright.' Diodotos stood back. 'Take it easy.'

Themis lifted his hand to show the drawing of the goddess Athena. She was standing by a chariot in full armour with her helmet in her hands.

Her face was that of Xenovia.

'Oh. I see.' Diodotos pressed his lips together and nodded. 'She's actually really good.'

Themis looked again at the drawing as though through someone else's eyes. '*Nearly as good as Panainos*,' he thought in surprise. But he didn't answer.

'Look. Themis, I wanted to talk to you about Mama,' Diodotos said. 'Come into the andron.'

They sat opposite each other. Themis did not meet Diodotos' eyes.

'Themis, this is important and we need to talk about it. Can you grow up just for a bit so we can discuss it?' said his brother.

Diodotos' face was totally serious. Themis relaxed his shoulders and nodded. 'Go ahead.'

'I'm still pretty sure that Nikanor is involved in Myrto's accident, whatever Phidias says,' said Diodotos.

'Why?' said Themis.

'It's just … He came to the farm the other day and started to look around all by himself. I found him staring out over the wheat fields with a nasty look in his eye.'

'What sort of nasty?'

'Proprietory,' Diodotos said. 'As though it was his and he was measuring up the takings from the crop.'

'He was here talking to Mama about ten days ago. He looked at me as if he really hated me. And he gave her a perfume jar full of stuff they use on dead bodies. She broke it.'

'I heard about that. As she said, he wants to marry her. Compared to him, she's prodigiously wealthy.'

'Is that what she meant by "other motives"? He wants her money.'

'Exactly. And to get it he needs to marry her and either have her fortune transferred to him by law, which could take years, or for her to have no children to inherit it or part of it.'

'But she has four children,' said Themis.

'Two of whom have had almost fatal accidents since their father died.' Diodotos was looking steadily at Themis.

Themis looked back. 'But mine was due to a thunderbolt. I don't think anyone could have arranged that.'

'But someone did try to smother you when you were unconscious – neither you nor I believe that was a mistake, do we? And the original thunderbolt could have given Nikanor the idea that his sister-in-law's children are mortal …'

Themis was silent for a moment. 'But what can *we* do about it?' he asked. 'No one seems able to prove anything.'

'I'm not sure,' said Diodotos. 'Yet. But we need to be vigilant, as Uncle Panainos said. You be careful on your journeys and stick close to him. I'll make sure Melanas and Menelaus are on their guard as well. If I learn anything, I'll send you a message. Maybe I could find out what Nikanor's thinking by getting to know him better.'

'Will you tell Mama about his visit to the farm?'

'I told her already. She's furious about it, but not surprised,' Diodotos said.

'Melanas says he's a bear without claws. Is he really dangerous?'

'It depends how much money he owes and, more importantly, who to,' said Diodotos. 'In the past, he hasn't been a real threat, but …'

Themis took a deep breath. 'Do you want me to stay?'

Diodotos shook his head. 'You'll be safer away to Olympia,' he said. 'One fewer for Mama and I to worry about!'

Themis was relieved. 'Well, you'd better be careful too, trying to be friendly with him,' he said. 'He really looked like he hated me when he looked up at me. And you're his biggest obstacle if he's planning to get rid of us all. Won't you be our legal guardian when you're eighteen, and even Mama's?'

'I will. So just be glad you're six years younger than me!' said his brother with a wry smile.

Later, Diodotos came out of his mother's salon with a nod to Themis. 'Suspicion is the order of the day,' he said. 'Keep in touch and be careful!' He picked up his travelling hat.

'Themis!' came Eirini's voice. 'Come and help me pack your box.'

Themis looked up at Diodotos. 'You're not so bad,' he said, 'though you do use words I don't always understand.'

Diodotos laughed and went off to the stable. Themis waved a hand and went into Eirini's room.

'Phidias leaves tomorrow on his ship,' she said as he joined her. 'But Panainos couldn't be ready in time, so he sent his slave on ahead. You'll leave with him in a few days. Is this tunic still long enough for you?'

'Not really ... What about my lessons?' asked Themis. He didn't want to leave without seeing Photios again.

'Panainos will sort something out.'

'No, I mean here.'

'You'll go to them as long as possible,' insisted Eirini, assuming he did not want to. 'These sandals?'

'They're worn through. Look!'

'You'd better go shopping with Melanas,' Eirini declared. 'And Arianos thinks you should go to the gym every single day until you leave, just to get you started again on regular training.'

Themis was as excited about the gymnasium as he was about the journey. 'Really! That's great! I'll go now. Can I take Frog with me?'

'No, I need him. You know where it is. Can you go alone? You used to before ... ' Eirini was on her way upstairs.

Themis called after her, 'Of course. I'll be back for the midday meal.'

'Just don't do the full programme,' called Eirini. 'Be careful! Whatever Zeus says, the healers say no boxing or wrestling!'

At the gymnasium, Themis was counting in his head, 'Forty-six, forty-seven, forty-eight.' The flautist and drummer kept a steady pace and the music had already taken him past the pain. He, Photios and seven others were doing sit-ups with elbow-to-knee twists. His stomach muscles were complaining, turning to wood. He knew he had to stop or suffer badly next day, so he raised a hand and Arianos grunted, 'That's fine, Themis.' The others went on in time to the lilting tune.

Themis stood up. The feeling of oil and sand on his skin as he walked over to a bench in the shade stirred a memory, but it was gone almost before it came.

A slave brought him water, and he sat under the colonnade studying his fellow students as he sipped it. They were all about the same age, some with very tanned legs and arms and paler bodies. One had a great scar on his thigh and another had a bruise on his bottom. They all had scars on their arms and hands, some new and raw-looking. Themis felt he was probably thicker-set than some, but not heavy or soft like the fat one. He watched their muscles and sinews working under their hairless skin. He promised himself he would balance his new training to give him as much strength in his legs as in his torso.

As he watched the boys, Straton came in to the workout yard. He was naked like they all were, and Themis could see the difference between Straton's bulging muscles and his own less defined, almost childish shape. Straton even had a shadow of pubic hair and a moustache beginning. He came over to Themis, rubbing oil into his forearms.

'So, you've finally found the courage to come,' he whispered.

Themis was concentrating on when the others would finish so that he could start the next exercise with them. 'Not a matter of courage,' he whispered back. They weren't supposed to talk during exercises.

'We'll see about that,' said Straton and ran out to join the class.

Later, after the lifting exercises and before Arianos called the pairs for boxing practice, Themis began scraping off the dust and oil. Photios was helping him when Straton appeared beside them.

'Still not allowed to fight, Themis?' he asked snidely. 'Your hair's almost grown back now. It won't be long … ' he added with relish.

'I have to go away for a while, Straton,' said Themis in a friendly tone, 'but by the time I get back I'm sure I'll be allowed to give you a thrashing.'

'You may have been champion material before, but you haven't got the spirit for it now. I'll wipe the floor with you.' Straton's sneer deepened at the confusion on Themis' face. 'Can't wait,' he said with a laugh.

Photios laughed too. 'Just leave him alone, Straton. He's still a bit odd in the head,' and he tapped his temple.

'Huh!' snorted Straton. '"Under the wing of a god" you mean? Soft in the brains?'

Themis stepped up close to Straton. His sweat smelled of garlic and raw meat. 'I'm not what I was, it seems,' he said deliberately. 'But that doesn't mean I won't be again.'

'Too right,' said Straton. 'It'll be a long time before you get another chance at – '

'Remember the curse, Straton!' Photios said suddenly.

Straton pursed his lips, blew down his nose in disdain and walked away. Photios called after him 'I'd quite like to see you call it down on yourself, but we did all swear the oath.'

'What curse?' asked Themis. 'What oath?'

'Ach, it's nothing,' said Photios, bending down to scratch his ankle. 'I must have a flea bite. It's just that we all agreed that we wouldn't challenge you to fight or overdo the stamina exercises. Just until you were fit, of course.' He stood up again. 'Where are you going – and when?'

'I had a different kind of dream, and it seems to mean that I have to go to Olympia,' Themis answered.

'Olympia!' Photios was genuinely shocked. 'Really? You dreamt that? And your mother has agreed? When?'

'In a couple of days,' Themis said. 'I'm going as apprentice to my uncle Panainos.'

'Olympia. Wow! When do you get back?' asked Photios.

'Photios with Kimon!' called Arianos.

'Don't know,' answered Themis. 'Maybe a couple of months.'

'Gotta go,' said Photios. 'Don't wait around. Go home before Straton starts on you again. Can I come by your house later?'

'Of course. But I'll be here again tomorrow.' Themis watched as Arianos helped the pairs of boys wrap their hands in leather thongs. When they were ready, they warmed up doing a series of stylized movements. Then they began truly lunging and punching, mainly at each other's heads.

Themis thought, 'So that's where we all get these scars on our hands.' He watched Straton so that, if necessary, he would know what to expect. Straton was strong, but he was slow. Themis smiled and went to dress.

Later, in his room, Themis was working on the goddess while Eirini added to the things in his box. She turned when Photios came in.

'Good afternoon, Mrs Eirini,' Photios said to her, and Themis noticed he nodded slightly.

Themis' quick glance at his mother showed her head tilted as though asking a question.

'Hello, Photios. It's good to see you,' she said with a slight smile. 'As you see, Themis will be going to Olympia in two or three days, apprenticed to my cousin … to paint some screens.'

'Lucky him,' said Photios. 'They say it's really pleasant at this time of year, not like later in the heat.'

'He'll be back here before the summer, of course,' said Eirini. 'Would you boys like something to eat?'

'No need to ask, Mama!' laughed Themis as he put his work away. 'Come on, Photios. Are you free now? Let's get some food and go down to the river.'

They sat eating their buns and watching a large bird with a blue flash on its wing scratching at the bank of the river.

'What's that bird?' asked Themis with his mouth full.

Photios swallowed. 'A jay,' he said, 'digging up acorns. They bury them in autumn.'

'Brilliant colours,' said Themis. Then he added, 'But what was all that "They say it's really pleasant" rubbish, Photios?'

'Your mum was worried we might have incurred the curse, that's all,' answered Photios.

'Who set up this curse?' asked Themis.

'Oh, the priest thought it best, when you finally came out of your coma that first time by the bridge. He and Sacred Lady Asterodia agreed on the form and we were all told about it.'

'How does it work?'

'Well, the priests have made offerings to Apollo, Poseidon, Athena and Hermes at their respective altars to persuade them to curse with a wasting disease anyone who … let me get this right … who allows you or persuades you, to do anything that might make your injuries worse.'

'Did they ask Mighty Zeus to do the same? He's the one who seems to want my hide.' Themis kept his tone light-hearted.

'I'm not sure. It cost a serious amount of money, Themis. Maybe it would have been more than your mother had, to deal with Zeus.'

'I don't think "dealing with Zeus" has a price,' said Themis quietly.

Photios jumped up, frightening the sparrows that were pecking up his crumbs from the dust. 'Come on, let's go to the pool above the Gymnasium. There are kingfishers there we can watch.'

As they walked along the busy road by the river, Photios told Themis about his grandfather who had been to Olympia just after the last Persian war, fifty years before. He'd competed in the pentathlon and been beaten. 'You used to boast about your dad doing the same in the year of Kallias,' he added. 'But your dad didn't win either. Only the victors are remembered,' Photios concluded sadly.

'Maybe,' said Themis. 'But the training's good fun, too, I imagine.'

Photios stopped and looked at Themis for a moment. His blonde eyelashes shone in the sun. 'That's the kind of thing you used to say,' he said. 'Are you sure you don't remember anything?'

Themis thought for a moment. 'Once or twice a smell – or a feeling – seems to knock on the door. But it hasn't opened yet. Come on!' He set off at a run, avoiding a string of laden mules coming the other way.

Chapter 16: curse

The next day Arianos asked Themis to wait for him at the end of training. So he watched the boys fighting again, although this time it was wrestling. He felt envious as they rolled around in the dust, trying to get a hold on each other's wrists or to pin down each other's shoulders. Photios did a lot of slithering to get out of holds as he was too small to pin his partner down. Straton was much better at wrestling than boxing.

At last Arianos sent all the boys off to scrape each other down and wash. He signed to a slave as he walked over to Themis.

'So you're off to Olympia at last?' he growled.

'It's only been two days since it was decided,' laughed Themis, 'but yes, it does feel like "at last".'

Arianos looked alarmed for a moment. 'Oh, I didn't mean … Well, anyway. You'll be gone for a month or two, I'm told, leaving tomorrow. So here's my suggestions for getting yourself back in trim.' The slave appeared with a tablet.

'Do you think,' asked Themis, 'that I'm a bit more developed on top than in the legs?'

'P'raps,' growled Arianos. 'But that's your family shape, too. Your father was deep-chested.'

'I was thinking I'd better do extra running, then,' said Themis, looking at the tablet. 'And you've got something here about leg push-ups. What are they?'

'You lie on your back with a weight on your feet and lift it as often as you can. Simple.'

'Right. And running up steps?'

'Certainly,' grunted the trainer. 'And I've addressed the tablet to Kadmos, a trainer who works in Olympia. He should be able to sort out a regular programme for you with the local boys.'

'Thanks,' said Themis. 'Can I ask you something else?'

'Of course,' said Arianos, watching as the first boys came out of the changing rooms.

'Are you involved in this curse business?'

'Hmph. What did Photios tell you?'

'Just that the priests had asked some of the gods to curse anyone who made me fight.'

'So just remember when you're tempted to answer an insult with a punch, you may be condemning that person to … what? What did Photios say?' Arianos asked.

'He called it "a wasting disease",' said Themis.

'Hmm,' said Arianos with a twinkle in his eye as he got up. 'So, no fighting! Follow those suggestions and come back fit as a flea. Have good journeys and the gods go with you.' He clapped Themis on the shoulder and strode off.

Photios and Themis walked back together. Today Frog was with them and carried their things. Photios had a recitation and music lesson immediately after the gymnasium, but Themis had no more lessons. He had packed some tablets and styluses to take on the journey, as Panainos had threatened maths, manuscript and music every day.

'Your scabs have all gone,' said Photios.

'Hmm, but it still itches, especially at night,' said Themis.

'Nah. That's your fleas,' said Photios seriously. 'You really ought – '

Themis turned and grabbed him round the neck from behind. 'Be careful,' he warned as Frog squeaked with worry and dropped the bags. 'I'll fight you,' declared Themis, 'and then you'll get thinner and thinner, until all I've got is your bones, and I'll boil them up to make varnish for my paintings.'

'Peace, peace!' Photios could hardly speak from laughing.

Themis let him go with a grin. Frog picked up their bags again. As they walked in through the city gate, Themis said 'What were you and my mother talking about so quietly yesterday?'

'I was reassuring her about us all biding by the curse,' said Photios.

'Did she say anything about Zeus?' asked Themis.

'No, but I was there when she sacrificed a white goat to Zeus of Hymetos not long after you were injured. The priests agreed that the message in the entrails was to beg Apollo's and Demeter's help. So that's what she did.'

'And that was when I woke up at the bridge?'

'Yes.'

'So you were there that day, too, as well as when I got injured?'

'Yes. I couldn't see very well because your family were all around, but I could hear Priestess Asterodia calling to Apollo, and the music and drums.'

'I hardly remember anything about that day … '

'But it seems Zeus was right,' said Photios, 'and you are usually Apollo's responsibility. When they called on him, he gave you back a certain amount of … intelligence.'

Themis elbowed Photios in the ribs.

Photios stopped walking and looked at Themis mock-seriously. 'But it's sad so much is still missing,' he said, his head on one side.

Frog snorted, but Themis nodded and bit his lip. 'Hmm. And now it seems that Zeus even wants part of what's left.'

'Not yet, he doesn't,' Photios reassured. 'Not till you've helped your fat uncle decorate his throne.'

'Yeah. That's going to be … well, it feels to me like it's meant to happen.'

'Ah, like your statue with the face of Xenovia?' Photios teased.

Themis turned on him, a blush rising up his neck. 'What do you know about that?!'

'Couldn't help seeing your drawings.' Photios walked on. 'They're very good.'

'At least that part of my mind is still better than yours,' said Themis.

'And you can still write, so send me a message now and again,' said Photios. 'Or even a drawing, as long as it hasn't got Xenovia's face.'

Themis was suddenly exasperated. 'Race you to the music school!' he said and the two boys set off, zigzagging through the busy streets, leaving Frog to follow as best he could.

When Themis and Frog got back to the house, his travelling box and bag were closed and ready in the portico. Eirini called him in to her salon. The garment she was working on was dark red and trailed from her lap in a large pool around her feet.

'You will leave here at dawn tomorrow,' she said, looking up. 'Panainos has found a cheap ship.'

Themis grinned with excitement. 'Really?'

Eirini went on. 'Melanas is in the andron. He's been to the farm and has something for you from Diodotos.'

As Themis entered the andron, Melanas came towards him with a small package in his hand.

'Your brother wants you to take this with you on your travels,' he said, looking down at Themis with sad eyes. 'You can wear it under your tunic and, if the gods are willing, you won't need it. But just in case ... '

Themis took the linen-wrapped bundle. It contained his father's dagger in a sheath on a belt of plaited leather. The blade was inlaid with a design of swallows in flight in silver.

Melanas showed him how to strap the belt round his waist so that it would not show or obstruct his movement. There was also a pouch on the belt. Themis opened it and found five silver, four-drachma coins, wrapped in fine linen to prevent clinking.

'So this is my survival belt,' laughed Themis.

'A gift from your father and brother,' said Melanas. 'Diodotos' message is, "Try not to lose, or use, any of its contents".'

'I doubt I'll need them,' said Themis. 'Mama is giving Panainos money to feed me until I begin to work for him.'

They went out into the sunny courtyard. Melanas said solemnly, 'Never let your mind sleep, young master. Always assume that even your best friend has other thoughts in his head than your well-being.'

'Do you mean Panainos?' asked Themis in surprise.

'No. I do not mean anyone specific,' answered Melanas. 'These were the words my father said to me the last time I saw him. I was going hunting along the River Nile with his steward.'

'What happened?'

'When I got back, my parents had been killed by raiders and I was captured and sold.' Melanas turned to Themis. 'So you see, you never know what might befall you from one moment to the next.'

Themis nodded, shocked at Melanas' story. 'Yes, I do see,' he said.

'Thank you, Melanas … Thank you for bringing these from the farm. And please thank Diodotos for me, too, and tell him I will take care of my survival package.'

'Safe journeys,' said Melanas with a smile.

They nodded to each other and the slave left.

Themis stood in his father's room, turning the dagger over in his hands. He longed again to remember the man who had worn it. The swallows seemed to move their wings.

Then he went and added his design for the statue with Xenovia's face to his travelling box.

>>>

From Bernie's Facebook Wall. March 8th 2010, Monday

Suzanne is here! She's in the Jubilee Ward at the hospital. You can visit anytime between 6 and 8 pm. She's still in a coma but there are signs that she will be out of it soon. The nurses say no point in grapes or flowers yet, and to remember the hygiene rules.

And just so everyone knows, Ian actually phoned me! He said to tell Suzanne when she wakes up that he's sorry he dumped her like that. She's too good for him and he hopes she'll be fine soon.

No comment!!!

From Bernie's private diary. Monday March 8th 2010

Trying to be upbeat. It's great that Suzanne is back home, but that doesn't change the fact that she's still not with us and could have all sorts of things wrong when she does wake up.

And the worst thing today was seeing what happened to Mrs Jenkins when they'd got Suzanne settled. We were told 'she'll be fine now and you should leave'. We went out into the foyer and Mrs J kind of collapsed. I had to drag her onto the bus to get her home. She's just like a zombie. When we got to her house, I helped her straight up to her bedroom. She didn't speak to her husband or the two boys.

This was all in the lunch hour. I left her there, lying on her bed, face down. When I got back to school, everyone was asking how things had gone. I couldn't pretend, and when I finished telling them, they just wandered off. It's really depressing. Laila actually gave me a hug.

And now I've got a load of studying to do to catch up.

It would be useful to know more about praying …

<<<

104

Chapter 17: departure

The ship was called the Pelican. The cargo was oil in huge jars. As Themis and Frog stepped onto the ladder from the quay, the last of these amphoras was being lowered onto a bed of straw in the open hold. The squeal of the pulleys and the shouts of the stevedores drowned the voices of Eirini and Chloe as they called farewell wishes. Asterodia had come to officiate with the priest of Poseidon at the leaving ritual. The smell of incense overlay the tang of drying seaweed and the sweetness of newly scrubbed wood.

The old priestess had said to Themis, 'I know it cost you dear when you lost your father, although perhaps you don't remember your pain.'

Themis had looked into those startling eyes and shrugged sadly. She'd gone on, 'But it seems sure you are under the protection of Zeus, at least for now. Don't forget that we can never know all that the Fates and the gods are preparing for us. All we can ever do is be grateful to be alive.'

Themis had taken her right hand and kissed it as he'd seen others do. 'And I am,' he'd said simply.

Now Asterodia stood by Eirini, her wide eyes following Themis' every move. He had been too shy to ask after Xenovia and no one had mentioned her.

Once on the deck, the boys turned to watch as Panainos was led up the ladder. The whole ship wallowed as he arrived on board. A mischievous smile flitted across Frog's face.

'Behave!' whispered Themis, and they both straightened their faces to receive the trunk and two bags that were all their luggage. The stevedores readied a net full of cargo and swung it aboard. It landed on the wooden half-deck with a thump.

Panainos called out, 'Steady there!' and fussed round as the sailors removed the net. 'Precious stuff in there. Come and help me stow my boxes,' he said to the two boys. They dragged the boxes into the small area of decking in the stern, where there were lockers against the hull. A wooden ladder rose from this deck to another smaller deck above. Near the ladder, also against the hull, were four cages containing pigeons.

As they bent down to stow away Panainos' things, a shape ran down the ladder and stopped. Themis turned and found himself looking into the curious brown eyes of a large, slim dog. He was a bit like Panax, but not quite as big, and darker, like brown marble. He had cocked his head on one side at the spectacle of the bottoms of two boys and a fat man.

'Leave some space for *my* gear,' came a loud voice from the quay. A wiry man with a deep tan and wild dark hair and beard danced from rung to rung of the landing ladder. He jumped lightly onto the deck and came over to them.

'Move, Beast!' he commanded the dog as they scrambled up from their knees by the lockers. The dog loped back up the ladder to the top deck and stood looking down at them.

'I'm Captain Stomio,' he declared. 'You'll be Panainos, the Master Painter?'

'Indeed I am,' said Panainos. 'And this is my cousin's child, Themistokles.'

'We'll be off shortly. Is everything of yours aboard?'

'All aboard and shipshape, Captain,' declared Panainos with mock subservience.

The ship lurched a little as someone else ran up from the quay. It was a young man in a fine-patterned green cloak with a large bag over his shoulder. The captain turned and said to Panainos, 'One of yours?'

'Not mine.' Panainos shook his head.

'I'm a temple messenger,' said the young man, catching his breath. 'I've been asked to take a sealed message to the Judge called Iasos at Elis. Can you take me?'

Themis had an uneasy feeling that he knew the youth's face, but as usual could not be sure.

'Do you have food for the journey?' The captain sounded impatient.

'No, but I have coin,' the young man said.

'Then you owe me for the passage and you'll buy stores at the first port,' said the captain, running up the ladder to the top deck.

Eirini and her household were waiting for the ship to cast off. Artemisia and Panainos' daughters had not braved a visit to the port. Themis stood on the narrow walkway inside the hull and leant on the rail. He waved. Eirini stared back up at him, standing tall and proud beside Melanas and Mika. Chloe was dancing and singing a 'wish' chant for good weather for them. Asterodia still watched his every move, though he felt her mind was far away.

'See you in sixty days,' Themis called cheerfully. His mother suddenly turned to Asterodia and hid her face in the old woman's shoulder. Melanas raised his hand, his smile a beacon in his dark face. Chloe stopped dancing.

A man with a striking resemblance to Captain Stomio reached for the bow rope and lifted it off the bollard. 'Safe journeys, my brother,' he called, 'and may Poseidon be kind.'

The rope slapped into the water as he dropped it and one of the ship's sailors pulled it on board. The bow began to drift round towards the harbour opening. Captain Stomio himself pulled up the aft hauser and started releasing sail ropes from his position by the tiller. The mainsail, which had been hanging in festoons from the gaff overhead, began to unfurl. The breeze filled it and tugged the ship away from the quay. The captain steered the heavy Pelican between the crowds of other vessels, large and small, and headed out into the bay.

Themis ran up the steps to the stern rail of the top deck beside the captain. He waved both arms. Chloe waved both hers back. The others stood watching as the gap between them grew. Beast came up, sniffed at Themis and stood to attention beside him.

Themis' small family group faded into the crowd as the ship picked up speed. His heart sank for a brief moment when he realised he could no longer distinguish their faces among the many others.

He put a hand on Beast's smooth head. 'Will I ever see them again, I wonder?' he whispered, tears stinging his eyelids.

The captain was shouting at the crew as Beast raised his muzzle to the increasing breeze. Themis felt the Pelican coming alive. Water hissed under the keel and churned into a wake across the outer harbour. The three sailors darted from adjusting ropes, to lacing the cover over the hold, to stowing the anchor. Panainos had retired to the lower deck beneath where Themis stood. That area would be home to all the passengers and crew for the next few days.

The ship began to rise and fall as they left the shelter of the harbour and set off across the Gulf of Salamis. They were heading southeast, to leave the island of Egina, with its single, pointed mountain, to their right. Slim white birds fussed and whirled around the Pelican and over her wake. Themis held onto the rail and looked around for his slave.

'Hey,' called Frog's voice from above. 'Look over there!'

Themis looked up and saw Frog lying along the gaff, above the brown-red sail. 'How did you get up there?' he shouted.

'Climbed the mast,' said Frog. 'Come on up!'

'No thanks!' called Themis. 'Too high for people with holes in their heads.'

'Look over there!' Frog pointed to the west as they drew level with the island of Salamis.

Two huge war-ships were running south quite a distance away, with all oars out and working. They were going more than twice as fast as the Pelican. 'There must be a hundred men rowing each of those,' called Frog.

Captain Stomio said, 'More like two hundred. They're training in case of war.' The Pelican was like a fat sparrow in the presence of falcons.

'And will we have war this summer?' asked the young man in the green cloak. He was sitting on the steps between the decks.

'Sorry, young man, but you can't sit there,' called the captain. 'Someone might need to get up or down in a hurry. You can sit on the rail there, or on a stool or the floor on the lower deck.'

The young man narrowed his eyes, but he moved to sit on the rail by the steps. The pigeons cooed quietly beside him. 'They say Sparta and Corinth are gathering their troops.'

'We'll have enough on our hands with the spring winds,' said the captain. 'If there's going to be a war, it won't start till we're back from this trip.'

He turned and pulled on a rope. The sail moved to catch the wind better. 'What's your name?' he asked the young man.

'Molon, son of Lykiskos of – '

'With this wind, we'll be at Ydra mid-afternoon. You can buy your provisions there.' The captain ran down the ladder and walked forward, checking the lacing of the hold cover.

Frog climbed down the mast and he and Themis went forward to stand in the bow, watching as the ship cut into each wave and sparkling drops were thrown up on either side.

They swayed with the waves with wide grins on their faces. It was exhilarating, thrilling. The light was so brilliant it forced them to slit their eyes. The wind lifted their hair and filled their lungs. The rise and fall of the waves made Themis feel that the sea was breathing.

He gazed at the horizon, his mind worrying at where he'd seen Molon before. When? Before the accident? At the Diasia? Suddenly a picture of Straton and his brothers came into his head. The eyes, the chin, the hair, all similar to Molon, and yet not quite Molon.

The captain came along the catwalk with Beast behind him. 'Got our escort already,' he said, pointing down into the water.

Themis shook his head to dislodge the Molon problem and looked where the captain pointed. At first he could see nothing but swelling dark blue water. Then a dolphin broke the surface in a shallow leap as it swam beside them, and another and another – tens, perhaps scores of them – appeared and disappeared in graceful curves with hardly a splash.

Beast let out a deep, excited bark. The boys laughed and pointed and punched each other's shoulders, the distance between master and slave forgotten.

As they were gathering to eat their midday bread and olives, Themis asked Molon, 'Are you related to Straton, son of Ypatos?'

'That hot-head!' said Molon with a hoot of laughter. 'Yes, he's my cousin. Ypatos is my mother's brother.'

'I have the same trainer as Straton,' said Themis.

'Arianos. Yes, I know,' said Molon. 'Bit of a clod, isn't he?'

Themis didn't answer. He took his food forward and sat on the anchor with Frog, throwing olive stones into the sea.

They docked in Ydra harbour in the late afternoon after a day of glorious motion, distant mountains, and groans from Panainos as he succumbed to seasickness over the stern. Themis thought it unlikely that there would be maths, manuscript and music for a while. He and Frog went ashore with Beast on a string and followed Molon to the chandlers'.

When Molon had finished his purchases, they walked behind him as he strode back towards the ship. The quay was busy. Some men hurried along with loads, others sauntered between heaps of fishing nets and cargo, sniffing the scents of food from the waterfront taverns. Molon carried his bag with a swagger and looked around him with an air of possession. He stopped and turned to them.

'I'm going in here for a glass of good wine and a pie,' he said, waving a hand at an open shop front with two long tables in front. 'Tell the captain I'll be on the boat by sunset.'

The boys looked at each other. 'We'll come with you,' murmured Themis.

'Not a good idea,' said Molon with a shake of his head. 'I'm not paying for you boys.'

'We can pay,' said Themis.

Molon turned with a snort of disgust and went up to the counter. He ordered good local wine, and a pie straight from the oven. He took these and sat on a wicker stool at the head of a table, looking out to the harbour. The boys stood back, watching. Themis was tempted by the smells, but did not want to reach for his money in public.

A man with a large cup in his hand went and sat near Molon.

'You going far?' he asked.

'The ship is going across to Tarentum in Greater Greece, but I shall probably leave it at Pheia for Olympia,' said Molon, gazing out at the bustle in the small, rock-bound harbour.

The man cleared his throat. 'It's just, I've got a small package I need to get to Olympia and I thought you might take it – for a fee, of course.'

'I'm sorry, I'm on Temple business and I'm not allowed – '

'But it's for one of the craftsmen working at the Temple of Zeus in Olympia,' said the man with an engaging smile.

'Who is the head priest here, in Ydra?' Molon asked, his nose rising.

The man was not to be diverted. 'It's not a big package. It'd fit into your bag there, easy,' he insisted, laying a hand on the bag.

Molon pulled the bag to him and shook off the hand. He said haughtily, 'There's a chance I won't be going all the way to Olympia. I may have to find a courier myself from one of the stops along the way.'

'You could just put your message together with mine in the same package,' said the man, a slight edge in his voice. 'This is really very important to us.' Molon ignored him.

Themis looked at Frog. 'I'd better call Molon to leave.' he whispered. 'This man may be a thief.'

'Let's see what he does,' said Frog with a wry smile.

The man took a swig from his cup. He looked at Molon sideways. 'Which Temple are you from?' he asked.

'My business is in the name of Apollo,' Molon answered, nose to the sky.

Themis whispered to Frog 'I thought he said he had to see a judge in Olympia?'

'He did,' said Frog with a shrug.

'So …' began Themis.

The man stood up and spoke suddenly slowly and loudly. 'Apollo is known to favour the Spartans. Could it be that your business is in fact in Lakonia? Could it be that we have here a Spartan spy?'

'Come on,' said Frog, grabbing Themis' arm.

Themis let Beast go. 'Back to the ship, Beast,' he hissed, as Frog pulled him towards the table. They slid in behind Molon, one on each side, put their hands under his arms and lifted him off his stool, bag and all. Themis said in Molon's ear, 'Captain Stomio needs you.'

Molon managed to get purchase with his feet on the ground and ran between the boys as they headed for the ship at the end of the quay. Beast danced around them, barking joyously.

'Hey!' the man shouted out. 'They are on their way to Lakonia with information from Athens. Stop them!'

Luckily the crowd either didn't believe him or was not prepared to deal with Beast. They ran up the ladder immediately they reached the ship, setting it rocking.

The captain came out from under the deck in the stern. 'What have you stolen?' he asked wearily.

'Not a thing!' Molon protested. 'Some idiot decided we were spies for the Spartans. And just because I mentioned Apollo.'

'We'd better cast off then,' Captain Stomio sighed. 'There's not much daylight left.'

'Where are we going?' came Panainos' weak voice from under the awning. 'My stomach won't take any more of these stormy seas.'

'Little place I know with a good spring and an easy mooring,' said the captain as he set about casting off.

Themis went and sat beside Panainos. 'It isn't stormy today, Uncle,' he said quietly.

'Tell that to my stomach,' groaned Panainos. 'We've been bucking like a newborn colt all day. I shall be as slim as Phidias by the time we get to Olympia.'

Themis helped Panainos take a drink from a water skin.

Panainos wiped his lips with the corner of his cloak. He asked quietly, 'Why did they think Molon is a spy?'

'He mentioned being on business for Apollo,' said Themis.

'I don't think there's an administered shrine to Apollo in Olympia,' mused Panainos. 'And that's not what he said when he got on the ship.'

'He said something about a judge,' said Themis. 'And he's related to a schoolmate of mine, but it's not a family known to sympathise with the Spartans.'

'Of course, everyone in the Peloponnese will be on the lookout for spies, but we'd better keep an eye on young Molon ourselves.' Then Panainos groaned and sighed as the ship picked up speed. 'Ergh … Go away, Themis, and let me die in peace.'

The sun had gone and the mountains of the mainland were layer upon layer of flat grey shapes against the burning western sky. They turned into an inlet with low rocky hills on either side. The inlet snaked deep into the land, and at its end branched into two. One branch offered a tiny beach, pale in the gloaming. The other was choked with steep rocks. Captain Stomio ran the ship onto the sandy bottom of the beach. One of the sailors jumped overboard with the anchor and took it up onto the land, hooking it securely round a large rock.

Beast bounded into the water with a splash, then disappeared silently over the headland.

'If you're prepared to wet your feet, you can sleep on land tonight,' said the captain. 'The spring is near the top of the leaning rock up there.'

'What is this place?' asked Molon.

'The island is called Dokos. There's a village of rather irritable locals on the western end, not far away, so don't wander. But we won't be seen here, even if we light a fire.'

Molon said, 'I bought bread and fruit and cheese in Ydra. Will we eat on land?'

Panainos stepped shakily out from under the deck, holding on to the rail. 'We will,' he said firmly. 'Even if I have to swim, I shall eat and sleep on land tonight.'

Later, round the fire, Themis offered Panainos a piece of cheese.

'No, no,' said Panainos. 'I'll stick to rusks and water for tonight. Ah, thank you, Frog,' he added, as Frog brought two full water skins from the little spring among the rocks and joined them.

'I never thought I'd hear you say no to food, Uncle,' teased Themis.

'It won't be a permanent phenomenon.' Panainos managed a smile.

Molon poked the fire with a stick. 'It's good for the soul to avoid excess in everything,' he said, nodding his head gravely.

Themis had to stand up and leave the group to hide his smile. Frog made a better job of it and stayed where he was. Themis walked up above the tumbled rocks. He could still hear the conversation, but also the sounds of the lapping sea and the breeze in the bushes. The sky was clear so it was going to be a cold night. He turned to look back at the fire-lit faces. He could hear Panainos talking kindly to Molon, trying to explain that an attitude of arrogance would only bring him trouble in areas beyond the influence of Athens.

'And this island is beyond the rule of Athens?' asked Molon, obviously surprised.

'Here we are on land held by Argos,' answered the captain, 'but from morning we'll be in Spartan controlled lands while we pass Cape Tainaron and skirt Messinia.'

'Pass?' queried Molon's voice, too loud in the still of the evening. 'I thought we would be sure to stop at Tainaron.'

'I avoid habitation if I can,' said the captain quietly. 'Tainaron is a busy city, what with the sanctuary and the oracle and the three harbours. Many ships have to put in there because of the currents and wind changes round the Cape. And there are always desperate men on the run or looking for work.'

'But I have to report to the priests at the Sanctuary of Poseidon,' said Molon crossly. 'I was charged with a … er … a message for them.'

'It's not somewhere I visit unless I'm forced to,' said Captain Stomio as he stood up. 'I'm off to sleep on board. Any of you who wishes can sleep here on the sand. We'll fill up on water when we wake, and leave before dawn.'

Just then, Beast joined Themis at his vantage point and put his nose into Themis' hand, giving him a fright. The nose was sticky.

'Ach! Beast,' said Themis quietly, 'what have you been doing?' He sniffed the slime. It smelled of blood. 'You've been hunting hares,' he whispered to the dog.

He climbed down to where the spring trickled into a little basin in the rocks and washed the blood off his hands and the salt from the day's sailing off his face. The water was icy but tasted sweet. Beast joined him and drank deeply.

'Where are you, Themis?' called Panainos. 'I've persuaded the captain to tell us a story before he goes back to the ship.'

This turned out to be short and a little disappointing as Themis had heard about the speedy but thoughtless hare and the trudging but determined tortoise before. But the captain did give it his own flavour by joking about which one would survive an encounter with Beast.

Later, rolled in his blanket under the sky, Themis wondered which god it was that Molon really served. He had now mentioned both Apollo and Poseidon. But, in spite of his family's general reverence, it was only Zeus that Themis felt might truly exist. His dream had felt so real. But even that, maybe, had been a memory of something Phidias had shown him before his accident. If it was true, though – and in his heart he believed it was – then the question of what Zeus wanted from him was going to keep turning his belly to water.

Better to think of other things. Frog had snuggled up for warmth and was asleep. So Themis looked up in awe at the millions of stars. How could one earth-bound god be responsible for so many stars?

Chapter 18: voyage

Themis woke to the sound of creaking rigging and found he was the last to rise. He and Frog scrambled to get on board before the ship began to move.

The sky in the east was turning from blue to green to yellow and the breeze strengthening as they left the lee of the inlet. Soon the Pelican's sail was straining at its ropes. Panainos didn't even have the strength to complain and seemed unconscious, wrapped in a blanket by the rail in the stern.

Themis and Frog knew they had four more days on the boat if all went well. They tried to play fivestones for a while on the unsteady deck. Then Themis plucked up the courage to climb the mast. He made it part of the way up at least. Later they spent a while happily oiling and removing ticks from Beast and dropping them in the sea.

The pigeons, it turned out, were not for food as Themis had thought, but carrier pigeons. They would take messages back to Athens from wherever the captain delivered them.

Themis dug out and read again the tablet that Arianos had given him. He asked Frog to tap out a rhythm and count while he did some sit-ups and arm-swings. Then he lay on his back with his feet in the air.

'Come and sit on my feet so I can do some leg-pushups,' he said.

'What will you pay me?' asked Frog with a laugh.

'I'll comb your hair for nits,' said Themis. 'Very gently, I promise.'

'Ha!' snorted Frog. But he sat carefully on Themis' upturned feet.

A corner of Panainos' blanket stirred. 'You'd be better off lying across them so that you can hold on,' came his voice. 'The ship is moving enough without going up and down like a yoyo.'

The boys exchanged winks and Themis began lifting Frog and then letting him sink down.

'That'll do,' he said after twenty. 'It's hard not to drop you because of the swell,' he said breathlessly.

'Of course,' agreed Frog, escaping happily. 'It's not as though I'm very heavy, is it? You could probably lift me a hundred times on dry land.'

'At least,' agreed Themis. 'Want to try lifting me like that?'

'Pass,' said Frog, rolling his eyes.

Themis' favourite place was at the bow. In the glittering light and constant motion, he was never plagued by the vision of Zeus' great hand trying to pluck something from his head. They watched dolphins and sea birds and sang songs with the sailors. Themis tried to accompany them on his flute, which caused a certain amount of hilarity.

The captain spent the day on the top deck, controlling the rudder. Molon lay near him, reciting the Odyssey out loud. He told with relish of how Circe turned Odysseus' men into pigs and made them eat acorns and chestnuts. After a while the captain asked Molon to shut up. He went down to the lower deck and carried on under his breath.

The stiff breeze held, and late in the afternoon the captain steered so that the land was quite close on the right. An endless series of headlands and rocky bays ahead became clearer. They sailed along parallel to the coast with the wind almost exactly behind them, sometimes catching the scents of earth and herbs warmed by the sun.

'We've made good progress today,' said the captain. 'We've already passed the place I was going to put in for the night. We'll go on a bit further and may even round the Cape before we anchor.'

Molon looked up. 'Which Cape is that?' he called.

'Cape Malea, the first of the three great peninsulars of the Peloponnese,' said the captain.

A loud groan came from Panainos. 'Only the first. Apollo, preserve me.' Themis glanced at him in the shadows and could see that his face was an unusual shade of pale grey instead of its normal florid pink. For the first time Themis realised Panainos was not immortal. He got out his wax tablet and began drawing his two uncles' faces. As he drew, he found he was praying that Panainos would survive the voyage.

The sun was going down behind the high mountains to their right. With the light fading fast, the Captain called an order and they headed directly for a high rocky wall. Magically, a tiny cove with a white beach opened in the cliff. They pulled up the sail and lost speed as they approached. The oars came out and the ship slipped in between two craggy headlands. White water showed on a line of rocks to the left as they gently bumped onto the sandy bottom.

Around the fire later, waiting for the stew to cook, Molon turned to Panainos, stubble-faced and still wrapped in his blanket, but now able to drink a little watered wine.

'You know, Master Painter, I appreciated your effort to show me how I appear to others last night.'

'Did you now,' said Panainos. His terrible pallor was fading as the wine began to revive him. Or perhaps it was just the firelight.

'As you said, I am rather young for my mission and I am a little worried that I may fail.' This was the first time Themis had seen Molon smile. It was disturbing. 'So I would beg you,' he went on, 'to use any influence you have with the captain to secure at least a short visit to the port of Tainaron. I understand that the Sanctuary is only a few steps from the quays.'

'I have no idea about that,' answered Panainos with a little more of his old spirit. 'But if the captain says it is to be avoided, we must comply. We are entirely in his hands.'

At that moment the captain joined the circle round the fire and signalled to the sailor who doubled as cook to stir the pot.

'Of course, I realise that,' replied Molon, settling himself closer to the fire and including the captain in the conversation, 'and I understand the possible difficulties that might arise. But it is imperative that I speak to someone there.' He turned his slimy smile full on to the captain. 'I do of course have authority to offer a considerable sum of money to ameliorate the inconvenience.'

'To what?' asked the captain.

'To make it worth your while,' said Molon, his head inclined at an ingratiating tilt.

The captain looked thoughtful and rubbed his bearded chin. 'I'll think about it,' he said, 'but we'll have to make good time again to fit it in, and the signs are that the wind will be almost in our faces once we round Cape Malea.'

The sailor-cook was taking the pot off the fire, so Themis began to hand round the bread. Panainos even managed a little of the stew.

And while they ate the captain began another story. Themis didn't really listen at first, but then he thought he heard his trainer's name.

'Arion overheard the sailors,' Captain Stomio was saying. 'They had just broken into his travel trunk and found his hoard of gold.'

'This doesn't sound like Arianos,' thought Themis. *'Who is this Arion?'*

'The sailors were deciding when to throw him overboard.'

'Not a good advertisement for your colleagues, dear Captain,' said Panainos, one eyebrow raised.

'They were Corinthians,' said the captain. 'What d'you expect?'

Molon looked shocked, but Panainos and Frog laughed.

The captain went on. 'Arion was a famous musician and had become rich from his profession. But there was little he could do. He offered to give them all his gold if they would spare his life. But the sailors just jeered at him. So he dressed himself in his richest performance robes and, standing on the bow of the ship, he played his best kithara and sang his favourite song as an offering to Poseidon.

'The sailors enjoyed the song, but showed no mercy. So, avoiding their drawn daggers, Arion leapt off the ship into the sea, kithara and all.'

Captain Stomio stood up to kick the fire. 'Dolphins like music,' he said, as he sat down again. 'The ship sailed away, but a group of them had gathered to listen to Arion's song. They carried him with them on their backs for two or three days. They chattered and clicked at him to show they wanted him to play for them and so he did, all the time hoping they would take him nearer to land. At last they understood he needed food and fresh water and they brought him in to the west port at Tainaron still wearing his magnificent costume and carrying his kithara. He stood on the end of the quay and gave them one last song. Then, when he'd drunk and eaten, he set off for Corinth to find and punish his would-be murderers!'

'And did he get his gold back?' asked Panainos.

'Who knows?' answered the captain. 'But he may have, because he had a bronze statue of a man on a dolphin cast and set it on the quay-side in Tainaron as a thank offering.'

The sky had darkened to black and to the east the stars glittered. But to the west they were veiled by thin, high cloud. Frog dropped off immediately, but Themis dozed fitfully, warding off un-nameable threats, until Beast came and joined them, adding his welcome warmth to their shallow, sandy bed.

>>>

From Bernie's private diary. Wednesday March 10th 2010

Suzanne hasn't moved today. She's completely still. I talked to her for half an hour, but it was like talking to a stone. She's just a body with no person living in it, no mind, no soul, nothing. All she does is breathe. They keep telling us that that's normal and doesn't mean she's going to die. But it frightens me more than anything else. I don't let on, but she is 'deader' now than she was even in Athens.

I haven't put this on Facebook or the blog, of course.

<<<

Next morning, the captain hugged the coast as they ran before a wind from the north. High mountains came down to the sea in spurs that seemed cut off at the ends by the waves. The cliffs were often convoluted, their many colours and strange shapes lit crisply by the rising sun. Thousands of birds had streaked them with white, birds that swirled in the breeze, their calls echoing off the rocks. The Pelican met and passed three other merchant ships too far out to hail.

Headland after headland appeared before them until suddenly there were no more, and the sea stretched to the south, empty as far as the eye could see.

'We turn westwards round the Cape soon,' called the captain from the top deck. 'Once we do, we'll have to tack and turn the sail more often, so the crew will be moving around a lot more. Passengers must stay in the stern, on the lower deck.'

'Will you tell us when to leave the bow, Captain?' called Themis.

'I'll give you a shout – and mind you move sharpish!'

Panainos' voice boomed out from the lower deck, 'Aye, Aye, Sir!'

Themis turned to Frog. 'He's feeling better!'

The boys watched the land as the captain brought the ship nearer and nearer to the cliffs. Here, great slabs of grey and white rock seemed about to slip off the mountains into the sea. They filled half the sky and were entirely empty of life, even birds. Not a village or path showed on their barren, contorted slopes. At their feet a fine border of white marked where the dark blue waves broke against them.

'Everyone to action stations!' called the captain.

Themis and Frog raced back along the walkway and dived into the lower deck. There they found Molon sitting calmly on a stool beside the stem of the great rudder that groaned as Stomio turned it from above.

And Panainos was sitting on the floor, his blanket over his knees, and a large piece of bread in his hands.

'Ah, Uncle,' said Themis breathlessly, 'you seem a little better.'

'Yes, thank the gods,' said Panainos with a mischievous smile. 'I haven't … er … disposed of last night's supper.'

The ship heeled over as the wind hit it from the side. The sailors leapt to pull in one lot of ropes and let out another. The captain leant on the rudder and called his orders. Beast let out an occasional bark at the wind. Sunshine poured onto the lower deck from the left. More huge cliffs slid by on the right, getting further and further away.

Then at another order, the ship heeled the other way, the sunshine moved round to the stern, and the cliffs came nearer and nearer again.

The morning wore on. The boys fed the pigeons and annoyed Beast for a bit. They counted seabirds, the only visible inhabitants this side of the cape, and watched them fishing.

They sailed across the mouth of what seemed like a large bay. Molon told them it was the Lakonian Gulf, but the captain snorted, so they did not believe him.

'Should I be working on some mathematics?' Themis asked Panainos.

'Mathematics, my boy?' groaned Panainos. 'Ask the captain to oil the sea with some of his cargo so we can have an unmoving floor, and then we'll see about mathematics!'

So Themis did some more of Arianos' exercises. Frog sang and beat out the rhythm. Molon joined in some of the songs and even the sailors added their voices to the ones they knew. As the day got warmer, they fell silent and dozed in the swaying sunshine.

'Storm to starboard, long way off,' came a call around midday.

The ship was passing a steep headland on the right, the last of a series they had come to after the bay. Far ahead, another line of mountainous land could be seen faintly against the western sky. This bay was huge, much larger than the first one.

Over the hazy mountains at the head of the bay, there was a dark blur in the sky.

They were moving away from it, but just then the captain called the turn and they could see the clouds stacking up in a dark line.

The wind freshened. 'We'll try and beat it across,' called the captain. 'But make sure everything is stowed away safely. Get yourselves some rope to tie yourselves on with, and make sure the knots are strong!'

'By all the gods!' exclaimed Panainos. 'Just as I get my sealegs we're in danger of being swept off the boat!'

'A bit of excitement at last,' said Molon enthusiastically. 'Shall we pray to Poseidon?'

'Go ahead,' said Panainos with a comic look at Themis.

Molon began a long, monotonous prayer.

The storm hardly seemed to be moving. The Pelican caught the extra wind and her churning wake sparkled behind them.

'Where are we headed?' asked Molon when he finished his prayer. He was standing at the bottom of the steps up to the top deck.

The captain looked down at him. He was using his legs to steady the rudder and hold the Pelican on course. With his hands he was tying a harness onto Beast.

'This is the real Lakonian Gulf. Cape Tainaron and its port are dead ahead, at the left hand end of that peninsular, on the far side, so still out of sight.' The captain finished knotting the rope round Beast's chest. 'You may be lucky yet, Molon,' he added. 'We may need to put in there to recover if the storm catches us.'

The storm hung over the land ahead and to the right of the Pelican, as if it was afraid of the sea. The afternoon wore on. Everyone was quiet but tense, watching the clouds churning as they clung to the mountains.

They saw four other ships fleeing eastwards, the way they had come. Only one was following their own westward course, forty or fifty stades ahead.

The wind was now slicing glistening streamers of white spume from the tops of the indigo waves.

The captain came down to the lower deck with Beast. He showed Themis and Frog how to lower canvas blinds to keep out the flying spray. Themis noticed for the first time the calluses and the ridged and blackened nails on his hands. His jaw was set and he hardly spoke as he tied Beast carefully to a stanchion. The Pelican had started shipping water over the bow. Most of this ran off before it reached the stern.

Pananios tied a rope to an upright, then round his chest, and disappeared under his blanket. Molon stood with his legs apart as though riding in a chariot, swaying with each rise and dip of the ship. Themis sat by Beast, talking to him quietly about Panax and his family, caressing the soft forehead. Frog climbed halfway up the mast and sang a taunting song at the top of his voice, challenging the god of the wind to silence him.

'Who taught you that song?' shouted Themis.

'You don't want to know,' called Frog with a laugh.

Panainos' head poked out from his blanket. 'Behave, boys!' he bellowed over the slapping of the ropes and the hissing of the waves. 'We may not see the end of this day.'

'Storm approaching!' called a sailor.

Frog turned to look, and swore. He came skittering down the mast and grabbed the security ropes he'd made ready for himself near Themis. He didn't stop singing, but he now chose a more respectable kind of prayer.

The black clouds had strung out from the land in a long line, pushed over the water towards them by the northwest wind. Under them, the waves were flattened by curtains of leaden rain.

'We might just make it!' shouted the captain, turning the Pelican more south than west, away from the Gulf and the storm. 'Hold on and pray!'

Chapter 19: storm

To their left the sun was still shining, while the darkness of Hades advanced rapidly from the right. Just as the clouds covered the sun, a great gust of wind flipped the sail inside out and the Pelican's bow rose high in the air. It seemed to hang there for a moment, and then came slapping down onto the slope of the next wave in an explosion of spume. The starboard end of the gaff had snapped and began to crash around at the top of the mast. Beast let out a single howl of dismay. Ropes from the broken gaff thrashed and coiled in the tearing wind.

'Catch them!' shouted the captain. 'Drop the gaff! Drop the gaff! Don't wait to pull up the sail!' Two sailors jumped for the ropes and Molon ran forward along the walkway to help. The sail flapped wildly. The third sailor was aloft, trying to untie the gaff from the mast as it swung. Frog ran forward on the other side from Molon to try and catch one of the flailing ropes. They were both reaching for it when a wave caught the little ship broadside. She wallowed and tipped in the deep trough. The rope wrapped round Molon's arm.

'I've got it!' he shouted as the ship sank into the next trough. The other rope whipped across and wound itself round his neck and shoulders, pulling him off his feet. Molon rose into the air, his legs and arms windmilling. As he was slapped back onto the heaving canvas cover of the hold, Frog ran over it to him.

The wind had passed and now the rain pelted down, soaking everything within moments. The sailors brought the gaff and sail down almost on top of Frog and Molon. The Pelican ran on smoothly now, with hardly a roll. Molon lay on the canvas cover of the hold. Frog knelt beside him, frantically unwinding the ropes from his body.

Themis was having trouble undoing the wet ropes that tied him to the rail. Once free, he dashed out into the deluge to join Frog and Molon. The canvas covering was not meant to hold weight, so he dropped to his knees and crawled out onto it. From what he'd seen, he guessed that Molon must be injured. When he got to them, Molon's head was rolling backwards and forwards as though it was only attached to his body by the skin.

'Frog,' he said through the rain. 'He's dead, isn't he?'

'Tell the captain,' said Frog.

Themis put his hands to his mouth and yelled through the drumming of the rain on the ship. 'We think he's dead!'

The captain signed to a sailor to take over the rudder and ran down the steps to the edge of the canvas. He threw a rope from there.

Frog and Themis crawled beside Molon, as the captain pulled on the rope they'd tied round his ankles. In that strange little canvas room, with the rain roaring on the deck above, the captain said, 'Yes, he's dead.'

The rain stopped as suddenly as it had started, and all was quiet.

The pigeons cooed in the stillness. Beast sniffed at Molon, snorted, and then sat still. They all stared at Molon's lolling head, trying to take in what had happened. The silence dragged on.

Finally, Captain Stomio stood back. His voice was almost a whisper as he said, 'We'll take the body in to Tainaron, and leave him with the priests of Poseidon. The god seems to want him, but he didn't wash him overboard, so we'd better respect that.' Then he turned away and ran nimbly up the ladder to the top deck. The sailors had already started replacing the gaff. Soon they raised the sail and the Pelican was underway again. Molon's head rolled worse than ever.

'Get him against the hull and cover him up,' said Panainos, offering his blanket. 'I'll throw up again watching that.'

Later, Panainos remembered Molon's bag. He got it out of the locker where Molon had locked it before the storm. He called the captain, who came down and watched with the boys as Panainos opened it.

Inside were two closed tablets with seals, and a bag of coins. There was also another tunic and an old dagger in a sheath that had seen better days. The smart green cloak was stuffed into the locker under the bag.

'Should we hand these over with his body?' asked Panainos.

'No,' said the captain without hesitating. 'We'll see if we can deliver the tablets ourselves to the right people. The cloak and tunic belong to the Pelican now. If anyone asks in Tainaron, Molon had no possessions, just a little money and this old dagger. I'll keep the rest of the money as my fee for stopping at Tainaron. He did say he would pay for that.'

Their progress was brisk and the sun was in their eyes as they neared the last low headland of the peninsular.

'Tainaron is just behind that spur,' called the captain from the upper deck. 'We'll have to guard the ship all the time we're in port. It's a rough sort of place.'

They came round the spur. Ahead, the wide inlet was split into three by two low promontories. A busy city covered these headlands and each of the three bays was full of merchant ships tied to the wide stone quays that lined them. Opening onto the quays were long, low warehouses. Behind these were streets of mean-looking houses, and huge, square water cisterns. At the top of the right hand promontory, the roof of a small temple was visible above a strong sanctuary wall. The roof was white against the pale sky, but the wall was bright cornflower blue. The only visible trees in the whole city were inside that wall.

Hundreds of people bustled along the quays and streets. Snatches of shouted instructions and songs reached the Pelican. Strong smells of cooking, smoke, and sewage met them as they turned in to the middle inlet.

The captain shouted, 'Stay!' to Beast, but jumped off the ship himself as soon as it touched the quay. He disappeared into the back streets without a word, but reappeared almost immediately with two men in tow.

'These guys will carry the body up to the sanctuary,' he said. 'Panainos, you go with them, and take Themis. Frog can stay and help me get supplies. We'll sail again before sunset.'

The two men came on board, looking hopefully around the ship. Beast growled very quietly, looking down on them from the top deck. Themis saw one of the men narrow his eyes at the open doors of two of the lockers in the stern. Themis and Frog stood in front of them as the men lifted Molon's body and carried it off the Pelican.

Themis signed to Frog to close the lockers and ran up the ladder. He whispered to the captain, 'I think they're planning to come back later.'

'No doubt,' the captain said with a wry smile. 'So don't be long.'

Panainos was already off the ship and waiting on the busy quay. Themis leapt down and joined him. They walked fast through the crowds, following the two men up a steep street with their stiffening burden.

At the sanctuary, the men turned right and walked along under the blue wall to the high wooden gate that faced away from the port.

'Can't go in,' growled one of them. 'Leave it here.'

They put Molon down without a care for his lolling head and shambled off down the hill to get their pay from the captain.

Panainos banged on the door with the hilt of Molon's dagger.

Nothing happened.

A group of men playing a game in the dust outside a nearby drinking house turned to watch.

Panainos tried again. The sound echoed round the walls inside.

'The door's not locked,' came an angry voice, and the door flew open.

'We don't lock up. Poseidon never sleeps,' said the priest. He was not very tall, and gave the impression of an old tree stump, brown and gnarled. 'You'll be from Athens,' he said, eyeing up their clothes.

'Indeed we are,' agreed Panainos in a formal voice. 'There was an accident on our ship when we were hit by a storm this afternoon.'

'And this is the result?' said the priest, indicating Molon's body wrapped in the blanket.

'He was caught by ropes loosed from a broken gaff. One whipped round him and broke his neck.'

'Right,' said the priest, and he called out, 'Get two men out here now,' towards the temple.

Themis was craning to see into the sanctuary. The temple was much smaller than the one in the Agora he had been so thrilled by. It only had columns along the front and was plain with cracks in its steps. There were other low buildings all round the inside of the wall, their roofs sloping down towards the middle.

'I know about the storm. Come on in and tell us about the dead man,' said the priest.

The door shut silently as they walked across the courtyard towards the temple. The two acolytes had carefully picked up the blanketed Molon and carried him into one of the buildings. The priest beckoned Panainos to a bench along the temple's side wall.

'So,' he said as he and Panainos sat down, 'who was he?'

'You may know him,' said Panainos. 'His name was Molon, son of Lykiskos. He said he was a temple messenger, but the only god he mentioned was Apollo. Later, though, he did say he needed to stop here to deliver a message to the "priests of Poseidon".'

'Did he say who from?'

'No. Nor did he say what the message was.'

'Hmmm,' said the priest, standing up. 'Not much help, really.'

'No,' agreed Panainos, also getting up. 'He had this dagger on him and these few coins.' Panainos handed them over.

'I'll make inquiries,' said the priest. 'Molon, son of Lykiskos, you say?'

'That's right. Will you arrange to let his family know?'

'No problem,' growled the priest. 'We'll have to put him in the catacombs until we can get him cremated properly. I'll send a pigeon to Athens tomorrow.'

'Do you have pigeons for specific places, then?' asked Themis.

Panainos frowned at him for interrupting, but the priest seemed pleased. He smiled, showing teeth almost as brown as the rest of him as he said, 'Yes, for most of the major sanctuaries.'

'How does it work? Do you buy them from ships from those places?'

The priest sat down again and gestured to Themis to sit on the ground by his feet. 'Some we buy, some are sent to us for future use. Have you got any for sale?'

'There are four on board, but I think the captain is taking them to Olympia,' said Themis, hugging his knees.

'That's fine,' said the priest. 'We have a couple from Athens, and there are at least five at the Oracle.'

'What's the Oracle?' asked Themis, ignoring Panainos' sign to him that they were in a hurry.

'It's where people come to speak to the dead,' the priest explained. 'It's down in the town. There's a garden with dreaming couches where you can stay the night and maybe dream of the dead. Or you can visit the cave that goes directly down to Hades. The spirits come up into the deepest chamber if the right words are said.'

'And if the necromancers have been well rewarded,' said Panainos with a false but charming smile.

'Is this the only place with a cave like that?' asked Themis.

'No, but it's the most well-known. Are you wanting to talk to the dead, then, boy?' The priest was ignoring Panainos but he had a slight gleam in his eye that unnerved Themis. The vague thoughts he'd had about contacting the underworld evaporated.

'No, no. I was just curious,' he said as he stood up and dusted off his tunic.

Panainos said quickly. 'We'll be off then, your holiness.'

'Right. Well, we'll sort out your corpse.' The priest stood and moved with them towards the gate. 'Drop in on your way back and we may have some news of exactly what his mission was.'

'Thank you,' said Panainos smoothly. 'That would be of great interest.'

As they climbed aboard again, Captain Stomio called from the top deck, 'We'll have to stay here overnight. There's going to be another storm.' A large pot of thick fish soup spread its inviting smell from the lower deck. A heap of bread loaves lay on a cloth beside it. 'Eat and bed down as best you can,' he added as he came down the ladder. 'We'll set guards all night and sail at first light, whatever the weather.'

'Have you been using up Molon's money?' asked Panainos, opening a locker which contained one of his boxes.

'No,' said the captain. 'Yours.'

'Ah,' sighed Panainos, running his fingers round the outside of the box. 'That's a relief. The water has not got through the waxing.'

'Is that your colours, Uncle?' asked Themis, settling down beside Frog and the pot.

'Colours, and other important things.'

'Put them away and don't talk about them,' said the captain, looking meaningfully at the ships moored on either side. 'We don't want to encourage visitors.'

Themis and Frog stayed awake a long time, listening to the sounds of the wind among ropes, and the songs and arguments that rang out across the harbour. Frog had hardly spoken since Molon's death and lay very still. Panainos was pretending to be asleep, but Themis could see that he was holding his blanket round him too tightly to be sleeping. The captain and Beast were on the top deck and they and the three sailors took it in turns to keep watch.

Themis dozed, but was suddenly awake as the ship rocked. He sat up and made out Beast in the starlight, standing at the rail, growling with teeth bared at two men on the quay. There was a whispered argument going on between them and the captain.

'My life's worth more than that,' Captain Stomio was saying. 'And if they don't get to where they're supposed to go, I'll be dead meat.'

'Just the boys, then,' came the harsh whisper from the quay. 'We can give you forty drachmas each for them. In silver.'

'No deal, gentlemen,' said the captain pleasantly. 'They're under the protection of Poseidon. Imagine what he might do to Tainaron – and to you – if we cross him.'

Their grumbling voices gradually faded as the two men walked on to a boat two berths down to try their luck there.

'What did they want with us?' whispered Themis to the captain. Frog sat up beside him, wide-eyed.

'To buy you as pretty boys for some rich old Corinthian, I dare say,' he answered grimly. 'Or maybe for ransom.'

'You could have made a lot of money,' said Themis.

'Perhaps, but I could have lost my honest reputation and that's worth more. Anyway, I wasn't tempted.' He started up the ladder again. 'If Molon had still been with us, now…'

'How long till dawn?' came Panainos' voice.

'Not long now,' said the captain.

Chapter 20: father

The expected storm was only a squall and passed over a short while later. There was not much rain, but the accompanying gale set all the ships bumping into each other and against the quays. As soon as the wind showed signs of dropping, the captain backed them out of the inlet with the oars.

As they passed the headland between their harbour and the one to the west, the captain said, 'If it wasn't dark, you'd be able to see the statue Arion dedicated. He's on the waterfront, just over there.'

The sky was beginning to pale as they passed the last moorings and raised the mainsail. It caught the stiff south-easterly breeze as they headed south with a long headland to their right. At last they cleared this, just as the sun rose to their left.

The Pelican heeled over as the captain turned her northwest, along the other side of the headland. The sail swung round, snapped and then bulged full.

'We'll make good time if this wind keeps up,' he called. 'Any of that bread left for breakfast?'

Later in the morning, he joined Panainos and the boys on the lower deck. He brought Molon's bag with him. 'I went through this again during the night,' he began. 'I think we should take a look at those tablets in daylight. There's writing on the outside.'

He gave the tablets to Panainos. 'What does this one say?' the captain asked.

Panainos tilted the smooth wooden tablet to the sunlight. The letters incised into the wood became clear and Panainos read out loud: 'To His Eminence, Judge Iasos at Elis. Cursed be he who opens this and is not the Judge. He shall be fetched to Hades by the Furies.'

'Better leave it be then,' said the captain with a smile and a shake of his shaggy head.

'This one has nothing on it,' said Panainos as he turned the other tablet this way and that in the sunlight. 'Nothing at all.'

'Let's see what it is then,' said the captain. 'If it says inside who it's for, I might be able to deliver it.'

Panainos looked at the seals on the sides. He handed it silently to Themis. The impression in the wax showed a rounded leaf with a central vein and three other veins on either side at right angles to it.

'Do you recognise the seal?' Themis asked.

'No,' said Panainos. 'The design is childish, but neat.'

Themis handed the tablet back. 'Will you open it?'

Panainos gave it to the captain. 'It is part of your ship, now, Captain. It falls to you to open it.'

The captain took his knife and carefully broke the seals on three sides of the tablet. The two pieces of wood were joined down the other long side by a fabric hinge and opened out easily. He laid the tablet on the deck in a patch of sunlight. The writing in the wax was clear. Panainos read it out.

' "To Diokles, Necromancer of Tainaron and Messenger of the Mighty Hades, greetings and felicitations. May the spirits speak truth through you." Huh!' added Panainos. 'It's a bit late to find this now. No wonder Molon wanted to land at Tainaron.' He went on reading. ' "The bearer of this tablet will bring you a boy, Themistokles, son of Kallistos." '

They all looked at each other in surprise. Panainos read on.

' "He will ask to speak with his dead father. You will arrange for his father to tell him … " ' Panainos looked up, horrified. Themis heart was beating so hard he could hardly breathe.

'Go on,' growled the captain, unsurprised.

' " … You will arrange for his father to tell him that he must do as he has been chosen to do and uphold the honour of the family." ' Panainos turned to Themis, his face grey. 'This must be a joke,' he said.

'But what does it mean?' asked Themis. 'What have I been chosen to do?'

'This kind of message must be going backwards and forwards to the Oracle all the time,' said the captain. 'I've been asked many times to deliver boxes of tablets or other messages to the necromancers there.'

'Does it say anything else?' asked Themis.

Panainos read again: ' "… the honour of the family. For his father was also chosen, and yet, in his stupidity, failed to do his duty more than once.'

'What?' exclaimed Themis. 'Father failed? Failed to do what?'

'"Bring the tablet to me afterwards",' Panainos went on in a monotone. '"You will reap a silver reward of great value."'

'Is there a signature?' asked the captain.

'Nothing,' said Panainos, with a wondering shake of his head.

'Is this … does the person who wrote this want me to hate my father?' said Themis.

'I've never seen that seal before,' said the captain. 'But I've seen messages like that again and again. Do *you* know what it's about?'

The captain looked at Panainos, who looked back, his eyes wide open. After a moment he shook his head emphatically.

'No,' he said. 'I have no idea what it means. When did Kallistos fail in his duty, or in anything? I know of nothing. He was certainly not stupid, so I don't understand this at all.' He snapped the tablet shut and handed it to the captain. 'You had better deliver it to its rightful recipient when you get back to Tainaron. But it won't have any meaning by then, of course.'

'So what was going on?' Themis asked. 'Was Molon going to arrange for me to hear a voice at the Oracle that was *pretending* to be my father?'

'Many people believe that *all* the voices heard at the Oracle are false,' said the captain as he got up.

'That's what it looks like,' said Panainos. 'I suggest we wait till we get to Olympia and talk to Phidias about it. He knows a lot more about what goes on in temples and oracles than I do.'

'Does the other one have the same seal as this one?' asked the captain.

Panainos took the judge's tablet from the bag. 'Yes,' he said.

'Phidias might know who the leaf seal belongs to,' said Themis. But he was thinking that the judge certainly would.

'He might,' said Panainos.

Themis turned away and walked alone towards the bow. He felt sick and lost again, like the first days after he came round, when he didn't believe he was who everyone said he was.

He stood holding the rail and watched the dark sea, swell after swell rising and falling in front of the bow. It calmed his tangled thoughts as he adjusted his stance to the movement of the ship.

Suddenly, as he was taking a slow, deep breath, he saw his father laughing, his arms open towards Themis. He heard him say, 'You won, my son. You did it!'

Themis' eyes sprang open. He gripped the rail, tears welling up. 'That was real,' he said to himself. 'It *was* real,' he shouted to the sea. 'I saw him! I know what he looked like! I remembered him!' He turned and ran back over the canvas to the lower deck. 'Uncle! Uncle! I remembered my father!' He was panting, looking down on Panainos.

'Sit down, boy, and tell me,' said his uncle, looking concerned.

Themis sat. 'I saw my father in my mind. He was coming towards me with his arms open. He was laughing, and he said "You won, my son. You did it." When was that, Uncle?'

'I have no idea, Themis.' Panainos shook his head and shrugged his shoulders, his stomach lifting in unison. 'You've had a shock – we all have. Are you sure it was a memory and not just a … a … ?'

'I'm awake, aren't I?' demanded Themis. 'I was watching the sea and rocking with the ship, and suddenly I saw my father. I remembered him.'

Frog stood up. 'Let's see if you can do it again,' he said quietly.

Themis smiled and jumped up. 'Yes. I'll do it again.'

There was a look of regret and pity in Panainos' eyes as they turned to run forward to the bow.

Themis stood a long time watching the waves, feeling the movement of the ship, breathing. Frog waited in silence.

'It's not working, Frog,' Themis said at last.

'Never mind,' said Frog. 'Tell me what you saw in your … memory.'

'Father had a beard – very black – and a garland on his hair. He was running … no, he was hobbling towards me and his robe was slipping down from his shoulder. I think it was … dark green with a purple pattern. I could see his stomach muscles. There was a lot of dust … Why was he hobbling?'

Frog answered, 'He lost part of a leg in a battle.' Then he said 'I know when that was. Your uncle wasn't there, but I was.'

'Tell me!' Themis grabbed his shoulders. 'When did my father say that to me?'

Frog looked down. 'I can't tell you when, because I will bring the curse on myself.' He looked up into Themis' face. 'But I want you to know that it *was* a memory, not a dream.'

'So where was it then?'

'I can't tell you that either.'

Themis wanted to shake Frog, to force him to say more.

Instead, he drummed on the rail with both fists in his frustration.

Frog said, 'When you get home, I think you'll find that green robe in the chest in the salon.'

'What is all this about?' shouted Themis. 'Everyone is hiding something or lying to me, or to each other. Even the gods are made to lie through the Oracle. Why? Why?' He turned and ran back to the stern.

'I'm not lying!' called Frog.

Themis spun on his toes and ran forward again to the bow. He longed to be on dry land where he could run till he dropped. Beast followed him, barking with excitement.

The captain shouted from the top deck. 'Themis! Stop dashing about and climb the mast. Let me know what you can see ahead.'

Themis beat the rail again, took a couple of furious breaths, and then did as the captain asked, climbing fast without a second thought.

From the top he looked carefully all around. 'There's a long line of land just showing in the haze a bit to the right,' he called down. 'Is that where we're going?'

'Good,' called the captain. 'We're going to round the left hand end of it. It'll be just after midday when we do, if this wind holds.'

Themis stayed where he was. It wasn't frightening at all. It was exhilarating! He moved through the air with the gentle sway of the mast and felt his anger retreating. He tried to empty his mind hoping for other memories, but nothing came. The sea was dark blue, almost black, in all directions. Under the surface, Themis could see a group of dolphins keeping pace with the Pelican.

'Look out there, Frog,' he called. 'Dolphins.'

Calmer now, he climbed down slowly. The two boys stood by the rail watching the dolphins.

'You've been very quiet since Molon died,' Themis said to Frog. 'Are you all right?'

'It gives me nightmares,' said Frog sheepishly. 'His head rolling like that. Makes me glad I don't have your kind of dreams.'

'Oh, I've learned to ignore them. Bad at the time, but gone in the sunlight.' Themis grinned. 'And now I have a memory, a real memory. Perhaps there'll be more. Perhaps I'll remember what my father was talking about. It must be something to do with training or fighting or you wouldn't be afraid of the curse.'

Frog opened his eyes wide with horror. 'I didn't say anything about that! I just wanted you to know it was a real memory. The gods will understand that, won't they?'

'I'm not sure,' teased Themis.

The sail swung round and threw its shadow over the boys.

'You keep an eye on those dolphins, Frog,' said Themis. 'I want to ask my uncle something.'

>>>

From Bernie's private diary. Friday March 12th 2010

SUZANNE SPOKE TODAY! I mean really spoke. Can't believe it!!!

She's been so still and quiet, I almost didn't bother using my two free periods to visit her this morning. But I had promised I would go every day and I knew there wouldn't be time tonight (had a date at Laser Wars with the usual gang).

When I got there, there was no one by Suzanne's bed. I sat with my hand on her good arm, watching the pulse in her neck and thinking how long it was going to take to pay back all my loans.

And Suzanne suddenly opened her eyes and looked at me! She looked around for a few seconds in a kind of panic. I was so shocked I couldn't move. Then she said, 'Not pelican.' That threw me a bit, but I stayed calm and said 'No. We're in a hospital – in Penrith. No birds in here.'

She looked from side to side, a bit scared, and said, 'Frog?' I didn't know what to say to that, so I told her she'd hit her head in an accident and was in a hospital, not a zoo. I said she was very ill, but she was getting better now.

She tried to move her right arm and it obviously wouldn't, so I explained about the collarbone. She just looked at me, confused and wary. Then she noticed the drip and seemed to panic. 'Snake!' she whimpered. I laughed and she looked at me as if I was mad. 'It's your drip,' I said. 'It's keeping you alive.'

She lifted the back of her hand really near her eyes and looked at the cannula carefully. Then she stroked the sheet. She still looked amazed, but I could see she was beginning to drift away again. I said her name, but she didn't react and her eyes lost focus and closed.

I ran and got a nurse and told her what had happened. She was like, 'That's a good sign.' 'But she was talking rubbish,' I said. And she was like, 'I'm not an expert, but I would think that any words are better than none.'

But her mind is full of animals! Her dreams must be really weird. I called her mum and told her. At first she didn't believe me, and then she began to cry. I think she thinks Suzanne will be a vegetable until she dies.

I stayed for quite a while longer. Suzanne seemed to be on the edge of consciousness sometimes, but she didn't open her eyes again. Mrs J came about lunchtime but by then Suzanne was deeply asleep.

Can't wait to put this on the blog! I've already called Laila and Gina, and Miss Rallis.

<<<

Chapter 21: brother

Panainos was standing looking out from the stern. Themis went and stood beside him. His eyes were on a level with Panainos' nose. He took a deep breath.

'Uncle,' he said quietly. 'I am truly very confused. Please tell me what you think is happening to me.'

Panainos turned to look into Themis' face. 'I think you had a shock and that stimulated your mind to – '

'No. I mean in general,' said Themis. 'Why would someone want me to believe my father was a failure?'

'*Do* you believe that?' asked Panainos, one eyebrow raised.

'Well …' Themis hesitated. He sighed and went on. 'At first, it felt possible. It seems to me that all men are hiding something, lying about something. But then I *saw* my father. I *remembered* him. And that has confused me. What could that happy, powerful man have failed at?'

Panainos shook his head slowly. 'I really cannot imagine.' Then he chortled. 'But perhaps he made someone jealous and so the writer of that tablet has a jaundiced view.'

'And another thing,' said Themis, ignoring this, 'what is it I have been chosen to do?'

'Now that is quite beyond me,' said Panainos with an almost comical shrug.

'Oh, Uncle!' Themis was exasperated. 'You are such a bad liar, you know.'

Panainos looked astonished. 'But that's the truth! I don't lie!'

'Yes, you do. You and everyone else.'

'When have I ever lied to you?' Panainos was shaking his head in amazement.

'Well... For instance, when you told me that Xenovia is a virgin.'

'What? But she *is* a virgin. That's what she told me, and I believe her.'

Themis felt anger close to the surface. 'How can she be? She was flirting with my brother in a way no virgin would behave. I saw her.'

'Is that a suspicion of jealousy I hear in your voice, dear Themis?' Panainos teased. He went on more seriously. 'In my dealings with Xenovia, she has always behaved with complete decorum.'

Themis took a breath. 'And what are your dealings with her, uncle?'

'That, my boy, is none of your business.'

Themis persisted. 'I saw the way you changed when you saw her. If you don't have sex, what *do* you do together?'

'That's not something someone your age needs to know about, Themis,' said Panainos.

'Is it politics?' asked Themis. 'She's related to that supposedly corrupt politician who was exiled, isn't she?'

'It's not important, Themis,' said Panainos, beginning to frown for the first time.

But Themis was controlling anger himself. 'Please, Uncle. I am so tired of being told lies. What do you do with Xenovia?'

The captain's voice from above surprised them both. 'Is that the priestess with the herbs and the mushrooms?' He was leaning over the stern rail, peering down at them.

Panainos looked up and snapped, 'What do you know about that, Captain?'

'Enough to know that she has the best reputation in Athens for happy dreams and curing certain ... disorders.' The captain was laughing.

Panainos' face changed and he laughed with the captain. 'I don't know about that,' he said. 'But she *has* given me some powders in the past which gave me inspiration for my work.'

The captain leaned further over. 'Then you'd better be careful. Some of the women who sell those things are sorceresses. There can be effects you ... don't expect.'

Panainos was screwing up his eyes against the sunshine. Themis thought he saw him wink at the captain. He said 'There is no magic about Xenovia, except her beauty.'

'Maybe not,' replied the captain, 'and people say she knows what she's doing, but she's a powerful woman with potions as well as political connections.'

Themis rolled his eyes in disgust.

Panainos turned to him. 'In my experience,' he said seriously, 'Xenovia is a forthright and trustworthy person, Themis. Do not be disillusioned by what others say. *And* she approves of your coming with me to Olympia,' he added. 'You should be pleased and honoured.'

Themis felt suddenly tired. 'I can see, Uncle, that you will never answer me clearly,' he said. He turned away to join Frog at the bow.

They sailed fast with the wind behind them all day. As the sun was dipping westwards, they ran parallel to the cliffs of a tall narrow island lying across the mouth of a wide bay. They passed the channel from the open sea and Themis and Frog saw a town on the inner shore of the bay with a large harbour full of boats.

They ran up the ladder to the top deck to see better.

'That's Pylos,' said the captain. 'We won't be going in there. There's a better place further on.'

'Don't we need food?' asked Panainos from below.

The captain laughed. 'Ach, Master Painter. You mustn't fret. In the village we're going to, they know me. We'll have a meal fit for Herakles.'

Some time later, they turned into a bay on an island. A headland hid them from the mainland and the Pelican ran up onto a tiny white beach.

Beast was the first ashore as always. He knew the way and started off up the only path. They followed him into a world of sparse shrubs and rocks. The smells of thyme and oregano rose where their legs brushed against the bushes. There was no sign of human habitation, except that track.

It climbed gradually up the western side of the island's only mountain. At last, looking up, Themis saw low stone houses under an overhang. Two men were coming down the track towards them with Beast.

'Greetings, Captain Stomio,' the taller one called. 'It's good to see you back.'

'Nestoras!' called the captain. 'I've brought you some custom as well as your goods.' He indicated a bundle carried by the one sailor who had come ashore with them.

'You will eat well tonight,' laughed Nestoras. 'We have your favourite fish soup, but also a kid that fell and broke its legs today.'

'That sounds worth the climb,' panted Panainos.

They were taken to a shrine of Pan, spirit of wild places, built into a wall. His ancient wooden statue was wreathed in fresh cyclamen and daisies. A stream ran alongside Pan's wall, with a trough set in it. They washed there and then went inside a large square building. There was just the one room, with a huge fire on a round hearth in the middle. The smoke rose to the roof and filtered out through a series of slats.

'Welcome to our megaron,' said Nestoras. He showed them where they could sit on blankets round the hearth. Women began to bring in the food.

They ate from common platters that were passed round. The small pieces of meat that Themis took tasted of herbs, and were unbelievably tender.

'This is what the gods eat on Olympus,' whispered Frog. Nestoras must have heard, because he turned with a delighted smile to the boys, even though he was in a deep discussion about politics.

Themis listened carefully and heard of the long-standing unrest between the Spartans and the people of Pylos. The arguments and conflicts between the Spartans and the Athenians were also picked over. There were names that he recognised like Aspasia, Perikles, and the Athenian general Kallias. He heard others that were new to him, like Thukydides, who had been Perikles' rival as the head of the Athenian parliament, and Archidamus, who seemed to be a king of Sparta. Themis learned how Thukydides had been banished for ten years but was now preparing to come back. He realised this must be the politician related to Xenovia.

But the talk and the food and the warmth were making him sleepy. Frog was already curled up on the blanket beside him. Themis' head fell forward.

He woke in the dark. He could still hear men's voices, now talking of the old days, when war was war and men were men. But as he became more conscious of where he was, he realised that was a dream.

A dull glow from the embers showed him the other sleepers, wrapped in blankets, feet towards the hearth. There were two windows he had not noticed the evening before. Through them he could see stars and hear Beast outside, scratching at his fleas. Themis left his blanket and picked his way between the sleeping bodies until he found a door. He could hear the stream and, slipped quietly out. He'd been shown where to urinate further downstream. As he walked back towards the building to get a drink, Beast padded softly to join him.

After tasting the water and rubbing his wet hands through his short hair, he sat on a rock beside the quiet pool above the trough. 'How will I ever know whether what I dream is a dream, or something that actually happened?' he whispered to Beast. Beast, who was lying near his feet, made a noise in his throat. Themis heard footsteps and turned. He recognised Nestoras coming towards him in the starlight.

'It's all right, Beast,' he whispered.

'Themistokles? Is that you?' Nestoras whispered.

'I was thirsty,' Themis replied quietly. 'It's warmer in your region.'

'We are nearer the sun in the west,' said Nestoras with a glimmer of white teeth in the gloom. He dipped his hands in the pool and drank from them. 'Your uncle tells me Kallistos was your father.'

'That's right,' Themis heart missed a beat. 'Did you know him?'

'I didn't know he had died. That is very sad. You have my deepest sympathies. He was a good friend when we were young and wild together.'

'Tell me about him. Please,' Themis urged.

'Ah, well. You must know about your father competing in the eightieth Olympic Games?'

'A friend told me something, but I've lost my own memory,' Themis whispered, his heart thudding.

'Oh, of course. Panainos did mention … ' Nestoras sat comfortably on the rock beside Themis. 'Yes. Your dad and I were both competing back then, he in the pentathlon and I in the sprint.' He smiled again. 'I was stronger then, and very fit.'

'In the year of Kallias. Yes, my friend told me,' said Themis. 'Did either of you win?'

'Nah, … And history forgets the losers, so we never talked about it much. But we had an … interesting month at Olympia. We were both just eighteen and had begun enjoying women. That may be why we weren't as strong as our fellow competitors!' He chuckled as he gazed into the pool. 'Your father was very handsome and ended up with at least four girls begging to marry him. But in Athens it seems you don't marry until you've done some years in the army. He went off to be a soldier and I came back to the village to raise goats and harass the Spartans.'

Themis asked, 'Didn't you try again for the Olympics?'

'No point,' said Nestoras. 'When you see the calibre of the ones who are really good, you know you can't compete. And we were too young.

The best pentathletes are at least twenty-five and they train all day every day. And the sprinters are mostly small and light, not my build at all.'

'Nor mine,' said Themis, deep in thought.

'No. You're very like your father, though even sturdier, I'd say.'

'I really enjoy training, but after my accident everyone's being weird about it.' Themis looked up at Nestoras suddenly. 'Do you know anything about what I was doing before?'

'Mm, mm,' smiled Nestoras with a shake of his head. 'Your uncle warned me about the curse and that you might ask me something like that.'

Themis sighed and looked back at the stream. Nestoras went on, 'But in fact I have no idea about it. The last I heard was that Kallistos had three sons. I only just learned from your uncle that your brother had died.'

'No one will talk about him, either. What was his name?' asked Themis.

'I don't even know that,' said Nestoras. 'But you were obviously the strongest. Twins are often like that.'

'Twins!' Themis almost shouted. Then he whispered 'We were *twins?* My mother just said he came between me and Myrto. So he must have been older than me.'

'Hm. Perhaps by a few moments, no more,' Nestoras said.

Themis was quiet, trying to find some kind of memory of his dead brother, but nothing stirred behind the blank wall in his mind.

Nestoras stood up. 'Get some sleep while you can,' he said, tousling Themis' still-growing hair. 'It's a good half day's sail and then a long treck up the Alpheios valley for you tomorrow.'

Beast stood up with a low growl.

'So they say,' replied Themis, smoothing down his hair.

'Good night again, then,' said Nestoras quietly, as he walked away.

'Good night,' whispered Themis, his hand on Beast's warm neck. The dog laid his heavy head on Themis' lap, and snorted when tears fell on his nose.

Chapter 22: landfall

'So I had a twin brother,' said Themis to Panainos next morning as they settled onto the ship's deck. The Pelican had sailed out into the channel between the island and the mainland as they waved farewell to Nestoras on the beach. 'And my father *did* fail at something. Why do you keep these things from me, Uncle?'

Panainos was checking that the lockers had not been disturbed while he was off the ship. 'I'd forgotten all about them,' he said, straightening up with a groan. 'Losing your brother is something we don't talk about any more. There's no point. He's gone and remembering him is painful. As for your father's disappointment, it was long before I knew him. He married Eirini many years later.'

'What did he fail at?' asked Frog in surprise.

'Father competed in the pentathlon at the 80th Olympiad,' said Themis. 'Nestoras was there too, but *he* was beaten in the sprint.'

Themis saw a wary look between Frog and Panainos.

'If that's what the tablet refers to,' said Panainos, 'the man who wrote it must be old enough to remember twenty-eight years back. But it might be something else we know nothing about … something that happened when he was serving in the army, for instance.'

'I don't think "in his stupidity, failed to do his duty" can refer to the Olympics,' said Themis.

'No,' mused Panainos, 'nor do I.' He sat down with his back to the locker doors and sighed comfortably. 'Anyway, we need to think about your apprenticeship, Themis. We'll be arriving in Olympia today, or at the latest tomorrow morning. So let's make a start on how to prepare the design. We can do real lessons when we have chairs and a table on a floor that doesn't keep coming up to meet us.'

Themis spent the morning drawing long lines on the boards of the deck with chalk. He had to bend from the waist, hold the chalk to the wood and then move using his feet while he made life-sized drawings of people and animals. At first the deck moved so much and he was so clumsy that he and Frog couldn't stop laughing. But gradually he gained some control, and the figures improved as he drew, wiped them off, and drew again. He even managed to make them look like people they knew.

'Not sure I want a decorated deck,' growled the captain when he came down to see what the laughter was about.

'It washes off,' Panainos reassured him.

'A job for me,' said Frog, making a face that set them all laughing again.

'Ship astern and gaining!' came a shout from the bow.

The captain ran up the ladder. After taking a look, he leaned over the upper rail and said quietly to Panainos, 'It's mercenaries. They're probably working for the Spartans. Not a word about where we spent the night! We camped on a beach on the mainland, all right?'

'Of course,' said Panainos. 'Any danger for Athenian artists on their way to Olympia?'

'Of kidnap, you mean?' the captain asked. 'Not that I know of, though I could ask them to rid me of the nuisance of your company … ' he added with one eyebrow raised.

'Get me to the Alpheios and you'll get a bonus,' smiled Panainos.

The captain's head disappeared and they went on with their drawing lesson.

The ship was larger than the Pelican, using sail and oars. It came up on the lee-side, which showed they were not aggressive, Captain Stomio said.

'We're looking for a group of fugitives from Tainaron,' called the other captain. 'Heard you'd come there. Seen anything?'

'Some other boats going our way yesterday, but not near enough to count men,' called Captain Stomio.

'No sign of them on shore over night?' came the question.

'No. We stopped for the night on an empty beach. No one had been there for a while.'

'What are you carrying?'

'Mainly oil in jars. And three passengers from Athens for Olympia.'

'Keep an eye open. They could be desperate,' called the other captain and the ship veered off.

Themis heard the thump of the rowing master's mallet as the rowers started again. The ship pulled away fast, keeping close to the shore.

'Fugitives from what?' asked Themis.

'Probably Spartan slaves, helots,' the captain said. 'They have various kinds of slaves and some live almost free, like Nestoras and his village. But others are – '

'Nestoras is a slave?' asked Themis.

'Well, he and the village pay heavy tribute once a year,' said the captain. 'They also have to provide a certain number of boy-children for the Spartan army.'

'Not much different from Athens, then,' said Panainos with irony.

'A lot different,' insisted the captain. 'You don't want to be any kind of Spartan except the elite. And even they live a hard, uncomfortable life.'

Themis looked at Panainos and smiled at the thought of him living a hard, uncomfortable life.

The shore from now on became less and less rugged. They passed a town with an akropolis on a hill above a harbour. Then there were bays between low, rounded headlands, and ahead they could see a long sandy shore stretching to the north.

They packed up the chalks and ate the bread, cheese and olives that they had bought at Nestoras' village.

'This cheese is much harder than we get in Athens,' Themis observed with his mouth full. 'Is it like this in Olympia, Uncle?'

'By all accounts there are myriads of cheeses to choose from in Olympia and Elis,' said Panainos with longing.

'What's Olympia like?' Themis asked him. 'Have you been there? Is it a large town?'

'I haven't been there, but Phidias says it's a small town except when the Games are on. Then the plain up-river from the town fills with temporary dwellings and the rivers fill with rubbish. There's a place called Pisa nearby, but Elis is the nearest large town.'

'Will it have a gymnasium and a practice track?' asked Themis.

'I imagine so,' said Panainos. He added dryly, 'But that's not something I thought to ask.'

'Will we all stay with Phidias?' Themis went on, breaking more bread off the barley loaf.

'I have no idea,' said Panainos. 'But I'm sure he'll have found somewhere for us to rest our weary bones. The Elians are paying him enough to have built a house just for us!'

After the meal, the captain suggested that they prepare their luggage to disembark. 'We'll be at the river mouth mid afternoon,' he said. 'And make sure you scrub that deck clean!'

The land had lain down. Behind the great long beaches were dunes, and then wide flat areas, rippling with canes and marsh plants. Beyond them, low hills had fields and vineyards on their slopes. Further inland, olive groves rippled silver-green on the skirts of remote mountains.

Panainos dragged his boxes out and made a heap of them at the bottom of the deck ladder. Frog scrubbed the boards while Themis sketched a comic likeness of the captain on the door of one of the lockers.

'He'll make you clean that off, too,' murmured Frog.

'He won't see it until we've gone,' replied Themis. 'How else will he remember us?'

'By the huge sum of money I'm going to pay him,' whispered Panainos. He smiled. 'That's actually not bad, my boy. But you must get out of the habit of drawing recognizable portraits unless you are asked. In Athens we don't make likenesses of people until they are dead.'

'Why *is* that, Uncle?' asked Themis, carefully outlining the captain's gnarled hand.

'There are those who think part of the soul of a person is in the image, and that they can thus influence events in two places at once.'

'Well, this is where the captain lives, so he and his picture will be in the same place – most of the time, anyway,' whispered Themis, signing the drawing with a flourish.

Panainos shook his head and tutted, but with a smile.

'Get ready!' called Captain Stomio from above. 'See the spit of sand there? That's where the river Alpheios comes out. We'll go into its mouth a short way. The Spartans have occupied Pheia, the usual port, on that headland beyond. So we'll use the little local port in the river. It serves both Olympia and Elis at the moment, and some of my cargo is for Elis.'

The quay was on the right bank and two ships were already moored to it. Their painted bow-posts and furled red sails glowed in the westering sun. Bundles and boxes were being unloaded. Wagons drawn by teams of oxen waited by the waterfront. Beyond the quay were whitewashed warehouses, and behind them were two or three streets of neat homes, a group of public buildings, and a small temple. Further up the river, a short stone jetty was surrounded by brightly painted barges. Smells of woodsmoke, drying fish, and mud came to them across the water.

A group of stevedores lined up noisily on the quay, ready to unload the Pelican. She approached with her sail furled and her oars out.

The nearest building to the landward end of the quay was a busy tavern. Two or three of the men sitting outside stood up and sauntered towards the mooring bollards. One was dressed in a short, ivory-coloured tunic with sumptuous patterned borders. He waved a wide-brimmed hat.

A sailor slid out the landing ladder as they bumped gently against the wooden piles of the quay. Beast sat to attention. As Panainos and the boys disembarked, the man with the hat stepped forward.

'Agorakritos!' exclaimed Panainos. 'Did my brother send you?'

Agorakritos was slim with gleaming dark curly hair, longer than usual for a man. He was clean-shaven, his face almost as beautiful as Xenovia's, though with stronger lines. 'Panainos! At last you are here.' His voice was deep and musical, a contrast to his boyish grin. Themis was dazzled, and longed to draw him.

The sailors were piling Panainos' boxes onto the quay. They added two of the pigeons in their cages to the top of the heap.

Agorakritos held up his hand to help Panainos down the last two rungs. 'We've been expecting you for two days,' he said. 'We have horses and pack animals here at the inn.'

Panainos clapped him on the shoulder and turned to speak to Captain Stomio, who had arrived on the quay with Beast. 'Thank you, Captain, for our safe, though eventful, passage.' He handed over a small sack of coins. 'Would you like me to take that tablet for the judge and deliver it, or do you have your own means?'

'You have all been surprisingly little trouble,' growled the captain, handing the tablet to Panainos. 'If you need to send anything to Athens, I'll be passing through here on my way back in ten days or so.'

Themis was stroking Beast's forehead. 'See you again, Beast,' he said.

Agorakritos called out, 'Bring up the donkeys!' Two slaves appeared, leading two donkeys between the wagons. The slaves loaded them with the boxes and bags.

Themis ran a hand over the boards of the Pelican's side and waved goodbye to the sailors. Music and chatter from the tavern added to the noisy calls of the stevedores and faded as they moved away from the ship. Beast followed them as Agorakritos led them to three tethered horses in the comparative quiet of the street behind the waterfront.

'It's at least an afternoon's ride,' he said, indicating a mounting block to Panainos, who was looking askance at the large grey horse allotted to him. Agorakritos turned to Themis. 'Can you manage the black?'

'May I double up with Frog?' asked Themis.

Agorakritos looked surprised, but said, 'Of course'.

The little cavalcade set off with Agorakritos and Panainos in front, the boys on the black behind and then the two slaves walking with the pack donkeys. Beast followed for a short distance. Themis leaned down.

'Go back, Beast,' he said, turning in the saddle for a last look at the Pelican, which was still unloading at the quay.

'Go on, Beast. Go back to the captain!' he said sharply to the dog. Beast put his head on one side for a moment, gave a quiet deep bark, and loped back towards the quay.

Themis could see two other boats approaching the harbour, one from the right and one from the way they'd come. As Beast joined him, Captain Stomio raised a hand to Themis, and he waved back.

Chapter 23: road

'Not far now,' called Panainos to the boys. 'And Zeus waiting to greet you personally in the temple!' He gestured with his arm along their road.

During the voyage, Themis had felt his reckoning with Zeus was so far in the future he could ignore it. Now Panainos' words brought back that stone of dread in his stomach. He took a deep breath. Frog's arms round his chest tightened briefly.

The sun was half way down the sky. At first there were quite a few small farms and other buildings beside the wide road. They had to overtake huge wagons of pots and jars, sacks and bales drawn by long teams of oxen. Dust rose from the animals' hooves and drifted in the gentle breeze from the sea.

At first, they travelled along the top of a raised bank between the slow, silent river and a wide, still lagoon. The reeds and canes were full of fluttering, twittering birds. Turning to look at them, Themis saw a lone man on a pale mule keeping pace about a hundred feet behind their pack-donkeys. He kept checking, and the man overtook wagons, slowed down and speeded up just as they did, but always at the same distance behind. Perhaps he was just a timid traveller keeping them in sight as insurance against theft. But the straight back and broad shoulders seemed to Themis to make that unlikely.

Themis kept his thoughts to himself. Perhaps what the man was doing was normal practice. Agorakritos was singing heartily as they rode, songs from the army and the symposium.

'Shall we try a hunting song,' suggested Panainos during a pause. 'Themis might know the words, and they might be more ...

appropriate.'

Themis and Frog nudged each other, and joined in the latest popular song about a wily boar that evaded capture in various cunning ways.

After a while, they left the lagoon behind. The track, diverging from the river, turned from sandy to rocky. Low hills rose around them, and fields and orchards alternated with olive groves. Under the trees, carpets of red and white flowers stretched into the distance. Some of the trees were in blossom, a rain of petals and a thrumming of bees filling the air beneath them. The man on the mule was still there, the same distance behind.

Prosperous-looking villages in sheltered hollows appeared at the feet of the hills. The travellers fell silent, so as not to attract guard dogs.

Themis tried to imagine Olympia to stop himself thinking about Zeus, or the man behind. He thought of it as a kind of larger Akropolis, all temples and rock walls. Frog was chanting songs about Olympic winners quietly in his ear. Although the winners all came from important cities and were descended from gods, Frog knew such intimate details of their habits and weaknesses that Themis was sure these were not the official victory odes.

Later still, the road rejoined the river. Along its banks there were plane trees and rich fields of barley, rippling in the slanting sun like green hair. The man on the mule was still there, but Frog was quiet at last. Lulled by the rhythm of the horse's hooves, and with Frog's head heavy on his shoulder, Themis dozed too.

They jerked awake when the two animals ahead began to canter and their own black set off to catch them up. It was nearly dark now, and Frog had to cling tightly to Themis. Looking back, Themis saw the donkeys were out of sight, and so was the man on the mule.

Themis urged the black on, to join the men ahead.

When they were in earshot, Agorakritos turned and called over his shoulder. 'We need to get to a good camping place before it's too dark to see. It's not far now.'

The site he stopped at was an open knoll by the river.

'We're near the ford just down-river from Olympia,' he said as they dismounted. 'I was hoping to make it to the inn on the other side, but it's too dark to cross now.'

The donkeys and slaves arrived soon after, quietly trudging along by the light of a torch held by one of them. There was no sign of the man on the mule. Themis wondered if he had passed them in the dark. Or was he waiting further behind for an opportunity to rob them?

After their meal, they sat round the fire and looked across at the tiny lights of other camps on the opposite bank. One by one, these began to go out.

'We'll take turns to watch,' said Agorakritos. 'I'll wake you when I can't stay awake any longer,' he said to Panainos.

'Meanwhile, tell us one of your stories,' Panainos urged. 'At least until the moon rises.'

Agorakritos wrapped his cloak around himself against the growing chill. 'Now, let me think … ' he said. 'Oh, yes. I know.'

They settled themselves to listen. The voice Agorakritos used for story telling was even deeper and more melodic than his usual one.

'There was once an Old Lion who died,' he began. 'His Lioness roared her anger and pain across the valleys. Her children were young and she must now protect them and their territory alone.

'A Neighbouring Lion heard her voice. He had long been jealous of the Old Lion's rich lands. A river ran through them and herds of plump gazelles drank at it every day. Neighbouring Lion's own lands were on higher ground, clothed in dry brittle grasses. The gazelles were infrequent visitors.'

'This reminds me of someone we all know,' murmured Panainos. 'Are you referring to Nikanor?'

'Who is Nikanor?' asked Agorakritos.

'Oh, just a jealous, bankrupt relative of Themis,' said Panainos. 'Hardly a lion, I must say,' he added with a smile at his nephew. 'Go on, Agorakritos.'

Agorakritos went on in his sing-song voice. 'Neighbouring Lion wanted to add that river to his lands. So he had his youngest wife groom him till he shone. He preened and strutted, raised his tail in the air, and went on a visit to the Lioness.

'"Now you are alone, oh beautiful tawny temptress," he wheedled, "will you accept help from your neighbour to patrol your boundaries and protect your person?"

'"Not from you!" growled the Lioness in her pain. "Not from you or any of your kind. My sons are growing and will patrol the boundaries themselves. Leave our lands now, before I chase you off." And she roared at him, showing her impressive teeth.

'Neighbouring Lion was terrified, and left with his tail dragging on the ground.

'But he could not forget those plump gazelles, that lush valley. He knew the Lioness took her sons with her, one at a time, to patrol her boundaries each day. She left the other cubs in a cave in the cliff above the river. The Neighbouring Lion watched her as she passed on her patrol.

'Then he approached the cave from above. When the cubs came out to play in the sun, he hid behind a rock. When one of the cubs came near him, he dashed out and grabbed it by the throat. He finished it off before it could even squeak. Then he dropped it among the other cubs, and declared, with his tail in the air, "This is a warning to your mother. She should accept my offer." And he left.

'The cubs milled round their dead brother, mewing and crying. When the Lioness returned and learned who had killed her cub, she decided to visit her Neighbour.

'"I see now that you are strong and courageous," she whined. "Please protect me from the evils of other male Lions. Bring your other wives to hunt by my river if you wish, but come and live with me yourself in my cave."

'So the Neighbouring Lion brought his wives and set them to hunt down by the river while he climbed up to the cave. The Lioness invited him to lie near its mouth, and she brought him a titbit from her morning kill. As he ate, she crept up the cliff behind him and pushed a great boulder that teetered there. It rolled down the cliff and fell right onto the Neighbouring Lion, squashing him flat.

'The Lioness called to his wives. "Look at your magnificent husband in his grave. See him and be afraid."

'The Lioness had no trouble from her neighbours after that.'

They all clapped. Agorakritos stood and took a mock bow.

'I've always believed the female is more dangerous than the male,' said Panainos. 'Let us sleep now.'

And Themis did sleep, immediately and deeply. He did not dream of the man on the mule, or Zeus. He did not see the moon rise, not hear the change of guard.

A heavy dew had bloomed on their clothes and luggage by dawn. That, and the hundreds of birds singing to greet the sun, woke Themis.

He rolled over and stood up. Frog was nowhere to be seen. The animals and the slaves stood calmly waiting round a large tree by the river. So there had been no emergencies in the night.

Themis walked towards the water, shining ribbons between sandbanks.

The valley was still wide and flat with stands of large trees near its edges. On the opposite bank, looking into the sun, Themis could make out a jetty and the inn. People were already fording the river in both directions. Mist was rising from the river and the flood plain, draping itself over the steep slopes of the wooded hills. There was no wind, and the birds kept up their musical frenzy.

'Welcome to the Olympian Plain,' came Agorakritos' voice behind him. Themis turned and looked up at him.

'It's breathtaking,' he said. 'So lush, so many different types of tree.'

'The Alpheios is a strange river. He likes to wander across the plain, changing his course each time it rains. But he fills the soil below, so the trees grow tall. You can sink a well anywhere and find sweet water.'

Themis said, 'Useful if the Games are on, with all those people here.'

Agorakritos squatted down and gazed out across the rags and streamers of water and sand. 'Perhaps you can write for permission from your mother to stay until the Games,' he said kindly.

'Can you see Olympia from here?' asked Themis.

Agorakritos pointed. 'See that hill with the top like a pyramid covered in forest?'

'Yes?'

'At its foot is the Altis, the sanctuary with the temples and altars and statues. You can't see them against the sun and with this mist. Beyond it are the stadium and the hippodrome, on the flats between the bottom of the hills and the river. The village is further back, where there's no danger of winter flooding.'

Themis thought he saw a flash of gold where Agorakritos had pointed. Was it the rising sun reflecting on something, or Zeus polishing his thunderbolt ready for Themis? Themis swallowed and then asked, 'How … how long till we get there?'

Agorakritos stood up, smiled his charming smile at Themis, and raised his voice. 'Far too long, if we can't get the others up and be on our way.'

Frog came bounding back from further down the river. He was carrying a brace of fat ducks. 'Breakfast anyone?' he asked.

'No time to cook them now,' said Panainos grumpily. 'We've been ordered to saddle up and set off.'

Themis was watching Agorakritos, who laughed, slapped Panainos on the shoulder, and went to help strap the boxes onto the donkeys.

>>>

Chapter 24: Olympia

From Bernie's private diary. Monday March 15th 2010

Suzanne's gone back to being a vegetable after all. She has to be turned over by the nurses so that she doesn't get bed-sores. There's no reaction to anything. Makes me want to scream.

I was there again yesterday and her dad turned up. We had a chat about why she'd stopped training for the pole vault. He used to meet her at Sheepmount Stadium every Sunday morning. I told him about Ian dumping Suzanne by text. He looked about ready for murder. So I said she'd been talking about starting training again.

That made us both cry.

<<<

Themis sat eating barley porridge with honey and cream. The ducks were roasting at the back of the inn. From here they could see Olympia. 'That must be on the temple roof,' he said, pointing to the tiny gilded figure of a woman. 'I think I saw it from where we camped. The building in front of it looks like one big, long house,' he went on with his mouth full. 'People must be rich to have such big houses.'

'It's a place for visitors to stay,' said Agorakritos. 'A hotel. But it's old. The top floor needs a lot of work and the roof could do with patching. Phidias has tidied up the end nearest to where he works, and most of us live there or in the rooms by his Workshop. He's prepared an apartment specially for you, Master Painter.'

'I knew he'd have made arrangements for us,' said Panainos.

'So you work with Phidias?' said Themis.

'Yes,' answered Agorakritos. 'I'm a sculptor and a painter, too.'

'Are you working on the statue of Zeus?'

'It's almost finished. I've done what I can, so now I'm finishing off a pair of lions for Judge Iasos in Elis.'

'Do you see the judge often?' asked Panainos, with a dried plum in his hand.

'Every day when I'm in Elis,' said Agorakritos with a nod. 'Why? Is he a friend of yours?'

'Don't know him,' said Panainos. 'But we have a message tablet for him from Athens. Could you take it to him when you next go there?'

'Of course,' said Agorakritos.

The hotel was truly ramshackle and old fashioned. It was made up of two parallel buildings with wooden colonnades facing each other across a long, narrow yard. In this yard there were two wells and a series of benches and paths. Open stairways led to the upper floors, where the balcony railings were draped with vines, frilled with bright new leaves.

The eastern building was beside the main road. Its outer side had views of the massive stone Council House in a grove of trees opposite, and into the Altis precinct to the left. The roofs of two temples, the tops of trees and a few tall statues were visible above the precinct wall. The forested pyramid of the Hill of Chronos rose beyond.

But Panainos seemed glad to find that their apartment was on the ground floor of the western building, looking inwards.

'Away from the tourists and the wailing pilgrims,' he said approvingly to Agorakritos as they walked in under the colonnade.

'True,' replied Agorakritos, 'but there's a market in the streets to the west on most days, so you'll get the noise from there.'

'That's forgivable. Associated with food,' said Panainos.

'Among other things,' said Agorakritos as he threw open the double doors of the apartment. 'I hope you and Themis will be comfortable here. Your slave Niris has been preparing for your arrival.'

They were in a wide room with couches along the walls and two delapidated doors opposite. Wooden chests stood against the wall between them and they each led into a bedroom with a high window in the back wall.

'So it was quite luxurious once,' Panainos commented, indicating the pierced, white marble screens in all the windows. The walls had been newly painted dark ochre throughout, but the floor was pale, with vague shadows of a design still discernible in the chipped mosaic.

'Yes, once,' agreed Agorakritos.

Themis was torn. Part of him wanted to prolong these polite procedures of arrival to stave off the future. But another part wanted to dash off to Zeus' temple and confront the statue to see what would happen. He couldn't stop fidgeting.

Niris came running in to welcome them. He was small, dark brown and wiry, with a long, sad face and water dripping from his hands. Themis was taller than he was, which was satisfying.

'Niris!' boomed Panainos. 'Do we have water to wash ourselves? It's been a long journey.'

'Let me show you, master,' said Niris, bowing his head. 'Come out to the well and I will show you, master.'

Between the two buildings, the yard was in shade. The wells each fed a channel that ran into the middle of one of the buildings. There were banks of sinks and cooking benches with fires, and in a separate space, rows of latrines. The slaves of other guests were scurrying to and fro doing their chores. In one sink there was a mound of long narrow leaves that Niris was in the process of washing as part of their meal.

Panainos and Themis immediately threw off their garments. Clouds of dust rose from them as they tossed them to Niris and Frog. The slaves poured water into ground-level sinks, and there was a lot of splashing and laughter.

Agorakritos called over the clamour, 'You can bathe at the gymnasium later, you know. Come to the Workshop as soon as you've changed,' and he left.

Clean and in fresh clothes, Panainos and Themis walked the short distance to the sculptors' workshop.

The main road was busy with traffic for the market in the town and the precinct opposite. Panainos and Themis paused on the forecourt, looking at the front of the Workshop. It was a huge, rectangular stone building with a high-walled yard behind.

'He really did it,' said Panainos quietly.

'Did what?' asked Themis, surprised at the plainness of what seemed to him to be just another warehouse.

'He said to me he'd build the workshop the same size as the inner room of the temple, the cella, so that he could get the statue in the right proportion.'

'Why wouldn't he?' replied Themis. 'It's a very good idea.'

'Because it must have cost the Elians a lot more than they bargained for,' laughed Panainos. 'Phidias never lets mere price stop him when he plans a monument.'

No one seemed to be around, but the small, heavy door opened as they approached it. A guard in full armour with sword and spear stepped out and confronted them. With him was a scribe, tablet and stylus at the ready.

'Name and business?' growled the guard.

'Panainos, son of Harmides, brother of Phidias,' intoned Panainos, 'and Themistokles, son of Kallistos, my apprentice.'

The scribe wrote this down. The guard bowed his head slightly and stood back. 'Welcome, sir,' he said. 'Later you must furnish yourselves with a pass so that you are free to move around the site.'

'Thank you, officer,' said Panainos and they went in through the low doorway to a long, dark, narrow room that ran across the whole width of the building.

'Just a moment, my boy,' said Panainos. He turned right towards a niche in the wall. A lamp in a bracket lit a small bronze statue of Hephaistos, with his shrivelled leg and his hammer and anvil. Panainos dropped two small coins in the slot in the anvil, and rejoined Themis.

'I've never seen you give offerings before, Uncle,' whispered Themis as they walked to the other end of the room.

'I always bet each way when it comes to the smith of the gods,' murmured Panainos. 'Now let's see,' he added, as they turned through an open doorway.

'Wow!' breathed Themis when they stepped into the huge, bright space of the Workshop. Dust motes hung sparkling in the air and soft music played. It was as high as a temple, with pillars painted on the walls. Cupboards and storerooms lined the left side, workbenches the right. Light streamed in from windows half way up the walls, and from panels in the ceiling.

Panainos swept over to a long bench where four young men were bent over their work. Themis saw trays of labelled pebbles, rows of minute tools and the sparkle of cut gems as Panainos asked for Phidias.

One gem-cutter gestured to the high back wall that was almost all door. They could see a sunny yard beyond. 'Out there,' he said.

They passed a large round marble table with a pile of papyrus scrolls spilling onto stools beside it. Near the huge door, a man was working on the back of a statue of a woman. He was gilding her hair with intense care, working the fine layer of gold into the wooden plaits and curls, using cloth pads and his own fingers. Two students and an armed guard watched him closely. He looked up as they passed.

'Greetings, Master Panainos,' he said with a grin. 'You got here at last.'

Panainos just gave him a nod. Two more armed guards stood on either side of the doorway. They saluted Panainos as he and Themis stepped out into sunlight. Acrid smells of vinegar and burning bone caught in Themis' throat.

They looked around for Phidias. Panainos walked over to a strange framework in the shade of the one large tree. The framework supported an irregular wooden disc in the final stages of being carved into a face lying at an angle across it. This face was bigger than the table inside. A skin of ivory sheets was being moulded to its forehead.

The smell of vinegar was stronger here, and the sounds of hammering and polishing deafening.

Panainos looked straight up the carved nose, and then tapped the shoulder of one of the four masked men working on it.

'Phidias?' shouted Panainos.

'Mph!' said the man as he gestured along a row of water-troughs that ran into each other. Beyond them, three great cauldrons steamed and a huge oven, almost as tall as the workshop, cast a deep shadow.

And in the shadow they recognised Phidias, gesturing broadly to a grizzled man in a leather apron.

At that moment he looked up and saw them. He strode towards them, his bald head shining in the sun. 'Aha!' he called as he approached. 'You're here at last, brother! Come and see something miraculous that's just arrived!' He waved a hand at the nearest corner of the yard.

There was a bench there, against the wall of the workshop. A large wooden box sat on it, with broken lead seals all round the lid. A guard stood beside it, one of many in the yard.

Phidias lifted the lid of the box and plunged a hand deep into the woodshavings. He pulled out a small parcel wrapped in linen and sealed with wax. Quiet descended. Everyone stopped work to watch as Phidias cracked the seal and unwrapped the layers of fabric.

A single, rather flat stone appeared, the size of a large man's palm. But it was not like any stone Themis had ever seen. It was the colour of dark honey, a rich glowing brown. The surface was smooth and the shape perfectly round. Phidias held it up to the sun and the light fell through it, making a pool of gold on Phidias' pale robe. Within it shone fine golden veins, and one or two tiny specks of black.

'See how clear it is,' breathed Phidias. 'I insisted there should be no flaws. Some amber has whole insects in it, but they promised they could bring together pieces with none. This is almost perfect.'

He passed it to Panainos and pulled another parcel from the box. It contained an almost identical piece of amber. The light played through it as if it were alive. There were two more of these precious discs. Phidias held one out to Themis to touch.

'Take it. Feel it,' he said.

Themis held it in his hands, turning it over, watching the light play in it. He leant it against his cheek. It was as warm as his own flesh and weighed almost nothing.

Phidias chose the two most perfect of the discs.

A cheer arose from the workers and the music began again even more jauntily. Phidias turned to Panainos and Themis and sighed with relief.

'Well, thank the gods for that!' he said. 'Now we have these, we will finish on time.' He did some neat dance steps to the music as he led them to a place in the shade where there were stools and a table.

'Please, sit,' he said. 'I'm just going to give thanks.' And he bounced into the workshop, his robe swirling.

Water and sweet cakes were brought to the table and Agorakritos appeared and sat with them. Panainos was shaking his head in wonder. 'This is even more organised than the building of the Athena in the Hundred Foot Temple on the Akropolis in Athens,' he said.

'We learned a lot from that,' said Agorakritos with a wry smile. 'Phidias gets more like an army general every project he takes on.'

'What will he do with the amber pieces?' Themis asked.

'They will be the irises of the eyes of this Zeus,' said Agorakritos. 'Phidias is making the eyes himself.' He nodded towards the fires and troughs. 'The whites are from a particularly white ivory tusk that he's been saving. The irises will be the amber you saw, and the pupils will be obsidion, polished smooth. The first lot of amber they sent wasn't good enough.'

'Where does it come from?' asked Themis.

'The shores of a cold and stormy sea far to the north,' answered Panainos. 'It's common there and they have a secret way of amalgamating small pieces into these large discs. It contains magic that keeps it warm even in the coldest climates.'

'What's it made of?' asked Themis. 'Is it … baked honey or … ?'

Agorakritos laughed. 'I'm not sure how it's made, but definitely not by humans,' he said. 'By the way – '

But Phidias interrupted as he returned to them.

'Amber!' he called. 'Amber is magical. It is the resin from a kind of tree that we don't have here. They say it dripped into the sea thousands of years ago and solidified. Now, Panainos, come and see what we've prepared for you.'

Themis followed his two uncles into the Workshop. This was important, to do with his own work, but he found it hard to concentrate. Phidias led them to a side wall where four large frameworks were leaning. 'These are the foundations of your screens,' he said.

Panainos lifted one away from the wall and pushed hard to see if it would wobble. 'Good and firm,' he said. 'Wouldn't expect anything else, of course.'

'We'll go over to the Temple and see where they'll fit,' said Phidias. Themis heart jumped in his chest.

'I want to see the panels first,' said Panainos.

Phidias gestured to a cupboard beside the frameworks and a slave pulled the doors open. Inside were deep shelves with layers of thin wood panels. Panainos pulled one out gently and ran a hand over the surface.

Phidias said, 'They'll need priming, of course, but you'll paint your chosen labours of Herakles and shame of Ajax and so on, on these. Then we'll attach them to the frameworks and fit them in place under the throne. Come and see!' He whirled round and led them through the workshop and back into the street.

Fear made its familiar fist in Themis' stomach.

Chapter 25: temple

Phidias crossed the main road and strode towards a wooden gate let into the wall of the Altis. He pushed it open and walked swiftly through. But before Themis and Panainos could follow him, they were halted by a tall, armed guard who stepped into their path. Phidias turned back.

'They're with me,' he said pleasantly. 'We'll get their passes now from the sanctuary offices. They'll be working with me on the statue.'

The guard looked down at Panainos and Themis with care. He said 'I'll know you both now. Show me your passes when you leave.'

And so they were in the Altis at Olympia, the most sacred of all Zeus' precincts. In spite of the dread in his stomach, Themis found himself gazing around with wonder at a peaceful glade of tall trees growing among majestic stone buildings and monuments. Lining the avenues and among the trees, were statues on stone plinths, some single, some in groups, some dull with age, some gleaming with their new colours. Living people walked by purposefully, or strolled by in wonder.

To his left was the western end of the Temple of Zeus with the ancient olive tree nearby. Victors in the Games were crowned with wreaths made from its branches.

On the roof, at the very tip of the triangular pediment, was the golden goddess of Victory he had seen earlier. Her wings were spread wide and she had been sculpted to look as though she was just landing on one foot, her gleaming garments billowing behind her.

And in the pediment below her, there was a group of figures painted in glowing colours. Some of them were centaurs and some were men and women and they were fighting. But the central figure was calm and still, with his arm stretched out over the maelstrom of battle. He wore a golden garland and sandals, and a rich yellow cloak over his naked shoulder.

Themis thought, '*That must be Apollo.*'

Gooseflesh ran over Themis' skin. He understood now why people felt the presence of the gods here. As he stared, he felt a touch on his arm that made him jump.

'The Victories were only installed a month ago,' said Phidias, looking up with an edge of bitterness in his voice. 'They gave the commission to a sculptor who is hardly older than you.'

'Oh come on, Phidias,' chided his brother. 'You can't do everything. Or be twenty-five again.'

Phidias grunted. 'Huh! Come on, we go this way,' he said and he led them to a water spout in the corner to their right. They washed their hands, faces and feet in the basins there. There was a tray laid out with headband ribbons of many colours.

'My statue-craftsmen wear the red ones,' said Phidias, 'so you'd better wear the same.'

They chose their red fillets and left small coins to pay for them.

As they tied them over their hair, Phidias recovered his good humour. 'Luckily no one expects me to wear one of those,' he said with a smile. 'It would be forever slipping off.' He gestured back the way they'd come. 'This gateway will have to be closed up soon. We made it to help us get backwards and forwards to the workshop. The main gate is over there, ahead and to the right. We have to go that way now.'

They followed the avenue beside the high wall. There were blossoming trees along it, shading statues that seemed to watch Themis as he walked by. '*Are they all victors at the Games?*' he wondered.

Panainos took the opportunity of the comparative peace to ask, 'Brother dear, do you know of the practice of priming the Oracle of Tainaron to say what you want it to say?'

'Sadly, it happens in a lot of places,' said Phidias, 'though I'm pretty sure that Delphi is a true oracle. Why?'

'We had a temple messenger with us on the ship. He was killed during a storm and we found two tablets in his bag. One was without direction, so we opened it, and it contained instructions for what the Oracle was to say to Themis.'

Phidias stopped dead. 'To Themis! And what was that?' he asked, looking at Themis with sudden concern.

Themis waited a moment for Panainos to answer. But when he didn't, Themis said, 'It just said that my "father's voice" should tell me to do as I have been chosen to do. Oh, and it called my father stupid.'

'Hmph,' snorted Phidias, relaxing and walking on a little faster.

'Do you know what it meant?' asked Themis, running to catch up.

'Well, you've been chosen to work with us on the Zeus, and you've even seen him in your dreams, so I imagine that's what it means.'

'But it mentioned that Father had been chosen too and had failed.'

'Well, he *was* guarding a sanctuary on the Megaran border when he was killed,' said Phidias. They turned left and strode into a short avenue with statues between magnificent plane trees. 'Perhaps it referred to that.'

Ahead there was a row of what looked like small temples along the bottom of the steep Hill of Chronos. Gold and copper flashed in the sunlight from the armour and other decorations hung on their walls.

Panainos said to Phidias, 'The tablets were sealed with a stylized leaf. Does that mean anything to you?'

Phidias shook his head. 'Who was the other tablet for?' he asked.

'Judge Iasos in Elis,' said Panainos.

Phidias stopped for a moment and laid a hand on Panainos' arm. 'Judge Iasos?' he asked.

'Yes,' replied Panainos with a steady look at his brother.

'It should be delivered then,' said Phidias. They turned left again and suddenly Phidias was striding up the ramp towards the tall, heavy doors into the Temple of Zeus.

But Themis hesitated and looked around him.

Six mighty columns stood across the front of the temple. Up in the pediment above them was a scene of brightly painted men and women, horses and chariots. At the apex was the twin of the flying golden goddess. This one was standing above a round, golden shield.

'Are they preparing for a race?' asked Themis, as he brought his gaze back to earth. No one answered him. Phidias and Panainos were already inside the Temple. Themis walked reluctantly up the ramp, and hesitated again before going in.

Above the doors was a series of carved and painted panels. One showed a man lifting an enormous boar above another man in a huge pot. The next showed one man offering what looked like apples to another who was carrying a heavy burden on his shoulders, helped by a goddess.

Themis thought, '*So these are the labours of Herakles. Seeing them carved in stone makes them much more real – not just entertaining stories. Is that why I'm afraid of Zeus? I've seen so many statues of him, that I have to believe in him?*' He turned and looked back out at the Altis. '*Panainos said he didn't believe in the gods, but then today he made an offering. And Zeus was alive in my dream. So maybe he really does exist somewhere but we can only see him when he wants us to.*'

And if he did exist, was he watching what was going on in his honour in the temple? And was he waiting for his dues from the boy who was 'not ready yet'?

A great din was coming from inside the huge open doors. Themis could hear hammering and scraping and voices raised in song and frustration. Tentacles of dust drifted out towards him.

'*Asterodia said I need to name my fears. What I am afraid of is … being torn to pieces by a statue.*' He smiled wryly to himself. 'Seems unlikely, after all … ' he said aloud. He took a deep breath and walked into the temple.

He stopped just inside and waited for his eyes to adjust to the gloom. Then he laughed out loud with relief.

In the middle of the floor, instead of mighty Zeus (without his face as yet) there was what looked like a dusty hill covered in fabric that reached almost to the ceiling. Corners of wooden frameworks poked out of it here and there, and rickety-looking scaffolding towers stood beside it.

Looking up at the roof, Themis saw that the dull white light was coming through its translucent marble. Great wooden beams made dark lines across it, while the shadow of a tree outside made moving patterns in one corner.

There were two tiers of columns inside, like the painted ones in the workshop.

The cloths that made up the 'hill' were thick with dust. Men were working at various levels in twos and threes. Some of them were hammering, others were rubbing at what lay under the cloths. Clouds of pale dust rose, then settled on hair, on garments, on everything. Like the workers in the workshop, the men all wore masks and so seemed to have no faces.

Themis walked forwards, and almost fell. There was a step down in the floor in front of him. He followed Phidias and Panainos, who were being given masks. The dust tasted bitter, so he accepted one gratefully.

Phidias' voice was muffled when he said, 'Follow me. We'll lift the covers to show you your patch.'

The 'hill' was raised on a rectangular base, but its own bottom seemed square, the front bulging out towards them. They went round to the back of the base, climbed up some wooden steps there and walked to where a workman was lifting the corner of the coverings of the statue itself. They stepped through the opening.

Inside, by the light of a dozen or so lamps, they could see a complex framework of wooden beams and ladders reaching up high above them. There was a huge timber, like a ship's mast but square, in the middle towards the back. This was set into the stone of the floor. Four square black columns stood at the outside corners. These were the legs of the throne, it seemed, and were reinforced by four round wooden columns a couple of feet inwards from each corner.

More than twice the height of a man above their heads there was a huge grid of strong crossing beams, close together. Above that, the framework could be seen continuing upwards, always attached to that great mast. Shafts of dull light showed between the covers high up, and the sounds of the men working were muted.

'That network of beams above us is the seat of the throne,' said Phidias. 'Your screens will be suspended from each of its four sides, inside the legs of the throne, but hiding the weight-bearing columns and all the rest of the support structure.' He placed a hand on the nearest round column.

Panainos walked over to a front leg of the throne. It was of plain cedar wood. They could not see the decorations on the outer sides because of the cloth covering, but there was a suggestion of gold and carved ebony. Between each of the four legs there was a deep crossbeam at about their eye level.

'So the screens also go behind these?' said Panainos.

'Yes,' replied Phidias. 'You'll see the model. These are decorated with figures on the outside. Your screens can be attached to the insides. So your paintings will only be above and below the crossbeams.'

'Hmmm.' Panainos turned to Themis. 'Your first task, Themis. To measure the exact sizes of the areas we are to paint.'

Themis looked around, at a loss as to how to do this.

'Don't worry, Themis,' laughed Phidias. 'You can do that this evening or tomorrow. You'll need a tape, and a tablet to write the results down.'

Panainos began to cough, so they lifted the cloth and hurried outside.

'Thank the gods we'll be working in the workshop, and not in there,' said Panainos as soon as they were outside and he could take his mask off. 'May I borrow your Tilemachos, brother, to help us with the measuring?'

Phidias was standing watching the dust drifting out of the open doors. 'Of course,' he answered absent-mindedly.

'When will you uncover the statue?' Themis asked him.

'Not long now,' Phidias answered, setting off back to the workshop at speed. He began ticking things off on his fingers. 'Almost all the gold work is done. The face is late, partly because I wanted to make the eyes before we finalise the expression of the mouth. But his hair and garland, and his beard are all ready for fitting. The rest of the gems need to be set in the throne and his hands need just one or two more details before we fit Nike onto his right palm … ' He stopped and looked mischievously down at Themis. 'Why, young Themistokles? Are you impatient to have your next meeting with him?'

Themis smiled, but did not speak. What could he say? That he was afraid that the meeting would be his last day on earth? Or (almost as bad) that his dream would prove to be a result of his injury and nothing at all would happen?

A slim, very dark man was walking towards them from the gate.

Panainos said, 'Shall we take a quick turn around the Altis, boy, so we know where we are?'

'Go ahead,' said Phidias. 'This is Gulkishar, my scribe. Take him with you to the administration office and get your passes sorted out.'

Themis and Panainos walked all round under the boundary wall of the Altis with the inscrutable Gulkishar. Scores of temple staff, tourists and scribes hurried or dawdled about their business. Themis was glad the many statues of Olympic victors and heros, painted to look alive, were on plinths. Otherwise the sense of being watched would have unnerved him completely. The smoke of smouldering wood from the altars, some streaked with blood and ash, mingled with the sharp, clean smell of sun-warmed pine and myrtle.

They walked along in front of the small, temple-like buildings closely watched by a corresponding row of guards. 'This row of Treasuries,' Gulkishar told them in his stilted, foreign way, 'contains enough treasure to build four hundred of ships, they say.'

Themis had to marvel at the heaps and bundles of intricately worked weapons and ornaments that hung on the walls and were laid out on the steps of the treasuries.

'Is that why the guards are everywhere and we need passes?' he asked as he dodged out of the way of an old man carrying a huge load of firewood.

'Visitors from all over the world come here, and not all fear Zeus enough to keep their hands off his riches.' Gulkishar seemed to be quoting something.

'Then it might be wiser,' said Panainos with a grin, 'if they didn't have so many golden shields and tripods, and so on, out on show.'

Gulkishar ignored this. He waved a regal arm at a temple smaller than that of Zeus. 'This is the Temple of Hera,' he said. 'It's very old and has wonderful things inside. You can visit it another time. We must, before it closes, get to the office for your passes.'

They walked along beside the painted columns of the older temple and came to a series of administration buildings. They passed between two lines of sculpted figures with inscriptions, some offering thanks for victory and others begging for it, then up some steps and into a courtyard. Gulkishar led them into a room with a stone bench all along one wall. Four men were standing in the middle of the room, arguing about the benefits and drawbacks of what seemed to be a newly proposed sewage system. The clerk had to yell to get the next man to take his turn at the desk.

By the time their own turn came, all the disputers had gone. Gulkishar dealt with the clerk with deadpan politeness, and they soon walked out with a piece of papyrus each, stamped in dark brown wax with the seal of the sanctuary. This hung in a small fabric bag on a ribbon and they had to wear it round their necks all the time.

'Master Painter, Young Apprentice,' intoned Gulkishar as they came out into the sunlight. 'I leave you here.' And he stalked away.

'Phew,' sighed Panainos. 'He makes my hair stand on end. Come on, Themis. Niris promised quails' eggs for lunch, then it's the gymnasium for you.'

Chapter 26: work

'Are you Themistokles?' asked a young man approaching the pool.
Themis swam over to the side. 'Yes. Are you Tilemachos?'

Tilemachos was tall and skinny, with hands that were too big for the rest of him. He made Themis feel like a duck next to a heron. 'Come to introduce you round the workshop. Your Master's gone ahead. You ready?'

Work had begun again after the midday break, and everyone seemed to be hurrying to finish before the light faded.

'These guys are from Syracuse,' said Tilemachos as they passed the gem-cutters at their glistening bench, 'and this is Glafkos,' he gestured at the gilder, who was now working on the front of the statue's hair. Her face was lovely. 'He's from Miletus. Glafkos, this is Themistokles –'

'Panainos' apprentice,' smiled Glafkos. 'I saw you before.'

'Pleased to meet you,' said Themis formally. 'Is this Nike?'

'It is,' agreed Glafkos. Themis wanted to touch her, but Tilemachos was already outside, so he nodded to Glafkos and hurried on.

'The carpenters up on the face are from Tyre and the ivory-moulders are from Egypt,' Tilemachos went on. He turned and led Themis to a corner bench. 'And this is one of the gold workers from Ethiopia. He's making the final details of the mantle.'

Themis was fascinated by the long dark fingers working with tiny hammers, beating the shape of a leopard into a shimmering sheet of gold. When the embosser looked up, Themis caught his breath, surprised by the likeness to Melanas. The shape of the head and the amused look in his eye were similar, but he saw now that there was an intricate pattern of scars on the man's cheek and he was even talled and slimmer.

'Good to meet you,' Themis said. The man nodded and returned to his work.

'Come on, Themis,' urged Tilemachos, leading the way back into the workshop. 'We're going to prepare what we need tomorrow morning to start measuring in the Temple.' He went to a cupboard and began taking things out and putting them onto the round table.

Themis asked 'Are all the craftsmen from other countries? Aren't there any Athenians?'

'There's me,' laughed Tilemachos, 'and there are other sculptors who work in plaster and wood. We made the beard and hair, as well as most of the throne.'

Themis looked around. 'Am I the youngest?'

'You certainly are,' Tilemachos confirmed. 'Everyone will want you to run their errands, but you only work for Panainos – and me of course.'

'Right,' said Themis. 'Will we need a basket to put all those in?'

'Your first errand,' said Tilemachos. 'Get a basket from the pile in the corner by the musician.'

Next morning, before they went over to the Temple, Phidias and Panainos took Themis into a room he had not noticed before.

In a shaft of light from the roof stood a model of the statue. The skin was painted to look sun-browned, the hair dark, the robes golden. But it was half the size of an ordinary man, the face very stylized.

'When we have a question about proportion or colour,' said Phidias, 'we come to this model and sort it out.'

Panainos bent down as far as he could to look at the representation of his screens under the seat of the throne.

'Have to remember that what we paint is at eye level, easier for people to see than most of the rest,' he said to Themis. 'So we'll have to work with great care.'

When they left the room, the guards shut the door and stood to attention. The door had been painted to look like the stone of the wall.

'Can't have anyone see what we're up to until it's finished,' explained Phidias.

'Did you paint the door?' Themis asked.

'No. That was Alkamenes,' said Phidias with a grin. 'He's a great competitor of my dear brother's.'

'He's a better sculptor than painter,' Panainos said wryly.

>>>

From Bernie's private diary. Tuesday March 16th 2010

Laila and Gina came with me today. We were going to tell Suzanne about Miss Rallis and her (possible) affair with the llama farmer, but somehow we couldn't see the point with her lying there like a dead body. We took it in turns to hold her hand for a bit. She did stir at one point and mumbled something without opening her mouth. But then she was quiet again, so when her mum came in, we left. Very depressing …

<<<

'Add another couple of sticks to the fire,' Tilemachos told Themis.

'This stuff really stinks,' said Themis, poking the sticks under the cauldron of simmering glue.

Tilemachos tutted and rolled his eyes as he stirred the foul, dark mass with a huge wooden ladle.

'What kind of skins were they before they were cut up and boiled?' Themis asked.

'Mainly rabbit with some hare and antelope.' Tilemachos lifted the ladle out and watched as the glue fell back into the cauldron with a satisfying plop. 'Ready to strain,' he said.

Themis gagged at the smell as he checked that the fine muslin he had stretched across a large empty bowl was well tied down. He picked up some thick cloths to protect his hands and turned to help Tilemachos move the heated cauldron. A voice behind him said, 'Just leave that for now, young masters. You need to answer some questions.'

Two uniformed guards stood beside the fire, columns of muscle and menace with folded arms.

'Questions, officer?' asked Tilemachos. His voice wobbled. Themis frowned.

'There's been a theft,' said the one on the right.

'More than one,' said the one on the left.

'We'll need to search your accommodation,' said the first one.

'Now!' said the second.

'I have to pour this glue or it will spoil,' said Tilemachos, looking at Themis.

'No delays,' said the first guard.

'We'll be done in a moment,' said Themis. He and Tilemachos moved so fast that the two men found they were trying to lay hands on a burning cauldron instead of two disobedient workers who were pouring glue through a strainer. Themis noticed Tilemachos' hands were unsteady.

As the last of the glue sank through the cloth, Themis asked, 'Theft of what?'

'Can't tell you that, young master,' growled the first one. 'Come on. You've finished that now. Why don't you have the slaves do it, anyway?'

'I'm an apprentice. I have to learn myself,' said Themis. 'He's teaching me.' He gestured towards Tilemachos.

The guards indicated that they should leave the yard and go into the workshop. Themis and Tilemachos walked ahead, past Glafkos the gilder and the gem-cutters. Other guards were at the street door stopping anyone from going in or out. A couple of the ivory-moulders had been detained there and were joking together.

'What have you been up to, young Themis?' one called jovially. 'You've only been here a few days and they've already arrested you!'

Themis smiled back, but was hurried on by the guards.

At the hotel, the two guards went through every box, shelf, and dark corner of both Themis' and Panainos' rooms and the salon. Frog was made to stand still in the middle of the floor. When they finished, everything was put back exactly as it had been before.

'You could have searched without our ever knowing,' said Themis pleasantly.

'Now your place, Tilemachos,' growled the first guard.

'I have quarters in Phidias' house,' said Tilemachos apprehensively. 'I'm not sure his own guards will let you in.'

'Let's go and see,' said the guard with a grim nod. 'You are free to go, Themistokles.'

'Are you from the Altis Guard?' asked Themis.

'Yup.'

'So it was something from inside the precinct that has gone missing?'

'Got to get to Phidias' place,' said the guard abruptly and they left, herding Tilemachos in front of them.

'Phew!' said Tilemachos later as he joined Themis, who was squatting, painting the glue onto one side of a panel to prime it. 'They're going through everyone's stuff, including Phidias'.'

'And they didn't find your secret?' Themis looked up at him.

'What do you mean, secret?' challenged Tilemachos. 'I don't have any secrets. I just didn't want them to find my … wages.'

'And they didn't?'

'No.' Tilemachos tossed his head. 'They're hardly worth finding, anyway.'

'And did they say what they're looking for?' Themis took a deep breath as he stood up. The smell was less away from the panel.

'There's a couple of gold bridle bits and the boss of a shield missing from the Treasury of the Megarans, according – '

'According to rumour and gossip!' exclaimed Phidias' voice as he approached. 'Is Panainos here?'

'He'll be back soon,' Tilemachos answered. 'Shall I fetch him?'

'No, no. I'll talk to him later.' Phidias turned to leave, then suddenly whirled back. 'Does he have any lapis lazuli?' he asked. 'Dark, rich blue?'

'There's a small amount of Egyptian Blue,' Themis said.

'Not enough to paint three complete panels with?'

'No …,' Themis hesitated. 'Uncle Panainos told me yesterday it was rare and hard to get, so he was just going to use it for a couple of robes and a hint of the sea in a few places.'

'Right,' said Phidias and he swept away, his mouth in a hard line.

'Oops,' grinned Tilemachos. 'It looks like the Master's in trouble.'

'Lapis is very expensive,' Themis said. 'Perhaps there just wasn't enough in the market in Athens.'

'Arianos said I should give you this,' said Themis at the gymnasium that evening to Kadmos the Trainer.

Kadmos' stern face softened in a smile. 'He remembers me,' he said, looking over the tablet. 'Good. So, you'll join Pantarkes' group for strength training every second day.'

'Pantarkes?' queried Themis, looking round. Tilemachos was standing behind Kadmos. Themis saw him frown at this.

'You'll meet him later,' said Kadmos. 'It's a good idea to take a run in the mornings before work,' he added. 'D'you have company for that?'

Tilemachos stepped closer. 'I could join him for that,' he offered.

'It's alright,' Themis said quickly. 'My slave always comes with me.'

'Fine,' said Tilemachos. 'Tell me, do you take him with you to parties as well?'

Themis looked at him sideways. 'I don't go to parties,' he said.

'Well, there's one tonight at Phidias' house,' said Tilemachos. 'You should come. You'll get to know people…'

'Be careful!' Kadmos warned. 'Phidias will string you up by your thumbs if you can't work properly tomorrow.'

So that night, Themis went to the party.

It wasn't as wild as he expected from what people said about Phidias. He was cornered by Agorakritos and the painter and sculptor called Alkamenes. They offered Themis a lot of good-humoured but conflicting advice about representing the female form.

At last they noticed someone approaching.

'Ah,' said Alkamenes. 'It's Pantarkes the beautiful. Wrestled any monsters lately, Pantarkes?'

Agorakritos invited Pantarkes to sit with them. 'He won the boys' wrestling in the Games four years ago,' he explained to Themis.

'And he has a statue in the Altis,' added Alkamenes.

Pantarkes did not sit. 'Leave them to their technicalities,' he said with a laugh. 'Come and watch the dancing girls.'

'I'm in your workout group at the gymnasium,' Themis told him as they sat on cushions laid round the dance floor.

'You are?' Pantarkes was obviously only interested in the pretty faces and enticing bodies of the girl dancers. 'D'you think we can persuade one or two of them to stay with us afterwards?' he said to Themis, with a nudge of his elbow.

'Only if you've got something to give her. I'm broke.' Themis laughed a little nervously.

Pantarkes sighed. 'Me too. Phidias gives me everything I ask for except money.'

At the end of the dance, they picked up a couple of sesame buns filled with cheese and cumin, and went out into the garden. Many of the trees were in blossom, and glowed silver and white in the moonlight. They gave off a sweet, cloying scent.

'What do you do for Phidias, that he looks after you like that?' Themis asked, as they threw themselves down on the grass under a tree.

'He's in love with me so I don't have to do much, except the obvious. There are five of us who live with him, but I'm the only one he loves. Still, he's too busy to spend much time with me anyway, and mainly I do lessons. I'm quite interested in military history and engineering, but I'd rather be doing or making something than learning theory all the time.'

'Don't you work on the statue or with any of the builders?' asked Themis.

'I was the model for the statue called Beautiful at the entrance to the Stadium here.' Pantarkes preened, self-mocking.

'Oo-er,' laughed Themis.

'He doesn't want me mixing with workers, so I have to find other things to fill my days.'

'Like what?' asked Themis, his mouth full.

'Oh, I hunt duck and hare. I go to the gymnasium, as you know. And I swim in the river and try to catch fish.' He took a bite from his bun. 'And I look for girls,' he added with his mouth full, 'but the clean ones are usually well guarded or very expensive!'

'Doesn't Phidias mind?'

'He only cares about how beautiful I am,' said Pantarkes. 'It's nice that he looks after me, but it's not so nice being made to do all those lessons and not be allowed to have many friends. And I won't be old enough for the army for at least another year.'

'So perhaps I'm lucky I'm not so good looking,' said Themis.

'You're lucky you have a talent,' said Pantarkes, twirling one of his curls. 'And anyway, you're not bad looking. Strong and sturdy, with a good jaw and nice hair.'

'Maybe nice, but too short!' laughed Themis.

A voice from the open door to the house boomed out. 'Ah, there you are, boy!' Panainos came lumbering down the two steps. 'Time to go. We have three heroes and a lion to paint tomorrow.'

Themis jumped up and held out a hand to pull Pantarkes to his feet. 'Having a talent can also be a pain,' he whispered.

Chapter 27: mountains

'Good cheese, Frog,' mumbled Panainos through a mouthful at breakfast. 'Where d'you get it?'

'Special stall,' said Frog, bringing a platter of dried fruits. He and Themis were just back from their morning run.

'Have you answered your mother's tablet?' Panainos asked Themis.

'I just said we are well and have started work. She doesn't say anything about Nikanor …'

'No news is good news. Even that man on the mule you told me about hasn't reappeared and it's what, eight days now? So we haven't seen anything worth reporting either. But you'd better tell her that you're doing mathematics and logic lessons and we're looking for a music tutor.' Panainos split a fig open and stuffed it with a sliver of cheese.

'I'll add that,' said Themis. 'If we send it this evening, will it be in time for the Pelican?' He wondered if Captain Stomio had washed away his drawing.

'Possibly.' Panainos chewed thoughtfully. 'You know, young Themis, your calligraphy has improved enormously.'

Themis stood up. 'I like it to be neat,' he said.

'Before your fall, you didn't have the patience for neatness. Keep practising and you can do some of the lettering on the screens as we progress.'

'Thank you, Uncle,' said Themis with a grin. 'Will there be any on the blue screens behind Zeus' legs, the ones that everyone will see first?'

'There won't even be blue screens if I can't get any more pigment,' chuckled Panainos, 'and Phidias will roast me on a spit!'

Next morning, Themis topped the narrow pass and ran down the short rocky path onto a wide grassy shelf on the mountain. A small shrine stood at the point where the path he'd been following plunged down steps in a cliff. He sat gratefully on the base of the shrine, with his eyes shut and his back against one of the two columns. His heart and his breath were racing. The climb up the other side to this eyrie had been hard, but not as hard as the first time he had attempted it a few days earlier. He was getting stronger and could leave Frog behind now.

The little building had no walls. Two sturdy wooden columns at the front and two square ones at the back held up a wooden slatted roof. Under it, a stone statue of Artemis had been smoothed of features by wind and rain. There was a wide stone bowl for offerings. Today there were fresh flowers and a loaf of sesame bread in it. '*Someone was up early*,' he thought.

The view from this high place was glorious in the growing light. Layers of misty grey and blue hills lay between Themis and the pale green sea. Birds called and sleepy bees were beginning their day's work among the tiny hyacinths and daisies in the grass.

The hammering of his heart slowed as he breathed the scents of the new day. He bent to pick a hyacinth the colour of a jay's wing, then stood up to offer it to Artemis – and froze.

Beside the rocks to his right a brown bear swayed on all fours, watching him.

The hammering began again, but Themis stood quite still, his hand groping for his dagger.

He seemed to hear a voice in his head say, 'Give her the loaf from the shrine.' His own voice, or the goddess'?

The bear lifted its head, sniffing the breeze.

Themis moved very slowly to the offering bowl. The bear watched. 'Show her that you will give her the bread,' said the voice.

Themis picked up the loaf and held it away from his body, offering it to the bear. The bear took a step towards him.

He moved away from the shrine and laid the loaf on the grass. Then he stepped back.

The bear lumbered forward, its thick pelt loose on its bones. It held the loaf down with its front paws and growled as it took a huge bite.

Themis was back over the little pass and waving to Frog in the distance before the bear had swallowed its first mouthful.

'No work today,' said Panainos to Themis when he and Frog came in after their run. 'It's the equinox. Have a good scrub down and put on your best tunic and a flower garland. We'll be having food during the rites in the Altis.'

'I'll save you some honeycakes,' Themis whispered to Frog.

'Don't worry,' Frog laughed. 'I'm friends with the baker now.'

'Then you must tell him to put a touch more salt in the barley bread,' Panainos put in, as Niris tied the ribbons of his garland. 'And you, Themis, stay close to me today. Bad things can happen in big crowds.'

The procession had already entered the Altis when Themis and Panainos caught up. A group of priests in white robes led them into the large open space between the temples. At a stone altar beside a high mound stood a white ox, its horns garlanded with spring flowers. The crowd was in their most flamboyant clothes, women as well as men. They were singing a hymn of praise for the growing days.

Themis saw Phidias there with three of his students, including Pantarkes. Most of his work colleagues were there, too, and Kadmos and the young men from the gymnasium. For a moment, he thought he saw Xenovia among the priestesses. But then he was often reminded of her by the way a woman's hair was dressed or the shape of a cheek or a hand.

A fire burned in the centre of the altar. The priests began to intone a rhythmic chant and the ox looked up and around with shining eyes. The crowd sent up a cheer at this good omen.

The officiating priest stepped forward, a knife glinting in his hand. The other priests closed in and the ox sank silently to the ground. A large bowl collected his blood as it pulsed out of his slit throat.

Themis suddenly felt sick and stepped back from the press of people. The crisply scented smoke from the fire was blowing towards him. He leant against a statue base. As he watched, the horns and two large pieces of skinned meat were placed on the altar.

Tilemachos had seen him leave the crowd and came over.

'You all right?' he asked.

'I'm fine,' lied Themis. 'What happens next?'

'You really don't remember?'

'No.'

Tilemachos shrugged. 'They'll burn the thigh bones on the fire with herbs for Zeus and the rest is being cut up for us all to eat at the feast.'

'When's that?'

'Soon, over there under those trees. See?'

Themis turned and saw a series of tables laid out near the back of the Temple of Zeus.

'Next time they do this, they'll be able to go inside the temple and see the god,' said Tilemachos. 'That'll be at the Games, and then again at the next equinox. You going to be here then?'

'I doubt it,' said Themis. The smoke drifted over them and the first whiff of the burning meat reached him.

With his next breath he found himself standing on a high mountain top with a wide plain below him and the hazy blues of sea and islands in the far distance. Beside him, his father and his brother were dipping their hands in a bowl of blood. They turned and smeared it on his face and hands, slowly and carefully. A small crowd of onlookers sent up a loud rejoicing cry and a priest began a song of thanks to Zeus, the master of good fortune.

And then he was back, beside Tilemachos in Olympia, leaning against the statue base, his feet among wild flowers, smoke from the altar bitter in his throat.

'What happened?' asked Tilemachos. 'You made a very weird noise.'

'I ... I remembered something!' Themis turned to him, shaking his head in amazement and grinning. 'I remembered ... another time when we sacrificed to Zeus. On a mountain.'

'What brought that on?'

'I think it was the smell of the wood they use – or the meat cooking.' Themis wanted to tell Panainos and Phidias, but the ceremony was in full swing now. 'Er ... I ... I'm going to look for my uncle,' he said.

'See you later at the feast,' said Tilemachos, and joined the crowd again.

Themis felt he would be more vulnerable in the crowd than in an open space. So he left the Altis by the gate to the Council House where he could see all round him. The gateway was festooned for the festival with green branches and coloured ribbons that fluttered in the slight breeze.

He sat down on the low base of a large statue there, checked he was alone, and closed his eyes. He took long slow breaths, reaching inwards to bring back the memory of his father and the mountain top.

It came to him through clearing mist. He saw the hazy distance, the smoke of a fire, the brightness of the sun on white garments. Then he noticed drops of blood that had fallen onto his feet. He heard chanting, and the wind in the stunted trees. He felt the grip of his father's blood-streaked hand on his shoulder.

He turned to look up at his father's face. Kallistos was looking straight ahead, and Themis followed his gaze. They looked down the other side of the mountain, at the city far below, with the Hundred-foot Temple on the Akropolis like a toy, and Athena's golden helmet a shining star in the slanting sunlight. The fields and slopes of the Athenian plain were brown after a long hot summer.

'When your moment comes,' his father said, 'remember that you represent the city and your family, not just yourself.'

And Themis said, 'Will you be there?'

>>>

From Bernie's private diary. Wednesday March 24th 2010

This afternoon, I was in the ward, working on my tidal generator project for Environmental Science. A nurse called Mandy was checking her patients. She'd got to Suzanne and was changing the catheter bag, when Suzanne stirred and groaned. She sniffed like a dog and opened her eyes. I stood up and went over to the bed. The nurse stood still and signed to me to be calm.

'You OK, Suzanne?' she asked quietly.

'Meat!' said Suzanne. Her voice was croaky.

Nurse Mandy said, 'I'll get you some porridge,' and flashed a smile at me.

Suzanne's eyes closed and I think she went to sleep again.

The nurse wrote something on the chart at the foot of the bed, and then we did a little silent dance.

Later, when Nurse Mandy put the porridge down on the bedside cabinet thing, Suzanne opened her eyes and sniffed again.

'You be there?' she said.

'If you want me to,' answered Nurse Mandy, like she knew what Suzanne meant.

And Suzanne suddenly looked surprised. 'Where?' she said.

'Wherever you say,' said Nurse Mandy, smiling at her.

'Where now?' asked Suzanne, looking round. No croak in her voice now.

'This is a hospital,' said Mandy. 'You've been very ill, but you are getting better now.'

'Dead?' Suzanne didn't sound frightened, just quiet, dreamy.

'No. You're going to be fine,' Mandy answered, still smiling. 'Would you like some food?'

Suzanne said, 'We-ird,' very quietly and closed her eyes. And she was asleep again – a twitchy kind of sleep.

I wrote this down while I was still there. When Nurse Mandy had finished with the other patients she came back and we had a chat about it. But we couldn't work anything sensible out.

Yes, Suzanne. Weird! What ARE you dreaming about?! But THANK YOU FOR SPEAKING AGAIN!!!!!

<<<

There was something cold pushing at Themis' cheek. He opened his eyes to see a large liquid eye staring at him. He leapt up, his heart racing, and saw that it was a dog.

The dog sprang backwards in surprise with a short bark. It was a pale yellow, taller and slimmer than Beast, with a long, narrow snout.

'Have you found him?' called a man's voice from near the Altis gate.

Themis did not recognise the voice. He sprinted away, hitching his long tunic up into his belt. The dog stayed where it was. When he looked back it was alone, a pale shape in front of the dark-robed statue.

Without thinking, Themis took the road past the hippodrome to the river. He turned left and ran along beside the waters. When he came to the long stone bridge where the Alpheios narrowed, he crossed it and pounded up the zigzagging track on the other side of the valley. He turned off on a steep path to the right and came out of the trees at the top of a cliff. He stopped, sobbing for breath, and looked back.

The river, the fields, the buildings of the town and the Altis, where smoke rose among the trees, were tiny. There was no sign of pursuit.

An eagle was cruising the tree tops just below him, its wings motionless.

Perhaps he should have stayed to find out who the man with the dog was. *'It was stupid of me to run like that. Especially to such a lonely place,'* he thought. But looking round, he saw there was no cover nearby for an enemy, so he sat down on a rock with the path in full view and tried to think clearly.

His mind buzzed with questions. But the memory of his father had been crisp and true. Unless … Had he in fact remembered his father's words? Or had his mind rearranged what was on the tablet they read on the ship and it wasn't really a memory at all? Then again, it could just be a coincidence that the writer of the tablet wanted him to do the same things as his father had wanted.

Which was what? What on earth *was* it that he had been chosen to do? What was his 'moment'? Why did these memories not include other people, so that he could ask them questions? Not that that would help. Everyone still avoided straight answers when he did ask.

The eagle was gliding lazily back and forth below him. Themis watched it for a few moments. A pair of squirrels burst out of the trees, chasing and scolding each other over the rocks and clumps of pink cyclamen. Themis' stomach growled with hunger, and he stood up. '*I'll get no answers from you, either,*' he thought, looking at the eagle. 'Will you give me a ride down?' he said out loud.

It sheared off into the mountains behind him. 'Ah well,' he sighed and set off at a jog.

He met no kidnappers on the way back and grinned at his fears. At the long table in the Altis he joined his exercise group from the gym. Someone had been spreading the story of his vision of Zeus.

'Did he warn you about women and their demands?' asked Pantarkes.

'No, he wouldn't bother with that,' said a pale, skinny young man called Pyrros. 'He probably just wanted to prepare you for when he whisks you off to Mount Olympus and turns you into a feast for Hades and Poseidon.'

Themis choked.

'Those stories are old-fashioned rubbish,' said Kadmos while Themis coughed. 'If Zeus visited Themis in a dream then there's bound to be a better reason than that.'

Themis looked up and saw the High Priest of the Temple walking towards them.

The Priest looked angry, as though someone had insulted him. He called out, 'Which of you is Themistokles?'

Themis swallowed. 'I am,' he said, his skin crawling.

'What's this about Zeus talking to you in a dream?' The Priest stopped behind Pantarkes, opposite Themis. 'You must have made that up. He doesn't talk to mortals directly.'

Themis said, 'But he did …' and the Priest said, 'Stand up when you speak to me!'

Themis stood up slowly, deciding he had better make light of this. He said, 'I had an accident when I hit my head. I have all kinds of strange dreams.'

'Well, that explains it then,' said the Priest, relaxing a little. 'It wasn't a real visitation, it was just part of your craziness from the bump.'

'That's probably it,' said Themis quietly.

'No one I have ever met has actually spoken with Zeus the Father,' said the Priest. 'Our experience is that he lets us know what he wills through oracles and the weather. You must beware of sacrilege and profanity, young Themistokles! If you persist, Zeus will punish you severely.' And he whirled away in his long white robe, his thin nose in the air.

Themis sat down. The others looked at each other and shrugged. 'He's a real terror, that one,' said Kadmos, 'Better to keep out of his way.'

Themis felt a hand on his shoulder and jumped. But when he looked up, it was Agorakritos. Everyone laughed a bit nervously.

'So,' said the sculptor, looking down on Themis. 'Have you upset His Holiness the High Priest of the Whole World?'

Themis smiled. 'Yes, I suppose I have.'

'Just avoid him in future. He's a bit miffed because the administration is talking about letting in anyone who wants to see the statue as soon as it's finished.'

'What's wrong with that?' asked Themis.

'No applications for special permission – which of course, you have to pay for,' smiled Agorakritos.

'Ah,' said Kadmos, 'There goes his pension fund?'

'Perhaps. But I imagine the open-door policy will only be until the Games. Anyway,' said Agorakritos, 'I came over to see if you will be at the gymnasium later, Themis.'

'Yes. Around sunset,' answered Themis.

'Good. There's something … I need your help with,' said Agorakritos, with a glance at the other boys. 'I'll find you there.'

The boys looked at Themis as Agorakritos left. 'Bet he asks you to spy on Panainos for him,' said Pyrros.

'Nah. He just wants him to massage his feet,' laughed Pantarkes.

After exercise and bathing, and as they walked back to the hotel together in the dusk, Agorakritos handed Themis a small tablet.

'Sorry about my little deceit in front of the others, but this was given to me in Elis and it's addressed to you,' he said. 'I'm not sure who it's from, but I suspect it's from the judge. I was told it would be best if you kept the message to yourself for the moment.'

Themis stomach clenched up. 'Thanks,' he said. They had reached the hotel. He took the tablet. 'Goodnight, Master Agorakritos – and thanks again.' He let himself into the apartment he shared with Panainos.

No one was there and all was dark. Themis lit a lantern and took the tablet into his room. He broke the seals with his knife.

It *was* from the judge, and it said, 'Please come to see me urgently but secretly. We have something very important to discuss. When you arrive at my residence, send in your pass for the Altis, so that I know it's you.'

Themis read the message twice and thought for a moment. Then he went out to find Frog.

Chapter 28: revelation

'You see, Uncle,' said Themis as they prepared to sleep that evening. 'I only heard about it when I went to the market with Frog.'

Panainos lit a candle for Themis to take to bed. 'Who told you about it?' he asked as he picked up his lantern and turned for his own room.

'It was a man who sells face-paints to the ladies,' said Themis. 'He says they've just found a seam of blue rock in a copper mine on the way to Elis. He received a sample in powdered form yesterday. The women love blue to paint round their eyes.'

'Well I can't afford to let anyone else go when it's probably pointless, so yes,' grumbled Panainos, 'you can go and see. I've tried to change his mind, but Phidias is adamant that he wants those panels to be a rich blue. "Like the darkest kingfisher", he said, so they show off the gold and ivory of Zeus' legs and feet.' Panainos went into his room and brought out a purse and a slip of papyrus.

'Get me twenty drachmas' worth if you find any,' he said. 'And use the rest if you need to find lodging for the night. This is permission for Xenon the guard to accompany you.' He went back into his room, but turned and said, 'And take Frog with you – *and* some food. Goodnight.' He closed the door muttering, 'So unnecessary, and so expensive … '

Frog and Themis punched each other's shoulders in silent triumph.

They set off mid-morning. The copper mine was somewhere

beyond a town called Pylos, quite close to Elis, according to Frog's stall-holder friend. Themis said nothing about going to Elis itself.

Xenon was short and slim, with two knives in his belt. Once they had run till they were tired, he got out a flute and they played a few well-known tunes. When Frog and Xenon started on a less savoury repertoire of songs, Themis forgot entirely to worry about what the judge might say to him.

The road was wide and often paved as they climbed up the fertile valley going north. It ran over the col between two high peaks and then down beside a stream towards the town of Pylos on the Pineos river. There was plenty of traffic between Elis and Olympia, so there was no chance of their losing their way. Every now and again, there were springs and taverns. They stopped briefly at one called the Fountains of Pieria where there were banks of water spouts under the pine trees, and rows of food stalls.

'Are we're nearing Pylos?' Themis asked Xenon later when they stopped at a crossroads. It was already getting dark.

'It'll be black night before we get there,' answered the guard, his hand anxiously stroking the hilt of one of his daggers. 'There's a farm I know of where they'll give us lodging for the night, if you've a mind to stop here.'

They turned up a track and soon found the farm. They were shown to a sleeping patch in a hay barn by the cheery farmer's wife. She gave them a pot of bean stew and some bread to eat by the light of a lantern in the yard, among the goats, pigs and chickens. They were almost asleep before they finished the food.

Dawn was just a wisp of light on the horizon when Themis woke. Xenon and Frog were still asleep as he set off. Not far from the farm, he came upon the farmer and his slave, driving a cart along the track.

'I've left the guard and my slave sleeping,' he told them. 'I'll be back around midday.'

'That's fine young master,' growled the farmer. 'We'll take care of them, but mind you bring enough to pay for another night's hospitality if need be.'

'Of course,' called Themis, and he ran on.

The main road ran along beside the Pineos river, in its wide, shallow valley. The villages were prosperous and the fields flat and full of flax and wheat. As he neared the city of Elis he could see the temples and municipal buildings above rows of newly-built villas. The road was overflowing with carts and travellers. Both bridges over the river were almost at a standstill with traffic.

He asked at the first tavern for Judge Iasos and was directed to a large house which backed onto the river. The street entrance had two elegant Ionic columns with red and blue painted capitals, one on either side of a high, shady porch. At the bottom of the steps was a gilded modern Herm, a victory wreath on its curly hair. Themis touched it for luck.

His stomach in a solid knot, he beat the dust out of his tunic, ran his fingers through his hair, took a deep breath and knocked on the tall wooden door.

The door opened and a slim man with a brown skin in voluminous yellow and green trousers appeared. The austerity of his face reminded Themis of Gulkishar, but he had never seen anything like those trousers.

A female voice could be heard complaining loudly somewhere in the house. 'Sir?' prompted the man.

'My name is Themistokles, son of Kallistos,' said Themis, holding out his Altis pass. 'Judge Iasos is expecting me.'

'Please come in,' said the man.

Themis was shown into a small room where he sat on a cushioned bench to wait. The door was closed, but the female voice was still audible.

'But now,' it cried, 'I'm leaving to get married! I won't be living here any more. Why won't you let me take something with me that was my mother's?' She must have been standing in the hallway now. 'You don't even want it yourself. You just want to stop me having it!' and the front door slammed.

The butler in the yellow and green trousers opened the door and stood back. 'The judge can see you now,' he said.

He led Themis through a sunny courtyard, along a colonnade and into a large, pale room that opened onto a river terrace. Reflections from the water played on the complex mouldings of the ceiling. The judge was standing by a couch against the end wall. An elaborately carved low table and two stools stood in front of him. He was wearing a long, dark yellow tunic with a heavy border embroidered in black and gold.

'*Rich and powerful,*' Themis thought. '*I may have to adapt the truth if I want to find out who sent those tablets.*'

'Come!' said the judge. 'Sit here,' and he indicated one of the stools.

'I am intrigued by your story.'

They sat down and immediately a slave came in with a tray of drinks and sweetmeats.

'Will you have some cordial?' The slave lifted a jug ready to pour.

'Just water, please,' said Themis.

'I understand that you had an interesting experience at the Tainaron Oracle,' began the judge, as Themis poured a small libation.

'Well, … ' said Themis, playing for time. 'Yes, it was … interesting.'

'You communicated with your father, I understand.'

'Well, er … yes,' said Themis. 'He did tell me something, but it didn't mean much to me.'

'Something about being chosen to do something?' The judge's light brown eyes reminded Themis of a goat.

'You see, sir,' he explained, 'I have completely lost my memory of anything that happened earlier than forty days ago.'

'So I understand.' The judge stood up and walked towards the river terrace. He turned, silhouetted against the light outside. His movements were brisk, but he spoke slowly and deliberately. 'In that case, you do not remember … that, in the Agora in Athens, … you qualified last autumn … ' The judge paused and Themis stood up, the hairs on his arms rising, '…. qualified … as a contestant in the boys' boxing contest in the Olympic Games this coming summer. You do not remember that. Or do you?'

Themis stood very still, staring at the judge. 'Boxing,' he said carefully. 'I see.' He saw, but did not dare believe.

'That is what you have been chosen to do,' declared the judge. 'It is a great honour, the will of Zeus. And because it is the will of Zeus, I must arrange for you to compete, according to your father's wishes and plans.'

So this was what Eirini and Arianos – and everyone else – had been hiding from him!

He said, 'My father's wishes, yes, your honour. But, unfortunately, not my mother's. And since my father is now dead, she is my guardian. She is concerned that further blows to my head may make me into an idiot, or an epileptic, or kill me.' Themis was so tense that his voice kept cracking.

'That, it seems, is … unlikely,' said the judge as he sat down on his couch again. 'A more important consideration is that she – among others in Athens – has laid a curse on anyone … ' The judge hesitated.

' "Who allows me, or persuades me, to do anything that might make my injuries worse",' Themis quoted, sitting down warily, as though the stool would break, his mind paralysed.

'Exactly,' agreed the judge. He stroked his neatly trimmed beard. 'I think we can arrange, with time and a few carefully chosen offerings, to get that curse lifted. But that will have to be done in Athens. And you need to get back to your training now, if you are going to be able to take the oath that you have been training since autumn last year.'

'But I haven't,' said Themis in dismay. 'Not for boxing, anyway.'

'Only because … you have been in mourning for your father – and injured, of course. I can arrange for the oath to be reworded for you if necessary,' said the judge with a shrug, 'but you will have to work hard now, preferably without your Master Painter knowing, for he will surely try to stop you, according to your mother's wishes and the curse.'

Themis' mind suddenly cleared.

'Would it be possible,' he said, 'for me to leave actual boxing training until the curse is lifted? I can increase my general training now, of course.'

'A laudable compromise,' said the judge. 'I will begin on having the curse lifted and let you know when it is done.' He rose to call the butler.

'May I ask a question?' Themis stood up, too.

'Of course.'

'I was wondering why you are helping me, and who my … benefactor is. Who arranged for me to go to the Oracle, and who informed you about this? I would like to thank whoever it was.'

'I have been asked not to reveal that for the present, but I can assure you it is someone with your best interests at heart.'

'I can see that,' said Themis, allowing himself to grin at last. 'This is a dream come true!'

'And as for why I personally am doing this,' went on the judge, 'I have checked that you won your place at the Games fair and square in the competitions in Athens. The gods were with you then, and there are signs that they are with you now. I always try to do as the gods indicate.' He stood up. 'But there are times when that involves a little duplicity amongst us mere mortals,' he said, the suggestion of a smile in his unblinking eyes. 'And, in this case, a lot of hard work for you, young man.'

They walked to the door as the colourful butler appeared. Themis turned and bowed his head. 'Your honour, thank you,' he said.

'I'll be in touch. Have a good trip back,' answered the judge.

Outside, Themis ran down the street for a short way, jumping up to touch the branches of the shade trees, silently shouting 'Yes, yes, yes!' to himself. Then he turned and walked slowly back. He felt calm and sure now, some of those buzzing questions finally answered. 'It had to be something like this,' he said to himself. 'It's so obvious now I know. I wish I could remember! … I must be really good. You don't get to the Olympics unless you're the best.' He grinned and nodded to himself as he sat down on a bench to savour his joy and make plans.

He looked at his scarred hands. How was he going to strengthen them and his arms without actually boxing? Should he trust Frog, or anyone else, and tell him that he now knew what they all knew? What was he going to say to his mother? And all the while his heart was singing, 'I qualified!'

A young woman and her girl slave left the throng on the street to climb the steps to the judge's house. At the second step she tripped on her robe and ended up sitting in a disconsolate heap, her slave hovering over her.

'Oh do leave me alone!' she snapped at the girl. 'I'm not hurt.'

It was the same voice that Themis had heard in the house earlier. He looked at her, wondering what her fight had been about, and resisting the urge to tell her – and everyone on the street – his amazing news. Her brown, shiny hair was pinned and plaited in a style even more elaborate than Myrto's creations. Was she really the judge's daughter?

She felt Themis' eyes and looked directly at him. The grey-green of her eyes was eclipsed by the bright blue she'd painted on her eyelids.

'*Oh maggots!*' Themis thought. '*The blue pigment …* '

He stood up. 'Excuse me, mistress,' he said.

'What is it?' she asked as she gathered her skirts and got to her feet.

'A strange question, I know, but could you tell me where you get the colours you paint on your face?'

Her mouth fell open. 'What?' she asked.

'I … want to play a trick on some friends, so I need some face paint,' said Themis with a sheepish grin. 'Where can I get some?'

Her smile was mischievous. 'Ah, well, I get mine from Mrs Melpomeni's stall in the market. She's usually between the statue of Pythokles and the big mulberry tree.'

'Thank you, young mistress,' said Themis, turning away.

'She's not cheap,' called the young woman as she climbed the steps.

'Tell her Anthoussa, daughter of Iasos, sent you. She may give you a discount.' She pushed the great door open and disappeared.

The stall was obvious. The owner's face was a melee of colours and shapes that had nothing to do with its original form. Themis waited for a large, middle-aged lady to pay for a miniscule package. He spotted a little dish of vivid blue among the many colours on the stall. '*There's your kingfisher blue, Phidias,*' he thought with a smile.

'Can I help you, beautiful?' said Mrs Melpomeni. 'You want to enhance those lovely eyes a bit?'

'Well,' began Themis. 'I'm not quite sure how to explain this, but I need to know the origin of your blue colour.'

Mrs Melpomeni started to shake her head.

'I'm an apprentice painter, you see,' Themis said quickly. 'I need a lot of blue pigment for something my Master wants to colour, and we are having trouble getting enough. Does yours come from round here?'

'Oh, I see, young man. Right, well … ' and she looked around slyly. 'You got any money?'

'If you give me good information, I'll give you some money when I've checked it out.'

'Hmmm. Well, it's common knowledge anyway really,' she said with what was probably a smile on her multicoloured face. 'There's a mine near here. This blue is called azurite – comes as crystals. They found a good lot lately. It's across the river at Pylos, and up in the hills, they say.'

Themis felt this was too convenient to be true, though it did corroborate what the merchant in Olympia had said. 'What price can you give me for a sample of it?' he asked. 'Anthoussa said you would give me a discount.'

'Did she now? Well, I charge her a drachma for one of these,' she said, indicating rows of tiny, folded linen parcels. 'You could have the same.'

'I'll see what my Master says. Thank you,' he said as he placed an obol coin in her hand.

'Come back soon,' she called as he ran off.

Themis bought himself some breakfast and an earthenware pot with a lid. Then he ran all the way back to the farm, brimming with excitement. Life was perfect! '*Or it would be if I could remember more of it,*' he thought.

By the time he got to the farm, it was almost midday. Frog was in the dairy stirring goats' milk for the farmer's wife.

'Where did you go?' he asked. 'Look what I've had to do all morning!'

Themis ignored the question with a grin. 'Where's Xenon? We have to go to Pylos and see if anyone can tell us where the mine is,' he said. He picked up a cheese from the drying rack. 'Is this any good?'

'Too young, probably,' said Frog, looking at him with a slight frown.

'Ah. You know all about making cheese now, do you,' laughed Themis, looking around for some bread to have with his prize.

The farmer's wife called them into her kitchen. 'Your guard is just coming,' she said as she made up a parcel with more food and a skin of honey water, 'and I know about that mine,' she told them. 'There was talk because they say there's a lot of copper and someone is getting very rich. Our eldest son's gone off to work there. His name's Ilarion. Say hello from his mother if you see him. The overseer's called Jason. But mind your step with him. He's a nasty piece of work … '

'Thanks,' said Themis as Xenon came in. 'We'll probably be back later but let me give you the price of this meal now.'

'Nah. If you're going to make it back by nightfall, though, you'd better get a move on.'

Chapter 29: azurite

Pylos was much smaller than Elis, though also very busy with lots of large carts on the road. They found the market place, but it was deserted at the beginning of the midday break. The taverns were open, though, and they were told to take the road into the mountains to the north and east. The mine was only about fifteen stades away.

Themis could not tell Frog his news in front of Xenon, so he had to keep stopping himself from grinning. As they walked, he planned a large painting as an offering to Zeus, and perhaps Apollo, or Hephaistos, or maybe all three. Secret offerings, of course, and only when he was sure they existed …

He was so excited he felt light-headed, as if his body was working by itself. He could hear that sound in his head like water dripping or a single note played on a lyre. He let Frog and Xenon lead the way for a while.

As they walked they came in sight of large, newly built smelters some way ahead. One was already releasing pale smoke into the sky. They turned off the main road before they got to the smelters, and followed a narrow valley uphill. They could hear the noise of the mine long before they reached it. The track was broad and well rutted. Twice they had to stand aside while a large cart came down full of ore.

Themis' light-headed feeling passed and he bounded into the lead.

They came to a place where the track widened out and plunged down into a mighty quarry with steep, stepped sides and a flat bottom. On the opposite side, lines of slaves worked on each of the levels. Here and there, the mouths of tunnels pierced the cliff.

There was dust everywhere, and the sounds of chipping and digging. They asked for Master Jason and were directed to a small hut on a wider shelf cut into the steep slope.

Master Jason was a large man with a belly to rival Panainos'. A long string of people was waiting to talk to him and he was in no hurry.

After a few moments waiting in line, Themis said to Xenon in a loud voice, 'Of course, Master Phidias will be checking progress!'

At that, Master Jason looked them up and down.

'You work for Master Phidias?' he growled. 'Come here.'

'He's my uncle,' said Themis, approaching the foreman. 'I work for his brother Panainos.' Themis stood tall and looked the foreman in the eye.

'What d'you want?'

'I'd like a sample of the azurite you have here to show my Master. He may need a little more than he's got.'

'Must be rich if he's got a lot of that stuff,' said the big man. 'Tell you what, I'll give you a crystal or two and you tell him to come here in person and we'll see what we can do for him.'

'Thank you,' said Themis, 'but I have instructions to bring back twenty drachmas' worth so that he can test the quality.'

'And how much do you suppose that would be?'

Themis turned to Frog. 'Give me that pot I put in your pack,' he said.

Frog took out the little pot Themis had bought in Elis.

'Twenty drachmas' worth won't fill that,' said the foreman.

'Oh, I think it will,' said Themis, guessing that Mrs Melpomeni sold her tiny amounts of powder at an enormous profit. Frog looked at him in amazement. Xenon stood like a statue, his hand on a dagger.

'Well, seeing as it's for Phidias himself,' Master Jason conceded, and Themis didn't correct him. He ordered a slave to take them to a sorting shed and fill up the pot with azurite. 'You can pay me now,' he said.

'I'll bring you the money when I've seen the goods,' replied Themis. 'I shall need a receipt, please,' and he turned on his heel and followed the slave. Frog trotted behind with a wondering smile on his face.

As they entered the shed they had to cover their mouths with a corner of their tunics against the dust. Sorting benches with shallow compartments were filled with small pieces of rock. In general the ore looked brown and grey, but some pieces were crusted with rich blue crystals, and others with green ones. The slave was an old man whose bones seemed ready to pop out from his skin and whose smell enveloped them in a fog of sweat and garlic. He scooped up some of the blue crystaline fragments and offered to put them in the pot.

'Please include that piece,' said Themis, indicating a particularly vivid blue piece. 'And this one here.'

The slave did as asked. *'They're like bits of the deepest sea in sunlight,'* thought Themis happily, though he kept a neutral expression on his face.

'Do you know a miner called Ilarion?' he asked the slave as they fitted the lid onto the pot.

The old man nodded. 'He'll be at the face today, overseeing a team.'

'Please give him his mother's greetings. She has offered us hospitality for the night.'

'I'll do that if I see him,' said the slave, and they went out into the sunshine, where they took great breaths of the cleaner air.

Master Jason had a sliver of stone scratched with the price ready for Themis. He added an estimated weight on Themis' insistence and they left him staring after them with a set jaw.

Once they were well away, Frog said, 'Well! You dealt with him in no uncertain terms.'

'Yeah, maybe,' said Themis. 'I hope Panainos is pleased.'

'Much more like your old self,' said Frog happily. Xenon followed them silently.

From Bernie's private diary. Thursday March 25th 2010

Suzanne was awake when I went in after school today. Well, she had her eyes open and was staring at the ceiling. Her heart was beating faster than last time I saw her and the machine also showed she was breathing more deeply. The nurses had warned me to go along with anything she might say, or just to talk quietly to her if she was unconscious. Questions make her freak out, it seems.

I said, 'Hey!' and she focused her eyes on me. 'You feeling better?'

She just looked at me, but she was seeing me, at least some of the time. She reached out her good hand and I held it.

After a bit she looked at me again and then she smiled the most perfect smile. She was looking right in my eyes.

But she didn't speak and went back to staring at the ceiling for a bit and then sank away again.

But I know she saw me and I know she knew me. Why does that make me cry?

<<<

'You're soaked!' cried Panainos as Themis and Frog burst into the apartment next afternoon.

'It rained all the way back,' Themis told him with a laugh. 'But we got your rock!'

'Show me, show me.' Panainos pushed scrolls off the low table and they gently poured out the pieces of crystaline rock.

'And here's your change,' said Themis, placing the purse with the few remaining coins beside the meager heap.

Panainos did not hear. He was turning the glistening rich blue stones over and over with glee. 'Perfect,' he muttered. Then he looked up. 'Grinding day tomorrow for my apprentice!' he declared. 'But now you should get along to the gymnasium for a long hot bath, Themis. Niris will look after Frog. Meet me at The Musty Miller to celebrate. You deserve a real meal!'

They met Agorakritos at the tavern and the three of them made their way to a corner away from the splash of the rain outside.

'It took you a long time to find the mine, then?' Panainos said to Themis later, his mouth full of lamb.

Themis looked up grinning with a ghost of a wink at Agorakritos. 'It took us a while to find the farm where the woman knew about the mine. From there it was easy.'

Agorakritos smiled at his bowl of soup.

'I'll be sending Tilemachos to get more of the azurite,' said Panainos.

'That foreman, Jason,' said Themis sitting back, his stomach finally telling him he'd eaten enough. 'He'd sell you rotten eggs as solid gold.'

'What you got is good stuff. Phidias will be pleased when he sees his blue panels at last.'

'When will that be?' asked Agorakritos.

'Oh, within five days, I should think. Depends on the mixing process and then the weather for drying.' Panainos waved a hand for a waiter.

'So you … er … we may be leaving in ten days or so?' asked Themis.

'Surely not,' said Agorakritos with a look at Themis.

Panainos ordered some more wine and water with dried figs and apricots, and then said 'A bit longer than that. The designs will take at least a week to paint. Then we have to fit the screens in place. And there'll be the festival of dedication when it's all finished. It would be a shame to leave before that, wouldn't it? We might never get a chance to come back and see the completed statue.'

'Ye-es,' said Themis, remembering suddenly what that might mean for him. 'It would be wonderful … '

'Are you a bit worried about that?' asked Agorakritos.

'Well,' said Themis, his head now beginning to ache in the stuffy heat of the tavern. 'Zeus didn't actually say what he wants me for. He just said to come again when I am ready.' Themis looked into Agorakritos' kind, twinkling eyes. 'I don't know what I'm supposed to be ready for.'

'Don't you?' Agorakritos asked innocently. 'Well, I expect you'll know when it happens. You're growing up fast. Something will make it clear.'

'And until then we have a good excuse to stay and enjoy the luxuries of Olympia,' laughed Panainos.

'At Phidias' expense,' said Agorakritos with a smile. 'Yes, once your work is done you'll have more time to look around at the statues and paintings in Olympia. Perfect education for an artist.'

'The boy's got ants in his sandals,' said Panainos. 'All he seems to want to do is run and swim and exercise. He asked me as soon as he got back this afternoon if he could start work later in the morning and leave earlier each day for the gymnasium.'

'Ah, he must be in love,' laughed Agorakritos.

'Just make sure it's not with Pantarkes,' Panainos said seriously to Themis and then burst out laughing too.

The stuffy headache did not retreat, so Themis excused himself and went back to his room. Frog was already asleep on his pallet on the floor just outside his door.

Themis lay on his bed without even getting undressed. He felt dizzily exhausted, as though he was being turned on a spit, round and round at high speed. With his eyes shut he could hear that regular note again. He was in a strange, pale place that smelled of something sharp and clean. There were people around that he couldn't see. They spoke quietly and came and went, but took no notice of him. The headache was less but if he opened his eyes the dizziness took over. *'But who cares?'* he thought. *'Now I know what I have to do, even if I'm not sure how. And it feels so right, so like the real me, whoever that is.'*

>>>

From Bernie's private diary. Saturday March 27th 2010

Saw a documentary last night on TV about people who get knocked on the head and all the different ways they can recover – or not. Didn't sleep much.

But when I got to the hospital this afternoon, the nurse said Suzanne had spoken again! They weren't sure, but she had made sounds like talking and said something like 'headache'.

I went into her ward and she was asleep, so I sat for a while, telling her about the weather (nice to see the sun, but still so cold) and what we'd been doing in class – anything I could think of except the programme I'd seen.

And her father came in! He asked me at one point what Suzanne used to say about him and I told him that she used to feel the only thing he cared about was whether she would win the next competition. He looked unhappy at that and said, 'In a way she was right.' I thought he was going to cry, but he just sat and held her hand. She groaned a couple of times and muttered. She was uneasy, but smiled a lot in her sleep, so I hung around, waiting for Mr Short to leave.

Which he did at last, and then of course her mother came with the boys. They only stayed a few minutes though – too hyperactive. I didn't have a chance to say anything to Mrs Jenkins.

And at last, just as it was beginning to get dark, she stirred and turned her head a little. She opened her eyes and I think she said, 'know what'. Not 'no' like the negative, 'know' like you know something. And it wasn't a question.

I started to ask what it was she knew, but she drifted off again, happy in her world of dreams. So I left to go to the cinema with Tom and Alison. The film was crap but Kyle was with them, so we had a good laugh sending up Farmville and stuff.

<<<

Chapter 30: secrets

It was evening. Themis found the slaves doing the laundry.

'Come with me,' he whispered to Frog.

'Now?' Frog whispered back. 'I'm trying to get the pigment stains out of your work tunic.'

'Now,' insisted Themis.

He led Frog to the ruined end of the hotel and out onto the roof. The beams were rotting and some of the tiles had fallen in, but they found a strong place and climbed out into the sunset. They sat looking west over the market and the streets of small houses. The Alpheios reflected the fiery corals and golds of the sky, a tangle of gaudy meanders across the flat, black valley floor. They chewed on melon seeds and spat the husks onto the cracked tiles.

'D'you like being a slave, Frog?' asked Themis.

'Never thought about it,' said Frog. 'If your dad hadn't picked me up out of the swamp I wouldn't be anything at all, so … '

'In a way it must be nice not having to make any decisions.'

'I suppose … ' Frog paused, 'but sometimes it's difficult when I know someone is making the wrong decision and I can't do anything about it.' He looked sideways at Themis.

'You have to keep your mouth shut a lot with me, don't you?'

'Only now because of the curse, and your mother being frightened about your accident,' said Frog. 'Before that, I could always tell the truth.'

'I bet that got me into a lot of trouble,' said Themis.

Frog laughed. 'Well, I suppose I got good at telling just part of the truth. When you got punished, you usually punished me later.'

'Did I?' asked Themis. 'Is that how it works?'

'It's only natural, isn't it?' replied Frog.

'Well, now I want you to keep your mouth shut even more. Something has happened and I need your help, but we have to keep it a total secret for the time being.'

They were both looking at the fiery sky. Frog asked, 'You remembered something?'

'No, it's not that – although, yes, I remembered a couple of other things.' Themis shifted his weight on the tiles. 'No. It's about the Olympic Games.'

Frog breathed in and looked sharply at him. Themis carried on gazing at the horizon with its spectacular, golden-edged clouds. He said, 'I saw Judge Iasos in Elis while you were at the farm with Xenon.'

'Ah. I wondered … ' said Frog. 'An important man?'

Themis nodded. 'He's one of the two judges who are organizing the Olympic Games this year. He told me that I qualified for the boxing last autumn in Athens, and he says I shall be able to compete.'

Frog nearly slipped off the roof in surprise. 'He told you that!?'

'Whoever sent him that tablet told him to tell me. But we agreed I wouldn't train for the boxing until he'd got the curse lifted.'

'Lifted!' exclaimed Frog. 'Can he get it lifted?'

'He says he can, but he'll have to send messages to Athens. Anyway, the main thing is that I need to be fitter than I am if I'm going to beat other boxers at the Games.'

Frog grinned with excitement. 'So you're really going to compete?'

'Of course.'

'Your mother will go epileptic!'

'She doesn't need to know until it's over. But I must train, so I'm going to run for longer each day and do stuff in the gym for my arms and chest.'

'Sounds good.'

'But of course no one must know that yet. So I want to set off before you in the mornings and meet you on my way back.'

'That's fine. As long as you don't meet any more bears.'

'True. But I don't want people – '

'You mean Panainos and Phidias?'

'Not just them – everyone. I don't want *anyone* to know we're not running together as usual,' said Themis.

'So we don't mention about you competing to anyone at all?'

'No. No one.'

'That's fine.'

'Are you sure?' Themis looked hard at Frog. 'If you say anything to anyone, it's not only the curse you'll have to deal with.'

'I know that,' said Frog with a wry smile. 'You knocked a boy out cold in the qualifiers. He was older and bigger than you. I'm not going to risk you punching *me*!'

At the first glimmer of dawn, Themis took the road to the east, going up the Alpheios valley to the bridge and beyond. Some thirty stades out, he turned left up a tributary valley. He had never taken this turning with Frog. A river tumbled between rocks towards him. A wide stony track ran beside it. Wheels and feet had left imprints where there was mud.

The birds were waking and the sky lightening. The path forked to the left and Themis took it. He brushed through bushes on both sides of the path. There were short stretches where it was very steep with overgrown steps. In other places it was less steep but rocky.

Gradually the view of the valley below opened out. There was a village and some small buildings among the fields, but he couldn't see the river any more. On the far side of the valley the woods climbed up to the bottom of a steep cliff of light grey rock.

The path got fainter and the bushes smaller as he climbed. He found himself on a shelf under a similar cliff to the one opposite. His muscles were complaining, but there were still signs of a path, so he carried on up some more broken steps and finally came out at the top of the cliff onto a plateau.

Here the bushes were only knee high and the rocky grey tops of the mountain range were bare and clear against the paling sky ahead. He turned and stood still with his back to the peaks, catching his breath and looking at line upon line of grey-blue hills to the south. To his right he thought he could make out a hint of the sea and to his left the sky was glowing with the coming sun. He had time to run on a little further.

The going was almost flat. The path was faint and could have been made by goats. It turned towards a pair of small trees between him and the rising sun. As he approached the trees, he was looking far ahead to see where the path carried on. His foot caught in a root and he stopped to untangle himself.

When he looked up his heart leapt in his chest.

In front of him was a chasm, cut as though with a knife through the plateau. The cliff on the opposite side, which was only five or six paces away across the void, was vertical. *'If I'd been running at full tilt …'* he thought. He lay down to look over the edge. He could hear water running but it was too far down for him to see.

He held onto one of the trees and leaned out. A long way below, a river ran fast and deep between the cliffs. The sound he could hear was from a small fall in its bed to his right. And beyond that, at the end of the ravine, he saw the river disappear.

He could not believe his eyes.

As he went on looking, he made out a step of rock across the gorge under three feet of smooth water. But beyond that, where the bottom of the valley between the cliffs was visible as it wound down towards the Alpheios, there was no river. The valley floor was full of dry, rounded stones until it spread out to the farmland. Where had the river gone?

The tree beside him had what looked like tatters of rope tied round it near the ground. A deep scar circled the trunk above the rope. The tree he was holding onto had a similar scar. On the opposite bank he could see the remains of several ropes hanging into the abyss. This had once been a bridging point, but now the bridge had rotted and the path was almost invisible.

He turned and ran back across the plateau and down the cliff. At a point he reckoned was level with where the river disappeared, he looked for a way down. He wanted to see what happened to it. But the gorge was too steep and thickly overgrown with thorny scrub.

Anyway, the sun was almost up, so he hurried on down. In the lower, agricultural part of the valley, he could run faster. The shadow of the hills to the east suddenly disappeared as the sun rose and its warmth touched him. Frog would be waiting.

Their meeting place was a built-up spring on the outskirts of the village where this valley joined that of the Alpheios. Frog was there, talking to a stout woman who was sitting on a stone bench, spinning.

'Good morning, young man,' she said as he ran up.

'Mistress,' panted Themis, bowing his head.

He stood and watched her spindle rise and fall while his breathing slowed. Frog laid a sweat-cloth round Themis' neck, and then went back to chatting with the woman.

A picture came into Themis' mind of another woman, someone very familiar, sitting spinning on a stone by a sandy river beach. He turned away to the spring and put his cupped hands under the spout. He splashed his face and then drank a little. For a long moment he stood watching the glistening water falling into the basin. In his mind he and another small boy were pushing a very young Frog into the shallow water of a river. They were all laughing, until a sudden look of horror passed across Frog's face under the water.

Themis turned round slowly. 'Do you remember, Frog,' he said, 'a time when we were playing Hellenes and Persians by the Ilissos and we pushed you under the water?'

Frog looked up, his eyes sparkling. 'Of course I do,' he said with a laugh. 'You nearly drowned me and Ligya had to hold me up by my feet to make the water run out of me. The wool from her spindle unwound everywhere.'

'Who was the other boy we were with?' asked Themis, walking over to Frog.

Frog's face changed rapidly from smiling, to understanding, to excitement, and finally to sadness. The woman laughed as she watched it.

'You remembered … no one told you … ' Frog paused and bit his lip. 'He was called Nikitas and he was your brother, born on the same day.'

'My twin,' said Themis, tears starting in his eyes. The woman stopped laughing. 'I remembered him. A clear proper memory.' A wry smile twisted his mouth. 'My mind seems to be coming back to me, one tiny piece at a time, like grains of sand … '

And he suddenly sat down and began to sob.

He did not hear the woman's question and Frog's answer, because his whole body would not stop sobbing. But still there was a quiet part of his mind that was surprised at the strength of this grief. By the time he felt a hand on his shoulder he was gaining control and looked up.

The woman held out a dish of milk curds with honey and walnuts.

'Stop the wailing and get some food into you,' she said kindly.

'Thank you,' he said, wiping his nose on the sweat-cloth. He took the dish and spoon she offered. The honey smelled of pine trees. Saliva flooded into his mouth, and he ate. He offered a couple of spoonfuls to Frog, so the woman reached into her clothes and brought out an extra handful of nuts.

When the dish was empty, Themis handed it back. 'That was very good,' he said with a smile. 'Thank you again.'

'It's nothing,' said the woman, who had gone back to spinning. 'We're used to seeing young men coming through here on their training runs. Most of them look like they need a good meal. But they are usually in groups. Running alone can be dangerous. There are boys stolen every year by the slavers. You'd best stick together.'

Themis took a deep breath and stood up nodding. 'Thank you, mistress. I'll remember that. Now we have to hurry back, but there's something I wanted to ask you about.'

'Go ahead,' she said, her spindle whirling.

'Up at the top of the valley there's a place where the river runs through a gorge,' he said. 'It's a large river there, lots of water.'

'That's right,' she said. 'It's the River Vathonero.'

'So where does all that water go? The rest of the valley is dry.'

'It goes into a cavern under the cliffs,' she said. 'It comes out again lower down, just above the village.'

'So the river I saw near here, where it joins the Alpheios, is the same river as I nearly fell into up there on the plateau?'

'It could have been through Hades and back, as far as I know,' she said. 'But that's what they say.'

Frog turned to Themis. 'They were talking in the market about a village that was trying to get rid of some bears from a cave. They found an enormous river running through the back of it.'

'The mountains are full of surprises,' said the woman.

Themis smiled at her as they turned to go. 'Thank you again, and may the gods be with you,' he said.

Chapter 31: high places

'Where do you think you're going, young Themis?' shouted Panainos, grabbing Themis by the belt as he started up the steps inside the Temple.

'I'm supposed to help with the pulleys up in the ceiling,' said Themis. 'Phidias said I could.'

'And if you fall?' Panainos raised an eyebrow. 'Who is going to write the names and paint the feet on our screens? And how am I going to survive when your mother runs me through with your father's sword?'

'Quick, Uncle! The face is arriving. I have to get up there.' Themis gestured towards the roof. Panainos' hold loosened a little and Themis twisted away from him and ran up the steps. He grabbed a dangling rope and climbed up it behind one of the pulley men. He heaved himself onto a beam and sat swinging his legs. Here, above the worst of the dust, he didn't need a mask.

'Anyone would think you were getting over that bash on the head,' boomed his uncle from below as he dodged to avoid a group of men sprinkling the floor with water. He started slowly up the stairs to the gallery.

Not far from where Themis sat on the beam, men were uncovering the head of the statue. Its dark hair and golden garland gleamed in the diffused sunlight. Only the face and beard were missing now and Themis could see right through to the back of the head where a section had been cut out, like a window in the god's skull.

Inside the neck, Themis could see two workers waiting and watching until their moment came to ease the face into place. A platform across the mighty chest held a group of men laying out tools.

Above and behind the head, the back of the throne was rigged with ropes and beams and protected with padding. The carved figures on its endposts had thick bags over them. Men lay along the beams in the ceiling above it, arranging ropes and pulleys.

'Here, Themistokles!' shouted one of them. 'Catch!' He threw a coil of string to Themis. 'Pull it to you and when you get the rope it's tied to, thread it through the pulley behind you.'

Themis grabbed for the string and almost missed. A huge hand grabbed his belt from behind. 'Steady there,' growled the man he had followed up. 'No feathers on you yet. Give me the string.'

'Thanks,' said Themis.

He had dislodged a fall of dust. Panainos looked up as it drifted towards him. 'Tie him to the beam,' he called to the pulley man, 'and leave him there. Zeus can snack on him at his leisure.' He pulled on his mask.

Shouts echoed round the temple walls. Outside, the rumble of a large wagon stopped as its oxen drew to a halt. Themis lay along the beam and watched a huge parcel, wrapped and crated, being brought in through the doors by a team of ten men. He could hear the stamping of the oxen on the temple ramp as the hubbub inside suddenly stilled.

Phidias strode into the temple and stopped in the middle of the floor, in front of the cloth-covered statue. He turned towards the doors.

'Master Harpist!' he called, and a musician stepped out from behind a column. 'You and your musicians should be up in the gallery. When I make this signal with my hand you will play in the rhythm we agreed.'

'Certainly, Master Phidias,' said the harpist with a nod, and he and his two colleagues ran up the stairs to appear opposite Panainos.

The great bundle was carried into the open space beside Phidias. The slatted casing fell away and a sling of ropes was tied round the wrapped disc inside.

At the signal from Phidias, the musicians began to play. Themis and the men in the roof all shuffled into their places. Men on the floor and in the galleries pulled on their ropes. Curtains of dust drifted down as the wrapped disc rose towards the ceiling, swaying in time to the music. When it was almost touching the beams there, Themis and his team began work. They pulled and stopped as directed by the music. The disc moved towards the gaping front of the head. Men wriggled along beams, moved pulleys and re-laid ropes.

'Steady!' cautioned the team leader.

Themis' legs were wrapped round the beam and his neck and arms ached with the effort of controlling the rope. It slid a little through his hands as the face of Zeus settled on its edge on the platform across the god's chest.

The men there cut away its wrappings. The eyes were still empty, but the brows and cheeks, nose and mouth had all been painted with warm skin colours. Themis eased his shoulders and took up the slack again.

As the eyeless face rose from the platform it reminded him of the moon. Then it swung towards the hairline. Themis saw the men inside hold out their arms to grasp it. There was an audible thump as it fitted into place and he almost fell as the strain on his rope slackened.

A cheer rose throughout the temple. Phidias disappeared under the coverings and his voice could be heard as he climbed up inside the statue, directing the men who were fitting the internal props.

Themis' team began scrambling down the ropes. He arrived beside his uncle in the gallery in a flurry of dust.

'Ah, you're still alive then,' murmured Panainos behind his mask. 'No thanks to your sense of balance, it seems.' He brushed the dust off his protruding stomach and turned to look at the calm, benificent face of the statue. 'There are those who say,' he said thoughtfully, 'that the gods themselves do Phidias' bidding.'

Themis laughed. 'But we know it's just engineering, don't we Uncle?'

Panainos guffawed. 'Engineering, and a certain head for heights,' he said.

>>>

From Bernie's private diary. Tuesday March 30th 2010

When I got to the hospital today, Suzanne's mother was there with Elliot, her younger brother. She was lying on her side, fast asleep, but her teeth were holding her upper lip in that way she has when she's pleased or excited. I whispered to Mrs Jenkins, 'Was she laughing?' and she shrugged and was like 'A bit, but in her sleep.'

I stayed a while. Elliot was quite quiet on his own, so I told Mrs Jackson about the other day when Suzanne looked straight at me and smiled. And she told me the nurses had said Suzanne had been rolling around a lot today, and once or twice had said something about 'careful' in her sleep. And she'd been wincing from the pain of her broken collar-bone.

But she didn't come round while I was there this time.

We're on holiday now, so I'll go in for longer each time. She does seem to be coming out of the vegetable phase at last. I'll take things to read to her. I can't think of anything to tell her now. That programme really scared me. Most people who get hit on the head are never the same again.

<<<

'Over the bridge to the south bank?' Frog asked Themis as they jogged out of Olympia in the early dawn.

'Yup, then on a bit and up the valley to the left. Haven't been up that one yet.' Themis was keeping his pace equal to Frog's for the moment. After climbing for a while, they stopped for a breather under some crags.

'You coming on for a bit?' asked Themis.

Far below them, they could see a small town with a large temple. The river made a silver thread through the shadowy fields in the valley. The high hills lay in crisp layers against the pale yellow dawn.

Not far ahead, the path bent round a steep grey buttress of rock and disappeared.

'You go on,' said Frog breathlessly. 'I'll wait for you by that bush back there.' He gestured over his shoulder.

'I'll turn back when the sun rises,' said Themis.

He ran on. Beyond the buttress, the path was covered in a seeping patch of green, and after that it widened out into a natural balcony. There was a cave in the cliff to his left at the back. A tumble of brightly coloured flowers covered a boulder at its mouth.

Themis stepped carefully through the green slime. The flowers were purple, with great fleshy petals dangling in trusses. He stopped to lift one and was showered with chilly drops of dew. He could hear birds waking. Water dripped inside the cave.

He went in. It was cold and damp and made him shiver. A thin thread of water fell into a small pool in the floor. There were footprints of goats and some kind of large cat in the mud near the mouth of the cave. Ferns grew on the back wall. There was an unpleasant smell, as though something had died there. '*Hmm, better not drink this,*' he thought, and turned back to the light.

Hoofbeats were approaching from the way they had come. Themis hoped Frog was safely out of the way, because the rider seemed to be in a big hurry.

Suddenly a large bay horse leaped round the buttress and skidded in the slime. The rider wore the usual short tunic, but his face was covered by a cloth and his wide-brimmed hat was pulled down and tied in place.

The man turned in his saddle when he saw Themis. His right hand reached back and the thong of a whip flew out and lashed Themis' left arm to his waist. He was jerked towards the edge of the cliff as the horse turned and backed.

'Hey!' Themis shouted, pulling at the whip with his right hand. 'What are you – '

'Where's the other boy?' shouted the man through the mask.

Had Frog managed to hide? Could this be someone Nikanor had hired? From the voice it certainly was not the man himself.

The whip slipped and unwound. The rider swung his arm back again.

Themis turned and ran for the cave, expecting the sting of the thong at any moment.

But it did not come. Through the flowers, Themis watched pebbles flying through the air at the man on the horse.

One hit the horse near its eye, making it dance sideways and slide on the slime near the cliff edge. The man almost came off. He was looking around wildly, arm up to protect his covered face from the stones. And as soon as the horse had a firm footing, it set off without its master's command, along the path beyond the cave. The man swore at it as they disappeared round the next buttress.

Themis turned and ran back the way he'd come. Frog jumped out from behind a rock and they dashed back along the path under the cliffs and down into the valley. When they came to a thick copse, they stopped among brambles and convolvulus.

'Anyone you know?' asked Frog, bent double to catch his breath.

'Couldn't see his face. Didn't know the horse,' said Themis, hands on thighs. 'Thanks, by the way.'

'Slave catcher?' suggested Frog.

'He knew there were two of us.' Themis thought for a moment. 'But if he wanted to catch us and sell us, surely it would have been easier to do that down on the main road.'

'Too many people.'

'Hmm. Not once we were among the fields. No, I think he may have been hired by Nikanor. And I think he was trying to pull me with his whip so that I fell off the cliff.'

'Not quite the loving uncle, then,' said Frog.

They listened intently and heard cicadas starting up, and doves, and far away female voices calling to each other in the fields. But no hoofbeats. Themis began to shake.

'We'd better get back,' he said, and ran on.

Back in Olympia, Gulkishar led Themis upstairs and out onto a terrace partly shaded by vines.

'There you are,' said Phidias. 'Thank you, Gulkishar.' He took Themis' arm and led him into the sunlight. 'Come here where I can see you.'

'I'm fine, Uncle. Really.' The shaking had stopped and Themis was beginning to be angry with himself for being so soft.

'Is this where the whip caught your arm?'

'Yes, but it's nothing.' Themis rubbed a hand over the red wheal.

'Thank the gods you weren't alone.' Phidias stepped back. 'The guards know what to look for, so we should catch him soon.' He strode across the vine-roofed terrace to stare out at the view of the Alpheios valley, his fists on the balustrade.

'Your message said someone from Athens wanted to see me,' said Themis.

'Yes. She's on her way here.' Phidias noticed Themis' gasp as he turned. 'No,' he added. 'It's not your mother.'

'But I have a *tablet* from your mother,' said a quiet voice. Asterodia had appeared silently and now laid the tablet on a small table.

Themis bowed his head, hiding his disappointment that it was not Xenovia. 'Sacred Lady,' he said to his feet, 'what has brought you – ?'

'Our revered Asterodia has business with the priestesses of Hera in the Altis,' said Phidias.

'I am also concerned about you, young Themistokles,' said Asterodia, taking Themis' hands in hers. He looked up and she held his gaze, probing his soul.

'*She knows what the judge told me,*' thought Themis. He forced himself not to flinch, to go on looking at those strange hazel eyes with the vivid green rings.

At last she said, 'The damage is less. You are more yourself. It is true that you are managing without me.' She raised her voice, 'Come, Phidias. Let us sit in the shade while you tell me your news.' She sat in a chair by a low table under the vine, inviting Themis to sit on a stool near her.

'Oh, the statue is so nearly finished it makes me itch,' laughed the

Master Sculptor, his dark eyes glowing. 'The Nike is a marvel and will be put in place tomorrow.' He paced out into the sun and turned to them. 'Ach, I know I am swollen with pride, but it will be the most perfect statue ever seen,' and he threw his arms out and his head back.

Asterodia smiled and turned to Themis. 'And what is *your* work on this masterpiece?' she asked, as Phidias stretched out on the couch by the shady wall.

'I helped prepare and paint the screens round the seat of the throne,' Themis answered. 'I did part of the lettering to name the figures and painted some of their feet and garments and the rocks and trees.'

Her eyes teased him. 'So you are content, learning to paint?'

Themis looked at her steadily. 'Yes, Sacred Lady, although there are many other challenges I hope to take up as well.'

Phidias looked sharply at them, but Asterodia waved him to silence. 'And do you still dream?' she asked Themis.

'Sometimes I still see strange things in my dreams, but I have also had some real memories!'

Oddly, Asterodia did not ask about his memories. Instead, she looked at him seriously and said 'Do you ever see my daughter in your dreams?'

Themis felt a blush rising up from his belly.

'Xenovia?' exclaimed Phidias. 'Why would he see her?'

Asterodia paused. 'I feel you have a special bond with her, Themis.'

The blush reached Themis' face. His voice cracked. 'I … I see her as very beautiful. I would like to … make a statue – '

'I know little of her movements, but she did tell me she will visit Olympia for the Games, so you may see her then,' said Asterodia.

'I may not be … ' Themis shook his head in confusion. Did they *both* know he knew about the Games? Had they forgotten the curse?

The lines in Asterodia's face seemed to deepen. 'It has always been Xenovia's misfortune to be beautiful, has it not, Phidias?'

'Her face may be beautiful,' replied Phidias, 'but no soul is as lovely as yours, Sacred Lady.'

Asterodia turned back to Themis. 'What *do* you dream of, young Themis? Men on horses with whips?'

'It is strange,' said Themis carefully, 'that real life has become more dangerous, while my dreams are becoming less frightening. There is one place, with walls of pale fabric, that I sometimes see very clearly … '

Phidias leapt up. 'Dear Lady, I must leave you. I have to choose a team of men and women to take care of the statue after its dedication, and they are waiting for me by the temple.'

Asterodia stood. 'I too must go now,' she said. 'Thank you, Master Phidias,' she added with a formal bow as he rushed off with a wave.

At the door into the house she turned. 'Give my greetings to your Uncle Panainos, Themis. He is doing a difficult job well. Perhaps you should do your training closer to the town after today. And don't forget to read your mother's tablet.'

Themis opened the tablet sitting on his bed. His mother's handwriting was irregular and large. 'Soon Diodotos will leave to join the army,' it read. 'He will be in danger every day. Make sure you stay out of harm's way yourself, and come home soon. The statue must be finished by now. I expect you before the solstice. Work hard, study well, and stay alive!'

'*Thank the gods she doesn't know what I'm planning,*' he thought. 'But then,' he said to himself, 'she is right. If anything happens to Diodotos, I'll have to take over. If it is Nikanor who is trying to get rid of him as well as me, it would be easier to arrange an accident in the army.'

He stood up and paced the room. 'But that's ridiculous. Surely Nikanor is not that ruthless. We're his relatives, after all. It must be someone else after me. But who?' He sat down again and tried to think.

Was the attack on the cliff anything to do with his being a contestant in the games, perhaps paid for by the family of an opponent? Or was it connected with Zeus and his being 'ready'? At that his body went cold.

'Whatever it is,' he said to himself, jumping up, 'I have to do as Father wanted, not what Mama thinks is best. When I come home with a victor's wreath she'll be proud as a peacock.'

He put the tablet in his box under the bed and ran the short way to the gymnasium. Only there could he forget the questions in his mind.

>>>

Chapter 32: reprieve

From Bernie's private diary. Good Friday April 2nd 2010

Suzanne spoke to me today, properly!! When I got there, she was awake and they'd taken away the heart monitor thing. There are great black shadows under her eyes, like someone's punched her. But at least they were open and she was looking around.

'Hi,' I say as I sit down and grab her good hand. All very cool, but my heart's going bezerk.

She looks at me – intense, careful. Then she squeezes her eyes shut and opens them again. She looks scared, hunted.

'Suzanne,' I say, and she kind of shivers all over. And that makes her notice her arm is still bound up.

'Hurt,' she says. A real word that's relevant to here and now!

'You had an accident,' I say. 'Your collarbone broke.'

'Meerto?' she says, looking at me as if I was some kind of vampire.

'Er … I'm Bernie,' I say.

'Mama?'

'Your mum will be in later,' I say.

'Sick,' she says, looking down at herself.

'Yes.'

She looks all round. 'Hospital?'

'Yes.'

'Not Themis?'

'Not that I know of,' I say.

She lifts the sheet and looks under it. Then 'No willie?' she says.

I take a breath. 'No. Just a catheter.'

She looks me in the eye. 'Tell!' she demands, looking frightened but determined.

'We were on the school trip,' I say, 'in Athens. That's where you got hurt.'

'Atheenai?' she says.

So I start on about the hotel and the museum and I try to remember all the things they told us about that day on the Akropolis. But she only lasts about two minutes before her eyes glaze over and she's asleep again.

And I go out and call Laila and I dance about a bit! Then we agree to get together and try and remember everything about that trip so we can tell Suzanne if she asks again. She really is on her way back to us this time. Yeah!!!!!

<<<

'Where's Panainos?' asked Tilemachos as he and Themis ran up the stairs to the temple gallery. 'He should be here for the attaching of Nike.'

'He's changed the design of his picture of Prometheus,' answered Themis, 'so he's working on that.'

'You not on the ropes today?'

'No. This is too specialised a manoeuvre, they said.' Themis looked down from the gallery.

The only part of Zeus that was visible was his right arm, its elbow resting on the arm of his throne, the hand open, palm up. Above it, two men were waiting to step onto the hand from a tall scaffold.

This was the hand that Themis had sat on in his dream of Zeus.

'What's wrong?' asked Tilemachos, when he saw the expression on Themis' face. 'It's not going to come up and punch you, you know.'

Themis took a deep breath and turned to him. 'No. Of course he won't. He's … it's just a statue.'

'Not quite the real live god of your dreams?' Tilemachos taunted.

'Not quite,' Themis said evenly.

The palm of the god's hand had two square holes cut in it, but otherwise it and the fingers all had a skin of ivory, painted pale on the palm and tanned on the back – exactly as it had been in the dream. The Nike rose up to the ceiling in stages to the rhythm of the music, her cocoon of soft cloths shedding dust. It was almost as if she were swaying and dancing into position under her wrappings.

The two men on the scaffold guided her down onto the great palm. She was taller than they were. They slotted the projections on the soles of her feet into the two square holes and began to unwind her cloths.

Phidias' voice carried up from below. 'No, leave her wrapped up for now. Her wings will be ready tomorrow.'

Themis left Tilemachos and ran down the stairs. At the threshold of the temple, he turned and looked back at the statue in its shrouds. 'It's just a kind of building,' he insisted to himself. 'It's definitely not alive.'

As he turned to leave, he almost ran into Phidias, who was also standing, gazing upwards.

'Not long now,' said Phidias, his voice trembling with excitement.

'And there'll be a ceremony?' asked Themis as they took off their masks.

'Yes, of course,' replied Phidias. 'The Elians are putting on a feast and poetry and drama competitions with music and dancing and so on. They are planning it all for seven days from now. Haven't you noticed the crowds of tourists arriving?'

'No. I don't go into the town much.'

'Working too hard?' asked Phidias with a smile.

'And trying to stay fit,' said Themis.

'Not running on any more isolated paths, I hope?'

'Not alone,' said Themis. 'And they haven't found the whip man?'

'They'll summon you as a witness if they catch him. Have you written to your mother? Asterodia can take a message back with her, you know.'

Themis shook his head. 'I'm trying to think what to write. Shall I just say I'm staying on here until Zeus decides I'm "ready"?'

'Are you sure,' asked Phidias thoughtfully, 'that Zeus is going to decide that?'

'That's what it means, isn't it?' said Themis. 'He'll decide and call me and … who knows what he'll do to me then?' To Themis' surprise and shame, his voice wobbled.

'I'm not sure that that's what your dream meant,' said Phidias seriously. He led Themis out and down the steps by the ramp. He sat down on a stone bench warmed by the sun and gestured to Themis to sit beside him. 'You told us that night that Zeus had said to you, "Come again when you are ready".'

'Yes, that's what he said,' answered Themis, gritting his teeth against the wobble.

'Well, to me,' said Phidias, 'that seems to put the onus on *you*, to decide when you are ready.'

'What do you mean?'

'He didn't say "come again when I am ready" or "when I call you." He said "when *you* are ready".'

'That's right.'

'So I think he will wait until you decide you want to … communicate with him yourself.'

'You mean … until I need his help?' Themis did not dare believe this.

'Maybe that, or maybe until you have fully recovered from your fall and want to give thanks. How are you feeling these days?'

'I still have headaches and dizzy moments now and again. And I dream, but then everyone does.' Themis turned to Phidias excitedly. 'But I *have* started remembering things, Uncle. I remembered my twin, Nikitas, the other day. And I saw my father with me at a ceremony of thanks on Mount Hymetos near Athens.'

Phidias was very still. 'Did you remember what the thanks were for?' he asked.

Themis hesitated. 'Er … That didn't come into the memory.'

Phidias looked into his eyes for a moment and then sprang to his feet. 'Well, I don't think you should be afraid of what Zeus wants with you,' he said as he set off on the path round the temple. 'You can ask him what it is when you feel ready. Meanwhile, I think I shall write to your mother as well. You've worked hard here and you are showing promise and I would like you to be able to stay on, even if Panainos leaves.' He looked sideways at his nephew. 'Would that suit you?'

'Suit me?!' exclaimed Themis. 'It's … my greatest ambition.'

'Good. I shall ask her to agree to that. And I'll have a guard run with you in the mornings.' Themis was almost running now to keep up. 'So you don't have to be in a hurry to keep your appointment with Zeus. We'll start you with lessons in casting bronze. Then we can tell your mother truthfully that you are fully occupied and learning fast.'

Phidias stopped suddenly at the corner of the Temple and turned to his nephew. There was a twinkle in his dark eyes. 'Is that a good arrangement?'

'That would be perfect.' Themis was breathless with delight. 'Just perfect. Thank you, Uncle. But … '

'What is it?'

'Are you sure I deserve all … that?'

'Deserve, young Themis? Of course you deserve it. I promised your mother, and anyway, you are important to me.'

'Why, Uncle Phidias? Why am I important?'

Phidias' eyes were so serious that Themis took a step backwards. 'One day you will understand,' murmured Phidias. Then he smiled and said 'I have no son of my own, you see, just the girls. So you are very important to both your mother and me. Don't let us down!'

'Of course not, Uncle,' Themis answered, still confused. He took a breath to ask another question.

'Good.' Phidias said with a nod and a smile, and walked swiftly away.

Themis stood watching him go. He felt a shiver down his back and turned to see if he was being watched. There was no one behind him, but, high in the pediment of the temple, Apollo's still face shone above the battling stone bodies around him. He seemed to be looking down on Themis with his calm, painted eyes. Themis smiled, sending up a silent prayer of thanks in case either he or Zeus was listening.

Later that day, he found himself kneeling in the workshop, his forehead pressed to the floor.

'You did it again.' Tilemachos' snide voice came from above.

Themis got to his feet. 'Did what again?' he asked with a shrug, little points of light blossoming behind his eyes.

'Went … somewhere else.'

Themis bent back to his work clearing out a cupboard as the little lights faded. 'It's nothing.' He gathered up some scraps of tattered papyrus. 'These will be for the fire.' He took them outside to the yard with Tilemachos close behind him.

'What happens to you?' Tilemachos asked with genuine curiosity as Themis put the scraps into the fire trough.

'It doesn't matter,' he insisted.

Tilemachos took hold of Themis' shoulders quite gently and turned him to look in his face. 'You said a name. You said "Straton". Twice. So I'm interested.'

Themis' skin prickled. He looked into Tilemachos' eyes. They were dark grey, like stones under water. He said, 'Did I? That's strange. Why would you be interested in that?'

'Because you go to the same gymnasium in Athens where Straton, son of Ypatos, goes. And his mother is my father's cousin.' Themis stepped sharply back from Tilemachos who went on, 'and I heard, about a year ago, that Straton came back from exercising with a huge bruise on his face and a temper as hot as the Methana volcano.'

'You did?' prompted Themis warily. The hairs on his arms had risen. In his few moments "away" this time, he had remembered sitting in the sand of the boxing pit at the gymnasium in Athens after being knocked down by Straton.

'Yes,' said Tilemachos. 'That's what you were remembering, isn't it? I heard that Straton had knocked a boy down and was crowing about it when the boy tapped him on the shoulder and gave him a left to the jaw. That was you, wasn't it?'

Tilemachos' manner was almost respectful. Themis said, 'I thought he was dead, he fell so fast. But he was fine. They threw water on him and he came round spluttering and swearing.' He looked at Tilemachos. 'I didn't cheat, or kick him when he was down.'

'And then he threatened you, didn't he?' said Telelmachos.

'Yes,' said Themis with a sudden grin. 'He said he would never let me forget that.'

'Typical!'

'And I answered that I didn't want to forget it,' said Themis, looking Tilemachos straight in the eyes.

Tilemachos snorted. 'Huh! He tried to get all his brothers and cousins to give "the little monster" a good beating in the street. But the trainer said if he heard he'd been set on, they'd all get a whipping and be suspended.'

Themis raised an eyebrow. 'Really? And did you all make a plan to take me down?'

Tilemachos shook his head. 'Nah. I had more important things to do. It was just some kids in a spat at the gym.'

'How do you know it was me that hit Straton, then?'

'Just now, you said something like, "That'll teach you, Straton" to the floor. And that reminded me where I'd heard your name before.' Tilemachos suddenly stopped talking.

He had finally remembered the curse. Themis kept the disappointment out of his voice as he said, 'So you didn't know me then?'

Tilemachos lifted his eyebrows and shook his head slightly. 'No. And you're not doing that kind of training any more, so I hadn't connected you until I heard you mumbling just now.'

Themis looked hard at Tilemachos and said, 'So Straton didn't send you after me to … punish me?'

"Course not!' Tilemachos laughed. 'I don't do Straton's bidding. And he was too caught up in his erotic dreams of some girl last time I saw him, to worry about you.'

'Yeah,' said Themis. 'So he was.'

>>>

From Bernie's private diary. Easter Saturday April 3rd 2010

I posted on my blog that Suzanne spoke yesterday. Everyone but Laila's away. She called to say could she come with me, so we went this afternoon. She's still talking about studying medicine and she said she wanted to see for herself how Suzanne is getting on.

So we sit there with Suzanne asleep and we chat about drama club. They'll be casting The Taming of the Shrew the week after the Easter holidays, so we go through the list of boys and discuss who could play Petruchio. I say something about Tom, when Suzanne's voice says, 'Tom can't act.'

Total shock!

Laila and I look at each other and then at Suzanne, whose eyes are open and she's looking at us as if we're stupid.

All I want to do is jump up and down and hug her to bits. But Laila puts her hand on my arm to keep me quiet, and says to Suzanne, 'I thought he'd be quite good. He's grown a lot lately and his voice has gone deeper.'

Suzanne doesn't answer. She just looks around for a bit. Then she says, 'This real?'

I burst out laughing. 'D'you want to pinch me?' I ask.

'Pinch,' she says. 'Pinch. Punch. Punch not allowed.'

Laila and I are lost.

Suzanne says 'You're Laila.'

'That's right,' says Laila.

'And you're … not frog … Bernie!'

'No,' I say. 'I'm not a frog.' Very cool.

'Frog helps,' says Suzanne.

I don't know what to say to that, but Laila says, 'With what?'

Suzanne looks at her and says, 'Everything!' as if it's obvious. Then, 'Well, nearly everything.' And there's a naughty expression on her face, like a two-year-old. I've never seen her look like that before.

'What are you on about?' I ask, a bit sharp.

She looks like she's suddenly remembered something. 'School trip,' she says. 'Akropolis all fucked up.'

Laila smiles. 'Ruined, yes. We spent a morning up there hearing all about it. Remember?'

'Remember … ' Suzanne says, like she's not sure what that means.

We start telling her, taking turns, and she suddenly goes to sleep, like a switch going off.

'Are they giving her something that makes her sleep?' asks Laila.

I say I don't know, so she goes and asks the nurse.

They are.

<<<

Chapter 33: last task

Frog plunged Themis' running tunic into the washing sink. 'They are saying the statue is ready,' he said.

'The dedication is tomorrow,' said Themis, tying the red band round his clean, damp hair. 'Today is clean-up day. I have to supervise a group of sweepers cleaning out the cellar under the floor of the Temple.' He strapped a small but heavy leather pouch round his waist.

Phidias had given it to him with a solemn 'Guard it with you life' the night before. They had hidden it in an empty oil jar.

'Yuch!' laughed Frog. 'Spiders, snakes, rats and toads. Why you?'

'Because I'm the shortest, so Phidias said. But I think it's so I miss the unveiling in case I have a fit or something.' He grabbed two honey-and-walnut buns and set off.

His cleaners were in the Altis preparing their brooms, cloths, basins and torches. Themis showed them where the side door into the basement space was hidden.

'The Master said you'd have the key,' said Herakles, the team leader, a wizened little man with a twisted foot.

'It's here, Herakles,' said Themis as he pulled it out of the pouch. 'You light some torches and I'll get the door open.'

The thick oak door was very low. When they got inside, Themis saw that a normal adult would not have been able to stand up. The smell was choking: dust, damp and various rotting things.

There were three rooms, all quite small. In one, a large locked chest with some planks on its lid squatted in one corner. The second room was empty except for an obvious rat-run through the dirt on the floor. But the third was under a trapdoor from the huge chamber above, where the statue sat. Below the trapdoor, a great pile of rubbish had accumulated: pieces of cloth and stone, bones, broken pots and tools. When the light of the torch fell on the heap a great scuffling arose as the rats scattered.

'We'll need a lot of baskets to deal with that lot,' said Herakles.

'There's a stack by the back of the temple,' said Themis. 'Do you need anything else?'

'Just a polecat or a python to clear the rats,' smiled Herakles, his three remaining teeth shining in the gloom. They could hear thumps and music from above. 'You get along upstairs. We'll be finished before the main ceremony begins.'

'I'll come back and check when it's over,' said Themis. He left the stench and thick darkness with relief.

On the temple ramp he met Agorakritos, and they stood at the tall, bronze-studded doors together. The noise and dust were appalling. They tied their masks round their faces and plunged into a boiling fog.

A musician was playing a lyre and a drummer was beating out a strong rhythm in the echoing gallery above. They ran up to join them.

Up there the air was a little clearer. They could see that the top of the statue had been completely uncovered. The three Graces and the three Seasons along the back of the throne had their heads turned towards Zeus' olive-crowned curls.

His eyes were now in place – and they were glowing!

Light shone from the amber irises, gilding the dust in the air and bringing the huge face to life.

And the god was looking straight at Themis! He was about to throw off his cloak and rise, so that he could come over for a chat.

'He'll lift the roof off the temple if he stands up,' said Agorakritos, breaking the spell.

Themis shook himself, then grinned. 'And all those little men will slip off him onto the floor.'

The eagle they'd seen in pieces in the workshop was descending in its wrappings from the ceiling to its place on the top of the glittering staff in the god's left hand, its talons grasping the shining treelike twigs and blooms. *'Those weren't there in my vision,'* thought Themis.

As soon as the eagle had been secured there, its covers were removed. The rubies that were its eyes and the golden filigree of its feathers gleamed in the sunlight diffused through the nearby roof.

On the god's other hand, the Nike was now free of her protection. She wore a golden robe and her white and gold wings spread high above her head. She was holding up her pale arms and looking straight at Zeus' face. A man on a scaffold was placing a wreath of golden olive leaves and purple ribbons between her outstretched hands.

At a shout from Phidias and a change in the rhythm of the music, more coverings came loose and slowly slid to the floor. A row of slaves with buckets advanced from the main door, spraying water in a fine mist from their mouths to tame the dust. Themis could now make out Zeus' cloak lying across his lap in gigantic golden folds. It was chased and engraved with animals and flowers and glistened with gems – more ornate than in his dream, and presumably colder and harder.

The arms of the throne appeared as the covers slid down, revealing sphinxes, nymphs and heroes in gold on a ground of ebony. Then the main crossbeam that would be in front of Panainos' blue screens came into sight, with its eight golden figures shining against the black wood.

The dust was clearing to show the god's ivory feet in their golden, decorated sandals. They rested on the footstool, which was richly ornamented with more golden figures and two large lions, one at each end, with black manes and white teeth. Gooseflesh ran over Themis' skin. He looked up again at the god's shining eyes. *'It's just a building,'* he silently reminded himself.

As the coverings finally fell to the floor and the dust began to clear, a sigh went up from the scores of workers – and then cheer after cheer.

The musicians and singers began a paean of praise to the Father of the Immortal Gods – and his mighty sculptors! Agorakritos and Themis joined faceless workers dancing in circles, trying to sing and laugh and congratulate each other all at once. The water slaves tried to continue their work but were swept into the melee.

At last everyone quietened down and unmasked. The last of the dust settled round their feet. A drum-roll thundered from the gallery.

Phidias stood at the stone balustrade, mask in hand. 'This is a great moment,' he called in his musical voice. 'It is the fruit of fifteen years of my thoughts, plans and sweat. Some of you have worked with me since the beginning, but all of us who have helped to create this likeness of the mightiest god on earth, must congratulate ourselves on the largest and most precious statue ever made. Be proud! Be happy! And let's work hard now to prepare our god for his great day tomorrow. Everyone to their cleaning stations!'

The music began again, and men on ropes and swings at the top of the statue started to mop and sweep the back of the throne. Dust fell in trickles as they dislodged it. The huge covers were dragged along the floor, out of the doors and down the steps. Men crawled like insects over the god, his ornate throne and footstool, and the great decorated supporting base, creating lustre where there had been grime.

Phidias came over to Themis and Agorakritos.

'How are your sweepers in the cellar?' he asked Themis.

'They started well. I'll go and check.'

'I've sent someone to get Panainos,' Phidias went on. 'I need him to come and direct the placing of the screens.'

'Will that be now?' asked Themis.

'Later. As soon as the dust has been dealt with. Will your team be able to help up here this afternoon?'

'I'll bring them up when the basement is clean,' Themis said. 'They're impatient to see the finished statue.'

'The almost-finished statue,' Phidias corrected solemnly. Flinging up his arms towards it, he cried out, 'I give you Zeus, the Immortal Father, my greatest achievement. It will outlive us all by hundreds of years, a wonder beyond imagining.'

The god's eyes flickered.

>>>

From Bernie's private diary. Easter Monday April 5th 2010

When I got there today, Suzanne was in a room by herself, sitting up in bed and eating dry bread with her good hand! Two nurses had finished making her bed and were watching her enjoying it. She looked at me and said, 'Bernie. Here.' And she offered me a piece.

One nurse looked at me and nodded. 'Hi,' I said, and took it. I suppose if you haven't had anything in your mouth for seven weeks, even dry bread must taste good.

The nurses leave and there we are, eating dry bread as if it's chocolate gateau, natural as can be. But the conversation is really weird and goes something like this:

Suzanne says, 'I am themis.'

I say, 'You're my best friend,' quietly, matter of fact, like the website said.

'Yes. I know. Also themis.'

'What's themis?' I ask, forgetting about not asking questions.

'Boy.' She munches a bit. 'Drawing boy. Boxing boy.'

'Themis is a boy?' I ask.

She looks at me like I'm a Martian or something. ''Course. Strong boy.'

They say to keep talking whatever. So I ask, 'Does he have parents, this boy?'

'Dad's dead.' And tears run out of her eyes as though a tap has turned on.

By now I'm seriously wishing I hadn't come on my own, but Mrs Jackson comes in, right on cue. She doesn't seem fazed by the tears.

'Hello, Moomin,' she says and kisses Suzanne's dribbly cheek. Then she wipes it with a tissue.

Suzanne looks at me and says, 'Lovely Mum. Nicer than …,' and she puts her good hand over her mouth like a naughty child.

Mrs J laughs. 'I brought your iPod.' She gets it out of her bag.

'Will they let her?' I ask.

'Nurse said they have to lock it up during visiting hours.'

'No,' I say. 'I mean she could strangle herself with the earphone cord.'

'She has to use the dock, see?' and she's brought the dock and charger. 'She does love her dance music. And it's good she's in a room by herself,' she says, plugging it all in. 'Won't disturb anyone.'

She sits down and holds Suzanne's hand.

I ask, 'Do you know anything about this Themis?'

Mrs J says, 'Psychologists say people recovering like this can go through a second childhood, and many children have make-believe friends. That's who Themis is, isn't it, Suzanne? Your invisible friend.'

I say, 'But she says she is – '

Suzanne looks hunted and suddenly says, 'Themis comes when I'm alone.'

Mrs J nods. I look hard at Suzanne and she looks back even harder. Then she smiles and says, 'I'm mental.'

'No!' shouts Mrs J.

'Maybe,' I say. I can't pretend.

Mrs J goes on, ignoring me. 'You're only just beginning to get better. Things in your head need time to straighten out.'

I get up to go. 'Four days ago,' I say, 'you were in a coma. Now you can speak and know who you are and who we are.' I laugh. 'If that's mental,' I say, 'then you're mental.'

Suzanne laughs too, and Mrs J smiles.

I leave.

I've been doing some research, and so has Laila. There are thousands of ways a bash on the head can mess up people's brains, and most of them get a lot better over time, though some don't recover completely, and a few not at all, like that programme said.

Maybe Mrs J is right about the make-believe friend, but Suzanne did say, 'I am Themis,' to me. We'll just have to wait and see. Now Suzanne's got her own room, we can show her stuff that's on the internet. We weren't allowed to bring a laptop into the main ward.

<<<

The last screen was being manoeuvred into place. The dust had almost gone, although there was still a bright haze in the air and a gritty feeling in Themis' eyes.

Panainos stood on the base of the statue beside the bottom of the god's gleaming staff. High above, its golden stem seemed to burst into life, where the silver, gold and copper twigs and flowers sprang from it.

Panainos was talking to the men under the throne who were trying to line up the corners of the final screen-frame with the throne-leg, to close the structural secrets of the god's chair away from worshippers' eyes.

'Come and help here,' he called, tearing off his dust mask. 'For some reason it doesn't fit exactly.'

Themis and Tilemachos ran round the back and up the steps onto the dais that supported the throne. One of the two men inside called,

'We can't do this from in here. We need a third man out there. It just won't fit in the slot.'

'You'd better come on out, then,' called Panainos. He turned to Themis and said, 'The door at the back doesn't open yet and the access with ladders is really narrow. You're the smallest, so you go inside and tell us which way to move the frame. With Tilemachos, there'll be three strong men out here. Surely that will be enough to lift it into the groove.'

The men moved the screen-frame so they could get out and Themis could get in. He looked up at the wooden scaffold under the statue's throne. There was a network of narrow ladders leading to all the levels inside. One led up to the seat and a small gap. From there, another led down outside the screen, between Zeus' knees to his feet. That would be the only way out once everything was in place and until the door at the back was cut out.

Themis turned to the job in hand. The men were moving the last frame into place. Only the fingers of six hands were visible along its bottom edge. It approached the problem corner and came to a stop, leaving a tiny gap where light bled in. Panainos' voice counted, 'One, two, three, drop it!' The fingers all disappeared, and the screen fell a short way to rest crookedly against the leg of the throne.

Except for one lamp, Themis was now in darkness. He lifted the lamp down from its peg and went over to the corner. The screen-frame was less than a finger's width too long to fit into its allotted groove.

'Can you pass me a file through the gap,' he called. 'It needs a tiny bit shaving off.'

A file came sliding through the narrow gap. 'You'll have to lift while I file,' he called. He saw the fingers re-appear under the screen-frame and the whole thing lifted up a hand's breadth. While he filed he could hear oaths and prayers from the men. He worked as fast as he could. At last he estimated that the corner should fit.

'Try it now!' he called.

Again he heard, 'One, two, three, drop it!' and the screen in its heavy frame dropped sweetly into the groove.

The men outside congratulated each other loudly and Panainos called, 'Well done, Themis!' Themis had seen a broom and dust dish in a corner. He went to get them to deal with the little pile of shavings he'd made.

As he tidied up, he heard new and louder voices in the Temple. He put the dust dish and broom down near where the door would be in the back screen. It would be cut through and hinged next day. There were still quite a few such invisible details to be finished off.

He came back to the front and began to climb the ladder.

He recognised the High Priest's voice saying, 'It is an honour, Sacred Lady, an honour. We are all amazed at the size and the quality of the crafts the statue enjoys. We pray that Zeus himself will be impressed with his likeness.'

'It is indeed magnificent,' replied a voice that made Themis blush all over and brought his heart to his throat. 'And to think that no one except those who have worked on it has yet seen it,' said Xenovia.

Chapter 34: gone

Panainos' 'special' voice came from further away. 'You are the first, dear lady. Zeus could not wish for a more beautiful and accomplished first visitor.'

The voices moved round to the side. Themis wanted to rush out and show Xenovia what he had done on the screens, and of course, if he found the courage, to ask her to sit for him to draw her.

'*But not in front of the High Priest,*' he thought. So he stayed where he was, waiting for them to leave.

'There is something I have to discuss with His Holiness,' came Xenovia's voice clearly as they returned towards the front.

'We hope to see more of you during your visit to Olympia,' said Panainos. And there were receding sounds of agreement as he and Agorakritos left. '*They've forgotten about me,*' Themis thought.

'Your Holiness,' said Xenovia, now businesslike. 'As you know, I am on my way to visit my uncle Thukydides at his estate near Three Rivers. I am only in Olympia for this night and part of tomorrow.'

'Your message made this clear, Sacred Lady. Is there something you need from me?'

'I wish to spend some time in the Temple. I am preparing to make an important offering to the Father of the Gods, and would like to pray for guidance as to what that should be.'

'You wish to be alone for this?'

'If you please.'

'I can arrange that,' said the High Priest's voice, rich with self-importance. 'It would need to be during the hour after sunset, if that is suitable for you.'

'It is the convenience of the Temple, not mine, that we must take into account,' said Xenovia.

'That is settled, then.' Themis could imagine the High Priest rubbing his hands together at the thought of the 'offering'.

Their voices faded as they walked away. They must have been at the door when the High Priest called out to the Temple servants still working. 'Make sure all is finished by sunset. The door will be closed then and the guards will come on duty.'

Voices answered from various corners of the Temple, and then there was quiet.

Themis climbed down from his ladder and sat on the ground to think.

'The only way I'll get to be alone with Xenovia is to stay here and speak to her when she comes back,' he thought. *'Then I can leave her to her prayers.'*

'And what exactly do you think you are going to say to her?' he asked himself.

He thought for a moment. *'I'll just show her what I've done on the screens. And I could ask her how I will know I am "ready" for Zeus, because of something that happens or something I dream?'*

'But she's far too important to be interested in that … ' he told himself.

'And yet there is no one else I can ask about such things. The High Priest hates me and I don't know any of the other priests.'

He stood up and stretched. 'Admit it to yourself,' he whispered. 'What you really want is to draw her and be near her and even to touch her if she would let you.'

Another part of his mind was shocked. *'Of course I can't touch her,'* he remonstrated. *'She's not my mother.'*

He paced silently back and forth. 'Well, the only way you can be with her, is to have intelligent questions to ask,' he decided. 'So you'd better make yourself comfortable. It's a while till sunset.'

He suddenly thought that Panainos might come looking for him. What would he say if he did? *'That I was afraid that the High Priest was around.'*

And so Themis hung his lamp on the ladder and sat comfortably in a corner to wait. He began to plan the details of the statue of Xenovia. She would be Penelope at the moment when she realised the man standing in front of her was her long lost and much beloved Odysseus …

He was woken by the clang of the great doors as they shut, and had a moment of panic.

Then the High Priest's voice came from close by. 'Have you everything you need, Sacred Lady?'

'This is very good of you, Your Holiness,' said Xenovia. 'I am quite comfortable, thank you. Except – I did want to ask you whether there has been any evidence of the god having accepted his new likeness yet?'

'Not as far as I can tell,' said the High Priest. 'We have had no earthquakes or storms, and there were no clouds today or reactions from local wild animals or birds to show that he even knows it is finished.'

Themis could hear that the High Priest was going towards the doors so he began to climb the ladder.

'Well, perhaps the remaining details that Phidias was just telling me about, are preventing him from acknowledging it yet,' said Xenovia.

'Possibly. We will pray for a sign tomorrow, of course. But the Father of the Gods must be pre-occupied by the possibility of war between Sparta and Athens. He may not have time for our small ceremony.'

'Surely not "small", Your Holiness.' Themis could hear the smile in Xenovia's voice.

'I mean small in relation to our whole world that Zeus has to guide and govern,' said the High Priest huffily.

There was a short pause. 'Your Holiness,' Xenovia said, 'there is something else I would greatly value your opinion about.'

'Please … ' said the High Priest, a little mollified.

'I want to ask you about a family friend.'

'By all means.'

'He is an apprentice with Panainos the painter. His name is Themistokles.'

Themis nearly fell off the ladder.

'Ah!' said the High Priest briskly. 'The boy with the vision.' His voice was sour with irony.

'Yes, he had a vision – it seems,' said Xenovia.

'*She was there!* thought Themis. '*But she's being diplomatic, of course.*'

'Has he been working on the statue?' Xenovia went on.

'As far as I know. You must ask Panainos about that.'

'Ach, Panainos,' sighed Xenovia, ' – when I mentioned the boy to him he just changed the subject. So I wondered, have you noticed whether Themistokles is well now? He had a terrible blow to the head during an accident some months ago.'

The High Priest's voice was dry with boredom. 'He cited that as the explanation for the vision. He seems fine. I hear he runs and exercises as though he is in training for something. I have only spoken to him once.'

'Training?' echoed Xenovia with interest. 'That is … a good sign.'

'I shall leave you now to your prayers.'

'Thank you, Your Holiness. It is important to me that I should be entirely alone with Father Zeus.'

There was a rustle of robes as the High Priest turned away and Xenovia approached the statue. She raised her voice a little. 'Your Holiness, how shall I signal that I am ready to leave?'

The High Priest called, 'Use this staff by the door. If you beat on the door with the metal end, the guard outside will hear and let you out.' He demonstrated. Themis heard the door swing open and the murmur of people out in the Altis.

'I am eternally grateful,' said Xenovia.

'Sacred Lady.'

'Your Holiness.'

And the great door closed quietly this time, with a sigh and a thud.

Themis was in a quandary, 'What shall I do now? She won't be pleased to be disturbed at her prayers and yet … Ach. Perhaps this was not such a good idea after all,' he chastised himself. '*Then again, she'd probably be pleased to see me. She worries about me enough to mention me to the High Priest.*' He started up the ladder. '*I'd better show myself now, before she starts to pray.*'

A strange chuckle made him freeze on the third rung. Was there someone else out there with Xenovia?

But Themis could only hear one pair of feet. She seemed to be walking swiftly round the statue. At the back, she climbed up the steps onto the decorated base. He could hear her walking round to the front. Was she talking to herself? Themis heard, 'How do you get up to the main part of the cloak?' and, 'Is this supposed to be Prometheus? Too many chains.'

These were not prayers.

What was she doing? He certainly could not show himself now. He could hear her testing the ladder up to the god's lap. He went silently down his own ladder and pinched out his lamp.

There was still a distant glow up near the top of the statue. Themis looked up. A beam of light was shining in through the 'window' in the back of the god's head. '*So that's how the eyes glow,*' he thought. '*There must be a hidden lantern set into the back of the throne.*'

Meanwhile he heard Xenovia start climbing up the ladder. She seemed to be examining the statue's golden robe. Themis could see the light from her lamp reflected on the inside of the statue's lap, above his own head. Would she climb up inside and find him skulking there?

'Only gilded,' she was muttering. 'Not solid, like the Athena. Ach! These cheapskate Elians!' and she slapped a hand on something with a loud crack that set Themis' heart racing.

Her voice came again. 'And these gems. I doubt they're even real. More likely coloured pebbles. Phidias, Phidias, you have duped us all again.' She seemed to be going back down the outer ladder. Themis sighed with relief.

Now she was walking round the base towards the back. 'But those eyes. They give me the shivers.' Themis heard her climb down the steps from the base to the floor.

There was silence for a while. Themis was in an agony of doubt. Why did she think the stones were fake? *He* knew they were real. He had been there while they were worked. Could this really be the same Xenovia?

A cool, distant part of his mind reminded him that she was not always so perfect. 'Remember how she was flirting with Diodotos?' it said. 'And even Panainos?' The not so cool part of his mind insisted, '*Maybe. But she looks so lovely,*' and he blushed all over at the feelings her beauty always aroused in him.

That distant part of his brain cautioned, 'You can't know what she's thinking. Maybe someone has been telling her lies. Keep quiet and listen!'

But there was a long silence.

Themis was afraid he would have to cough. He sucked a corner of his tunic to make saliva and swallowed hard. He really ought to tell her he was there.

Then Xenovia's professional praying voice came from the front, between the statue and the doors.

'Mighty Zeus,' she said loudly. 'I beg you to hear your devoted child. Your daughter, Athena, knows me well.' The voice thickened and lowered. 'I see in your eyes that you hear me.'

Themis almost called out. He was appalled that Xenovia, perfect or not, was taken in by Phidias' trick of the light inside the statue.

But she went on. 'There are many favours I would ask of you if there were time. But the most important, the most efficacious for the sake of the city of Athens and for the whole of Hellas, is this.

'Dear Immortal Father, you who can achieve all things, I beg you to restore to my uncle, Thukydides, the power to rid Athens of the traitor, Perikles.' Her voice rose higher, now more a cry of despair. 'It is ten years since anyone had any control over Perikles. Give my uncle your help, and we will sacrifice to you a thousand oxen, or whatever you command. Athens cannot survive another year of the misrule of that man, with his weakness and his indecision. There will be war with Sparta if he is not replaced by a strong, diplomatic hand immediately. Grant us this, oh mighty Zeus. Grant continuing life and glory to Athens, through your daughter Athena and your brother Poseidon. We need your help.' She was sobbing now.

Themis felt he had to go to her. He began to climb, but in the darkness, he missed his footing and swayed. His shoulder knocked the metal lamp off its peg. It fell to the floor with a loud ringing sound.

At the same time a tiny draft made the flame high above flicker and strengthen.

Xenovia gasped. 'By all the gods, Father Zeus, do not harm me!' she exclaimed and ran to the door. She beat on it and it opened. Themis heard her feet run away from the Temple.

The guard must have stepped in and looked round, because after a few moments' silence, Themis heard him grunt and the door thudded shut.

He sat at the bottom of the ladder in the deep gloom. His first thought was '*Missed my chance!*'

And his second was, 'She thinks she can save Athens from war.'

The two parts of his mind began to debate.

'So why would she be interested in you?'

'*Perhaps she knows how much I admire her and …* '

'Go on. Admit you're in love with her. Everyone else is.'

'*No! I admire her beauty and her … energy.*'

'Phidias doesn't like her.'

'*She doesn't like him. She doesn't approve of his fame and how he lives his life. Perhaps she knows things about him that I don't.*'

'She changed her mind about your future that day in Athens.'

'*Because she knew about the Games and wants me to compete.*'

'Even when it could mean you might die of any injuries?'

'She knows the gods want me to take part, just as Father knew.'

'Are you sure your Father would want that now, knowing how dangerous it could be?'

'Of course he would. And anyway, that's just hypothetical. He did not know. Oh do be quiet!'

Themis felt out of control. Question was following question in his mind and he felt powerless to stop them.

'Have you still no idea who tried to smother you, or hurt Myrto, or who tried to grab you on the mountain if it's not Nikanor?'

'Perhaps he employed someone else to get rid of me and the others.'

'Who else might be a danger to you?'

'No one I can think of. Maybe a rival boxer. Straton's family don't seem likely. If only I could remember my life before, I might know.'

'Of course, it could just be someone wanting to make you a slave and use your boxing skills for fights to bet on.'

'What sort of idea is that?' Themis wanted to shout out loud with frustration. *'Ach, what is going on in my head!? I just wish I could remember!'*

And he found he was standing in front of the statue, in the large sunken space between it and the door. He had no memory of getting there. He looked up at the calm face with those living, flickering eyes.

Perhaps the real Zeus was truly somewhere nearby. Perhaps Phidias was right and Panainos was wrong, and the gods were real, and cared for and protected at least some of their human supplicants.

The face was looking down on him with sculpted compassion. 'What is happening to me, Father Zeus?' Themis whispered in desperation. 'So many of the thoughts in my head don't seem to be mine. So many of my memories might be dreams, not memories at all. I felt in Elis that I had been shown the real me, but I can't remember – my whole life before the accident is still a great, gaping emptiness. I often don't know what people mean or what they're referring to. How can I be clear in my mind who I am, if I don't know what I've done and what I haven't done?' And he sank to his knees and bowed his head in despair.

A quiet rumble echoed throughout the temple.

'Come here,' said a deep voice, a vibration in the air.

Themis looked up in wonder, his eyes wide, his mouth open. The statue of Nike was now standing on the arm of the throne and Zeus' right hand was moving, reaching towards him, beckoning. 'Come here,' the voice repeated.

Themis thought, '*And so it is time.*'

He grasped the huge fingers and was lifted onto the god's right knee. The gold of the mantle over the mighty legs gave off a living warmth as he was gently placed on it. He gathered his courage and lifted his gaze to the all-knowing face. A golden glow shone all around the god. Beyond was deep blackness.

The god did not speak or move again. Themis waited, all doubts of Zeus' power dispelled.

He knew he must speak – or perhaps pray – but the words wouldn't come. He breathed deeply many times, looking for truth in the chaos of his conflicting thoughts. Zeus was still, infinitely patient.

At last Themis looked up and said, 'I cannot ask you for things I do not understand. So I will not pray to help Athens, or even to be sure I can take part in the Games and win. These things will happen as you will, not as I wish.'

He was quiet for a moment. Then he said, 'I can only ask you for clarity in my own mind. I need to feel sure of who I am – and what you want me to achieve.'

He gazed at the god's face. The light was brighter now, warmer. The smooth, pale muscles of the chest and stomach gleamed as they rose and fell with the god's slow breathing. The decorations on the golden robe glowed and shimmered. Themis saw that Zeus was smiling in his beard. 'You came,' he said in his deep voice, and Themis caught a flash of white teeth. 'You are ready.'

Themis saw the right hand come looming towards him again. 'Will I die?' he asked quietly, as he lifted his head to meet it.

The smile on the god's face widened. 'No. From now on you will really live,' he breathed. 'Now you can manage alone, though there will still be times when you are not sure who you are, or what you should do.' His finger and thumb came together and touched the hair on Themis' head.

Then they lifted away.

Caught between them, suspended in the golden air above him, Themis saw the shape of a young woman, scantily clothed and with very short hair. She struggled up to kneel on the palm of the huge hand, and from there she looked down on him. She was crying and laughing together. Her tears fell on his face.

Their eyes met. Hers were grey, ringed with damp lashes, dark against her pale skin. They glowed with love and sadness. Themis felt she wanted to speak, but she just lifted both hands towards him, smiling through her tears.

Zeus' deep voice stirred the air again, reverberating in Themis' chest. 'She has given you a great gift,' said the god. 'Now you must let her go.'

And in that moment the knot of Themis' fears came undone. A kind of peace filled him as he gazed up at the shining nymph and the father of the gods. He held his open hands, one on top of the other, to his chest, then bowed his head in the gesture of gratitude.

When he looked up again, Zeus' hand was empty.

He curled up among the golden folds on the lap of the god and wept, mourning a nameless and inexplicable loss.

PART TWO
Apart

Chapter 35: paean

Themis woke shivering. Tears had run into his ears and gathered under his cheek where it had lain on the cold, hard gold. He rubbed at them with the hem of his tunic, just as he had when he finally understood that Nikitas was dead and would not be sleeping in the other bed in their room ever again. Eirini had held him and rocked him, but she had fallen asleep herself, leaving Themis feeling abandoned and truly alone.

With that same feeling, he looked up at the god's face, dark now except for the eyes. He heard again his father laughing and saying, 'But even you, Phidias, can't make a statue that size. The Elians are wasting their money.' The men were in the andron at home, and Themis was out in the courtyard with Panax and Melanas, painting the dog on a tile in white and black.

'You'll see, Kallistos,' Phidias had said. 'Zeus has to be that big. After all, Athena was born from his head. And now, at last we're beginning to add the ivory skin. You should visit Olympia again.'

Themis caught his breath and jumped up, almost losing his footing on the hard smooth mound of the knee. He stopped himself from crying out, even though he suddenly wanted to shout for joy.

'I'm remembering!' he thought. *'I'm remembering!'*

He stood still, his mind full of a thousand tumbling images: his first day at the gymnasium when he measured himself against the other boys and found he was stronger but shorter than most; the day Diodotos allowed him to borrow his big bow for hunting; the day he and Frog left a dead snake on the couch in the andron and Eirini made Kallistos whip him, but not Frog, because he should have known better than the slave boy.

More memories came back: Myrto's wedding; Chloe's first steps; his own oath before the boxing trials in the Agora in Athens; knocking out his final opponent, Mantius; arguing with his Uncle Panainos about the existence of Apollo; crossing the ceiling of the unfinished Odeum by balancing on the roof-beams when Straton dared him.

He stood on the lap of Immortal Zeus, breathless with wonder. *'Now I am me,'* he thought. *'Who or what that girl or nymph was, and how she was inside my head, I don't know. But now I know I am me, and only me.'*

And in his memory a song came back to him, a paean sung at thanksgiving ceremonies by the priests and the worshippers together. He let it fill his mind and began quietly to sing it to himself as his hymn of thanks to Zeus. And to all the gods. And to the nameless nymph.

>>>

From Bernie's private diary. Saturday April 10th 2010

Suzanne was sitting in her armchair today.

The nurse says to me in front of her, 'She walked to the loo and we'll be able to remove the drip tomorrow or the next day. She gets very dizzy on her feet. So if she wants to get up, give her your arm.'

'Right,' I say.

Suzanne's eyes look huge and bruised in her poor white face. She seems oddly wary, but gives me a bit of a smile.

When the nurse has gone, I say, 'You're looking better.'

And then she looks at me with a kind of confusion and horror and says, 'He ended it. Wanted to die.'

I'm like, 'Ended what? Who? Ian?'

'No!' She's angry. 'Bloody Zeus.'

'Zeus!' I squeak. Then I remember to be cool. 'The god Zeus?'

She looks at me under her eyebrows. ''Course,' she says.

'Right,' I say. 'Zeus ended something and you wanted to die.'

The frustration in her eyes is alarming. ''Zactly. Zeus pulled me out.' Then suddenly she's all proud, like a toddler who can reach a light switch. 'Got back later!'

'Out of where?' I ask, really quiet and cool. 'Back where?'

'Themis' head,' she says. 'Safe or what?'

I can't work this out. She's nodding, like she's congratulating herself. I say, 'I brought my laptop over. Your Facebook wall is a mile long with get well messages.'

Her smile goes out like a light.

'Bernie,' she says. 'My friend?'

'Sure,' I say.

'Themis' friend,' she states, QED.

'I don't know Themis,' I say.

'I'm Themis,' she says.

'Not to me, you're not,' I say.

She starts hitting the arm of her chair with her good fist. 'I am Themis, and Suzanne!' She chants this over and over.

The nurse comes in to see what the noise is about. The name on her badge is Jenny. Suzanne has started moving her head from side to side like some kind of zoo animal as she chants.

I shout to Nurse Jenny over the noise, 'What's the matter with her?'

Another nurse comes, and they get her back into bed and calmed down. They beckon me out. 'In the report,' says Jenny, 'it says she had a fit like this in the night. Music helped. You'd better go now, but come back another time. It's all part of the process. Patience.' And she smiles at me.

PATIENCE!!!!!!?

Suzanne is turning into someone else in front of my eyes and you say Patience! I can't deal with this. I need to talk to someone, p'raps Laila …

<<<

Themis was so excited by the flood of memories that for a long while he forgot where he was. At last he realised that dawn was beginning.

'*How will I get out?*' he thought.

He was still wearing the leather pouch with the key to the cellar in it. Perhaps he could find and lift the trap door. By his calculations, it should be near the back wall of the temple.

He climbed down the ladder from Zeus' lap and walked round the base of the statue in the dim light. Along by the back wall, behind a screen of embroidered panels, was a narrow trestle table on top of a dusty piece of woven rug.

Themis had to move them aside to see if the door was under the rug. He worked carefully in total silence in case the guards outside heard anything. When he slowly pulled the rug away, there was the trap door, its bronze handle set into the heavy wood. He planted his feet and strained to lift it, almost falling over when it opened easily and silently.

But there was no ladder, just complete blackness.

'*If I jump down and can't open the outer door, how will I get back up?*' he thought. Then, with a wry smile, he added, '*Just pray that was a ladder I saw on top of the old chest.*'

He lifted the door right back so that it rested on the floor. He grasped the edge of the hole and swung himself down.

As he landed, he heard someone swear. His heart raced. He could see a faint light in the next room. He crept to the doorway. Two men were cowering in a corner beyond what seemed to be a frame holding a great barrel on its side. It stood in the middle of the now spotless floor, pierced through the ends like an animal on a spit.

'By Heaven and Hades,' said Gulkishar's voice in the gloom. 'It's not Father Zeus. It's the boy, Themistokles!'

'What in Hades are you doing, boy!?' growled the other man, approaching Themis. He was on his knees, bending his head so as not to crack it on the ceiling.

Themis shook his own head in disbelief. 'What's happening?' he asked.

'Where were you hiding?' asked the scribe suspiciously.

'I came down from the temple to check the cellar,' said Themis. 'I … I fell asleep down here and just woke up. I'm starving hungry!'

The big man had opened his storm lantern and he and Gulkishar stared at Themis in its light.

'How did you know about this cellar?' asked the big man.

Gulkishar answered, 'Cleaning it yesterday morning was his duty. It must be he who has the second key.'

The big man growled deep in his chest and moved on his knees towards the door. 'Well, we've finished in here, haven't we? Let's go.'

Gulkishar went over to the barrel. He also had to stoop so as not to hit his head. One end of the 'spit' was bent into a handle. He gave this a small push and the barrel made a part turn before falling back again. A slight rumble came from it.

'Yes, it is ready. We can go,' he said, standing back so that Themis could pass.

They came out into the growing dawn. Gulkishar stretched, then turned and locked the door behind them. The big man stood up. They walked in single file towards the gate to the workshop in the Altis wall.

There the big man slipped away among the early workers on the road.

Themis asked Gulkishar, 'What's the barrel for?'

'It is the voice of Zeus,' said the scribe with a cold stare at Themis. 'In case it is needed.' And he walked briskly away.

'Are you alright?' whispered Frog when Themis got back to his room at the hotel.

'Have you told anyone I was out?' Themis asked.

'No. No one asked, but if they did, I was going to say you had a headache and were sleeping. I was a bit worried though.'

'Sorry! And thanks. I'm starving. Can we take something and go out?'

'Then you are alright,' said Frog, gathering food into a bag.

'Yes, I'm fine.' He led Frog into the growing traffic on the main road. 'In fact I'm extremely fine,' he said with a laugh and a skip in his step. 'I've just had my talk with Zeus.'

'What!'

'Well, it was a kind of vision again,' Themis said as he danced along. 'And he didn't want me to give him anything after all. He just took away the feeling I've had since the accident, the feeling that I'm not really me.'

'I have to say, you have been different – more … er …'

'Soft?' said Themis with a smile.

'Just … more polite,' said Frog carefully.

'Perhaps even a bit feminine sometimes?'

'Well, yes,' said Frog with a grin. 'A bit feminine about describes it!'

'You be careful!' laughed Themis. He stopped and looked around to see if anyone could hear him. Satisfied, he said quietly, 'You won't believe this, but it seems I've had a woman in my head all this time. Zeus just pulled her out, and now I can remember life before my fall.'

'You can remember? Everything?' said Frog, his eyes wide with apprehension.

'Well, maybe not every single thing,' said Themis. 'I don't remember learning Papa was dead, for instance. But lots of things. Like when you "lost" my flute for me so I wouldn't have to go to music lesson.' He pulled a bun out of the bag. 'And about the dead snake.'

'Which one?' asked Frog with innocent eyes.

Themis laughed. 'Hey, come on. I want to get some flowers to give Zeus a garland later. We don't need a guard just for that.'

'Flowers? Are you sure you got rid of that woman in your head?' asked Frog.

'Oh, shut up!' Themis grinned through a mouthful. 'And don't you go telling anyone about it. No one else must know! Partly because I want to go on using it as my excuse for staying here, and partly because … well, I'd feel a fool.' He finished his bun. 'And remember, I know stuff about you now that you were glad I'd forgotten. So behave!'

'Were you in the temple, then?' asked Frog, as they reached the last houses and began to speed up.

'Yes, but not a word about that, all right? Everyone must believe that I was asleep in the temple cellar. The story is that I went to check that the cleaners had done it properly and fell asleep. Got that?'

'Of course.'

'I met Gulkishar down there at first light.'

'Gulkishar? In the cellar?'

'Yes. He was arranging "the voice of Zeus" for later.'

'Oh!' said Frog. 'That reminds me. Panainos said to tell you … you'll be needed mid-morning for the thanksgiving ceremony and then the handover of the statue.' He was quoting word for word. 'Everyone in Olympia will then go to the stadium to hear the odes and a play.'

'Are they opening the temple?' They were running uphill now and getting breathless. Themis was heading for a particular olive grove he'd passed on training runs.

Frog went on with his chant. 'After the handover, the doors of the temple will be open until sunset, for anyone who wishes … to see the statue … that is the new wonder of the world.'

'Sounds like they expect a lot of people,' panted Themis.

'Thousands,' said Frog shortly as they topped a rise. Below them lay the olive grove, grey and silver in the morning haze. The ground under the trees was crimson and purple with tulips and iris.

'By the way,' he added, 'what is "the voice of Zeus"?'

'A barrel full of stones that thunders when you turn the handle.'

'Hah. Naturally. Like in a theatre.'

'It's a pity religion has to rely on theatrical tricks,' said Themis, bending to pick some flowers. 'I'm surprised they haven't found a way to make lightning, too.'

'Perhaps they have,' said Frog, his hands full of irises. 'Though rain would be truly difficult.'

Chapter 36: lightning

Themis could see Xenovia from a distance among the temple dignitaries, as beautiful as ever, standing straight and proud beside the Priestesses of Hera. There was no sign of Gulkishar.

The sun was high, and the flying goddess on top of the temple pediment glistened, making the other statues below her look dull in spite of their bright colours. The strong breeze came from behind her. She seemed about to take off on its updraft. Themis wondered whether, in view of what Xenovia had been praying for, perhaps sculpting her as a flying Nike would be a better tribute to her beauty and angry patriotism than the doubting but faithful Penelope.

The crowd was gathering under the trees near the bottom of the temple ramp. Guards kept the people back as more and more tried to get a good view of Phidias and the High Priest standing between the two central columns in front of the great studded doors. These were closed to hide even a glimpse of the statue.

Beneath the colonnade to the left side of the doors stood the most important of Phidias' colleagues, including Panainos, Agorakritos and Alkamenes. And on the other side next to the High Priest were the City Archon of Olympia, the City Archon of Elis, Judge Iasos, another judge, and other dignitaries from the two cities. They all wore magnificent, colourful robes, the sun sparkling on gold borders and belts, embroidered ribbons and cloaks. The scent of rosemary and frankincense drifted from braziers on gleaming bronze tripods.

The High Priest was making a declaration. 'For Olympia, for Elis, for all people across the Hellenic World, this is a momentous day.' He paused and the crowd clapped politely. 'From this afternoon, all the world will finally … finally, I say, … be able to see what Elis has spent so much time and treasure to give to Zeus himself. I call upon Phidias, Master Sculptor, to officially deliver the statue of Zeus the Immortal Father to the Council of Citizens of Elis. To symbolise this, Master Phidias and the City Archon will exchange gifts.'

There was a sudden fanfare of trumpets from a platform under the roof of the temple. Themis looked up at the musicians as a flock of pigeons were startled into flight. They whirled against the churning grey clouds that had appeared behind the temple. Rays of sunshine drove down like spears, appearing and disappearing. A sudden breeze made cloaks flap and flutter. Only the robes of the flying goddess stayed still.

Phidias and the Archon of Elis stood forward side by side, between the columns. Phidias held up a huge key on a thick golden ribbon for the crowd to see. Then he hung it round the neck of the Archon.

The Archon took a large gold dish from its linen wrappings and held it out to Phidias with both hands. Phidias took it and held it up. It was more than three feet across and, filling the centre, was a depiction of Phidias' statue of Zeus, embossed and inlaid in silver and copper.

At that moment, the clouds covered the sun, and the dish no longer glowed.

'My thanks to your worship, the Archon of Elis, and all those you represent,' called Phidias in his rhythmic public voice. 'I accept this magnificent gift as part of my payment from the city of Olympia and the municipality of Elis. I thank, too, all who took part in creating this unique offering to our forefather, and the father of our Olympian gods, Immortal Zeus, the Benevolent and Wise. Fifteen years have passed since I felt the call to create this likeness. Others have spent as many years assisting me. There is no payment on this earth that can equal the devotion and care we have all invested in our work.' He stepped forward and, turning to the Hill of Chronos, raised his voice even more.

'And so I call upon you, most beloved and feared of Fathers, tell me that we have done well. Your pleasure will be our payment. Have we pleased you? Are you happy with your new gift? Will you give us a sign?'

As his voice died away, there was complete silence in the Altis, except for the gusting wind. Themis wondered how long the men in the basement had been told to wait before turning the barrel to make the 'voice of Zeus'.

Time passed. No one moved. The wind pulled at tunics and cloaks, bent branches and grasses, swished and groaned in the trees. Clouds boiled and shredded above.

A sizzling, searing light and a huge clap of thunder suddenly leapt upon them.

Themis let out a cry of surprise, like many others all round him. He heard Xenovia scream, 'Have mercy!' Everyone crouched down, trying to protect their heads and ears from the noise.

The light was immediately extinguished.

In the echoing gloom that followed, the churning clouds swept across the sky. The thunder growled up and down the valley, then died slowly away. There was a strong smell of burning.

Phidias and the Archon had been shocked into stillness. At the bottom of the steps, on the paving just in front of the crowd, a black and smoking flag-stone had cracked in the shape of a star. Three men had fallen on their faces a few feet from it. Others were helping them get up, while their hands groped and their eyes stared unseeing.

Phidias ran down the ramp and reached out towards the blackened stone. He pulled back his hand as if he'd been burned, stood up and cried, 'Thank you, Father, for your appreciation and acceptance of our gift. We will honour you in this shape, and in our hearts, for ever.'

As he turned to go back up the ramp, rain began to fall. The blackened stone steamed. The rain was gentle at first, giving time for the crowd to disperse and find shelter. But within moments it was turning the pathways to streams and the rivers to torrents.

Themis fled to the hotel and found Panainos already there.

'Was that, or was that not, the act of a god?' Themis asked him as they stripped off their soaking garments, laughing at the wonder of it all.

'That was a weather phenomenon which arrived at just the right moment,' chortled Panainos.

A song of glory and thanks could be heard from the Altis, sung by the professional worshippers. People in the buildings all around took up the song and it echoed through the streets, accompanied by the drumming of the rain on the roofs and the thunder rumbling up and down the valley of the Alpheios.

'Wake up, sleepy head!' came Panainos' loud voice by Themis' bed next morning. 'Just need to remind you that I'll be leaving in a day or two and that you might like to send something to your mother.'

Themis groaned. He had a headache. 'I'll think about it,' he said and sat up wincing. 'Does that mean I don't work for you any more?'

'No, not for me, you don't. But you'd better not leave Olympia until you've done what you came here to do,' said Panainos. 'I'll leave you to the tender care of my brother, who has to stay a while and oversee a couple of details.' He walked to the door. 'He tells me he'll apprentice you to a bronze caster, and will feed and house you until your appointment with Zeus. Then you can come back to Athens and we'll teach you to paint properly.'

Memories of the feasting and dancing of the evening before, and a crazy moment when he tried to kiss one of the slave girls came back to Themis. He had a horrific thought. 'Did I say some stupid things last night?' he asked.

'Oh, nothing spectacular, boy,' Panainos said with a smile. 'Just something about no girls in your head any more (in spite of your actions, it seems). Oh and something about warm glowing flesh, and someone "not called Penelope",' said Panainos from the doorway. 'You're growing up fast, young man. No harm done. Phidias scooped you up and brought you back here to sleep it off.'

>>>

Made myself drop in on Suzanne this evening. Laila had said she'd come with me but at the last minute she couldn't.

'Tell me about my accident,' Suzanne demands before I've even got in the door. 'You were there.' That's the longest sentence she's said to me since February 15th.

I've got my laptop, so I read her my blog. Her eyes glaze over after a couple of minutes, so I stop reading.

She says, 'Where 'zactly was I?'

I find the street map and show her.

'No river,' she says.

'Mr Green said there's a river under the road near there,' I tell her, the hair on my arms standing up.

Her eyes fill with tears. 'Twice in the same place,' she says.

'Twice what?'

Now she's telling me a secret. 'I sing the notes,' she whispers, 'and breathe in, very slowly. Then he's there. Usually.'

I don't get this. 'Twice what?' I ask again.

'No one will talk about Themis,' she says. 'Mum doesn't believe he exists.'

'Does he?' I ask. Then I see that was a mistake.

Her face goes all closed up. 'You don't like Themis,' she says.

'I don't know Themis.' I shrug.

'You don't want to,' she accuses me.

This makes me want to cry. 'No,' I say. 'I don't. I want to know Suzanne, my best friend. I want her back.'

'That's me,' she says. 'Don't cry.'

'I'm not!' I get up and pack up my laptop.

'Don't go,' she says.

'I'll come back tomorrow.'

I bump into Mrs Jenkins in the doorway. 'She seems a lot better today,' I say and run down the corridor.

This is really, really hard to deal with. Suzanne and I always made decisions together. Now she's someone else and I can't talk to her. Josh just laughs at the whole thing. 'She's awake and chatting, isn't she? She'll be fine.'

But she isn't.

<<<

'You'll never grow taller if you stunt your growth with wine and women,' said Pyrros at the gym that afternoon.

'Rubbish!' laughed Kadmos, the trainer. 'They'll put hair on your chest and give you something to fight for.'

'Fight for?' asked Themis, deliberately innocent.

'Why are you all training?' asked Kadmos. 'To be fit to be soldiers when the time comes.'

'Of course,' put in Pantarkes, 'most soldiers don't need women or even wine to prove they're tough men ...' Themis dived at him and they fell in a tumble in the sand.

'Enough of that!' called Kadmos over the rumpus and the encouraging shouts of the other boys. 'Let's use our time to really strengthen our bodies.' He signalled to the flautist and they began the usual series of exercises.

Themis was still left out of the last few that focused on stances for wrestling and boxing, so he scraped off and then swam in the pool instead. The sunset made him feel he was swimming in red and orange paint.

When he got to the end nearest the river for the fourth time, he found Agorakritos waiting for him.

'Are you ready to stop?' he asked with his infectious smile. 'I have messages for you.'

'Sure,' said Themis. 'I'll meet you at the snack stall.'

'There'll be no wine,' called Agorakritos as Themis ran in to dry off and dress.

'*Last night has given me a reputation,*' Themis thought with a wry smile. '*Good!*'

'First of all,' said Agorakritos over their spiced milk with sweetened must and cheese rolls. 'You should be ready to congratulate me.'

Themis frowned a little. 'On what?'

'On my betrothal,' laughed Agorakritos.

'You're going to be married?!'

'Yes. Judge Iasos has finally agreed that I may broadcast that I am to marry his daughter, Anthoussa.'

'*You!*' gasped Themis. 'You are the one she is marrying?'

'Yes. Why? Do you know her?' Agorakritos' handsome face shone with amusement. 'You do get around, don't you?'

'You know I went to Elis,' said Themis.

'Yes, I do.' Comprehension dawned and Agorakritos' almond eyes opened wide. 'Ah... you're the one who asked about the face paint.'

'That's right. She's very … pretty,' said Themis carefully.

'Only when she doesn't paint her face!' said Agorakritos.

'Congratulations. You'll make each other very happy,' said Themis with a touch of irony.

'I doubt it,' said Agorakritos. 'We'll probably make each other very cross, but hopefully we're going to have some strong, clever children.'

'You are?'

'Yes. We're expecting the first at about the time of the Games.' Agorakritos looked as though he would burst with pride. Themis had to stop himself from saying, 'In that case, I shall see your firstborn.'

'Double congratulations,' he said instead. 'Will you live in Elis or Athens?' Themis longed to talk to Agorakritos about training and his own future challenges, but he could see that the sculptor was only interested in these banal domestic issues. And anyway, it was still a secret because of the curse, of course.

Agorakritos was saying, 'We'll be staying in Elis until the baby's born. Then I have commissions waiting for me in Athens. The judge is giving me a house there, and a large flax farm near Elis as Anthoussa's dowry. He has two other girls to marry off, and so that's all he can give her.'

'He must be very rich,' Themis said seriously. 'Why would he accept a disreputable sculptor as his son-in-law?'

'Disreputable or not, my mother owns part of the Paros marble quarries,' said Agorakritos with a laugh. 'She is richer than the judge will ever be.'

'Ah,' said Themis with a sigh and a nod. They lifted their cups, touched them together, poured a few drops onto the floor for the gods, and drank to the betrothal.

Agorakritos handed Themis a tablet. 'By the way, the judge gave me this for you,' he said.

Themis' fingers trembled as he opened it. 'The curse is now lifted,' said the first line. 'Your brother, Diodotos, has made the necessary payments. You are now free to publicise that you will compete in the Games.'

Themis looked up at Agorakritos, eyes alight. 'The best news ever! Thanks.'

'The curse is lifted?'

'Thanks to my brother, the curse is lifted,' said Themis, bursting out laughing. He jumped up and spun round on the balls of his feet. 'Now I can really train! I'm going to be a real boxer!' and he began feinting and dancing around.

Agorakritos stood up. 'Come on,' he said, delighted. 'Let's catch Kadmos before he leaves and tell him you can start normal training from tomorrow.'

'Lie still,' Frog was saying, trying to hold Themis' shoulders down on the bed. 'You'll make it worse if you thrash about like that.'

Themis tried to relax. He was breathing heavily and concentrating on not groaning. They had just brought him back from the gymnasium on a stretcher. While sparring with Pantarkes, Themis had thrown a strong punch to the chest and Pantarkes had instinctively thrown one back – to the jaw.

'The healer will be here with the sleeping draft soon,' said Frog. 'At least you're not unconscious.'

'No,' groaned Themis bitterly. 'Far from it!'

'What d'you mean,' asked Frog, laying a damp towel on Themis' forehead.

'It's obvious, isn't it? My mother was right,' said Themis between clenched teeth. 'I can't do fight training, even with special rules at the gym … Pantarkes did me a favour, hitting back at me like that.' He choked on a groan. 'It hurt so much I couldn't see, or even stay on my feet … Now I *know* I won't be able to compete in the Games. I won't survive the first round.'

'See what the healer says,' said Frog.

'He can't see inside my head,' said Themis, his jaw rigid. 'No one can.'

He was holding his head together with his two hands, rocking himself and trying not to sob with the pain and anger and disappointment.

The healer finally arrived.

The sleeping draft was bitter and left his mouth feeling shrivelled as a walnut. But by then he would have done anything to lessen the pain throbbing behind his eyes. He sank gratefully into unconsciousness.

'No, Pantarkes,' Panainos was saying. 'You didn't kill him. Look, he's coming round.'

Themis could hear other voices around him talking quietly. His head felt lighter, as though it would float off. But at least it hardly hurt.

He opened his eyes. Pantarkes was sitting on a stool by his bed, looking anxiously at his face.

His expression relaxed as Themis focused on him. 'Seems I didn't hit you hard enough,' he said gently with a rueful smile.

'Oh, you did!' said Themis. 'What did they give me? I'm flying.'

Another voice came from the foot of the bed. 'That will pass. Just stay still. How is the pain?'

'Just enough to remind me what it was like,' said Themis.

'Good,' said the healer's voice. 'I'll come back this evening.'

Pantarkes got up. 'You'd probably better sleep again now, Themis,' he said. 'I'll see you later.'

Panainos settled himself on the small stool and said quietly, 'I'm going to stay a bit longer – just to see that you are recovering properly.'

'Thanks,' said Themis faintly.

'Also, if you're well enough, you and I have been invited to a large country estate near Three Rivers the day after tomorrow. We'll see how you are nearer the time.'

'Can we talk about it later?' Themis asked, closing his eyes.

'Of course. I just wanted you to be able to relax knowing I'm still around, dear boy.'

'Right,' murmured Themis. 'Thanks.'

Chapter 37: despair

Someone nearby seemed to be murdering a pig while playing on a harp. It took Themis a few moments to understand that there was hymn practice going on by the well of the hotel.

And then he remembered he would not be able to compete in the Games and his disappointment filled him like an icy torrent. He groaned, turned over and shut his eyes.

Frog said, 'That's enough lying in bed,' as he bustled around. 'It's a lovely day outside, birds singing, bees buzzing, Trainer Kadmos swearing. You going to get up now?'

Themis grunted.

'Come on. There's food,' tempted Frog, standing over him.

Themis opened one eye to look at him. 'Not much point really,' he murmured.

'There's lots of point,' laughed Frog. 'You need to get up. Panainos wants to talk to you about something important. And the food is duck and mushroom stew.'

Themis groaned and rolled out of bed.

He ate in silence while Panainos chatted on about some battle in Homer that he was going to paint when he got back to Athens.

'You need a walk, my boy,' said Panainos at last, as he stood up. 'Come with me.'

Themis followed meekly, his mind dull and empty.

They walked towards the entrance to the Altis. It was early evening and there had been rain, so everything sparkled with drops in the slanting rays of the sun. But Themis was watching his feet as he walked on the paving stones. His sandals were getting too small.

'It's such a shame about your injury, you know,' said Panainos as they walked into the gate and joined the strolling crowds along the avenue towards the Treasuries. 'You were a real terror in the qualifying bouts in Athens. I saw you beat the first two boys hollow, but then I had to leave.'

'I can remember some of that now,' said Themis numbly.

'It's a relief not to have to keep quiet about it, I can tell you!' Panainos tried to lighten Themis' depression with one of his big laughs.

Themis pressed his lips together. 'But I'm a different person from that Themis,' he said. 'He was powerful, sure of himself … '

'Oh, come on,' said Panainos. 'Cheer up. You're still the same person. You don't have fits and you have the use of your arms and legs, and even some memories. Now you're not just a boxer. You're an artist, too. All is not lost.'

They came to the ramp up to the Temple of Zeus and the seat where Phidias and Themis had talked. It seemed years ago. Panainos wiped off the last rain drops with his cloak before they sat.

'But I feel as if all *is* lost,' said Themis. 'Uncle Phidias is arranging work for me here, but what's the point of staying in Olympia if I can't compete? It's hopeless.' Ironically, he was free to go back to Athens now, although no one knew that Zeus had released him except Frog.

'You can't go back without having your "little talk" with Father Zeus,' said Panainos kindly. 'Have a word with your trainer tomorrow. He'll know what to do. Now,' he added, turning his bulk towards Themis on the bench, 'I have an invitation for the next few days that you may want to consider.'

'Invitation?'

'Yes. I mentioned it to you. You and I have been invited to Thukydides' country estate at Three Rivers. You can bring Frog and carry on with the running and so on. We'll have meals with the other guests. It's a magnificent farm, by all accounts.'

'Why would Thukydides invite me?' Themis asked. All he knew of this man he had heard from Xenovia in the temple.

'Actually, it was Xenovia who arranged the invitation,' chuckled Panainos. 'I think she wants me to consider a new commission in Athens. But she specifically mentioned you, too.'

It crossed Themis' mind that, if he went, he might find out why Xenovia took such an interest in him. And he could see if she would let him draw her. But even planning his statue seemed pointless now.

'How long would we have to stay?' he asked.

'Maybe three or four days,' said Panainos.

'Phidias wants me to start work with the bronze casters,' he said without enthusiasm.

'He's still waiting for an answer about that from your mother.'

Themis sighed. 'Then I suppose it will pass the time.'

Panainos stood up. 'Wonderful! I'll make the arrangements while you go and see your trainer. See if he has any suggestions about other healers or priests who might help with your … er … head problem. Do you want to give thanks now? It might make you feel more … ' his voice faded away when he saw the expression on Themis' face. 'Never forget to be grateful!' he remonstrated, and turned and marched away through the never-ending line of pilgrims.

Themis joined the line into the temple, behind a group from Akragas in Sicily. They were arguing about whether their own Temple to Zeus was more beautiful than this one. Inside the great doors he was recognised and allowed to take the staircase up to the gallery on the left. There he could be closer to the god's face.

He leaned his elbows on the balustrade between the columns and looked at the Nike. How could victory ever be his now?

'Never forget to be grateful,' Panainos had said, though he had not said to whom, or for what. Nor how hard it could be.

Themis deliberately turned his thoughts to the girl-nymph who had cried as she was drawn out of his head. He sent up a silent prayer. *'Whoever you are, or were, and whatever it is that you did for me, I do thank you for helping me get this far.'* Then he whispered to Zeus, 'She's gone, but my head still hasn't healed inside. Will I ever really recover?'

Other worshippers arrived behind him, jostling for a place at the rail.

'Why did you take her so soon?' he went on, and then answered himself, 'Because I asked you to, of course.'

Zeus' eyes glowed.

Themis pushed his way blindly down the stairs.

>>>

From Bernie's private diary. Friday April 16ᵗʰ 2010

Couldn't face Suzanne yesterday, but today Kyle asked me if he could come with me to see her. Kyle? Why? Anyway, I thought I'd better ask her permission first. So I went round to the hospital before meeting up with him for our date.

I'd called Mrs Jackson to see what to expect and she told me Suzanne had asked for pen and paper.

When I get there Suzanne's in her chair, hiding something under her blanket.

'Your mum said you wanted things to write with,' I say. 'Is your arm better enough?'

She lifts the blanket and shows me she already has a small notepad and a biro, and she's been writing. 'Just use the other hand,' she said.

'Want to walk a bit?' I ask.

'OK.' She stands up and almost falls on her face. We have to giggle. Then we get her upright.

'You bring me any paper?' she asks.

'Yes. You hold onto the bed and I'll get it.'

She stashes the exercise book and pencil case I've brought in the drawer of her cabinet.

'Don't you want your laptop?' I ask as we set off along the ward. She really can hardly stay upright at all.

'Screen jiggles. Makes me want to puke,' she says. Suzanne never used to use language like that.

'What are you writing?' I ask.

'*You* don't want to know.' She is gritting her teeth.

'Right,' I say. We walk up the ward and through the corridors and come back to her room. We don't speak.

'Bed,' she says. So I help her in. She lies down exhausted, eyes shut.

'Would it be OK if Kyle comes to see you with me?' I ask.

'Kyle?'

'Yes, you know. Under 18s goalie. We're going out later.'

'Goalie,' she said with her eyes closed. 'Not boxer.'

'No. Though he's tried it,' I say. 'Not his thing.' I've started talking in short sentences like her now!

She sighs deeply with her eyes shut.

'Problem?' I ask.

The anger in her eyes when she opens them shocks me. I step back. '*You* should believe me,' she says, accusing me. 'You're my *best friend*.'

'You need a doctor, not a best friend,' I say, almost in tears.

She says, 'Knew you'd say that. Everyone says that.' Then, 'Go now.' And she closes her eyes and starts to hum to herself.

I met the nurse on the way out. She told me Suzanne will be going home in a day or two. Doesn't seem to me like she's ready for that. The nurse said not to give up on her, it's just a phase.

<<<

'I've contacted a healer who knows about head injuries,' said Kadmos by the pool. 'He should be here by the time you get back.'

Themis sighed and said, 'Thanks.'

'Meanwhile,' said Kadmos, 'you can work on your belly muscles so you can take punches to your stomach.'

'Right,' said Themis. 'No opponent is going to be kind enough to only hit me there … ' He sighed. 'I'll see you in four days.'

He and Panainos had borrowed Agorakritos' horses to ride to Three Rivers. Phidias had not been able to lend them his as he was busy preparing for the arrival of his wife and daughters. This involved moving out of the magnificent townhouse he shared with his students and friends and into a smaller villa nearby.

'You'll have to cut down on the parties,' Panainos had teased.

Phidias had just laughed and said, 'I'm looking forward to a little female company.' Then he'd added more seriously, 'But you be careful of Thukydides and friends. Don't let him embroil you in his politics.'

'Thukydides estate is more a village than a farm, I hear,' Panainos said as they were passing near the spring where Themis had remembered Nikitas, his twin.

'Is it?' Themis replied automatically.

'There are some special cows from the north that give milk that is all cream,' went on Panainos, 'and Thukydides breeds the fastest horses in the Peloponnese.'

'Really?' said Themis.

'I wonder whether I shall finally lose my temper with you, Themistokles, son of Kallistos,' said Panainos without a change in tone.

Frog, who was leading the mules with Niris just behind them, snorted with laughter.

Themis did not react.

'Perhaps you should go back, and I'll tell Xenovia that her kind invitation was not to your taste?' Panainos asked mildly.

Themis looked up. 'How far is it now?' he said. Xenovia might be backing the wrong political horse, but she did seem to want him to compete in the Games. And she was supposed to know about herbs and medicines. Perhaps she knew of something that would help …

'Hmm. All day at this pace,' answered Panainos. 'Should we try a gallop?'

Frog laughed, but Themis gritted his teeth and said, 'Whatever suits you best, Uncle.'

Just as the distant town was coming into view, they turned in at a large gateway, waved through by two armed guards. A long, curving gravel track led them between tall slim trees that swayed in the strong breeze. To their left, vines striped a field sloping up towards the skirts of steep, craggy mountains.

The track curved further to the right, past a dense stand of wind-ruffled oaks and they came in sight of the farm.

A large, two-storey house was set round three sides of a courtyard with sturdy columns. Beyond were two rows of cottages, a small temple, a gymnasium and countless stables, barns and workshops.

Aristocratic estate this might be, but the noises and smells were those of the farmyard. Panainos turned in his saddle and wrinkled his nose at Themis, which finally made him smile.

They were shown to rooms in one of the wings of the house.

'Aha,' said Panainos. 'A room of your own, Themis. So you won't have to listen to my snoring after all.'

'Do you snore, Uncle?' asked Themis with a wide, innocent stare.

Panainos ignored this. 'Come with me and let's find our host,' he said. 'He bought this place a few years ago so as to be nearer to Athens. He travelled to the far west at the beginning of his exile, but soon learned that he still had a following at home, and so may well get a second chance at political leadership.' They left Frog and Niris to put things away. Music was coming from the garden terrace of the main house. Panainos grabbed Themis' arm and set off to see what was going on.

People were listening to the music on couches in the undulating shade of a spreading plane tree beyond the low terrace. Panainos swept down the two steps and approached a white-haired man with a nose like the beak of a hawk, who was standing by a natural pond.

'Thukydides!' said Panainos heartily. 'I don't think you've met my nephew and apprentice? Themistokles, meet your host.'

'Sir,' said Themis, interested in spite of himself by the bold lines of the old man's brows and hooked nose. They bowed to one another.

'You are both very welcome. You're a boxer, I hear?' said Thukydides.

'Not any more,' said Themis bitterly.

'Themistokles had an accident which damaged his head and he cannot take punches any more,' explained Panainos. 'He is very disappointed.'

'I'm not surprised,' said Thukydides. 'But we may have just the remedy for you. Many of my guests are … herbalists. We will be trying out various remedies in our meals.'

'Nothing too noxious, I hope,' laughed Panainos.

'Nothing noxious at all. Everything is guaranteed to make you feel better than you have done for a long time. Come, sit with us.' Thukydides led them to the couches. There was no sign of Xenovia.

Themis had forgotten what boredom was like. He had not sat in a philosophy class or been forced to listen to older people setting the world to rights since before his accident. He soon found that he couldn't keep his eyes open, so he excused himself and went off to find Frog.

'Training time,' he said. 'Can you come?'

'Thought you'd given up training now you're an official invalid again,' said Frog, setting down the jar of lamp oil he was carrying.

They ran out along the drive, through the town and up beside one of the three rivers that gave the area its name. Themis pushed himself hard and was far ahead of Frog by the time the heat got too much and the way too steep.

He stopped for a few moments in the shade of the last tree before the path climbed into some crags. The view did lift his heart a little. Lines of mountains and valleys to the south-west, one behind the other, faded from green to hazy blue to deep grey where they met the deep blue of the sea. Perhaps these hills contained a wonder herb that would cure him, after all. He set off back to join Frog.

At the estate, they found they'd missed the midday meal. Someone had left a plate laden with cold meats, rolls and chutneys for Themis.

'We've got hare in wine with fresh bread in the kitchen,' said Frog.

'Sounds better than cold meat to me,' Themis replied.

In the kitchens they found another boy scrounging a meal.

'I'm Zephus,' he said to Themis with his mouth full. 'Want to look round the farm after?'

They were counting the piglets and it was getting dark when they heard a great clamour of voices from the house.

It came from the servants' quarters. Themis could hear Thukydides voice booming above the others. 'Give him space! Call the healers!'

At the sound of that voice, Zephus disappeared. Panainos came rushing across the yard to Themis and Frog. He stumbled in his haste and distress. Tears were running down his cheeks.

'It's Niris,' he gasped. 'He's convulsing, frothing, vomiting … ' He grabbed Themis' hand and pulled him into a small courtyard. 'What can we do? What can we do?'

They pushed their way between the on-lookers. On the flagstones of the yard, Niris' was straining to rise from a pool of vomit and faeces. His brown face was set in a horrible grimace, his eyes bursting out of his small head. The fear in them lessened when he saw Panainos, and he reached out a dripping hand. As Panainos stepped forward, Niris gave a shuddering sigh and fell back, his eyes blank in the set stare of death.

'No! No!' wailed Panainos. 'No, this can't be true.' Many hands held him back from kneeling in the slime. He turned to Themis, his eyes wide with disbelief and horror.

'What killed him?' murmured Themis, staring at the distorted body.

Thukydides put an arm round Panainos' shoulders. 'It looks like some kind of poison,' he said. 'Perhaps a mistaken mushroom of some kind.' Then he raised his voice. 'Nobody touch the slime! Take the body and wash it and prepare it for the pyre. Bring water and scrub this area clean.'

Panainos sank to the ground wretching.

Frog appeared at Themis' side. He was shaking. 'Come and see something,' he whispered.

The guests were moving into the main house. Two of them helped Panainos up and supported him as they took him inside.

Themis followed Frog. They went to his own room.

There, near the door, the platter of cold meats and relishes had fallen and scattered its contents all over the floor. The dish was in two pieces. Frog pointed at smeared footprints in the mess.

'I often saw Niris take a little piece of food from a dish. He would rearrange things so you would never know,' said Frog in a whisper.

'Do you think that's what he could have done here? Taken a bit, started eating it and choked, or … '

'That dish was meant for me!' said Themis suddenly.

They stared at each other in horror.

Chapter 38: poison

In the kitchens, between mouthfuls of soup, Zephus told them, 'A man died out in the woods last year. They found his body with the same kind of slime all around, just like Niris.'

'Bad things, mushrooms,' nodded the cook. 'I only use the ones with the white tops and black gills – autumn mushrooms. Those others had spots on – black spots on brown.'

'So Niris could have eaten one and *then* gone to get the platter?' suggested Themis.

'Mmm. The poison will have grabbed him as he was carrying it,' said the cook. His chins wobbled as he nodded sagely.

'We'd better get to bed,' said Themis. 'They gave my uncle a potion, but he's too upset to sleep long.'

He and Frog left Zephus with the cook and bedded down together on a mattress on the floor, like they'd done as children.

Themis dreamed he was swimming in green froth and having his belly bitten into by huge bears. Frog woke him up because of the noise he was making. He did not sleep again.

Niris' body lay on the heap of hastily assembled logs. Thukydides thrust a torch into the mound. As soon as he saw that the fire was going well, he left the private cemetery. Themis, Frog and Panainos stood and watched. It was not a heroic pyre and there were still recognizable pieces of Niris left when the flames died down and the slaves began tidying up.

Themis led Panainos to his bedroom and sat him on the bed. Themis took the only stool.

'What should we do now, Uncle?' he asked.

Panainos was taking a weary breath to answer when a bustle in the corridor revealed Xenovia. She hurried in, her eyes green pools of concern.

'I've just got back from the Temple of Athena at Scillus, south of the Alpheios, and heard about your slave,' she said. 'Are you well yourself, dear Panainos?'

Themis stood up from his stool and offered it to the priestess. She did not seem to see him but sat on the stool. Themis caught the scent of jasmine as she moved. Two tendrils of her hair had come unpinned and spilled onto the shoulder of her ivory linen gown.

Panainos said, 'You are kind, Sacred Lady. I am well, but deeply saddened and shocked.' His face had sagged into vertical lines.

'As am I,' said Xenovia. The straight lines of her profile were austere, her curls soft in contrast. Themis stepped slightly nearer.

'I will return to Olympia today and leave for Athens immediately,' said Panainos.

'I cannot tell you how sorry I am.' Xenovia leaned forward on her stool, hands spread open towards Panainos. 'If I had been here the mistake would not have been made.'

'Mistake?' asked Panainos.

'One of the kitchen slaves had brought in some mushrooms from the forest and left them in a basket for me to see. It seems your man took one to taste before …' Xenovia sat back. 'I've had them disposed of safely.'

Themis breathed a sigh of relief.

Panainos looked down at his belly. 'It was a terrible way to die,' he said quietly. Then he raised his head. 'But now we will gather our things together and leave, won't we, Themis?'

'Yes, Uncle,' said Themis. He was looking at the point where Xenovia's nose joined her upper lip in the perfect right-angle, beside the neat curl of the nostril.

Xenovia stood up. 'I will send a man to help you.'

'And so we bid you adieu, Thukydides,' said Panainos, obviously impatient to leave.

'This has been such an unfortunate visit for you, Master Panainos,' growled the older man. 'I pray that you will not wish to avoid me now that I am free to return to Athens.'

With a set smile on his face Panainos replied, 'Of course not, my old friend. I shall be seeing you there soon, I hope?'

'Thank you.' The older man inclined his head. 'And you, young Themistokles. I'm sorry about this death, but I hope your stay with us was memorable for more pleasant reasons, as well.'

Themis saw Xenovia coming out of the house. 'It certainly was, sir,' he said. Then he turned to Xenovia. 'Will you be visiting Olympia again, Sacred Lady?'

'Oh, yes. Many times in the next few months,' she said with warmth in her eyes. 'I was so glad to hear of your continuing recovery. Soon you will have your memory back too, I am sure.'

Themis shook his head firmly. 'I doubt it,' he said. 'There are still long periods I cannot remember. Will you be here for the Games?'

She smiled sadly. 'I shan't be able to watch you compete, Themis. Women are not allowed in the precinct during the Games.'

'Well, it seems my injury will stop me from competing after all,' said Themis, his jaw set. 'But I'd very much like to see you there anyway.'

A little frown of curiosity passed across her face. But all she said was, 'I'm sure we'll meet again soon.'

Themis bowed to them both and turned to mount his horse. Thukydides called, 'Go well on your journeys!' above the din as they rode out of the yard.

Themis wanted to ask Panainos whether he had learned of any herbs that could heal the weakness in his head. It was clear that there were some strong medicines available. But the master painter leaned forward and urged his horse to a canter. Themis hauled Frog up behind him and followed. Foot travellers scattered as they passed.

Phidias was waiting for them at the hotel. 'You have different rooms this time,' he said, leading them to the upper floor. 'And it is not an apartment, I'm afraid. This is yours, brother,' and he showed Panainos into a large room at the end of the outside walkway.

'This is fine,' said Panainos, as he threw down his hat on the bed.

'And you are along here, Themis,' Phidias went on. Themis' room was three doors along, just over the kitchens. 'Best I could do at short notice,' apologised Phidias.

'No problem, Uncle,' said Themis.

'We're expecting you for an evening meal as soon as you're able.' There was an unusually hard edge to Phidias' voice.

'Is something wrong?' Themis asked.

'I would say that the death of a faithful servant in circumstances that smell of murder is something wrong, wouldn't you?'

'But no one believes … '

'Come to dinner and we'll talk about it,' said Phidias more gently. 'And make sure my brother comes with you. He may want to opt out.' He turned on his toes and disappeared down the stairs.

The meal was over. Ismini had been in to the andron to wish them welcome and, later, goodnight. Frescoes of intricate flowering bushes against a fading sunset sky glowed in the lamplight.

'But it *was* the mushrooms,' insisted Panainos. He looked straight across at Phidias.

Phidias swung his legs round to sit upright on his couch. 'Think about it, brother. What kind of mushrooms do you get in late spring? None.'

'Not in Athens,' agreed Panainos. 'At least, not that I know of. But here it's damper, cooler. There are fungi all year round. There was a dish of them fried at the midday meal, and Frog made a duck stew with some three days ago. We were talking about it in the andron afterwards. No one had any problems with them at all.'

'Well, you know my opinion of Xenovia.'

'Don't be ridiculous. Why would she lie?' challenged Panainos.

'It would not be the first time,' Phidias smiled wryly.

'So what do *you* suppose happened to Niris?' asked Panainos.

'I *suggest* that Niris ate something that was intended for someone else.' Phidias was looking hard at Panainos.

Themis said quietly, 'The dish of food that was spilled all over the floor was left out for me.'

Phidias turned to him sharply. 'Are you sure?'

'We'd been out, looking round the farm. When I saw the dish of food in my room I assumed it was for me because I'd missed the midday meal, but Frog said they had better food in the kitchen, so I ate there.'

Panainos' face was grey. 'And when Niris was clearing away later … ' His voice faded to nothing.

'How do you know it was for you and not for your uncle?' snapped Phidias.

'We had separate rooms,' said Panainos wearily, rubbing a hand across his face. 'Going to Thukydides' place was clearly one of my worse ideas.'

Phidias was triumphant. 'I told you that having anything to do with that Spartan-loving old oligarch was a mistake.'

Panainos sighed. 'But Phidias, what is the point of getting rid of either me or Themis? Thukydides thinks of me as a political bridge to you and Perikles. He needs me. He told me so. Unlike Perikles, *he* is trying to *stop* the war.'

'Aren't we all?' said Phidias impatiently. He stood up. 'So, you believe that what Themis reported from the kitchen is true. Niris ate something he shouldn't in the kitchens, then went to tidy Themis' room and the poison caught up with him as he worked?'

'That is what I believe,' said Panainos, grief thickening his voice.

'Well, I have more faith in Niris' knowledge of fungi,' declared Phidias. 'I still believe there was foul play there. But, as you say, there is no obvious reason for *you* to be poisoned in the house of a man who is a traitor to Athenian democracy.' Phidias was striding up and down in the middle of the room, swishing his robe at each turn.

'Oh, Phidias. Drama, drama, always drama,' groaned Panainos as he stood up. 'How can an opposition leader be a traitor in a democracy? Thukydides is a man of integrity and vision.'

'And his vision will ruin Perikles, and Athens, and possibly me,' said Phidias. Then he relaxed with a sigh, and came to stand by his brother. 'But in spite of your political views, I'm glad the world has not lost its best painter, and I do wish you a safe journey home.' He put an arm round Panainos' shoulders.

'Well, thank you for that, brother,' said Panainos wryly.

>>>

From Bernie's private diary. Monday April 19th 2010

They took Suzanne home yesterday. Kyle and I dropped in today and she was in her own room with her computer on and all her stuff tidy, the way her mother likes it.

Kyle got dragged off by Elliot to see his latest video game. Suzanne's skin looked two shades more transparent than in hospital.

'You don't look too good,' I say, tactful as always.

'Yesterday was … knackering.' She looks at me sideways. 'And … my shoulder aches.' It's the first time I've ever seen hollows in her cheeks, and her eyes are too wide open.

'Have they given you some new drug or something?' I ask.

'No. Blue pills morning, orange pills evening.'

'Do you want to tell me what's really wrong?' I ask.

'Not sure.' She looks away.

'It's about your dreams?'

'Yes.' She looks back at me, suspicious, ready to get angry.

'I'm just frightened for you,' I say very quietly.

'No point,' she shrugs. Her shoulder doesn't seem to hurt after all.

'Go on then,' I say.

'I don't see so much now – as Themis.'

'That doesn't sound so bad,' I say.

'I have to guess the in-betweens.'

'Right,' I say.

'But … since I got home yesterday … ' she's looking out of the window, '… it's the same stuff, over and over. It's … ' Her voice is wobbling, rising. But then she stops.

'What?' I ask. 'What happens?'

She looks at me, a moment of aggression. Then she whispers, 'One of the slaves is dying in a pool of sick and shit. The food he ate was supposed to be for me ... er … Themis.'

I think about that for a moment. Then I say, 'You don't suppose this is brought on by the pills you take, or by the changes cos of coming home, do you?'

She takes a breath to swear at me, then decides not to. Her mouth is a hard line.

'Never seen things more than once before.' She looks at the posters of Taylor Lautner and Kate Dennison above the door. 'Home's better.'

'You happy to be here?'

'It's OK. Computer still makes me dizzy.'

'Your mum took time off, didn't she?'

'One week. Nurse from Monday. Dad's paying.'

'How long for?' Even Mr Short isn't rich enough for a full time nurse for ever.

'Not sure.' She begins to hum, her eyes going blank.

'D'you want to sleep?' I ask.

A door downstairs slams and a voice I don't recognise calls out, 'I'm ba-ack!'

Suzanne stops humming and makes an OMG face. 'Steve's mum,' she whispers spookily.

'Your step-father's mother? What's she like?'

'Don't know. Granola.' She makes an imp face.

'Granola?!' I laugh.

'The boys call her that.'

She gets up and walks over to the window. 'Woo-oo. Dizzy,' she says.

I go and stand with her, looking out.

'I must be mental,' she says quietly. 'Can't stop seeing it.'

'Watch some TV,' I say. 'You've got some great DVDs here.'

'My eyes jiggle about,' she says. 'But books are OK.' She has an idea. 'Get me some library books?'

'OK,' I agree. 'What kind of books?'

'Pictures. Old times. Perikles.'

'Perikles! You doing research for your project?'

'Can't stop seeing it.'

'What does your doctor say?'

She puts her nose in the air and speaks over her shoulder, like some kind of diva. 'I have a date with a shrink.'

Kyle comes back just then.

'Who *is* that woman,' he whispers.

We all giggle. Suzanne says, 'Grows lilies.' She puts on a silly voice. 'Mind the pollen.'

We crack up. 'Tuck your shirt in,' she goes on in the voice. 'Go on, eat it. It's got no calories.'

'Stop it, Suzanne,' I shush her. 'She'll hear.'

Suzanne switches back to serious. 'Get me library books,' she says.

'Now?'

'It's open isn't it?'

'Sure. I'll see what I can find,' I say, and we leave.

Later

Suzanne opened the front door to me. 'You got some?' she asked before I was even inside. Elliot and Robbie were playing F1 on the Wii and Steve was grinding something in the kitchen, so she had to shout.

I'd found some Groovy Greeks stuff and one huge volume at the library. I laid them out on her desk and said, 'You'd do much better on line.'

'Later,' she said, and sat straight down to look stuff up in the index. I had a look at her CDs and the playlists on her iPod, but she ignored me. She's really into Mozart all of a sudden …

She muttered something like, 'What about Phidias' wife?' so I gave up. 'I have to go, Suzanne,' I said. 'Kyle's waiting.'

'OK,' she said without looking up. 'See you.'

<<<

'You'll start in the wax-melting sector,' said the senior caster, Kleandros. He led Themis through a large complex of yards and buildings. The smells of burning wood, hot wax and that odd, floating odour of hot metal reached Themis. In the huge room they entered, two men and two slaves were already working at enormous fires with shallow cauldrons hung over them. They were naked except for loincloths. The heat made Themis come out in an immediate sweat.

'Your first job is to help load the cauldrons with the raw wax,' said Kleandros. He led Themis over to an unstable stack of baskets by the wall. 'Unfortunately,' he went on with a twinkle in his hooded eyes, 'all the honey has been extracted. But, as you can see, there are often dead bees and twigs and suchlike in the lumps of wax. These float to the surface during the melt. That's when you start your second job, skimming them off. With this.' And he handed Themis a wooden skimmer with a handle longer than Themis was tall.

The older of the two men came over. 'You'll learn to be careful with that,' he said. 'It took me a while,' and he showed Themis his hands, deeply scarred and twisted. 'Those are old scars. We have bands of leather we make to protect our hands these days.'

'Themistokles, son of Kallistos.' The voice rang out over the din of work and song.

Themis swung the skimmer over the debris bin, knocked off the skimmings, and stood it against the wall.

A slave was waiting for him at the door.

'You have a message? I'm Themistokles,' he said to the man.

'Phidias wants you. Please go to his workshop at once.'

Themis found Phidias at the round table, now covered in drawings and the small model of a temple, discussing earnestly with an overseer.

'Ah, Themis,' he said with a nod at his colleague. 'I thought you should know that the guards have learned that a gang of slavers has been active down near Pylos. There have been no other raids here, so they think your attacker has left the area.'

Themis nodded. 'That's good,' he said.

Then Phidias pulled a small scroll from his belt and led Themis out into the yard.

'Meanwhile, this arrived from your mother. It came on the boat that Panainos left on.'

'What does it say? How is she?' Themis' mouth was dry.

'She seems to be fine. And so are the rest of the family, thank the gods. But, and this is not good news, she insists she is not going to sign the permission necessary for you to take part in the boxing contest at the Games, always supposing you're well enough.' Phidias pursed his lips gravely.

'But my father wanted me to ... '

' "Uphold the family honour"? Yes, she mentions that and says that there's not much point doing that if there's no family left and you are dead or epileptic. Also,' said Phidias more gently, 'she thinks it would be a shame if you damaged your hands and could not paint any more.

You can see her point.'

Themis sighed in exasperation, 'Huh! Damage my hands,' he said. 'It's the wax that will damage my hands. Anyway, women don't understand about things like this. Especially older ones.'

'She *is* getting old,' agreed Phidias. 'She knows it's unlikely she'll have any more sons, so she's trying to protect those left to her.'

Themis' shoulders drooped. He felt on the edge of tears again. 'Well, I doubt I can compete anyway,' he said hopelessly. 'There's not much point training when you can't do one-to-one fighting. And no one seems to know how to cure me of fainting every time I get hit.'

'But Kadmos is finding a way to solve that problem. He holds out great hopes. He says your left fist is deadly and you are fearless!'

'He hasn't said that to me.'

'Well, we'd better not tell your mother anyway. She's definitely not going to agree to your competing.'

'So.' Themis swallowed, trying to clear the lump in his throat. 'I'll *have* to leave now.'

'That's not what she says, though I imagine that's what she wants.' Phidias held out the scroll with a smile. 'She says you can stay and learn your craft as long as I am here. Of course, she also wants you to have your audience with Zeus.' Phidias was looking at Themis with one eyebrow raised.

'O-of course,' stammered Themis.

Phidias came a little closer. 'Am I right in understanding that your memory of before your fall is improving?' he asked.

Themis thought, '*He knows. I haven't been careful enough.*' He said, 'I do get more flashes of memory these days.'

Phidias nodded slowly. 'That can only be good.' He indicated the scroll. 'Your mother asks me to bring you back to Athens on my ship.'

'Really?' Themis said in relief. 'On your ship? Wow. When do you leave?'

'Well … I was going to slip over to Egypt now the weather's better. Then I'll be back here for the Games and off to Athens after that.'

Themis was still. 'So … I suppose I could at least watch the Games?'

'I'm sure that would be fine – as long as Eirini doesn't learn that I left you here for a while, on your own.' Phidias looked hard at Themis.

Themis smiled slightly. 'Oh she won't learn anything from me!'

'Nor from me,' said Phidias, handing the scroll to Themis.

>>>

254

Chapter 39: special rules

From Bernie's private diary. Saturday April 24th 2010

'How did it go with the shrink?' I asked Suzanne today, thinking about how upset she'd been about the man dying over and over in her mind.

But she seemed to have forgotten him, cos her head went back and her eyes got huge. 'His name's Nigel. Nigel! Yuck! He says, "Your fantasies are how your brain is curing itself".' She put on a slimy voice. ' "They're like a scab over a graze on your knee or a plaster when you cut yourself. They protect you while you heal inside. Soon the scab will peel off and disappear".'

'Don't you believe him?'

'I have no idea!' she shouted. 'Never had scrambled eggs for brains before, or … ' She stopped.

'Or what?' I asked.

'Or … a complete other world in my head.'

I said, 'That's … scary, but he might be right. You are changing. You just told me all that in whole sentences. Perhaps that world really is a kind of retreat.'

That made her swear!

It was amazing. She stomped around her room yelling stuff I can't believe even her father would say. Nigel was a bald caterpillar fetishist with his tests and his lists and his long words, and I'm the misbegotten spawn of a mangy squirrel! But most of it was to do with not being able to check things cos the computer screen makes her feel sick, and our all being stupid donkey turds because we don't believe her.

In the end I shouted, 'Shut up!' And she did!

'Look, Suzanne,' I said. 'You have to stop obsessing about this stuff. Can't you come out with us yet? Kyle and I and Tom and Alison are meeting at Laser Wars tonight. Come with us.'

And Mrs J said ok, so I helped Suzanne into her tightest jeans and we put a bit of makeup on her face. She still wants to cover up that mole on her upper lip with foundation. I told her that even top models have moles, and she said, 'You always say that!'

So she really does remember everything from before. And at Laser Wars it was great. Everyone was so pleased to see her, we stayed till late.

<<<

'Oh, come on,' said Themis wearily. 'He'll never finish at this rate and I'm tired.'

'Shhh,' whispered Frog. 'He'll be done any moment. He said I was to make sure he got to speak to you or he would whip me.'

'Agorakritos? Whip you?'

'That's what he said,' said Frog.

Themis looked sideways at him and sighed pointedly.

They watched as Agorakritos sweated and grunted through the leg lifting and the final push-ups. He came over to them as soon as the trainer released his group. Frog got him a sweat-cloth.

'Thanks, Frog,' he said breathlessly, sweat dripping from his curls. 'I gather from Kadmos that you haven't trained for some days now, Themis.'

Themis made a face. 'No need! Work at the foundry is really hard. Better training than anything we do here. Look at these biceps.'

'Hmm. Will you get a day off?' asked Agorakritos, rubbing the cloth over his hair.

'In three days.' Themis looked at the sculptor suspiciously.

'Well,' said Agorakritos. 'I shall be in Elis by then. But I want you to come to the gym and report to Kadmos as if there were no doubts about your place in the Games. Things can change, and if they do, you don't want to have lost your edge. Just do a couple exercise routines on your day off.' He stood up. 'I'd better get cleaned up.'

Themis murmured bitterly, 'And I was so looking forward to spending my day writing a long, obedient letter to my mother and drawing some sketches of the statues of heroes in the Altis.'

Agorakritos laughed. 'Phidias said you'd need an eye kept on you. And how can you draw – or box, even – with those hands?' He held Themis' hands and turned them over to look at the blisters.

Themis looked up at him. 'What does it matter? I'm under age and Mama won't sign. End of story.'

'For now.' Agorakritos walked towards the dressing rooms. 'But the judge is my future father-in-law … ' Then he called over his gleaming shoulder, 'Make sure he eats properly, Frog. I'll be back in five days.'

When Kadmos saw Themis, he showed no pleasure.

'So, Themistokles, you are honouring us with your presence today,' he said.

'I've only missed a few days,' said Themis. 'I get tired at the foundry, but look at the muscles I'm building.'

'Join the back line.' Kadmos was unimpressed. The group of boys and young men began their exercise routine. Kadmos called out the moves and the flautist played the rhythms.

The routine was longer and harder than the last time Themis had attended. He was exhausted by the end, and collapsed in the shade, sweating and trembling.

'Pair up for wrestling practice,' called Kadmos. He started calling the names of the pairs.

'I'd like to work with Themis,' interrupted one young man.

'We have special rules for Themis,' Kadmos said.

'I know,' said the young man with a pleasant smile at Themis. 'That's why I'm interested. No blows or holds on the head.'

'All right, Lysimachos, you and Themis work in that corner,' agreed Kadmos.

Lysimachos was a small, slim man of about twenty. He and Themis went through the stylized approach-and-retreat routine with the music. Lysimachos moved gracefully and took great care where he put his feet in the soft sand.

Then Kadmos gave the call for free practice and all the pairs began to grab and tumble each other. Lysimachos was relatively fresh and got Themis round the waist, tripping him quite easily.

Themis grasped Lysimachos' right arm on the rise, and twisted it up behind his back. Lysimachos sagged as though submitting and, when Themis' hold slackened a little, he leaned forward. This upset Themis' balance and Lysimachos hit back hard with his other elbow. It found Themis' left ear with a crack. In automatic reaction, Themis pulled hard upwards on Lysimachos' right arm and they both fell on the sand. But whirling grey had filled Themis' head.

'Not again,' he thought as pain dragged him into a roaring blackness.

Coming round, he could feel the resident healer wiping sand from his face and hair with a damp cloth. Kadmos and Lysimachos were arguing.

Kadmos was saying ' ... agreed that there would be no blows to the head.'

Lysimachos whined, 'But there was no other way to get out of that hold.'

'There are lots of ways to get out of it, and anyway, you should have submitted. That's why you got a whipping. You are the one who said you wanted to work with Themis.'

Lysimachos conceded, 'Well, perhaps I should have submitted, but in the heat of the moment ... '

'There *is* no "heat of the moment" in practice,' bellowed Kadmos. 'How many times have we chanted that and worked on it?!'

Themis heard someone kneel down beside him. A hand felt for the pulse in his neck and Themis opened his eyes.

'Ah. You're conscious. Any pain?' Kadmos asked with concern.

'Dizzy,' said Themis trying to focus his eyes. When he shut them he was less dizzy, so he lay like that for a while. Then he heard a new voice.

' … not heat of the moment. I was watching. Lysimachos was angling for that blow. I could tell by the way he got into just the right position.'

Kadmos' voice said, 'Oh no you don't, Lysimachos! You'll stay here and answer what Amintas says. Did you do this on purpose?'

'Of course not!' came Lysimachos' voice, fearful now. Then, 'Ouch! Let me go!'

Themis risked a look. He could see a blurred Lysimachos on his knees with four or five gashes across his back.

Amintas was standing over him with some kind of hold on his fingers. Themis shut his eyes again.

'Aaagh! Please! Let go of my finger!' squealed Lysimachos.

'Why did you do it?' growled Kadmos.

'I was paid,' sobbed Lysimachos.

'Who paid you?' asked Kadmos in surprise.

'I don't know him. A man in a long black cloak – last night when I was leaving the brothel. I'd lost a lot of money betting on … Aaagh! … betting.'

'Let him go, Amintas,' said Kadmos wearily. 'Old man? Young man? What was he like?'

'My height, youngish I think, but I couldn't see and his voice was muffled.'

'Get out of here,' said Kadmos. 'There's no place for you in this gymnasium any more.'

It was morning. Themis sat up. Frog was sleeping on a mat beside his bed but no one else was there. He swung his legs off the other side of the bed, expecting pain or dizziness, or both. He stood up – and immediately sat down again.

Frog's head appeared. 'You planning your escape?' he asked sleepily.

'Just looking for the latrine – and some food,' said Themis. 'Are you going to help me?'

Frog got an arm under Themis' shoulder. 'You're not so bad this time.'

'Huh!' grunted Themis. 'Any news about the man in the cloak?'

'Lysimachos works in the administration offices,' said Frog. 'We can't prosecute him because what he did isn't against any law. And he doesn't know any more than he said. Kadmos went to see him.' Frog nodded happily. 'He won't bother you again.'

'Photios, dear friend,' wrote Themis. *When I wrote to you about getting my memory back, I thought everything was going to be fine and nothing more would go wrong. But now everything's going sour. And with the work in the foundry and boxing practice, my hands are a mess and holding the stylus is difficult, which is why the crooked letters. I can't believe I'll be able to take part in the Games, even if I'm fit and Mama changes her mind about the permission. There was a man at the gym who was paid to hit me on the head by someone in a long cloak. This took me a day to get over, feeling like I'd drunk a whole jug of undiluted wine. Do you suppose Straton or his family really are out to get me? Could they have sent this man? And I've been followed by a man on a mule, and a man with a dog, and a man with a whip! Are they all the same person? Are they sent perhaps by Nikanor after all? Mama doesn't mention anything else nasty happening to my brother and sisters, unless she is hiding things from me. Could you check if that's true for me? Or is it the family of that boy, Mantius, that I beat in the finals to qualify? If I'm going to be beaten up so that I can't compete, I can't see any real point in staying on here. All these attacks make me angry, but I don't know how to fight back because I don't know who is behind them. It must be someone in Athens, mustn't it?. I'm thinking of using my emergency money for the passage back, so don't be surprised if I turn up at your gate in ten or fifteen days. At least Mama would be pleased, and I could compete again in four years' time. Just one thing seems to be going better, and that is that I don't dream such horrific dreams any more. Now I see people I know, like Kadmos and Kleandros at the foundry. And I often dream of Xenovia (Don't you dare tell anyone else that! You will drown in the Ilisos after running mad and going green if you do. Zeus is watching you!) and that nymph I mentioned. The others say and do frightening things, but* she says *things to me like "don't give up because you'll regret it later". Really spooky, and yet she gives me courage. When I'm awake, though, I find everyone irritating, even myself. Write back soon and let me know what*

>>>

From Bernie's private diary. Saturday May 1st 2010

I went round to ask Suzanne how her interview at school had gone yesterday. Her mum drove her there to be 'assessed' while we were all in class.

And she was furious! She kept saying, 'Why can't I concentrate? Why can't I concentrate?' They had an outside psychologist and the Head and Miss Rallis talking to her. She'd got confused and hadn't understood some of the things they asked her.

She yelled at me, 'They say I can't do a full day at school until after half term. Or maybe later!'

'Don't yell at me!' I yelled back. 'You're getting better all the time. You make proper sentences. You can keep your mind on one subject for more than a minute now. You're beginning to use complicated words.'

'Words!' she spat out. 'I have to look everything up! It comes of … ' and she looked like she was going to cry for a second.

'What?' I shouted.

'Oh, nothing,' she said, with her 'you'll never understand' look again.

I stared out of the window for a bit to calm down. Josh and I were planning to drive along the lake and go for a walk cos it's May Day. No daffodils now, but rhododendrons everywhere. So I said to come with us. Her house is so noisy and chaotic, I felt I couldn't leave her there on such a lovely morning.

And she agreed! So we went to the little beach Josh and I used to play on when we were in junior school, beyond Waterside campsite. Josh got her talking about how she used to train for pole vault. He said she should get back to it and to ask her doctor if it would be ok, with her collarbone and everything.

I asked, 'How are you getting on with that shrink?'

'Makes me do questionnaires and write a log. Like I'm a dead tree. He's a twat,' she said. End of conversation.

But she had been mostly talking sense and not losing her temper for at least an hour!

<<<

Chapter 40: float and sting

Frog would be out looking for him by now, but Themis did not want to be found. He ran up a small hill among the orchards just out of town and sat on the cool rocks at the top under an old oak tree covered in shining new leaves.

'I'm losing what mind I have left,' he thought. *'I'm working like a slave for something that isn't going to happen. But then again, it might … '*

He held up his hands and looked at the scars: lines from the boxing thongs, and dots where the wax had fallen beyond the protecting bands. *'How do I fight without getting hit?'* he thought. Then he said aloud 'Tell me that, all you gods! How do I fight without getting hit? And should I go home to my mother like a whining child, or should I fight for my father, like a man?'

He turned his hands over and looked at the palms as though the answer would be there.

A butterfly came tumbling towards him, bright orange with tiny black spots at the tips of its wings. It landed on his finger. He held his breath. It opened its wings and closed them again.

'What are you doing here?' he whispered. 'I'm not a flower, you know.' He tried to put his other hand over it, but it avoided him. It wavered and drifted around him, like a flake of glowing ash. It even almost landed on his nose.

His heart lifted for the first time in days. He tried again and again to catch the butterfly between his hands. Its flight seemed so random and pointless, and yet it always eluded him.

At last it departed, floating on the breeze above the fruit trees below.

Themis started to walk back down the hill with a smile on his face. Falling apple-blossom petals had turned the ground pink, although the trees were still flowering. Their fragrance filled the air and he could hear bees at work.

He saw Frog crossing a field below, peering all round to find him.

He shouted, 'Hey! I'm here!' Frog didn't hear him. He waved his arms and began to run. 'Here! Frog!'

Just then, something hit Themis on his bare shoulder. He stopped. There was an angry buzzing and something brushed through his hair. The buzzing became louder and the bombardment more often. He was being attacked by bees! He ran through the trees as fast as he could until he met Frog.

'Where … Hey, what's the matter?' Frog asked. 'You seen a ghost or something?'

Themis was breathless. 'No. But I upset some bees … by calling to you from up there among the orchards.'

'I didn't hear you. Did they sting you?'

'I can't feel any stings.'

Frog looked him over and shook his head. They started jogging back.

'The bees were so fast,' said Themis, 'I hardly saw them. By the time I heard them they'd hit me.'

'A bit like your left fist,' joked Frog.

Themis stopped dead. 'Butterfly,' he said. 'And bee … '

'Sorry?' said Frog.

'You can't catch a butterfly because it's so random, so unpredictable. And you can't catch a bee because it's so fast you don't even see it.'

'So?'

'So that's how to fight!' laughed Themis. 'Frog, you're a genius!' And he ran on, leaping up every few steps with a shout of joy.

Frog followed, smiling and shaking his head.

From Bernie's private diary. Tuesday May 4th 2010

Suzanne showed me the log she writes for her counselor today. It's just an exercise book and she writes by hand because she still has trouble with screens. She writes like she talks, jumping from one thing to another. Also she sometimes uses her right hand and sometimes her left. I never thought about that before, but her writing looks different with the different hands. I suppose her shoulder bothers her sometimes, so she switches. I wish I could write as well with my left as my right.

Oh, and she's so angry. But sometimes it's funny too.

'Can't say anything about Themis to Nigel, though,' she said. 'He thinks I'm making it up.'

'But surely it's his job … ' I began, though I wonder if Nigel isn't right.

'Hhhm!' she snorted. 'He asked me a load of questions. Gave me a score. Said it told him I'm not schizophrenic, and I don't have dissociative something or other.'

'Dissociative Identity Disorder,' I said. 'No you don't, because you remember everything. I checked it on the web.'

'So whatever I *have* got, no one wants to know about.' She slapped her log down on her desk and looked out of the window. 'Gets a bit lonely.'

That made me feel bad. 'If you start writing down exactly how you feel, just for yourself, you'll feel less lonely,' I said sympathetically.

'Got an answer for everything, haven't you?' she mocked.

When she's cruel like that, it hurts me and I have to tell myself that it's just the accident talking. Mum says I should make a joke of it, but I haven't managed that yet.

I asked Josh to come with me when I go to see her this evening, just to keep things on a fun level. He's much better at that than I am. And he's worshipped by her brothers.

From Suzanne's secret diary
May 5th, 2010, Wednesday

Can't say what I want to in Nigel's idiotic 'log'. Can't tell anyone what's important. They all think I'm mental. P'raps I am. Sometimes think Bernie believes me. Then I see she doesn't. Pisses me off.

Have to type this in bursts. Messes up my eyes.

BUT – got something very important to say …

Today is best for weeks. Themis got my message!!! Unbelievable. Been well depressed cos of him. Why does he want to box, for God's sake? He'll get killed. Can't tell him. Doesn't hear me. But today he did! Heard (can't watch yet) this documentary on TV on Mohammed Ali in 1960s. Started boxing when he was twelve. 'Youngest boxer to win world champion heavy weight title from holder.' He said things like 'I float like a butterfly and sting like a bee.' And 'Your hands can't hit what your eyes can't see.' Wrote them down so I could tell Themis.

Since then – days now – been trying to get the idea into his head. And today he got it! Maybe chance, tho. Or maybe some god ...

Everyone's out except Granola. She's on the phone to a client. She makes cakes – it's her job. I didn't know. Sour old bat makes sugar roses. Wants me to help with the housework.

Sunny there. Who needs clothes? All-over tan very sexy.

Nigel looks like a heavy in a spy movie – shaved bald with black t-shirt, grey suit. Smells of … ? rubber.

Granola says, 'Even if you're doolally you can fold clothes from the dryer.'

Don't know what to say in the log. He doesn't want to know about Themis. Nothing else happening.

Home's just like before. Mum's out or on automatic pilot. Steve's out or taking the boys to football. Or swimming.

Kadmos was explaining anatomy to a group of boys sitting round his feet under a tree. Themis signed to him that he wanted to speak to him urgently, and went to the wrestling area. He passed the time punching one of the bags of wool and sand that hung there. He was going to be late to work, but nothing could depress him now.

The sun was throwing shadows of the wooden columns round the practice area onto the sand. The sand in the shadows was the colour of the sky as the last light leaves it at night. He loved looking at the shining green of the pine trees against the bright morning blue above. Life was good. He sent a silent thank you to any gods that might be listening.

And a vow to his father. He *would* compete! He would change his mother's mind and get the permission and take part in the Games. He would write to her today.

Behind him, Kadmos cleared his throat.

Themis turned and said to him, 'I … came to apologise for being so —'

'No apologies,' said Kadmos. 'You look like you're ready start again.'

'Yes. I'm ready. But I want to ask for your help with something.'

'Go ahead.'

'I need a sparring partner I can trust,' said Themis. 'I think there's a way that I can fight without getting hit on the head. But I don't want other contestants to know about it, at least not yet.'

'Hmm. The officials could object to that as unfair.' Kadmos' eyes were questioning.

'It's not against any rules,' said Themis. 'It just involves training differently so that … well, mainly so that I can avoid my opponent.'

Kadmos smiled. 'So your magic weapon would still be your left fist?'

'Of course.'

'I'll look around for a strong partner. Can't think of anyone just now. Neeeds to be incorruptible,' said Kadmos thoughtfully.

'Or threatenable,' said Themis.

'Hmm,' said Kadmos. 'Come on. At least I've got just the place.'

He clapped Themis on the shoulder and led him to a small walled yard with a sandy floor. Along one wall was a line of enormous jars. 'Just don't break any of these. They're full of the oil we use in training.'

'This is perfect,' said Themis. 'I'll join the normal class after work this afternoon. Is Phidias still paying my dues?'

'Yours and a few others',' grunted Kadmos.

>>>

From Suzanne's secret diary
May 15th, 2010, Saturday

Optician (looked it up) couldn't help. Pressure from inside my head. Said it'll get better on its own. She's right – I can look at a screen for half an hour at a time now.

Looked up schizophrenia, too. Learned how to spell it, but don't understand it. Still don't know if that's what I've got. I know it's a Greek word. Funny how I understand Greek fine with Themis, but can't remember a single word here. Not funny – totally petrifying. Don't think about it!

Nigel wants me to talk about how I feel. Want to scream, 'Everything's on a slant!' But I don't.

He means about Mum and Dad, the divorce and all that. Do I get on with Steve? And the boys? Gossip spy, that's him.

Put in his log about playing football with Elliot when he was little. Oh, and Steve being miffed when I stopped. Don't mention Dad. None of his business.

Themis very busy these days. Seems he's just training and training. All obsessed with their bodies. Not just the dangly bits, either. Scraping off and massaging and washing and rolling up their hair. Amazing for men! And he's working every day in that foundry place. Hell, with wax and flutes.

Try to find him every day. But he doesn't come through most times. Can't believe he's just a scab, tho, protecting me while I recover, like Nigel said. Much too real.

And I think I've found the right Olympic Games – in 432 BCE. Start of the 87th Olympiad. Someone called Lykinos of Elis won the boys' wrestling. But no mention of boxing, or Themistokles of Athens. Lots of other things are right, tho – blue screens on the statue, sacrifices with

<<<

Themis joined the queue that was moving slowly into the Temple of Zeus. He'd made a drawing of a bull to leave in the temple as an offering to Zeus. A cool hand touched his shoulder.

'Themistokles?'

'Anthoussa!'

'Ssh! Agorakritos brought me so I could make an offering to Hera. But I really came to see the statue of Zeus.' She dropped a layer of linen back over her face.

'And where is Agorakritos now?'

'Oh, dealing with some cedar merchant.'

'So you shouldn't be here?'

'Officially, I'm not,' she whispered. 'Don't say a word!'

They shuffled further up the ramp and into the shade of the pediment.

'I'll make my offering here,' she said and showed him an embroidered ribbon, red and gold.

'It's … exquisite,' he breathed. 'There's a table behind the statue where you can leave it when you finish your dedication.'

They came to the threshold. As with all the pilgrims, they fell silent as they gazed upward in awe. Anthoussa almost stepped down into the reflecting pool in the floor, so Themis took her arm, noting he was now the same height as she was. A harp played quietly up near the roof. Hundreds of people were moving slowly and silently round the pool and the base of the statue. Gold and gems gleamed and sparkled. Zeus smiled down, blessing them all with his honeyed stare.

When Anthoussa had laid her ribbon on the table and Themis his papyrus, he led her to the gallery steps.

'Can you manage these?' he whispered, gesturing vaguely at her belly.

She started up briskly.

In the gallery they were alone for a few moments. Anthoussa threw back her veil and leaned over to look at the Nike. 'Which hand did he hold you with?' she whispered in Themis' ear.

Themis was startled. 'When do you mean?' he asked.

She put a finger to her lips, took one last look and ran down the steps.

Themis just wanted to stand and gaze. But the gallery was filling up with pilgrims. The incense could not compete with the miasma of human odours they brought with them. And Anthoussa hadn't answered his question, so he followed her down.

She was waiting for him.

'Agorakritos told me about your vision,' she said. 'Forgive me for surprising you, but everybody knows about it.'

'I know.' Themis shrugged.

'I just wanted to ask you what it was like. And if you've "seen" him again.'

'Why?' Themis asked sharply. He had told no one about the second time, except Frog.

'Ah ha!' laughed Anthoussa. 'So you have! Why aren't you telling?'

Themis was angry that he had given himself away. 'My mother wants me to give up on the Games and go home.'

'Don't blame her,' said Anthoussa. 'But you, being a man, want to stay and face the fight.'

Themis had to smile. Anthoussa had such a charming way of saying annoying things. 'One reason she agrees to that is because everyone knows Zeus is going to call me back.'

'And no one knows he already did?'

'Exactly … So if you promise not to say anything, I'll promise not to mention your visit, in your present … interesting state, to Zeus.'

'It's a deal!' She put her head on one side. 'But you could always deny it, you know.'

'Of course.' He put on a disappointed, despairing voice and rolled his eyes. 'I'm still waiting for my call from Zeus, you know.'

Anthoussa giggled. 'Oh come on. Please tell me about it!'

>>>

Went in to school today with Granola. We walked. The traffic noise is scary. Makes me think I'm going to pee myself. She helped me across the lights. She wore green shorts and has black veins in the backs of her knees.

Double period biology on speciation. I got the gist some of the time. Mainly lost and panicky. Nigel says to expect that.

And I'm not good with so many people. But everyone was nice. Teased me about my hair. Bernie in tears cos she was 'so happy to see me there'. Can't imagine the teachers are, tho.

Miss Rallis came to see me after the lesson. She's trying not to feel guilty. Mr Green has left. Bernie says there's been an inquiry. No one asked me anything. But then I don't remember anything.

Had to find my own way home. Got lost! More panic. Ended up in MacDonalds. Couldn't bear the smell. Called home and Granola came out for me. Lots of pigeons in Castle Park. Not as many as in Themis' Athens.

Maybe going to Florida with Dad over half term. The next MRI will decide. That's tomorrow. Don't like that tunnel. But if it's ok, I might be able to start dancing lessons again. Maybe just the gentle, warm-up stuff at first.

Found Themis later – at last. So he's not a scab. But he is turning into a real flirt.

Watched TV a bit with Elliot and Robbie tonight. Olympic hopefuls. Made me cry.

From Bernie's private diary. Tuesday June 1st 2010

Near Rockcliff, Dumfries and Galloway, Half Term Holiday

Just got back from a walk with Mum and her new dog (known as Rolls – another Labrador, of course). It was fabulous. And I didn't want to come here! Huge cliffs with loads of seabirds, beaches made completely of irridescent shells, views across to the Lakeland Fells. Texted Kyle he should wave a towel from the top of Helvellyn and I would see him. He's working at the outward bound school this week, to make money for his trip to the States in the summer.

Mum and I talked a bit about Suzanne. I haven't seen much of her lately except at school. And now she's gone to Florida with her dad. Mum asked me how she was getting on and in the end I blurted out all about feeling so betrayed because she seems to be someone else now, someone difficult and angry and ungrateful, and even unkind at times.

Mum said I should tell Suzanne that she has changed for the worse, and explain how. 'She's battling with problems we can't even imagine,' she said. 'Give her the benefit of the doubt.'

And she told me about a friend's grandfather who had been in a house that was bombed in London during the war. He was on leave from the army, and the ceiling fell in on him. He was very strange for years – angry and unmanageable – until his older brother came back from the Far East. The brother just refused to take any notice. 'He treated him as he always had done, whatever he said, however he reacted. And slowly the young man came back to being himself. He even married my friend's grandmother, as they'd planned before the war,' she told me.

Really hope Suzanne is having a good time. Have texted like I used to: 'Brill walk 2day with new k9 and mum gr8 crunchy shell beach howz florida?'

From Suzanne's secret diary
June 7th, 2010, Monday

I thought I'd be petrified on the plane. But no open-mouthed monster, no dripping saliva. Poor Themis. In fact it was fun. Dad kept making me laugh. The food was good, and I slept through a lot of the crappy movies. Granddad and Granny were fine, always out playing golf or in the boat fishing. Dad took me to Disneyland again. I was afraid of mashing my brains even more, but actually felt better!

And I'd forgotten Oreo biscuits! And cousins Rachel and Mike. Amazingly, they were OK. We went to movies and a disco, but they really only think about baseball and cheerleading.

Bernie texted a few times. Didn't answer. Too much or too little to say.

Dad and I ran together a bit each day. Nice and flat there. I'm getting faster.

Granddad asked me about giving up the pole vault. He doesn't know about Ian and thinks I stopped training cos I lost my nerve. 'Too much imagination, that's you,' he said. 'They say here "courage is fear that has said its prayers".'

They do say a lot of prayers in Florida. For big fish, to get a home run, that the soufflé will rise. Not many thank yous … And nothing like the praying people did in Olympia.

Couldn't get in contact with Themis while I was away. I played the piece of Mozart's clarinet concerto which has the same notes as Themis' song lots of times on my iPod. And I sang them over and over. It used to work as often as not, but nothing happened. Maybe he really was a scab – totally impossible thought! Don't believe it. And I won't give up trying to reach him. Other people may think I'm crazy, but he's what keeps me sane.

Going to school for a couple of hours again this afternoon.

<<<

Chapter 41: permission

'So there is hope for the Games yet,' wrote Photios. 'As for my own news, I have entered a drawing in the public competition for drawings of Attica. I went to the bridge where Blaze threw you to draw from reality. But I put the lightning in my picture and the hint of the hand of Zeus in the shapes of the clouds. I'll share the prize with you if I win!'

Themis rolled up the little scroll and slid it under his belt. He would read the rest later. Earlier in the letter, Photios had reminded him of something very important, something he needed to discuss with Phidias. And now they were at Phidias' house, where the Master was expected at any moment.

'Ah, there he is!' called Agorakritos as Phidias swept into the open courtyard. 'Welcome back, dear friend. What did you see in Egypt?'

Phidias laughed. 'A lot of reeds, birds, river fish, and a crocodile or two.'

'I heard they eat people,' said Phidias' daughter, Io, as she emerged from his embrace.

'Only juicy young women,' joked her father. He took a cup of wine and poured a libation at the shrine. 'There were some buildings, too, of course.'

'Stone buildings?' Agorakritos asked as the men stretched out on couches.

'Mostly,' answered Phidias. 'They bring the stone down the river from Ethiopia ... '

This was not the moment for his own news, so Themis wandered off along the colonnade and came out into another courtyard with a table along one side. Most of the women were here, admiring the wreaths and ribbons Ismini had made for the apprentices to wear next day. Musicians played quietly in the corner.

'Are these for the Stadium-clearing Festival tomorrow?' asked Themis.

'Of course,' said Anthoussa. 'Isn't this one glorious?'

She put the most elaborate wreath on her head, and twirled round so that she was visible from every angle. The ribbons and long narrow flax leaves lifted away from her head like a coloured wheel. Her growing belly was only obvious when the fine linen of her robe swished against her as she changed direction.

'You'll trip, Anthoussa,' laughed Ismini while others clapped.

A rhythm grew and the music followed it. The women moved into a dance, singing a song about swallows lining up to watch the threshing of the new corn. Themis remembered something similar in Athens and joined in the circle of 'swallows' with one or two other men. He was opposite Anthoussa. She and Agorakritos were married now and she glowed with health and confidence. She smiled across at him and he grinned back. It was hard to believe she was the bad tempered girl he had met nearly three months ago on the judge's steps in Elis.

Phidias had come in. He waited for the dance to finish and then took Themis by the arm. 'Have you heard from your mother?'

'I wrote to her about my new technique,' said Themis breathlessly.

'Which is?'

'A secret,' laughed Themis. 'It helps me protect my head and confuses my opponents.'

'Sounds perfect,' said Phidias.

'But it hasn't changed her determination. She scolds me properly and still refuses permission,' said Themis ruefully.

'Hmmm,' grunted Phidias.

'But I did get a message from my school friend, Photios.'

'Significant?'

'I think so. He reminded me that my brother Diodotos will be eighteen, head of the household and, according to my father's will, my legal guardian from the middle of this month.'

'Ah. Clever Photios.' Phidias' eyes shone. 'You'd better write to Diodotos in time for it to arrive by his birthdate.'

'I'm working on it,' smiled Themis.

'Wake up!' came Frog's voice from far away.

Themis was dreaming of a writing tablet that glowed with many colours. '*At least it wasn't the Niris thing again,*' he thought as he stirred.

'Come ON,' insisted Frog. 'You shouldn't have put your name down for the first group of weeders. Get up!'

Themis sighed and sat up. 'You shouldn't have let me!' But he was grinning, because there would be no foundry work today.

In the Stadium, members of the Olympic Council were organising the rows of weeders. The flat running surface had plants up to three feet tall after almost a year with no use. The sloping sides, where most spectators would sit on the gournd, had already been scythed.

Kadmos marshalled his group. They all wore flower garlands and ribbons, carried a wooden two-pronged fork to dig with and a basket to put the weeds in.

'There's water from Chronos' spring and fresh rolls made from the new harvest corn waiting for you at the other end of the stadium,' he told them. He pulled one young man to stand beside Themis. 'You two might like to work together,' he said. 'This will be your sparring partner, Themis. He hardly ever speaks, but comes with the best recommendations!'

Themis looked at the youth. He had seen him before, at Thukydides estate. It was Zephus, but with very short, lighter hair!

Zephus said, 'Hi. I'm Efthimios.'

At that moment, music for the starting ritual began, so Themis did not answer, but all his senses were on full alert. Once the short ceremony was over, the two boys worked side by side, digging with their forks and chanting in rhythm to the music. They threw the plants they uprooted into the baskets on their backs. Their heads and shoulders were gradually covered with sandy soil.

Under cover of the music, Zephus/Efthimios whispered, 'I ran away. My uncle accused me of stealing and beat me unconscious. Now I'm apprenticed to a weaver. Don't give me away.'

'Of course not,' said Themis. 'I just hope you can box!'

'Better than I can weed,' said Efthimios.

Some days later at training, Themis was given an official note from Judge Iasos. The tablet said, 'In fifteen days you will report to the Olympic Gymnasium in Elis for your official month's training. As you are still under fourteen, I shall need the permission of your legal guardian for this. Please arrange for it to be delivered to me directly.'

Themis closed the tablet and put it in his bag. He knew Efthimios was waiting in the oilstore yard. He went through, put his bag on top of a sealed jar and began wrapping his hands. The sun almost never reached this yard, so it was cool. Kadmos came in.

'You can use this every second day, in the hour before sunset,' he said. 'I'll set you off and come back to check on you regularly.'

'Frog will be on watch at the door,' said Themis, and he turned to Efthimios. 'You warmed up?'

'Done some work on the punch bags and been running.'

'Me too,' and they squared up to each other.

Themis had been asking around about the weaver's apprentice. His story seemed to be true, but Themis was still wary of someone who was from the house where Niris was poisoned.

They began with the prescribed steps, but Efthimios lashed out at Themis before they had completed them. Themis swayed backwards avoiding the blow, and began dancing backwards and forwards on his toes. Efthimios tried again and again to close in, but Themis managed to keep out of his reach by ducking and weaving.

Themis said between breaths, 'Shall we stop for a bit? I want you to think about ways of dealing with my avoidance tactics.'

'Oh, I am,' said Efthimios. 'No need to stop.'

When Kadmos came back he watched carefully as Efthimios darted in and out, trying to land a punch. Themis danced around on his toes, unpredictable and always out of reach.

'Stop,' called Kadmos when he'd seen enough. 'I can't see anything against any rules there. But you'll need to be able to do that for a very long time if you are going to beat some of the boys I've seen.'

'D'you know who they are?' Themis asked.

'Of course,' said Kadmos. 'And so should you. Come and get the names from me later. There are two or three that don't look like they'll give up just because they can't reach you.'

'And I won't give up, either,' said Efthimios.

'I wasn't sure of you until today,' said Themis approvingly. 'You are a worthy opponent.'

'Hmmm,' grunted Efthimios with a slight smile.

'So, work on the endurance of your legs, Themis,' said Kadmos. 'It looks as though you won't need the head healer after all. And whatever you do, don't knock Efthimios out with your left fist!' He was smiling as he left them.

When it began to get dark, the boys stopped and went into the main rooms to clean up. They were both trembling with exhaustion and agreed to meet again in two days.

'Anyone here know what I know?' Themis asked Efthimios.

'Kadmos,' grunted Efthimios, shakily scraping the sand and oil off his slim thigh.

'You getting paid for this?'

'Yup.'

'Good.'

'I'll find a way through, you know,' Efthimios said looking straight into Themis' eyes.

'Good,' said Themis again, meeting the look. He thought, *'Mustn't let myself like him. We need to think as enemies.'* So without a word, he turned away.

>>>

Found Themis a couple of times in the last few weeks. I can feel how much stronger he is than he was. He can dance around for ages and his legs don't ache. It's like being on springs – or somewhere with lower gravity. Something for me to aspire to! His sparring partner's really fit – in both senses.

But they smell like shit, what with their bad breath and sweat and olive oil with herbs in. And the sand gets into their foreskins so they tie them up with thread! They box with horrible leather thongs tied tight over their knuckles and right up their arms. Why doesn't Themis wear those almost-gloves he wears at the foundry? Against the rules, I suppose.

It's all very unhygienic. But maybe all the garlic they eat helps.

Saw Ian today. Said a few choice words to him. He looked a bit sick!

<<<

'Themistokles? From Athens?' A youth in trainee priest's robes called to Themis as he was on his way to the foundry.

'Who's asking?' asked Themis.

'I'm from the Altis administration. The High Priestess Xenovia would like to see you if you have time. She says she has something that may be useful to you, as you are now in full training.' The young man had learned this by heart.

'She's here?' exclaimed Themis. 'That's wonderful.'

'She has been on a tour of Athena's precincts in the Peloponnese and is here for only one day this time.' The trainee was leading Themis past the Altis towards the River Alpheios where there was a small temple to Athena.

Xenovia was instructing a group of acolytes under the river trees. She left the group when she saw Themis.

'Themistokles! Both my mother and I have been wondering how you are.'

Her perfume reached him and Themis breathed deeply. A pulse drummed in his belly. 'Fine, Sacred Lady,' he said, hardly daring to glance at her. 'And you and your mother?'

'She and I are both well. And you are glowing with health! You have grown a hand's breadth since I saw you last!'

Had she guessed he'd been in the temple? He couldn't meet those powerful eyes. 'Training is going well,' he said to his feet.

Xenovia placed a hand on his shoulder to turn him. A shiver ran through him. 'Come, walk with me,' she invited and they joined the path beside the river. 'I wanted to see you because I still feel so concerned about what happened at Thukydides' estate.'

'I had forgotten about it,' lied Themis. 'Panainos is in Athens and has bought a new body slave.'

'But such things can leave disturbing memories, even in the minds of adults who are used to dealing with illness and war. For a child who has lately been injured … '

'It does not affect me, Sacred Lady. But thank you for your concern.' Themis certainly did not think of himself any more as a child. And he wanted to talk to her about the statue he was planning. He took a deep breath. 'There is something else I – '

'And how is your memory now?' Xenovia interrupted a little breathlessly. Perhaps Themis was walking too fast. He slowed down. She went on, 'I understand that you have recovered completely and your whole childhood is now back in your mind.'

'I can remember a lot, but I'm not sure that it's everything. My slave, Frog, teases me that I do not remember some things, but they may just be things he makes up to suit himself.'

'Very astute of you. I have been praying to Athena to grant you such wisdom – and to keep you safe.' She looked at him sideways. 'Do you pray to Athena?'

'No, Sacred Lady.' Themis said. 'If … I usually pray to Zeus or Apollo.'

Xenovia stopped walking and turned to him. 'Your father served Athena as officer of the guards to her precincts for many years.'

'Three,' said Themis. 'From when he lost part of his leg at Samos.'

Xenovia walked on. 'You accompanied him sometimes, didn't you?'

'I only remember once or twice,' Themis said.

'I'm sure it was more often than that. Why, I remember one day when you were there myself. You were on the Akropolis with your brother and sister. We met at the top of the steps at the entrance, early in the morning. It was the Panathenaia – a very happy day.' Xenovia looked at him with a beaming smile.

'My apologies, Sacred Lady,' Themis replied, catching his breath. 'But I don't remember meeting *you* there. We were watching the procession from the building site at the new gates.' He grinned. 'Myrto was newly married and veiled for the first time. She was looking out for Menelaos. We kept teasing her by saying "There he is!" when he wasn't.'

Xenovia turned to walk back the way they had come.

'I understand your father was serving Athena when he ... was killed?'

'Yes. At a precinct on the border with Megara. He could still fight and ride.' Themis looked a question at her. 'I thought you knew.'

'I did.' Her voice was quiet, but her eyes were sparkling, rimmed with black. 'I only mention this because I feel that, because of all these things, Athena would be willing to help you. I just wanted you to know that, in the hope that it will comfort you.'

'Thank you, Sacred Lady, but I'm fine. In fact, I wanted to ask you ... I am thinking of designing – '

She had produced a small cloth bag from her robe and pulled out a tiny, lidded pot. 'I'm sorry to interrupt you, Themis, but I only have a few moments. And I want to give you this. While I was praying a few days ago, Athena gave me the idea. It is to help your hands heal between training sessions.' She handed him the pot.

It was decorated with tiny swirling designs. Themis lifted the lid and sniffed the contents. It smelled of newly cut grass. 'This is ... very kind of you, Sacred Lady,' he said, looking up again at her perfect face. 'And kind of Athena. I will not forget her in my prayers.'

'The gods are with you, Themis,' she said.

'I have been feeling that very strongly lately,' ventured Themis.

'You have?' Xenovia asked.

'Yes. And I have a plan ... to ...' but now that it came to it, he just could not say it. So he went on awkwardly, 'I was praying one day and an idea of how to fight but protect my head came to me.'

'That is … very interesting,' said Xenovia. She began walking faster.

'Yes. So now I shall be able to compete properly. I was sure for a long time that that would not be possible.'

'Very good news, young Themis,' Xenovia said. 'Now you must excuse me. My girls are waiting.' She strode ahead, turning off the path towards the temple.

'Thank you again, Sacred Lady,' Themis called after her.

>>>

**From Suzanne's secret diary
June 25th, 2010, Friday**

Don't know what Themis sees in that Xenovia woman. Obviously never plucks her eyebrows.

School is easier now, but they still won't let me go full time, even though I've so much to catch up on. We've been given a project on Ancient Greece to do during the summer holidays! Bernie's doing hers with Laila, but I said I'd do mine on my own. Bernie spends a lot of time with Kyle, too. I see Dad most weekends now. I think he has a girlfriend, but he hasn't let me meet her yet. Call her the ISO (Invisible Significant Other). Got one of those myself – sort of.

From Bernie's private diary. Friday June 25th 2010

They are giving us homework for the summer now – only three more weeks of school. With Suzanne, we've been out a couple of times and had a great time. But she always comes out with some nasty comment or sharp reply at some point. So in the end I've decided to do my summer history project with Laila. I just can't deal with the sort of 'you know nothing about it' looks Suzanne gives me when we start work on anything Ancient Greek.

Kyle will be working all summer at the outward bound until he goes to the States. It's hard to find time to meet up just the two of us cos he's had a lot of revision to do, but the exams are over now. He says I should ignore Suzanne altogether until she realises how unhappy she makes people. Secretly, I often find her comments on other people funny, and I know I should laugh when she's hard on me, too. But somehow I can't. No mention of the Greek boy lately.

<<<

Chapter 42: casting Dionysos

'Ouch!' Themis exclaimed as the healer cut the last strap of his sandal and unwound it from his swelling ankle. He'd leapt away from a falling stream of molten bronze and sprained it, it seemed. The liquid metal had missed him – except for two or three droplets that had bounced up from the ground where it hit. He was sitting on a table by the back wall of the foundry with his legs stretched out in front of him. The healer had made room for him by pushing aside a heap of sections of plaster moulds for cauldrons and was now applying something disgusting to his foot.

'You were lucky,' he said to Themis. 'From what I heard, you could have been scalded all down your side. Men have died of less.'

Themis nodded. 'I know,' he said. He'd stopped shaking now and just felt sick.

'How did it happen?' asked the healer, working on Themis' ankle. 'Sorry if this hurts, but it'll recover faster. At least nothing's broken.'

Themis said, 'Good. I'm in training.' He went on through gritted teeth while the healer ground his bones together, 'The Master Caster had just called forward the largest casting mould. The slaves were pushing it … argh! … along on the rollers so that it would be under the pouring spout. It was nearly as tall as me … and I was guiding it. Then just as I came exactly under the "line of pour", something fouled the rollers.'

The healer's fingers felt as sharp as knives. Themis took a breath and went on, 'Kleandros has this rule, "Nothing but the mould in the line of pour." Someone shouted at me to jump, so I did. I landed badly and turned my ankle.' He groaned again as the healer gave his foot one last painful wrench. 'But, thanks to that shout, I did avoid the "line of pour".'

'Not quite,' said the healer as he probed the small burns on Themis' leg. 'These will also need attention.'

Just then, Phidias came in. 'How's the patient?' he asked calmly, though he was vibrating with tension. 'No permanent damage?'

'He'll be fine in three or four days,' replied the healer, beginning to bandage Themis' ankle. 'The burns are minute and not deep. The sprain is more important for an athlete.'

'Did you learn who warned me, Uncle?' Themis asked.

Phidias looked down on him. 'I think it was the same slave that put his foot between the rollers and caused the whole thing, which is really odd. But he's not admitting it, though his foot's in a far worse state than yours.'

'But surely it was an accident,' said Themis. 'Who would want to sabotage the casting of part of your new statue?'

'I can think of one or two,' said Phidas grimly.

The healer was tying off the ends of the bandage. 'Did they finish the casting?' he asked. 'What was it of?'

Phidias nodded. 'It's the head and torso of a Dionysos commissioned by the town of Olympia for the entrance to the little theatre on the hill. And yes, it's all done now. We've still got to remove the runners and risers. Then we'll see if all the parts fit together.' He twisted his mouth. 'Meanwhile, we have yet another failed attempt to get rid of you, young man.'

Themis shook his head, relieved now that the manipulations were over. 'I can't believe that, Uncle,' he said. 'A bronze casting is much too unreliable as a murder weapon, isn't it?'

'Well, it's not a method I would trust, except perhaps as a warning,' said Phidias as the healer packed up his salves and bandages. 'And it may be hard to prove that it was deliberate. But you've been a target for trouble so often lately that it does seem likely.'

'You mean it's some god or nymph or spirit trying to punish me – or to tell me something?' Themis asked.

Phidias shook his head. 'I doubt that,' he said. 'I'd say there's definitely a mortal – or mortals – behind these attacks. But it does occur to me that the fact they've all failed may indicate the involvement of a god ...'

Themis took a moment to think about that. 'You mean I'm being protected?'

Phidias shrugged. 'It's just a hunch. But the sooner you are at Elis for your official month's training, the happier I'll feel,' he said, handing some coins to the healer. To him, he said, 'Thank you for your prompt attendance. Themistokles is staying at the hotel just beyond my Workshop. Could you send his slave Frog to help him get back there? Ask him to bring a stick or a crutch or something.'

The healer nodded as he turned to leave. 'Of course.'

When he'd gone, Phidias said, 'My contacts in Athens tell me your other uncle, Nikanos, has found a different way to pay his debts. So, assuming it's not him, who do you think your enemy could be?'

'I've tried and tried to think,' Themis said, testing his foot gently on the ground. It wasn't going to take his weight without serious pain. 'I suppose it could be someone in Straton's family, but most likely it's something to do with a future opponent. That's what Kadmos thinks, anyway.'

'Your fame flies before you.' Phidias smiled grimly. 'You'd better not walk on that foot for a couple of days. Ah. Here's Frog.'

>>>

**From Suzanne's secret diary
Sunday, July 4th 2010**

Themis was attacked again! This time at work. That's all he does, work and train. It could have been an accident but Phidias obviously doesn't think so. He's suspicious of everybody – have to be in his position, I suppose. And he's not convinced that the attacker is something to do with one of Themis' opponents in the Games. But who else could it be? Whole thing feels very ominous to me …

But Themis is on a high. When he trains on his own it's more like dancing, though not quite my style! He holds stones in his hands and straps sandbags to his ankles. He practises changing direction a lot. More like a cat with wet feet than a butterfly, tho. And of course there's no music, so no predictable rhythm.

I don't get through very often lately and I don't talk about him to anyone, not Nigel, not Bernie, no one. I know I'm missing bits of what's happening to him, but I'm pretty sure he's not a scab now.

Which means I'm probly mental. I'm sure anyone who heard about my 'dreams' thinks I am. Sometimes, *I* think I am.

Anyway, what is mental? Seems to me it's when your head is full of stuff irrelevant to what's really going on, but you don't know it.

But I *do* know it. So, I'm not mental …

Really behind at school. Trying to catch up.

And trying to be patient and not be rude to people. But most of them are really stupid, so illogical – at least, that's how it seems to me these days.

I go running with Dad every weekend – went this morning. He's paying for me to go back to dancing lessons on Wednesday evenings. But Mum's worried I might start serious training again. She says she can't afford the costs.

And I fancy Josh like mad. Nigel says I'll have lots of crushes, like I'm growing up all over again. Told him where to go – politely!

I reckon it's from spending time with so many naked boys when I'm with Themis … Hold your nose and enjoy the show!

From Bernie's private diary. Monday July 5th 2010

Suzanne came over last night. She brought her photos of Athens in February and we had a bit of a chat again about the trip. But she kept looking at the door. In the end Josh came in. He'd been out with his mountain biking group. Suzanne went all silly when he was there, but back to 'normal' when he went upstairs to shower.

'Josh is so nice,' she said. 'I've known him for years and never thought about it.'

I started checking out what was on TV, as she obviously wasn't about to leave. Then she said, 'It must be the accident. Nigel says I'll get lots of crushes, like we did when we were eight and nine.' She stood up and turned to me. 'I do know when I'm being weird, you know.'

I looked up at her and said, 'It's not the weird that matters to me. It's when you say hard, nasty things to me or look at me as if I'm an idiot. That's what hurts.'

'I thought you found things I say funny.'

'I do, when they're not about me! Which isn't fair, I know … '

'So weird is OK, but hold the pointless criticism?'

I swallowed. 'Something like that.'

'Right.' She marched up and down a bit. Mum came in from walking Rolls.

Then Suzanne came over to me again and sat down. 'If I promise not to criticise you, will you listen when I talk about Themis?'

Better to lose a friend cos I can't take ridicule, or to be told a load of stories about another world?

I said, 'I'll listen.'

**From Suzanne's secret diary
July 7th, 2010, Wednesday**

No more news of Themis. I keep trying, especially now that Bernie is prepared to accept his existence.

Tiny glimmers now and then of sore hands, and erotic dreams of Anthoussa and other girls. Boys get it worse than girls, I reckon.
I had a weird visitor yesterday.

Granola let him in and gave him tea. So I had to be polite and listen to him. He said Miss Rallis had told him about my 'dreams' of Themis. (How did she know? From Nigel? Or Bernie?!) He wanted to talk to me about them. Lots more long words. Wanted to scream at him, but I'm trying to be nice.

If I got it right, he's here on holiday in the Lake District, but he works with psychiatric patients at a hospital in Edinburgh. He's doing research on memory and he wants me to go to his laboratory for tests.

He asked me to write down what I see 'via' Themis and show it to him. But 'Only if I feel entirely comfortable, and only parts of it, if you prefer.'

He says there are other people who get similar 'dreams' and I can meet them if I want. So basically he's studying freaks, and I'm like them.

So now I'm a freak – mental *and* a freak!

Left me his card – Gordon Keely with loads of letters after. But I only recognise the PhD. 'Postgraduate research fellow in cognitive neuroimaging, University of Edinburgh, with emphasis on cases of "parallel lives".'

Is it him who's crazy, or me? He insists I'm not, by the way. Which is nice ... even if it turns out he's wrong.

<<<

Themis heard the whip whistle over his head. It cracked on the shoulder of his opponent, a youth from Massalia called Esperos. A fine line of blood appeared. 'Kneeling down is for wrestlers, not boxers,' growled the trainer with the whip.

Esperos stood up. He was a head taller than Themis. He had slipped in the sand and ended up on one knee. He raised his hands again and they went on sparring.

He was quick with his hands, but not as quick with his feet. Themis had to concentrate hard, and eventually won the match by landing a punch on the target painted on Esperos' chest. Themis' target was on his shoulder today.

Later, as the boys were all scraping off, Esperos came up to Themis. He said, 'Where do you disappear to every second or third evening? Most of us never leave the training precinct.'

'I have friends in Elis,' answered Themis, rubbing ointment into his bruised hands.

'Friends related to judges, from what I hear,' said Esperos, his eyes hard with suspicion.

'True,' agreed Themis. 'The wife of my friend is the daughter of Judge Iasos. But they live in a separate house. I don't see the judge at all.'

'And I hear you haven't got official permission to compete yet.'

'Not yet. But it'll be here soon.'

282

'I hope not,' said Esperos.

'I take that as a compliment,' laughed Themis.

'Take it as you like,' Esperos muttered. He turned away, rubbing salve on the cut on his shoulder.

>>>

**From Suzanne's secret diary
July 14th, 2010, Wednesday**

Themis is training in Elis, staying in like an athletes' compound. His ankle's recovered. God, they stink, those boys – but some gorgeous bodies among them. It's hot, clouds of flies. Slaves with fans can't keep them away. They are obsessed – addicted. Bit different from how my training used to be!

But it reminds me that I miss that team feeling. Dr Grant (GP) says I could run with the school team at least, even if I mustn't jump. At dancing it's different. Miss Stefi won't let me do much except the strength exercises, and the girls in the class seem to be waiting for me to faint on the spot.

Emailed Granddad in Florida today. He mails me every week. He sent my last mail back with grammar corrections! Tried to write full sentences this time. Looked back over this diary. I'm improving.

Facebook friends want pictures of me now my hair's getting longer. Bernie took some after school today. Awful, but they're already out there. The boy from Queen Katherine's who was on the school trip is asking if I'm feeling better. His name's Ron. I seem to be over the crush on Josh. He's amazingly bossy to Bernie. She says she's learned to ignore it.

Gordon called from Edinburgh. He wants to set me up in his system and asked me what I want my code name to be. Said I'm not sure yet if I'll take part.

School breaks up tomorrow. I have catch-up projects for three subjects and text books to read for the others. No holidays planned. And no job. But then I'm not competing, so I don't need money. And Dad gives me guilt money now and then.

Sometimes get panic fits, tho not as often as before. I catch sight of myself in the mirror and it doesn't look like me. My hair's changed and I'm soft looking. It's going to be a bit lonely now school's closing. Everyone on Facebook is just doing rubbish. P'raps Ron will get back to me.

<<<

'When you jump up,' said Anthoussa 'you can kick your bottom with your heels. This can make a noise like a slap.'

'Good for confusing an opponent,' said Themis, and tried it, but his tunic killed the sound.

'You look like a colt with hiccups,' giggled Anthoussa, as he continued to practise.

'I won't be so rude as to tell you what you look like,' he countered breathlessly. 'Show me that cross-over step you told me about.'

She took a small step backward on her toes, crossing one leg behind the other so that she was turned sideways to him. She looked at him over her shoulder. Then she changed feet and did the same on the other side, very quickly. This made her belly shake and sway. She began to giggle again and it danced so that she had to support it from underneath with her hands.

'What's so funny?' asked Themis, laughing too.

'I can't see my feet,' she managed to say.

Agorakritos came into the courtyard. 'What do you think you are doing?!' he shouted in angry surprise. 'You'll hurt the baby!'

Anthoussa smiled at Themis and went over to her husband. 'Of course I won't,' she soothed. 'Here, feel. It's enjoying the ride.'

Agorakritos was not prepared to touch his wife's belly in male company. He turned to Themis.

'Phidias is here,' he said sharply, 'in the andron. He wants to see you.'

Phidias was stretched out on a striped couch with Pantarkes sitting at his feet. There were bowls of fruit and nuts on the low table beside him.

'Ah, Themis,' said Phidias, tossing a peach to Pantarkes. 'Sixteen days to go and you look wonderful. What's the food like?'

'Lots of meat – they say it's a new thing.'

'Good. And you won't be allowed out again, I imagine?'

'No. From now on they'll be monitoring every meal, every training session, every cup of water.' Themis was watching Pantarkes eating the peach, licking the juice from his fingers as he looked up at Phidias from under his eyelashes.

'So no more cheating,' said Phidias, his eyes on the peach.

'I don't cheat, Uncle.'

'No, of course not. But others do.' Phidias sat up. 'Look, I'm concerned there's still no news from Diodotos. Perhaps the message went astray, or something has happened to him. I want you to agree to my sending a pigeon to a friend in Athens who will take your message to him personally.'

'Of course,' said Themis. 'Why do you need me to agree?'

'It's an official communication,' said Phidias, 'on behalf of an official competitor during the official training month. How are you finding it?'

'It's very hard for some of the contestants,' said Themis.

'But not for you?' Phidias raised an eyebrow.

Agorakritos heard this remark as he came in. 'Themis was training so hard, now it's almost a holiday for him,' he teased.

'Hardly,' protested Themis with a laugh, glad to see Agorakritos had got over his irritation. 'The best thing is seeing future opponents train.'

'Anyone important?' asked Phidias.

'One, maybe two,' answered Themis. 'Apollodoros of Korkyra could be a problem. He's small and fast and fights like a snake. And perhaps Esperos from Massalia. He's tall with long arms.'

'If anyone asks,' drawled Phidias, looking at Pantarkes, 'I'm your temporary guarantor for the guardian's permission.'

'Thank you,' said Themis. 'How did the statue of Dionysos turn out?'

'You wouldn't know it wasn't alive, except for the colour,' said Phidias.

Pantarkes smiled coyly and said, 'And it hardly looks like me at all.'

Themis laughed, then said, 'There was no news about the foundry accident when I joined the trainers here in Elis. Have you heard anything?'

'They interrogated the slave, of course,' said Phidias. 'But he just said he was pushed from behind and his foot fell between the rollers.'

'Where is he now?' asked Themis.

'No idea,' said Phidias. 'Anyone suspicious among your opponents?'

'Not that I've noticed. No one seems to hate anyone else that much. Not even as much as Straton hates me. We've all won our places here, and we're being tortured together, so we get on fine most of the time.'

'Like in the army,' said Agorakritos.

Phidias looked over at him and he nodded and went on, 'I'll send a couple of men back with you to the precinct later, Themis. It's the last time you'll be alone on a public street until after the Games now.'

One of the men had a lantern as there was no moon that night. They were almost at the gates of the gymnasium when they heard someone running towards them. The larger man stepped in front of Themis to shield him. They stood back against a stone wall.

The runner appeared. 'Themis, is that you?' called Frog's voice.

'It's my slave,' said Themis, grinning with relief.

'I just got to Elis. Confusing town,' said Frog between breaths. 'Agorakritos told me you might have already gone into your "prison".'

'Not quite,' Themis gestured towards the precinct. 'What's wrong?'

'The slave who caused the trouble during the casting gave me a message for you before he died.' Frog was frowning in the lamplight.

'Died!'

'Yes, yesterday. He asked to see me and told me he believed he'd been pushed so his foot fell between the rollers by a man he believed was in the casting team. He said the man had disappeared but he'd seen him earlier that day, talking to someone in a long black cloak …'

'What?!' exclaimed Themis. 'D'you think it's the same person that paid Lysimachos?'

'Could be. So I thought I ought to warn you,' finished Frog.

'Thank you, Frog. You deserve at least a decent meal for that,' said Themis. 'And I'll make an offering to thank the slave. He saved my life … But I have to go in now. You go back to Agorakritos' house and tell Phidias. Ask them to feed you and tell them I'll be on my guard.'

'Right.' Frog stepped up to Themis and took his hand. 'I brought you this.' He put the little pot of Xenovia's salve into Themis' palm.

'Thanks, but you have it. Or give it away,' said Themis. 'They have really strong stuff here.' He gently pulled his hand back from Frog's grasp. 'And thanks again.'

'Good luck,' Frog's voice wavered.

'Look on the bright side,' Themis said. 'We made it to Olympia! My dream come true.'

'And mine,' called Frog as he turned and ran off.

>>>

Chapter 43: tent city

From Suzanne's secret diary
July 19th, 2010, Saturday

Bernie came over yesterday. I'd made a garland for her with ribbons and flowers from the garden (not that there are many that aren't weeds). It wasn't as good as Ismini makes.

Bernie hardly looked at it. She wanted me to go to the cinema, so we spent ages getting ready. We tried curling my hair but I looked like a sheep in shock, so we gave up and washed it again and plaited it. It's hardly long enough. I told her about Myrto dressing her mother's hair. She said she wasn't interested in fashions thousands of years ago, just in what's going on now. A while back she said she would listen about Themis, but she doesn't really want to know.

It looked OK in the end, I suppose. Then we went out. But we never made it to the cinema. We met some of the guys from school and ended up at the Warehouse. We danced like idiots for hours to music that was so loud I couldn't even hear the notes. I left and came home with a headache. Modern people may not have much muscle, but they smell quite nice.

Mum and Steve let me sleep in this morning. And I found Themis! He's locked in now for training. If Anthoussa wasn't pregnant, he'd be in love with her – or maybe it's just a crush, like mine was on Josh. Ron's gone to visit his relatives in Cape Town. Have to remind myself it's winter there so I won't be jealous.

From Bernie's private diary. Saturday July 19th 2010

Suzz had made me a wreath! She called it a garland. It was ribbons plaited together with garden flowers. Did she really think I'd wear it? I gave it back to her and she hung it on the wardrobe doorhandle.

I just wanted her to come to the cinema and stop living in her dreamworld. We curled her hair and I thought it looked great, but she freaked out!

'It's like a sheep that's had an electric shock,' she said. So she had me wet it and plait it in about six plaits and pin them back.

'It looks a lot better with longer hair,' she said and started to tell me about Themis' mother's hair.

But I told her we're not interested in thousand-year-old styles nowadays. (Doesn't she realise how totally … elsewhere … this all is to me?)

She laughed and said 'Well, I may have plaits, but at least I'm not blue, like Neytiri in Avatar.'

'Have you seen that already?' I said.

'No, but I've seen the ads.'

We got sidetracked to the Warehouse when we met some guys from school in the street. Later, I was dancing with Kyle, and Suzanne waved at me and left. Maybe she needs a different kind of friend …

Going away next week to Ibiza with Mum and Dad, scuba diving. Josh might come for a few days, but Kyle's working.

<<<

'Themis? Remember me?' the young man asked as he wriggled his way onto the theatre bench beside Themis. His hair smelled of camomile.

'Something to do with Photios?' asked Themis.

'Cousin,' said the youth. 'Name's Ariphron.'

'I've seen you training. For the pentathlon?'

'That's right. I heard you'd been in another accident – something at the foundry?'

'Yeah,' said Themis, suspicions galloping through his mind.

'You seem fully recovered,' said Ariphron.

'Better than ever.'

'Are you still having trouble remembering things? Photios told me how you'd completely lost your memory.'

'It's coming back.' Themis said. He remembered painting a pot for Photios and then smashing it because it was not good enough. Ariphron had mended it because he liked the picture on it of goats reaching up to eat olive leaves.

'You painted the goat pot,' said Ariphron. 'And you lost your twin brother when you were little.'

'Yeah. Can't say I was very happy to remember that,' sighed Themis. 'But I remember the pot, and a few other things – but there are important things I can't remember.'

'Like what?'

'Well, I can't remember hearing about my dad being killed. That day is a complete blank.'

'He was a brave man, your dad. Not like mine!' Ariphron made a rueful face.

'Why, what's wrong with yours?' The benches were filling up and they had to raise their voices a little over the din.

'He got into debt from gambling. Photios' dad had to bail him out.

He's dead now.'

'I don't remember that,' Themis said.

'Your dad fought all over the place and always seemed to be on the winning side.'

'Even when he lost half his leg!' laughed Themis. 'That was in Samos, and he used to say "Samos is calling" when the wooden bit hurt him in the cold weather.'

'You see?' said Ariphron. 'You remember a lot of things.'

'Not much about Dad. I didn't get my memory back till after I left Athens.' The ushers called for silence, so Themis whispered, 'And there aren't many people here who know me that I can ask.'

The songs began. Some were odes to past victors in the Games, some about battles and others about journeys. There was dancing to some of them, which reminded Themis of Anthoussa, but it was all by and about men. Girls were not even spoken of. Themis wondered if Anthoussa had had the baby yet.

There was a break after one particularly tedious poem about soldiers who ignored Athena's warnings. A few of the athletes had dropped off to sleep, sitting on their benches.

Themis and Ariphron got up and went through into another courtyard. There were torches lit all round it and drinks laid out.

'That poem reminded me,' said Ariphron. 'D'you remember that day your dad was on duty up on the Akropolis? There was a festival. When we got there he was really aggravated because he'd missed searching one of the priestesses as she left the precinct after the night of prayer. I remember he was – '

'He kept calling himself stupid and punching his hands together.' Themis interrupted, with the sudden memory of his father, beard bristling, hair flopped onto his brow, swearing quietly at himself. Themis caught his breath. 'It was Xenovia he hadn't searched,' he said in surprise.

'There'd been thefts from the Temple, bits of gold and gems off the Athena that Phidias made.' Ariphron chuckled. 'It was the day I first saw your sister. She lifted her veil a couple of times. Out of reach, of course, but made me grow up fast!'

'And Dad was the commander of the temple guard. So he felt he hadn't done his job properly.' Themis shrugged. 'Still, she was probably the most trusted person there, so it can't have mattered much in the long run.'

'And I remember another time, you and Photios – ' Ariphron was interrupted by the call for everyone to go back to the show. 'Ah. They said the best bit was at the end.'

'Just dancing with the audience, I heard,' said Themis as they sat down again.

>>>

Those Greek guys can really dance! How do they do that? Throw each other in the air, turn upside down? Useful for vaulting! But I'll never learn anything like that at my classes, and anyway, I'd still be too dizzy upside down! Some of them even turn somersaults in the air. Just everyday guys, not what we would call gymnasts. We think we're fit nowadays. Everyone should see their coordination – and their muscles!
Saw a few muscles on Sunday, too, tho much wimpier! Went with Dad to the trials in the Sheepmount stadium. The cherries were dropping off the trees by the highjump. Like last year when I won the under 15s pole vault and came second in the 100 metres. Difficult to believe that now.
Lots of people I know there, all saying how good to see me well. And I have a date with Ron! Friday. There's a gig at the Sands Centre. I'll stay over at Dad's. Ron was there with the team from Kendal. He throws the hammer.
Am I excited or what?!
And Cassie wants me to think about getting back into training. 'Still got springs in your shoes,' she said. 'Joy to watch.'
But I did say some stupid things like, 'It's a lot easier without clothes' and, 'less sweat, less smell,' when Ron mentioned the lousy weather. Thinking back, that's probly what made him ask me out. He thinks I'm a nudist or something. Poor guy. He'll never know the truth.
In fact, no one else must. Most people who do know, think I'm nuts – or I was nuts but I'm getting better. I know that because Nigel still won't talk to me about Themis. Even Bernie gets that panicky look on her face.
I'm kind of addicted to the history. Most of it checks out on-line, but not all of it. So how do I 'know' all this stuff? *Am* I sick? Or am I a time-traveller, like in Heroes or Doctor Who? It'd be wicked to know how to control it! It's not difficult to open my mind up, especially with the right music, but the actual connection – seems to come from somewhere else. And it's happening less and less often.
I can look after myself better now – haven't got lost for weeks. Cycling freaked me out though, the balancing thing. I spend more time at Dad's. I

<<<

Themis could hear a donkey complaining bitterly in the freight yard behind him. It had begun just after all the prayers and hymns had been sung and made it hard to concentrate on the two judges.

They both stood on the dais the priests had vacated. They wore their official purple robes. Judge Iasos was proclaiming in his firm, clear voice: 'You have come from all over the known world. You have taken the oath that you have lived blamelessly and trained hard for your event during the last ten months.'

The other judge, an older man called Perilaos, took over, his voice thin in the cool dawn air: 'Your trainers have confirmed this for the month you have spent here in Elis. If you have also behaved with honour and energy throughout those ten months, then know that Zeus, and all of us who wish to please him, will welcome you in Olympia for the competitions.' At last someone had silenced the donkey.

Judge Iasos took over: 'If you cannot declare that, this is the moment to leave and go wherever you wish. In Olympia we will be watching every contest, making sure every rule is kept, every law upheld. Now,' and his voice rose, 'let the march from Elis to Olympia, for the eighty seventh Olympiad … begin!'

A fanfare played as the judge swept down from the dais and led his colleague through the crowds. A double row of Olympic Councillors in dark green followed them and then the Guardians of the Laws in crimson. The crowds began to cheer as the athletes joined the procession, each in a clean white shift.

The sun rose above the horizon and shone into Themis' eyes as he began to move off. He caught sight of Agorakritos to the left on his black horse, gesturing that Themis should go over to him. His heart raced.

'It's a girl!' called Agorakritos as Themis came nearer. 'They're both fine.'

'Congratulations!' Themis shouted back automatically. This was not the news he had been hoping for.

'Anthoussa says to "sting them all hard". Is that right?'

'Of course.' Then the excitement of the day banished Themis' disappointment. The permission *was* on its way. Phidias had promised. Themis laughed up at Agorakritos. 'This is a great day. You must call your daughter Melissa!'

'Sweet but with a sting,' Agorakritos quipped. He was walking his horse along beside the procession to keep pace with Themis. 'I won't wish you luck because all you need you have. Zeus is with you. See you there!'

He waved his wide hat and disappeared at a canter.

'That your Uncle?' asked Esperos, who was suddenly beside Themis.

'No. He's the friend I visited in Elis.' Themis was surprised Esperos had not dropped out before now. He felt pretty sure the Massalian had not behaved with 'honour and energy' throughout his training.

'Thought you'd have dropped out,' said Esperos. 'Your permission doesn't seem to have come.'

'It's on its way.' Themis had been allowed to receive a note from Judge Iasos which said Phidias was adamant it would arrive in time, but if it did not, the Judge would be forced to disqualify Themis before the contest.

'If I were you, I'd drop out now, while you still can with honour, rather than being disqualified at the last moment.' Esperos would, of course, be concerned about Themis' honour!

'What?' said another voice. 'And miss all the fun?' It was Ariphron. 'Who cares if you win? This is going to be the experience of a lifetime!'

'We all care,' replied Esperos in surprise. 'What are you doing here if you don't want to win?'

'Of course I want to win,' said Ariphron, 'but you could get so obsessed by that that you would miss all the other fun things that are going on. Isn't that right, Themis?'

Themis thought for a moment. 'Perhaps. But to win you have to be obsessive. Then you can enjoy the other stuff afterwards.'

'Such a diplomat!' laughed Ariphron.

They were now walking in twos and threes on the road into the centre of Elis from the west. The trainers were trying to organise them as they approached the main street of the town. The music ahead got louder and drums set up a marching rhythm.

'Get in line!' came the call and the scores of young men suddenly went from being a muddled crowd into three straight lines.

Themis marched to the beat and sang the prescribed songs as loudly as he could, crowding the fears out of his mind. He remembered much of the way from his visit to Elis with Frog and Xenon in the Spring.

By midday they were at the Fountains of Pieria. As Themis jostled for his turn to wash and drink, he could hear a ceremony going on nearby in the forest. There was loud, stately music, with lots of cymbals and drums. Then suddenly the two judges came dashing down to the spring covered in spatterings of blood. The crowd made way and the two older men washed themselves in the basin, soaking their robes. The water ran red, then pink. The athletes had to wait for it to clear.

Themis found a rock to sit on in the shade of the pine trees. Other athletes threw themselves down nearby. It was time to eat and rest before the next stage that would get them into Olympia sometime after sunset.

'What did they sacrifice?' Themis asked, his mouth full of bread.

'Just a pig,' said Esperos. 'We'll be seeing some sacrificing in a couple of days that'll fill your stomach a treat.' He gestured at the meal they had been issued of bread, hard cheese, olives and walnuts.

Suddenly a group of touts was among them. 'Learn the future!!' one called as he quested among the crowd. 'Will you win? Will you get the girl of your dreams? Ask a question at the oracle. Only one drachma!'

'That can't be Zeus' oracle, can it?' said Ariphron as he joined them. 'It must be a fake.'

Themis laughed. 'There are about a hundred fakes. I heard the real one is very impressive, and very expensive!'

'It doesn't need to advertise, you mean?' sneered Esperos.

'That's right.' Themis turned pointedly to his meal.

Other touts were offering them good luck charms, super-oils that would' multiply their strength and beauty, tonics and potions to improve their performance. But the guards soon dispersed them with whips, and quiet fell.

Themis lay on the earth looking up through the grass-green pine needles at the deep blue of the sky. He ran through in his mind the memories of how he had arrived here. He remembered Mantius' lying in the sand, knocked out, on the day he won in the Agora in Athens. He saw again his father's joy and stumbling rush to embrace him. He remembered the grateful sacrifice at the top of Mount Hymetos with the whole of Attica laid out at his feet. He remembered the congratulations and excitement of his classmates and the start of special training with Arianos. He remembered the feeling of his fist hitting Straton's chin, his strength tingling in his veins.

But his memories from the day he heard of his father's death until

when he woke up with his "visitor" in his head were vague. They rose
reluctantly from what felt like a sea of thick grey mud in his mind.
There was something about his father's will that Phidias and Eirini
had argued over with Menelaus and Diodotos. There was a painfully
clear picture of his mother weeping over Kallistos' cuirass, her tears
splashing from it onto the stone floor. And a strange, eerie time
listening to Chloe and hundreds of other little girls singing in the newly
complete Odeum music hall with a storm raging outside. What had
that been … ?

'On your feet!' came the shout. 'Olympia here we come!'

By the time they finally arrived in Olympia the moon was high and
bright, and everyone was complaining of blistered feet.

'Follow me!' called the leader of the march, leading the athletes
across the bridge over the Kladeos, the tributary of the Alpheios that
fed the swimming pool. A series of fields had been cleared and rows
of tents pitched. Lamps glowed in each tent and torches burned in the
wide 'streets' between them. They marched to the centre of the 'city'
where a large open area was arranged for dining, with benches and
tables and a line of cooking fires along one side. A few tall, spreading
plane trees would provide shade during the day, but now were hung
with lanterns and coloured ribbons.

The athletes crowded into this open area.

'Welcome to Olympia!' called a loud voice and a huge man in a short
tunic leapt up onto a dais opposite the line of fires. 'And to our special
competitors' city! My name is Vion. I'm the chief administrator of
your new city – your Olympic archon! Now, you were all given a letter
and a number in Elis. The number is your tent and the letter is your
street.'

The crowd murmured. Vion went on 'But before finding your bed,
you probably need latrines and food. For the first you'll need to walk
along the path with the green lanterns until you come to the obvious.
Just don't fall in.' There was a laugh at this. 'Then you can come back
here and sit for a good meal with broth, bread and fruit.'

Groans of 'No meat?' and 'We're starving!' went up.

'There'll be meat in plenty on the third day, and even some
tomorrow evening,' promised Vion. 'Now, no leaving the tent city till
the morning, no brawling and no washing, defecating or urinating in
the river. Do as your trainers tell you and thank Zeus and all the gods
that you have made it this far!'

As Themis turned to look for his tent, he almost ran into Frog.

'Don't look so surprised,' Frog chided.

'How did you get in here?' Themis whispered. Then he noticed Frog was wearing the same tunic that he was.

'No one believes it, but it is legal if there's an urgent message. And I have one,' said Frog.

Themis looked at his face. There was no joy there, so the message was not the one Themis was waiting for. 'What is it?'

'You are to go to the Oracle precinct on Mount Chronos before sunrise tomorrow. "A consultation with the oracle will be possible as long as the moon is still the strongest light in the sky." '

'They won't let me out.'

'It's all arranged. I'll be at the gate. You'll go into the cave with the priest. Don't eat or drink anything beforehand. When you come out, Phidias will take you to breakfast. After that, you will come back here.'

'Why?' asked Themis.

'Phidias says it's something your father wanted you to do before competing.'

'He did?'

'That's what Phidias says. See you then,' said Frog. 'I'll bring you a cloak. It'll be cold in the cave.' And he ran off.

>>>

Chapter 44: oracle

Two big things in the last few days:

Friday, the date with Ron was brilliant. He's so easy to talk to. Doesn't comment, or criticise my opinions or clothes or anything. Plays chess! Does long jump as well as throwing hammers, fell-runs, and lives on a farm. I thought he was a city boy, he's so cool-looking! The gig was just local bands but it was pretty good and we ended up dancing. No headache! He had to catch a train, so we couldn't stay till the end. He just kissed me lightly at the station, but we text all the time. Seeing him again this weekend.

Had another email from Gordon in Edinburgh. Seems they want to wire me up and do MRIs and record my brainwaves. Told Dad about it and he asked why they were interested. He doesn't know about Themis and I know if I told him he'd freak out. So I just said it's standard procedure for injuries like mine.

'You're fine,' he said. 'No need to go through all that again.'

Texted Bernie. She texted back, 'Stall for time. C U in three days.'

Then Saturday Dad introduced me to the ISO! She's called Donna and she's from Southampton. Impressive figure and long pink nails. Silly voice. I asked her why she'd come to the grey and grizzled North. She said, 'to shine some light.' Hmm …

They took me to see Avatar. Mistake! Too long, too obvious, and I couldn't keep the 3D glasses on all the time because they made me dizzy. Funny how it's ok for people to change bodies in a film, but not in real life.

Cool hairstyles, though!

Donna's got two little daughters and we went round yesterday for lunch – proper roast chicken and three veg. No wonder Dad likes her! And the two girls mean the house feels different. You get to tread on ballet shoes and glittery exercise books, instead of bits of transformers and dropped hotdog.

Made contact with Themis, after about an hour trying. Why is it so difficult now? Is it fading away? I really really don't want it to, just when it's coming up to the Games. Will I learn how he got on? I haven't found any reference to him anywhere on the net or in the library even though it turns out it really was the 87th Olympiad. Can't imagine living without him.

<<<

'Scat! Get out of here, you!' hissed one of the guards at a dog.

'Always hanging around, that animal,' grunted another.

Themis held out a hand. The dog was small and painfully thin, not like the one who had found him near the Council House. 'Here, boy,' he whispered. 'What's the matter?'

'Don't encourage it,' muttered the first guard.

But the dog was licking Themis' hand and arm. He giggled as it tickled. 'It just wants the salt,' he said to the guards.

'Huh!' snorted the guard. 'They sell the stuff you guys scrape off yourselves after your competitions. And you're giving it free to a dog!'

'Not quite the same stuff,' laughed Themis as Frog appeared in the torchlight. 'Stop now, dog. I have to go.'

Frog lit their way through the trees in silence. As they walked he was looking at Themis in wonder.

'What is it, Frog?' whispered Themis.

'You know, the old Themis would not have chatted so easily with the guards.'

'Hmm!' Themis smiled. 'Seems I've learned a few things from my "visitor",' he said.

They came to the entrance of the precinct, a high gateway in a high wall. They waited with the guard until a priest Themis had never seen before came out to meet them with a small lantern. Frog gave Themis the cloak he had promised and disappeared.

Inside the precinct, the moon lit a large paved area with an altar in the middle. The moving shadows of tree branches made confusing black and white patterns. The altar's wide top had been cleaned of ashes but still smelled of burnt fat and bone. Beyond it there was a dark cave mouth like a deep vertical slit in the rock-face. On one side of the entrance was a pillar, and on top of that a green flame flickered in a massive stone crucible. On the other side was a statue of Zeus, older than any Themis had ever seen.

He stood dressed in real robes heavy with embroidery, and wore a garland of real flowers and leaves on his head and others on his arms. His face was wooden, carved with curling hair and beard, almost black with age. The eyes were inlaid white with green irises, giving the god a living, obsessive stare in the wavering light.

The priest led Themis to the gash in the rock and then moved behind him. Themis was suddenly apprehensive. Was any of this necessary? Did his father really want him to do this? He stepped forward uncertainly, vowing to challenge Phidias about it.

'Close your eyes and breathe in and out seven times. Let the god into your soul,' said the priest.

Themis obeyed, breathing in the smells of rosemary and damp that came from the cave. He allowed his shoulders to relax and heard his heart beating in the silence.

When he opened his eyes, he could see a faint glow in front of him. The air was chilly and Themis pulled his cloak tighter. The priest now had a torch and gave him a gentle shove. They moved into a large, sandy-floored space that faded to blackness beyond the light of the torch. Water trickled into a basin and the priest led Themis to it.

'Wash your hands and face here,' he directed.

Themis washed and was given a scented cloth to dry on.

Then they walked quickly to a screen. Behind the screen was another narrow entrance. The greenish glow came from the smaller cave beyond. In the centre of this cave sat a hooded figure muffled in pale robes, swaying and murmuring. Themis could not tell whether the seer was male or female. The light seemed to come from a boulder at the back of the cave.

The priest led Themis to stand close enough to be touched by the figure. A dull drum began to beat and a flute played long, single notes in an echoing melody. The walls of the cave glistened with crystals.

The priest spoke clearly but quietly. 'Themistokles, son of Kallistos is here. He comes to ask Mighty Zeus for his blessing and for his help in his trials and endeavours. He comes at the behest of his father, who is now with the multitudes in Hades. He comes to know that which Zeus expects of him and how he should achieve it.'

The drum and music went on, but the light became dimmer and greener. The robed figure swayed more vigorously and its mumbling grew louder. A new and repulsive smell emanated from the ground.

Themis felt slightly sick and began to shiver in spite of the cloak. The figure groaned loudly and suddenly froze, stiff with tension. A breeze lifted the corner of its robes and brushed Themis' hands and cheeks. The smell lessened. The priest readied his writing tools.

'When the boy in two minds,' whispered the seer hoarsely, 'wins without a fight, Athena will pay her dues.'

As the priest wrote this down, the figure began to fall towards them, drawing tight, rasping breaths.

Two men in black appeared, gliding rapidly from behind Themis. One politely moved him and the priest to one side while the other caught the seer before he – or she – hit the floor.

The first man whispered to the priest. 'Do you need interpretation?'

'Thank you,' said the priest quietly. 'The words are quite clear.'

Themis' teeth were chattering. The seer began to jerk and groan as they turned and left. The music had stopped.

Outside, dawn had lightened the sky and the birds were beginning their day enthusiastically. Phidias was waiting, sitting on a boulder. His face was carefully calm. Frog was sitting at his feet.

'Good morning, Your Holiness,' said Phidias, standing up. He nodded to Themis, but went on speaking to the priest. 'Thank you for officiating in person. Was there a result?'

The priest handed the closed tablet to Phidias. 'For the man who gave us a living god, I would do far greater things,' he said.

Phidias bowed slightly and the priest left them. 'So did you understand what the seer said?' he asked Themis as he unfastened the tablet. Frog was questioning Themis with his eyes.

'I could hear the words clearly,' said Themis, still feeling shivery.

And Phidias dropped the tablet.

His face was grey and slack with shock, and he took a huge breath as he sat down heavily on the rock.

Themis and Frog looked at him with horror. 'What's the matter, Uncle?!' Themis shook Phidias' arm. 'Are you ill? What is it?'

'I am not ill, no,' Phidias said, shaking his head in wonder. 'I am just … amazed. This is the exact same prophecy as I received from Apollo on behalf of your father at Delphi.' He jumped up and turned to the growing dawn with his arms flung out. 'Yes!' he shouted. 'Yes! We chose the right boy!'

There were people on the path from the precinct and the main road beyond. Some of them turned to look at the flamboyant Master Sculptor with speculative smiles.

Phidias swept up the tablet, grabbed Themis by the arm, and called, 'Come on, Frog.' He led them at a run towards the town.

Out on the road, Themis pulled back and said, 'Uncle, you have to explain. What does all this mean?'

Phidias walked on more slowly, heading for his house. 'I'll explain over breakfast. There's someone at home who wants to see you.'

The someone was Panainos!

'When Phidias sent the ship to get some scrolls and tablets he needed, I took the opportunity to return on it to watch the Games,' he explained after happy greetings and back-slappings.

'You risked the sea-sickness to come back and watch a crowd of athletes showing off?' teased Themis.

'It's not so stormy in summer and Phidias' ship is more luxurious than the Pelican,' said Panainos seriously. 'I wanted to see old Zeus again, and hear what the world thinks of his likeness – and the screens that hide the secrets of his structure, of course!'

Phidias said quietly, 'Everyone seems pretty happy with it.'

'You are not usually prone to understatement, brother,' said Panainos.

'True,' Phidias chuckled. 'For me, there are still details I would change, but it's too late for that now.' He waved impatiently at the couches. 'Sit. We have much to talk of, and look, there's breakfast!'

Panainos and Themis arranged themselves on couches. Frog and another slave served them or sat on the floor.

'You probably won't remember,' Phidias began, addressing Themis and choosing a crisp pastry from the dish by his couch, 'but your father and I used to spend quite a bit of time together when the Temple to Athena on the Akropolis was being finished off.'

'Oh, yes, I remember some of that. It was a good time because Dad was at home so much. And he had recovered from losing his leg, too, so he was fun and laughed a lot.'

'Well, in that time I … er … ran short of money to complete the statue.'

'But I thought parliament had agreed that the whole cost would come out of its treasury.' Themis remembered Diodotos taking an interest in this.

'True, but you know officialdom moves at the pace of the tortoise,' said Phidias with a twisted smile and raised eyebrow. Panainos snorted. 'There were some details we wanted to finish before the Panathenaia festival, so your father and I both chipped in and lent, so to speak, Athena our money.'

'Her "dues" in the oracle?' asked Themis.

'That's right. And I asked at Delphi, as I happened to be there around that time, whether this was the right thing to do.'

'You asked the Delphic oracle about something as small as that?'

'Oh ho, you'd be surprised what people ask the Pythia at Delphi,' Phidias laughed. 'And anyway, it wasn't so small a thing, and the city treasury was … not convinced the expense was necessary.'

'Oh … And what did the Pythia say?' queried Themis.

'She said, quite clearly, the same as is written on this tablet,' said Phidias, serious now. 'Exactly the same words, allegedly directly from the god Apollo.'

Panainos looked up from his food. 'What?' he gasped.

Themis took a breath to speak, his mind full of suspicion.

Phidias went on, 'And before you say the priests of the two oracles could have agreed what to say, when I asked the Pythia in Delphi I did not use my own name, or your father's name, and I went in disguise.'

'Really? Why would you do that?' Themis was surprised.

'Being famous is not always very comfortable,' explained Phidias. 'It can be difficult just to walk down a street, sometimes.' His brother hid a smile by biting into a large roll.

Themis said slowly, 'So Apollo in Delphi and Zeus in Olympia both say the same thing – that you'll get your money back when a boy in two minds wins something without a fight.' The hairs on his arms rose when he thought of the 'visitor' in his head. He risked a questioning look at Frog, who shook his head slightly with wide, shocked eyes. So Phidias knew nothing of that, and of course, neither did Kallistos. 'And you and my father decided that the boy in two minds was me?'

'We decided it meant that you, who had been a twin, were that boy.'

'Ah … Because I was a twin.' Themis looked at Frog again. Frog made an 'Imagine that!' face.

'So you probably won't need to fight to win the boxing crown,' Phidias smiled. 'You may win just by being there!'

Themis laughed wryly. '*If* I get permission. And after all this training, I hope I do have to fight!'

'Ah,' said Panainos. 'I can enlighten you about that. I have a message from Diodotos. The permission will arrive today.'

'Are you sure?' Themis leaned forward sharply, knocking his platter off his couch. Frog ran over to pick it up.

'Quite sure,' said Panainos. 'It's on a ship that docks today. It was loading as we left.'

Themis took deep breaths, letting the news sink in, allowing the thrill to run through his body. Frog covered his own grin with both hands.

'So, Panainos and I will be in the Stadium the day after tomorrow to watch you win, with or without a fight.' Phidias stood up. 'We'd better get you back to your trainers. The swearing-in ceremony begins soon.'

Themis stood, too. 'I'm glad you're here, Uncle,' he said to Panainos.

'Me too, my boy,' Panainos murmured.

Themis followed Phidias into the courtyard. 'But if I do win,' he said as the gate guard opened the outer door, 'how will you get your money back?' He did not need to look up so much nowadays to see into Phidias dark eyes.

'I have no idea,' said Phidias. 'Nor am I sure I ever will.'

'You said some of it was my father's?' Themis smiled but kept his voice firm.

'Indeed it was,' Phidias agreed, 'and, if it materializes, your father's share will go to your family. Take him away, Frog, and deliver him to his trainers. I'll send someone over with the permission when it comes.'

Chapter 45: scroll

'Been to see your uncle?' asked Esperos under cover of the noisy procession. 'Give you some good advice, did he?'

Themis shook his head and moved away from the boy from Massalia.

The procession was jubilant. Athletes, officials and trainers were making their way to the Council House between the Altis and the River Alpheios. They were led by drummers and cheered through the streets. Crowds of spectators lined the route, including friends and family who had come to watch sons and brothers compete. Flowers were thrown and names called out. Frog stood with some of the apprentices from the foundry and they yelled dubious compliments at Themis as he passed. He made a suitable face at them.

Stalls with awnings of every colour filled all the nooks and crannies between the buildings, and gave off enticing smells. Vendors with trays slung from their necks pushed through the crowd. Musicians and orators fell quiet when the drums and flutes that headed the procession approached.

And as they rounded the corner of the Altis wall, Themis could see along the valley. It looked as though half of the Hellenic world had come to Olympia for the Games. As far as he could see along the river, there were brightly coloured tents and prefabricated wooden shacks lining both banks.

The athletes were called straight into a large room inside the Council Buildings and chivvied into lines.

Here they stripped and were examined. There were questions about their home cities and their forebears. The boys had to show they were old enough for the contest, with the beginning of adult hair on their bodies. There would also be a check that they were eligible to compete for the city they declared as their home.

Themis was nervous because he had no moustache beginning yet, and also because of the business of the permission that had still not arrived.

The official who examined him asked, 'What age?'

'Thirteen summers,' said Themis, clearing his throat.

'Guarantor's name?'

All the other boy competitors were asked for their guardian's name. Themis answered, 'Phidias, son of Harmides.' The man ticked his tablet. Then he looked up at Themis. 'But your true guardian's permission will need to arrive by midday tomorrow.'

Themis nodded. The man moved to the next boy. Was the special treatment because the judges knew of the oracle's prediction? Or did permissions often come late? Did it matter?

Themis ran outside to join the naked athletes standing in lines and singing hymns. Crowds of spectators drifted by. They were all waiting for the examination of the horses at the hippodrome to finish. The sun rose higher and the shadows of the shade trees retreated. Themis began to sweat. An announcement that two men athletes and two horses had been disqualified was made, but they were no one Themis knew.

All competing athletes, their trainers and the officials who would control and judge the competitions now gathered in the wide space beside the Senate House. From there they filed into a small courtyard to swear before Zeus of the Oaths.

This statue stood on a plinth as high as a man. It was very old, but bright with new paint and robes. The god carried a thunderbolt and looked down on them with a stern frown.

The athletes all knew the standard words by heart, swearing that they would do nothing to jeopardise any part of the Games, that they had trained for the allotted time, would not cheat, and would honour any decisions of the judges. As they well knew, these oaths would be policed by men with whips.

They were dire words chanted to ominous drums. The oath-takers had to pass, one by one, in front of an altar at the foot of the plinth, where the butchered parts of a wild boar were laid out, dripping blood. A row of slaves in olive green tunics fanned away the flies.

The man in front of Themis, also from Athens but not a friend, was trembling slightly but gave the oath with a relieved smirk. Themis wondered what his guilty secret could be, and how many others were plotting ways to cheat.

By the time everyone had taken the oath it was past midday, and the heat and flies were difficult to bear.

Judge Iasos stood high on a dais against the Senate House wall. He called for silence and then made the proclamation:

'Our mighty Father Zeus, ruler of the skies and the hearts of men, has shown in the body of the boar that he is pleased by all that have gathered here.' There was a brief fanfare. Then he went on, 'And so I hereby declare the start of the Eighty-Seventh Olympiad in his honour, the greatest Games in the world!'

A huge cheer rose from the crowd. It was gradually taken up by people further away, in the Altis, in the streets and perhaps even in the surrounding villages.

The Games had begun.

As soon as Themis could find his tunic and get through the crowds, he hurried back to his tent. But there was still no news of the permission.

The other two boys who slept there with him were out in the town, making offerings.

Themis willed himself to be calm, trying to empty his mind of all the questions and dangers.

He was here, at Olympia, for the Games. Just that was a miracle.

'Face the fact that your life might be over anytime,' he said to himself, 'so fill it full while you can.'

He jumped up and set off into the town.

As he threaded his way through the festive crowds, he heard his name.

An old man was sitting on a box under a tree, reading from a scroll. He was saying, 'Themistokles, son of Neokles, who had just recently risen to a position of prominence … '

Themis had a sudden memory of a heroic statue of his famous, ship-building namesake. That Themistokles had persuaded the Athenians to build two hundred warships and later fought the Persians in a sea battle off Salamis nearly fifty years before. 'I have a good name,' he thought.

But the noise and heat, the smoke from the cooking fires, and the constant exhortations from the vendors made his head ache. He left the melee and jogged up the Hill of Chronos to find clean air. Up there, in a small clearing above a little shrine, he sat down under a pine tree to think through the experience at the oracle that morning, and the information about his father's partnership in debt with Phidias.

He had been there only a short while, when something cold butted into his neck. He jumped up, his skin prickling.

It was the pale yellow dog. It stood back, alert but still, a rope dangling from a leather harness over its shoulders. Themis looked around for its master. No one appeared. He approached it, but it growled and made a feint at him this time. Perhaps it was a different dog, though it looked the same. Puzzled, he turned away and began to walk down the wide path towards the town. The dog remained still.

A high whistle sounded and the dog lifted its head, gave a short bark at Themis, and turned to run further up the hill.

Had it been warning him? Or summoning its master? Themis set off back to the town at a run. It had been stupid of him to go off alone.

Back at his tent, there was still no news. He went to the gates of the tent city and asked at the manager's office. Nothing.

So he ran to Phidias' house.

He was shown in to Ismini's salon. She was closing a door to the inner house as he came in.

'Themis!' she exclaimed, 'How … !?' She smiled a secretive little smile. 'How … you've grown. I wish your mother could see you now.'

'Even though she hates my being here?' Themis asked, confused by that smile. Was Eirini here now?

'Ah, but if she saw you so handsome and so strong, her heart would swell with pride.' Ismini moved briskly towards the chairs and tables in the middle of the room.

'Thank you, Mrs Ismini. It's kind of you to say so, but I'm not completely sure of that.' Themis sat where she indicated. He rubbed his scarred hands together with impatience.

In spite of the twinkle in her eyes, Ismini spoke calmly. 'You've come to see Phidias, I know, but he's busy at the temple, I'm afraid.' She signed to a girl slave to place water and fruit on the table by Themis.

'Yes,' he replied. 'But I must talk to him. I'm worried about the permission Diodotos is supposed to have sent.'

A man's voice from the inner doorway said, 'Are you? But you needn't be.'

It was Diodotos himself!

He was sweaty and dusty and still in his travel clothes, but Ismini called, 'Come on in, Diodotos, do come in!'

Themis stood up and stared, relief spreading through him. Tears came to his eyes as he embraced his brother. Ismini said, 'The gods be praised!'

'Mrs Ismini's right,' Diodotos said as he drew back and looked at Themis. 'You've grown, Puppy Dog – and you're as brown and hard as old bronze.'

'I enjoy training,' said Themis, his smile so broad it was hard to speak.

Diodotos filled a cup with water and drank.

'Even when they tease you that you run better than the messenger slaves?' laughed Ismini.

'Even then,' Themis agreed. 'I like feeling the power of my muscles, especially when they've had a good rest. And,' he went on, 'it's beautiful round here, Diodotos. Much greener than Athens at this time of year, and some of the buildings are glorious and – '

'Always the aesthete as well as the athlete,' laughed Diodotos, setting down the cup. 'Look, I brought you your permission,' and he pulled out a scroll, damp with sweat, from inside his tunic.

'Yuch!' laughed Themis. 'How long has it been in there?'

'Just today,' Diodotos said. 'I rode quite fast from the port. That was the safest place.'

'I'd better take it to the administrators now,' said Themis. 'Can you come with me? They may need to see you, although I don't compete until the day after tomorrow.'

Next morning, Themis and Diodotos went together to the Temple of Zeus. Themis had made a small figure in plaster of his father sitting on a box with two small boys, one on each knee, laughing. Diodotos had brought money. They made their offerings and came out of the temple into the smoky morning sunshine and the Altis crowds. Sacrifices and processions had been going on since before dawn.

'There's nothing else like that in the whole world?' said Diodotos, shaking his head in wonder.

'Not that I've heard of,' answered Themis.

'They should be charging to see it,' declared his brother.

'They will, once the Games are over,' said Themis. 'That doesn't seem right to me, though.'

'But imagine the cost,' said Diodotos. 'You'd have to get some return on that.'

'I can't imagine the cost,' laughed Themis. 'It's beyond belief. But some people think it is really Zeus and it seems wrong to make them pay to see their god.'

'You got inside it, you said.'

'Yes,' said Themis.

'And frightened Xenovia?'

'Well, not on purpose,' agreed Themis.

'Those eyes,' said Diodotos. 'No wonder people think Phidias can do magic. What he makes frightens them.'

As they walked, Themis asked his brother, 'Will you fight if there's a war?'

'Of course,' said Diodotos. 'I've started training. It's a lot harder than I expected. Though I'll be in the cavalry, of course.'

'That will make Mama proud,' said Themis as they left the Altis.

'Yes. Although, she keeps telling me to take care. She says she's had enough of the men in her family dying and getting injured.'

'Has she gone to Vravrona yet?'

'She's there most of the time. Chloe goes with her. Myrto has completely recovered and is pregnant again.' Diodotos was eager to get to the hippodrome. 'Come on. They've almost finished the sacrifices,' he said over his shoulder. 'The chariot races will start soon.'

They pushed their way through the crowd and found a good vantage point high above the finishing line.

The names of the competitors in the first race had been called.

'The last time I watched a chariot race,' said Diodotos, 'your "friend" Straton's father won.'

'When was that?' asked Themis sharply.

'Oh, a month or so ago. The races were on the other side of the bridge where you came off your horse. They've made a temporary race track there.'

'Did you speak to Straton's father?'

'I went and congratulated him as he was thanking his driver at the finish. He asked after you.'

'What?' exclaimed Themis. 'Why would he do that?'

'He asked if you'd recovered and would be competing here after all.'

Themis wanted to ask Diodotos more, but silence fell as the lots were being drawn for who would start where. People believed that Zeus himself chose who would be in the best starting position.

A cheer went up from the other side when the results were announced.

'It's the Spartan,' Diodotos groaned in disappointment.

'Photios wrote that he couldn't find any evidence that Straton was carrying on with his vendetta towards me,' said Themis. 'Do you think he is?'

Diodotos shook his head. 'No sign I could see.'

'*So who is?*' thought Themis as the race began and the huge crowd roared. '*Someone with a pale yellow dog? But why?*'

The chariots dashed the length of the hippodrome towards the small temple at the end. Then they turned at the post and came hurtling back. The drivers wore long, billowing white tunics with sashes and headbands the same colour as their chariots. The scarlet Spartan was obvious among the competitors from elsewhere. He hugged the inside lane, hauling the horses tightly around the turning post by the sheer strength of his arms and his hold on the reins.

There were twelve laps. Dust rose and hooves thundered. Horses and drivers screamed when one chariot collided with another. The crowd called and whistled. Themis and Diodotos jumped up and down in their excitement, shouting encouragement to the two Athenians.

One chariot flipped over, throwing the charioteer into the crowd. The horses carried on pulling as it disintegrated. The other drivers tried to avoid the debris, but three of them failed and piled on top of each other. The thrown charioteer disappeared into the crowd to avoid his master's fury, but the other drivers were less fortunate. Two were knocked down and trampled, and one was dragged along until his chariot fell to pieces. Marshals dashed into the chaos and pulled them out. They left trails of blood in the sand.

But for all the excitement, the outcome was clear from the start and the Spartan chariot won.

As the crowd subsided and the dust settled, Themis heard a man behind him say, 'It seems that Zeus favours the Spartans these days – perhaps in more than just the chariot race.'

As the arena was cleared and the rows of slaves began to rake the sand, Themis said to Diodotos, 'I've had a lot of small "accidents" lately.'

'You have? Like what?' asked his brother.

'A man tried to pull me off a cliff with a whip while I was out running. Panainos' slave died from eating food that was left for me. Someone I was training with was paid to hit me on the head at the gym.'

'You think this has something to do with Straton?'

'I don't know what to think.' Themis was aware that the people around them were listening to their conversation. 'Sometimes I think I've upset a god somehow, if there are any, but Uncle Phidias thinks the gods are protecting me from a rather persistant mortal enemy or two.'

'Really?' said Diodotos thoughtfully. 'Someone did try to kill Myrto, remember? So it may be a family thing, or it could just be coincidences.'

'Has anything happened to you?' asked Themis.

'No problems at training camp, but a strange moment in one of those steep little alleys between the houses near the Akropolis.'

Everyone was sitting down on the ground to wait for the next event. Diodotos and Themis joined them, speaking quietly. 'I was the only person in the alley,' Diodotos went on, 'and I heard rumbling. Then a stone drum from a small column came rolling round the corner and down the steps at me. Luckily the wall beside me had a window in it and I jumped up and hung on to the sill while the stone passed.'

'What do you think is going on?' Themis asked.

'Oh, I doubt there's a real connection. One of the builders came rushing down after the drum shouting to warn people. Just coincidences. Some of *your* problems might be jealousy I suppose – or fear of your left fist. But probably just cases of mistaken identity.'

'I don't think so,' Themis said grimly. 'Too many of them.'

The single horses and their jockeys were being announced.

Diodotos gestured at the arena. 'Do you know any of these guys?'

'Nope,' said Themis, 'but the Scythian horse has the reputation of being so crazy he's unbeatable.'

The man behind them said, 'Poseidon's favourite!'

They stood up to get a better view.

'Spartan party at the Villa of Herakles!'

The rumour ran through the crowds as they were leaving the stadium later that afternoon, after the pentathlon.

'We should try going to that,' said Diodotos. 'We might get a free supper!'

'Their food's not exactly the most delicious,' said Themis. 'And won't that make it look as though we support Sparta if there's a war with Athens?' They were weaving their way along the crowded street and had to shout to each other.

'We're not important enough,' replied Diodotos. 'Phidias or Judge Iasos might have to be more careful.'

They came to a square full of stalls and the platforms where poets, philosophers and orators spouted their competing cascades of words. Onlooking groups shouted admiringly or heckled and ridiculed.

The brothers climbed up the steps of a small temple to see over the heads of the crowd.

'Ariphron could have won the pentathlon if he'd got a neck hold in the wrestling,' said Diodotos.

'Ariphron's not really a fighter,' Themis said to his brother. 'He can throw and run, but he doesn't have the fire in him for hand-to-hand fighting.'

'Not like you, huh?' smiled Diodotos, looking over the square. 'Look! Everyone's going that way. Let's see if we can get a Spartan dinner.'

They were separated in the crush as they moved out of the square into the wide street along the side of the hill. The villas on the right had steps up to them, while those on the left had steps down. Between them were narrow alleys.

Themis was ahead of Diodotos and turned to wave as he was pushed along. He took some steps down at the entrance to an alleyway to allow his brother to catch up.

'You look like a man in need of a little fun,' said a husky voice beside him.

Chapter 46: a bit of blood

Themis looked down to the step below and saw a woman in diaphanous clothes leaning seductively against the wall. Her face was subtly painted to enhance her wide eyes and she licked her full lips as she looked up at him.

'You are mistaken.' Themis smiled an embarrassed smile.

The woman came closer him. Her perfume was exotic and disturbing. This was no ordinary prostitute. Themis leant backwards and stumbled against the step above.

'Hey! Puppy Dog, is that you?' called Diodotos from above. 'Oh ho!' he added lasciviously. 'What have you found?'

Themis turned and ran up the steps to street level. 'She found me,' he said pointedly.

Diodotos looked down at the woman, a smile of appreciation on his face. 'What do you charge, beautiful lady?' he asked.

Themis watched with interest. The woman stared insolently at his brother and said, 'More than you'll ever have, little man.'

Diodotos was stung. 'So why are you soliciting my baby brother?'

The woman looked up at Themis again. 'Not such a baby,' she said. 'Come with me, young Themis. There are things I can show you – '

Themis turned his back and stepped into the river of men in the street above. His brother followed him.

'Why didn't you stay?' asked Diodotos.

'She knew my name!' hissed Themis. 'Someone sent her to find me.'

'She just heard me call out to you,' said Diodotos.

'No!' Themis was searching for a way to get out of the throng. 'No. You called me "Puppy Dog" like you used to. She knew who I was.'

'Another coincidence?' said Diodotos, sounding less sure now.

'Perhaps,' said Themis. 'But I think I'd better get back to the athletes' tents and stay there this evening. Kadmos will find me something to eat.'

'But there are the sacrifices to Pelops tonight,' Diodotos protested.

'I know, but I compete tomorrow, and it's stupid to risk being in a crowd any longer than necessary.' They managed to enter a quiet street. 'You go to the sacrifice and mention me in your prayers,' Themis said with a wry smile.

'Perhaps you're right,' said Diodotos. 'I'll see you to the gate,'

>>>

From Bernie's private diary. Thursday August 5th 2010

Near Port des Torrent, Ibiza

Been thinking about Suzanne a bit. She would have loved this place before her accident. I'm not sure now. We don't seem to laugh at the same things any more.

But I was thinking that I might ask her to check through our history project. If the world she visits *is* real, then she would know a lot of detail that Laila and I can't find out. We could say that we can't prove stuff, but think it *might* have been like this or that.

I had this idea cos I woke up today – our last in this totally brilliant place – thinking how I've been very offhand about Suzanne's other life. It's so important to her and I've been trying to ignore it. It just scares me rigid, and I don't even know why.

It's not as though she's really mad or anything. She's getting better at school – and at managing her difficult family – all the time. It's just that she's tuned into somewhere/someone none of us can see. It's kind of disturbing. But I'm going to try and learn more about it all when I get back.

And so we leave today. Dad says if we save up we can come again next year. I'm exhausted, dancing nearly every night till two and three am, then swimming during the day, but it's been awesome. Yesterday we were snorkeling near the Fish Farm wreck and some dolphins came to see what we were looking at. They made clicking noises and slapped the water with their tails, like they were laughing at us. We must seem really funny to them!

<<<

'Themistokles, son of Kallistos, of the Deme of Diomea in the city of Athens,' called the herald, and Themis ran forward into the Olympic stadium.

His heart was pounding so hard he could hardly hear the cheer that rose from his left, high on the northern slope among the huge crowd. He looked up. Diodotos was waving a bright orange kerchief. Ariphron and some of the other Athenian competitors were with him.

Themis raised his hand to them as he followed the oiled and gleaming back of the boy in front. They marched to the flutes and drums on a lap round the stadium. When he passed the enclosure for important spectators on the southern side he saw Phidias, Panainos and Agorakritos on the wooden benches, clapping and stamping their encouragement.

The boys' feet made a scuffed path round the sandy edge of the ground. The lines for the running lanes ran from end to end, the weedless gravel newly raked ready for the boys' sprint. Themis felt the sand between his bare toes. He still found it hard to believe he was really about to take part in the Olympic Games, and he shivered with excitement.

The sun was hot but not yet the fiery tormentor of midday. The boys returned to the shady support tent at the western end of the stadium, behind the starting line. Their trainers were waiting for them there.

The cheering quietened. Now was the time for the drawing of lots. First the seven wrestlers were arranged in a circle, each with a marshal standing beside him. Judge Iasos held up a bowl to each marshal. When they had all taken one counter, he went round and read out the letters on them, pairing up the boys with the same letters. One boy was lucky and had no partner for the first round.

Then it was the turn of the boxers. There were six. Themis stood with his marshal. He felt calmer than at any time in the last few weeks. He had done everything he could to train and prepare well. Diodotos' permission had been accepted. He had made offerings to Zeus and Apollo with a heart full of gratitude. Now it was in their hands.

He found he was paired with Apollodoros from Korkyra. He was older than Themis but smaller, with a vicious right fist. Today they would fight full out for the first time, trying for a knock out or a submission. Themis knew he had more stamina than the Korkyran. But did he have the fury of that strange, quiet young man?

With the lots drawn for their first round, the boys sat on benches in the shade of the tent awning.

The sprint was the first event, seventeen boys running one length of the stadium. The marshals spread out, evenly spaced along each side of the tracks and at the finishing line. The crowd massed near the eastern end, all vying for the best view of the finish.

The race was over in a few moments and a youth from Platea won, streaking home well ahead of the others. He was immediately given his victor's head- and arm-bands and a branch of the palm tree. He bounced round the Stadium waving this and acknowledging the cheers of the crowd as they moved back towards the starting line where the wrestling pit was.

And the wrestling began. Themis sat for a few moments watching the first bout. The boys started as usual with their foreheads together and the mandatory first moves. Two marshals with short whips stood by, ready to punish any cheating.

Then Kadmos came to bind Themis' hands with the leather thongs they had prepared so carefully. Themis stood up for this and felt his excitement building. His heart beat speeded up and a singing started in his ears.

The first wrestling bout ended with a submission in a cloud of sand and a shout of pain.

As the other bouts were fought, Kadmos silently re-oiled Themis' back and chest and insisted that he took regular mouthfuls from a cup of water. Marshals came to check all the boxers' bindings. The sun was halfway up the sky.

Suddenly, the wrestling was over. The winner was from Elis, a boy called Lykinos who was so arrogant that Themis had only spoken to him once. He had thrown his opponent three times in quick succession.

The crowd in the Stadium included thousands of people from Elis. It exploded with cheers and shouts and victory songs. Lykinos ran round with his palm branch, waving and shouting and bowing to his friends and family. Flowers and ribbons were thrown at him.

This went on for some time, as the sun rose higher. Finally, Judge Iasos called a halt and the marshals spread out and calmed the crowd.

The first boxing bout was between Esperos and Voithus from Sparta. Themis could not sit still. He walked up and down in the diminishing shade, keeping an eye on the fight, in case he had to fight its victor later. Kadmos stopped trying to calm him.

The Spartan caught Esperos a good punch to his eye which made Esperos so angry that he lashed out fast with both hands. The Spartan was knocked out.

'Themistokles of Athens and Apollodorus of Korkyra!' called the herald.

'*Now*,' thought Themis as he stepped into the square. And then there were no more thoughts, just complete focus on the fight, and keeping out of reach of any blows to his head.

Apollodorus was quick and angry, but Themis managed to be quicker. Once he slipped in the sand and almost went down on one knee. But he recovered and danced on, round and round, waiting for a chance to get through the Korkyran's guard. The heat caused them both to sweat through their oil and the sand stuck to their legs as though they were wearing leggings like Persians. The crowd shouted and roared and called out 'Shame, Athenian! Let him get near you!' Themis ignored them.

At last Apollodorus' concentration wavered for a moment when a flock of crows flew over the Stadium. Themis jabbed with his left to the chin. The Korkyran's legs buckled and a look of surprise came on his face as he fell. His eyes closed and he lay still. A tooth had landed in the sand beside him. Themis felt a marshal grab his arm as he stepped forward to give the Korkyran another blow if he tried to rise.

The other marshal stepped in to check that Apollodorus was still alive and gave a nod.

'You win,' he said, and Themis stood back. The marshal helped the Korkyran to his feet and led him out of the square, dripping blood from his mouth.

The Athenians all round the Stadium yelled encouragement and praise. Themis waved his arms to them briefly. Then the next bout began.

And it was very short. The winner, Tindareos from Taras, pranced around as his victim was carried from the square.

Lots were drawn again and Themis was matched with Tindareos. So Themis would have to fight Esperos if he won this bout.

'Try and get him quickly,' growled Kadmos quietly as he re-wrapped Themis' left hand. There was no blood. 'The heat's growing. You may have to go a while with Esperos – he'll be fresher than you with only one bout fought.'

Themis nodded and stepped into the square. After the obligatory opening steps, Tindareos began to talk. Themis darted and wove and stayed out of reach, but the boy from Taras' voice got louder and his insults more pointed. The crowd picked up on this and began to chant with him.

'Coward, coward!' they called. 'Mummy's boy!'

Themis didn't take his eyes off his opponent. Kadmos called out to him, 'Ignore it!' and went to speak to Judge Iasos.

'Dancing like a girl!' called Tindareos. 'Hello, darling!'

The crowd laughed and joined in. 'Give us a kiss,' they called. 'Sit on me, sweetheart!'

Themis watched Tindareos' eyes. Once or twice he glanced up at the crowd, enjoying his effect on them. Themis waited, dancing backwards and forwards and then round behind Tindareos. As they came face to face again, the boy from Taras was looking at a group in the crowd who were calling his name. Themis bounced in and hit hard.

Tindareos staggered back, shaking his head. Themis closed up and punched with a right and a left to the boy's ears.

The boy stood still, swaying, his eyes spouting tears and blood running from his right ear. Themis went in again, but Tindareos raised a finger. 'Stop!' shouted the marshal.

Themis bounced round the square and waved to the crowd, which was in turmoil, some cheering and some shouting out, 'Cheat!'. Those who were too far away to see were asking others what had happened.

'They like a bit of blood,' said Kadmos, pushing a cup of water into Themis' bound hands. He drank and returned the cup. Then he ran part of the way up the stadium and back. The crowd shouted and sang and chanted his name. His feet weren't touching the ground.

The bout with Esperos was called. The marshals quietened the crowd and the two of them took up their positions.

As Themis and Esperos finished the opening steps, Esperos tried to trip Themis under cover of a cloud of sand. Themis jumped back and almost fell.

'Do that again!' he shouted. 'Do it again so everyone can see.'

The marshals looked at each other and shrugged.

'No need,' smiled Esperos, standing quietly, his guard up, waiting for Themis to tire in the heat.

So Themis stood still too. Neither of the boys heard the crowd any more. They faced each other in silence, watching.

The crowd began a slow chant. The boys began to circle each other. The sun blazed. As he reached the spot where it was in his eyes, Themis realised he would be blinded for a moment. He danced a step or two and slowed again as Esperos moved into the blinded position.

Themis struck with his left. Esperos defended with his right forearm, but the power of Themis' blow made him stagger.

The crowd roared.

Then there was stalemate again as the two boys avoided the direct glare of the sun. The crowd began their chant. The marshals walked round the square, whips ready.

Themis began a complex dance. He approached and retreated, punching at Esperos' head and being countered again and again by the arms. He confused Esperos by coming almost within reach often and fast but from different sides. Esperos began to fight back, taking a firm stance and swinging hard. Themis used the brief moment this took each time, to come close, land a glancing blow, and dance away.

He caught Esperos on the chin and made him bite his tongue. He had to spit blood. The marshals were desperate not to miss anything so they kept dodging around the square. The crowd called out to them to get out of the way so they could see.

Sweat began to get into Themis' eyes. With a brief prayer of gratitude for his thick eyelashes, he brushed it away with his wrists, a trick he had learned on his long runs. Esperos was not as expert, and had to shake his head from time to time, blinking desperately.

Then Themis saw Esperos preparing to flick sand up with his foot. He had to look down for a moment. This was technically cheating, and Themis was so angry that when his left fist landed on Esperos cheek, the jolt went right up his arm and made him stagger.

The crowd thought he was hit and there was a sudden silence. Then Esperos began to collapse, blood pouring from his mouth where his teeth had cut into the inside of his cheek.

A huge roar rose as one marshal grabbed Themis' left arm while the other leant over Esperos, crumpled on the sand, groaning.

Themis stood stunned for a moment. Then the marshal raised his arm and shouted, 'The victor!'

He was led to the awards table where an official tied the victor's bands round his dripping hair and on his arms. Another handed him the palm leaf, and he found himself running a circuit of the stadium to the cheers and praise of the crowd. Diodotos ran out of the crowd and joined him. Panainos, Phidias and Agorakritos were standing and applauding as they passed, but Themis noticed that Phidias looked puzzled as well as pleased.

>>>

Chapter 47: prey

At Dad's, late afternoon

O. M. G. WE WON!! He won! We won!!!!!!! He got it right! All that training. All that obsession and sweat and repetition. It paid off and he won, with not a punch taken! I danced around my room so much that Dad came up to see if I was OK. (I told him I'd shut my finger in a drawer. He's not good with scrambled brains.) It was so good to feel Themis' joy and pride. Makes me jealous – in a happy way.

Mum and Steve announced two days ago that they were taking the boys to Alton Towers. They must have booked back when I was unconscious.

I'm supposed to be working on my projects, but I've found it so easy to be with Themis this last couple of days. I'm up to date now with inputting all I remember of his/our life. And in a way it is part of the Athens history project. I was thinking of doing weaving and clothes, but p'raps now I'll do sport. Everyone else has done things like building the Parthenon, or the war between Athens and Sparta. Even with Themis, I don't know much about any of those things, except that the war hasn't started yet. I wish I could tell him it really will!

And now he is the boy boxing champion of the 87th Olympiad! But, god, he loved it, but I hated the fighting. It was all testosterone and blind will power. Blood, broken bones, spitting teeth, cuts and bruises, heat, sweat, oil, fetid stink, yelling crowds, sand in all the crevices. And the pain! They have amazing tolerance of pain. I never watch boxing. At least they don't have to deal with the sand nowadays.

Bernie's back this evening and she's emailed me a draft of the project she's doing with Laila. It's on the gold and ivory statue of Athena inside the Parthenon. Phidias made it before the Zeus in Olympia. I've been reading through it. She wants my opinion 'As an expert' she says with a smiley. Huh. Now he's useful to her, she's prepared to accept Themis. Anyway, much of the project is boring and obvious. But they found out that Phidias was accused of stealing some of the gold from the statue's robes! And yet Phidias said to Themis that he paid for stuff with his own money – and Kallistos'. Bernie and Laila say there was a trial, but in the end there wasn't any gold missing! Perhaps that's what Phidias and Kallistos paid for, the replacements.

I wish I could make Themis do what I want. I could get him to find out what really happened. That would be awesome ...

Going out now with Dad and some friends of his for a meal. Sporty types, he said. Prob'ly rugby, yuch. Probly see Ron again tomorrow.

Yeah!!

Later

They were from a cycling team! And they talked about fitting their obsession into the lives of their families. Which made me think about how angry I've been with Bernie lately. I haven't been fair. She probly just wants to make things better between us. Dad was telling me about all the time she spent with me when I was in a coma. In fact, I've been pretty angry in general, I suppose. Nigel's on holiday, thank god, but he did say something about anger being one of the phases people like me go through.

Have to remind myself to relax, be nice!

<<<

'Are you feeling pleased with life, little brother?' yelled Diodotos with a laugh.

'It'll never be this good again! I'm going to explode,' shouted Themis over the sounds of the feast.

Diodotos clapped him on the left shoulder. Themis winced. Diodotos laughed again and rubbed the bulging bicep. 'Sorry! Forgot you'd felled an ox with your left today.'

'Not quite an ox.'

'You were talking to Phidias and Xenovia before the sacrifices to Zeus,' commented Diodotos.

'Yes. Phidias called me over,' replied Themis.

'What did he say?'

Great platters of meat from the one hundred sacrificed bullocks were being brought and set on the long tables. Bread, water and wine were already laid out and burnished lanterns lit. Throughout the town and the tent cities, there must have been thousands sitting down to Zeus' meat that evening. Diodotos and Themis were with the athletes and their families under the trees in a corner of the Altis. None of Themis' opponents seemed to be near them.

'Phidias was surprised I didn't win without a fight, like the oracle said.' Themis reached for a piece of meat.

'Perhaps to a god that wasn't a real fight, just a minor spat,' teased Diodotos.

Themis lifted his stiff, swollen hands in mock aggression. 'Want to see for yourself?'

Diodotos laughed, shaking his head. 'No need. I'm convinced!'

The official at the head of the table stood up. 'To our victors today, Timon of Plataea in the sprint, Lykinos of Elis in the boys' wrestling, and Themistokles of Athens in the boys' boxing, beloved of Zeus and dear to all the gods. May you live to see a hundred summers and win a score of crowns!'

Everyone at the table banged cups on the boards and cheered. Themis had finally begun to believe he had won. He was so excited he could hardly eat. He knew there would be celebrations and gifts when he got back to Athens and he would now be famous throughout the Hellenic world, at least for a year or two.

'Careful,' warned his brother. 'Your face will split open.'

'Oh, shut up and eat,' laughed Themis.

Later Ariphron's father urged Diodotos, 'Come on. You've had more than enough wine.' He turned to Themis with a broad grin and a nod. 'You'll be needing your sleep, young champion. I'll take your brother back to his lodgings. You get back to "Tent City".'

The men who would be competing next day were drifting away and the evening was cooling off as a tiny breeze rustled in the trees. The moon shone full, making black shadows with its stark white light. No one needed a torch to get home tonight.

'Night, little brother,' called Diodotos as he was helped off.

'Night, old man!' answered Themis.

He began to walk back to his tent. But suddenly he knew he wouldn't be able to sleep. He searched out Kadmos among the strolling crowd.

'I'll just go for a short run to calm me,' he said. 'I've got my pass so they'll let me in later.'

The trainer shook his head and shrugged. 'It's been a great day. Enjoy the flavour of winning, but don't go too far, and come and speak to me when you get back.'

'However late?'

'You're not going looking for girls are you?' queried the trainer.

Themis snorted. 'Not tonight! But I might tomorrow … '

Kadmos gave him a gentle push in the chest. 'Go on. Go and get the fire out of your blood.'

Themis started slowly, his stomach still working on the meat of the feast. He ran between the tents along by the River Alpheios. There were some enormous ones in the best positions beside the water, luxurious, multicoloured, and brightly lit. Some had fences around and guards. Themis knew these were for foreign ambassadors and even princes. There had been three kings represented in the chariot race the day before.

The furthest tents were the plainest and poorest, and at last they petered out as he ran on along the road to Three Rivers. Here there were almost no other people and he speeded up, his blood singing in his veins, his body as light as a bird.

At the spring where he'd remembered Nikitas his twin, he turned off up the valley. He had not come this way for months. The track was clear in the white moonlight and he enjoyed feeling his muscles begin to burn on the steep slope up to the cliff.

The path was wide now, and well worn from the feet of athletes. Some of the rocks had even been moved to the side and the steps up the vertical section of cliff made more stable.

He came out onto the plateau and turned to look back to the distant, shining sea.

'Wow!' he said out loud. The magnificent black and white view made him shake his head in wonder. This was perhaps the most perfect moment of his life …

As he stood there, basking in this heavenly feeling, he noticed a horse and rider on the track along by the river. They had passed the village and now turned to climb the first steps in the path up to the cliff.

The rider was wearing a long dark robe with a hood.

'*It's a bit warm for clothes like that,*' thought Themis idly.

The rider looked up, a pale oval face in the moonlight. The horse suddenly leapt up the steps towards the bottom of the cliff.

Themis stared, watching the speed and agility of the animal with admiration. He could hear the rider urging the horse to go faster. It must have been a young man as the voice was hardly broken.

Why would a man on a horse be hurrying up this hazardous path at almost midnight on the third day of the Games at Olympia? Was he a messenger from Kadmos? Themis stood at the top of the cliff and waited.

He could hear the horse's labouring breath and the rider's exhortations. Although he couldn't hear the words, the voice was furious, desperate, with an edge to it that couldn't be justified by haste to deliver a message to someone who was obviously waiting for it.

Themis suddenly realised there was no message. He was being hunted again.

Furious with himself for forgetting this possibility, he looked around wildly. The plateau behind him stretched out without cover until it reached what seemed to be sheer rock slopes. In front of him the cliff plunged into the forest, but there was no other way down except the path the horse was coming up.

He turned and ran out onto the plateau in the hope of finding a dip between the thorny bushes where he could hide. He zigzagged at speed, scratching his shins on the small thorny bushes.

The rider topped the cliff and stopped for a moment, the horse snorting and dancing. Themis was clearly visible and they came on after him. He ran along the path towards the only two trees on the plateau, those at the edge of the gorge. Wasn't there a ledge just below the lip that he'd seen when he was up there in the spring?

He could hear the horse gaining on him fast. He was a hundred feet from the two trees when he turned to see how far away it was. The rider's hood had blown off.

The rider was Xenovia!

He stood still in shock. Then he waved his arms to stop her. 'No!' he called out. 'Stop! There's a gorge!'

The horse came on. He could see the determined line of Xenovia's chin and her wide, furious eyes.

He ran backwards towards the trees. 'No, Sacred Lady,' he was shouting, waving his arms. 'Stop! Stop!'

But she drove the horse on towards him, its hooves thumping and scraping on the earth and stones. She screamed something at him and he saw the shine of her teeth.

He broke away to the side, but she turned the horse to follow and cut him off. He ran back towards the trees and she whipped round to cut him off again. The thunder of the hooves was upon him as he turned in desperation to face her. Her triumphant scream filled the air and Themis felt the breath of the horse on his face as he dived sideways. A hoof caught his right thigh as he landed face-down across tree roots.

There was silence.

Themis lifted his head and watched the horse and rider fly out from the cliff, then begin to fall. They parted company just as they were swallowed up by the black shadow of the ravine. A terrified whinny and a thin scream reached him, cut off by the sound of a splash, a pause, and then another splash.

He lay still for a long moment, completely stunned.

Then he jumped up and leant over as far as he dared. The depths of the ravine were totally black. He could not see the river, but he remembered its muscular surface as it raced through the gorge. He could hear the gentle swish of the water where it flowed over the step of rock and down into the earth. This was disturbed once, and then again, as something bulky caught on the step and then flopped noisily over it.

Themis ran faster than he had ever run before. He flew across the plateau and down the cliff, along the valley and then beside the Alpheios, between the tents, and finally to the Senate building outside the Altis.

The guards there refused to understand what he was saying to them. He felt the same panic he used to feel after his accident when he couldn't find words. He caught his breath and tried to slow down.

At last they grasped that someone had fallen into the Vathonero and was now underground. A group of six formed up and set off at a run for the village in the valley. Two men on horses rode after them with ropes and healing supplies.

Themis made as if to follow them. 'You'd better take a rest,' said the guard on duty. 'They'll find her and you look like you might drop dead at any moment,' and he gestured at a gash in Themis' thigh that was trickling blood.

'I'm fine,' said Themis, gazing at it with a surprised frown.

'Who's your trainer?' asked the guard.

'Kadmos,' whispered Themis as he fell gently against a column.

Then Kadmos was pulling him up to sit with his back to the wall. 'Drink this,' said the trainer, and Themis choked on the potion Kadmos poured into his mouth.

'That burns,' he managed to say between coughs.

'You want to tell me about what happened?' asked Kadmos.

'We need to find Phidias,' said Themis.

At last the temple priests and the judges had been found, Themis had briefly explained, the search party had been augmented, and Phidias had appeared.

He ushered Themis and Kadmos back to his house. Frog joined them and Themis felt himself being bathed, dressed and bandaged in clean linen in a trance. Whenever he closed his eyes, he re-lived the scene of the flying horse and rider as they came apart in midair. He had moments of uncontrollable shaking.

He was led into the andron, and helped onto a couch. Kadmos brought him something much nicer to drink. A slave slowly worked a huge fan and Frog sat wide-eyed at the foot of the couch on the floor.

Phidias came and sat on a stool beside him. 'It's very late, Themis. Do you want to sleep?' he asked in his lightest voice.

'NO!' Themis started up, his eyes staring. 'I want to know why Xenovia tried to run me down – why she fell … '

Phidias put his hands on Themis' shoulders and pushed him gently back onto the couch. 'Sit quietly,' he said, 'I'll tell you what I know.'

Themis subsided.

'Do you remember,' Phidias began, 'I told you that your father and I spent some of our own money to finish the statue of Athena?'

'Of course,' said Themis.

'In fact, we had to do this because there were small sections of the gold used for her gown and on her shield that went missing.'

'Missing?' Themis' voice came out much deeper than usual. It confused him.

'Yes. Stolen. It began with one quite large piece, and I was accused of taking it myself. Perhaps you remember? It was a very public accusation.'

Themis shook his head.

Phidias went on, 'Well, I replaced it from my own pocket, and the ensuing trial found me innocent. However – '

'You needed to know who had really stolen it?' Themis interrupted and finished for him. His voice sounded normal again.

Phidias nodded. 'Exactly. And your father was Commander of the Akropolis Guard, so he took it personally that someone was stealing right under his nose, so to speak. He instituted searches of all visitors and workers on the Akropolis at both the new gate and the back staircase. He doubled the guard and had everything locked up at night.'

'But – '

'But no one was caught, even though other smaller sections were disappearing. This went on over a long period. Then, on the day of the Panathenaia, your father took over from the night guard at dawn. He took you and Diodotos and Myrto up with him to watch the procession coming through the Agora from the best possible viewpoint.'

'I remember that day,' said Themis with wonder. 'Myrto was making an offering in the temple before the rush. She said her hair stood on end when she saw Xenovia in there. I was just dashing around outside, trying to find officials to annoy. When we got back to Father, he was angry because he had forgotten to search Xenovia … Oh … '

Themis looked at Phidias in horror.

Chapter 48: proof

'That's right, said Phidias. 'Your father was embarrassed that he had been chatting to Xenovia and forgotten to search her. I learned later that he sent someone after her to her house. This man saw a mounted messenger ride away with a heavy saddlebag. Kallistos waited until Xenovia had gone back to her duties on the Akropolis, and then he questioned her house slaves. She'd sent the saddlebag to Three Rivers.'

'Three Rivers!' echoed Themis. 'Where Thukydides lives?'

'Exactly. Thukydides is Xenovia's mother's cousin.'

'So the gold – '

'Was being sent to him by Xenovia. He is a political opponent of Perikles, as you know. And we think that Xenovia was trying to help him with his campaign for votes this coming winter.'

'But he's in exile,' said Themis.

'True, but the ten years' ostracism will be over in two months' time.' Phidias looked grim. 'If he can get enough votes in the Assembly this winter, he could oust Perikles altogether and let the Spartans take whatever they want from Athens without a fight.'

There was a stunned silence as everyone in the room considered that.

'Without a fight … ' said Themis after a moment. 'That reminds me. What about the oracle and my winning "without a fight"?'

'I still don't know what that means,' said Phidias. 'Did we get it wrong? You certainly had to fight for your victor's palm today!'

'Yesterday now,' growled Kadmos from his couch. 'I'll have to go, Master Sculptor. I have men competing this morning.' He stood up, bowed to Phidias and Themis.

'Thank you, Kadmos,' said Themis, sitting upright. 'Thank you for making me a champion!'

'You did that. I just watched,' said Kadmos. He lifted a hand and left.

Themis lay back and looked across at Phidias. He still felt very strange, as though his head was full of drifting feathers. 'So you believe that Xenovia was the one stealing from Athena's statue?' he prompted.

'We know that she was. Your father followed the messenger that very evening and finally caught up with him four days later as he was leaving Thukydides' estate – without the saddlebag. Thukydides himself was away hunting. Your father disguised himself as a beggar, got a meal and a night's rest from the slaves at the estate, and managed, with some difficulty, to steal the bag away. He took it into the forest where he had hidden his horse. There he opened it and found a wooden casket full of gold and jewels.'

'Jewels?!' exclaimed Themis. 'You didn't mention jewels before.'

'There were precious stones in the figures on the straps of Athena's sandals and in the eyes and scales of the serpent, Erichthonius, by her left foot. Some of these had been dug out and we'd replaced them. There are lots of others on the breastplate and necklace, but they're higher up.'

Themis suddenly exclaimed. 'I saw her!'

'Athena?' asked Phidias.

'No. Well … I thought she *was* at first.' Themis looked sheepish. 'But no. It was Xenovia. She was standing in the corner of the little walled yard beside the Vravronio, just inside the Great Gate. She had her back to me and I wouldn't have noticed her as I ran past, except that at that moment, the sun came up over Mount Hymetos and shone on her. She was alone, but she was talking – praying, I suppose. She was holding up her hands and they were full of coloured fire. I ran into the yard to ask her what it was, and she quickly shut her hands and put them inside her robes. When she turned, something banged against the wall, as though something hard and heavy hung from her girdle.'

'Ah,' said Phidias with a slow nod.

'Does that mean …? Is it possible … that it's Xenovia who's been hunting me ever since I started getting better?' Themis covered his mouth with his stiff and swollen left hand in sickening realisation.

'She wouldn't have known who you were when you saw her with the jewels,' said Phidias. 'Your father told me you were running wild somewhere among the temples and you didn't turn up until the procession was well underway.'

'That's right,' said Themis. 'At the time, she just said something like, "run away little boy," and hurried off. But forty days ago, when I met her here, she did say she had seen me that day, although she didn't mention where exactly. She must've been testing to see if I could remember … '

'That would be her greatest fear, I imagine,' said Phidias. 'That you would remember and be believed. So when all her efforts failed to get you killed, or knocked stupid during your boxing bouts, she must have made the decision tonight to kill you herself.'

They sat in appalled silence for a moment.

'But what happened to the casket?' asked Themis so as not to think of the scene at the gorge yet again.

'Your father was caught by Thukydides' men as he took a short cut through the mountains. There was a fight and the casket fell into a river. Your father was wounded but managed to get away and back to Athens.'

'So it's lost.'

'Yes. Unless Thukydides dragged the river and found it, which I'm sure would not have stayed a secret for long.' Phidias sipped his wine. 'Of course, someone completely unconnected might have found it and taken it without telling anyone, but that, too, would eventually have become known. Meanwhile, there have been other accusations of Xenovia from among the priesthood. She manages to discount them as jealousy, but I imagine that when she learned that the boy who saw her with the jewels was you and that you had lost your memory, she became afraid.'

'That I would remember and tell.'

'Exactly. Maybe she thought you know more than you do. She could be stripped of her titles and privileges if it was proved she was the thief. Her mother has been suspicious for some time.'

'Asterodia?'

'Yes.' Phidias sighed. 'Think how painful it must be to suspect your only child of being a crimimal.'

'I can't … '

'I also think Xenovia learned about your father's trip to Three Rivers and began a campaign to discredit him.' Phidias looked suddenly tired. 'Then he was killed while on duty anyway.'

Themis swung his legs off the couch which made him feel as if he was going to faint. 'I think I'd better go and get some sleep,' he said quietly.

Phidias stood up. 'Sleep here tonight. Any news of the search will come to me and I promise I'll wake you.'

When Themis woke it was day. Frog's pallet by his bed was empty. He could hear voices outside. Phidias was greeting a messenger. Themis joined them in the shade under the columns.

' … sign of the priestess, but they've found the body of the horse,' the messenger was saying. 'They can't dislodge it. One leg is caught in a cleft between rocks in the bottom of the river. It's very deep and fast-moving there.'

'We should go and see if we can help,' said Phidias. 'She may be nearby. Would you like to come, Themis, or do you want to watch the men's games in the stadium?'

'I'm not sure, Uncle,' he said. 'I really wanted to watch the men's boxing, but if I can be of help to you and the – '

'You stay,' said Phidias. 'Rest today. You did enough for twenty days yesterday! Diodotos is there now. I'll send him back. Panainos has gone to the temple. He rarely prays, but he wanted to today.' He set off briskly for the stables.

Themis watched the two men ride off and then went to look for something to eat before going to the stadium. His mind felt numb with shock. He wanted it to stay that way.

'Where were you this morning?' asked Pantarkes as Themis joined him in the crowd. 'The first two races are over.'

'I had a … disturbed night,' said Themis with a shrug.

'I bet!' laughed Pantarkes, his beautifully symmetrical face full of friendly cynicism. 'I didn't even go home. It's not often Phidias gives me a whole night off!'

'Who's that?' asked Themis, watching a young man, garlanded and beribboned, being led to a seat on the enclosure benches.

'Sophron of Ambrakia,' said Pantarkes, pushing his way through the crowd to a good vantage point. 'He won the men's sprint this morning, so this will be called Sophron's Olympiad.'

'I didn't mean to miss that,' said Themis as they stopped and turned to look down. Preparations for the final boxing bout were being made.

A man nearby recognised Themis and said 'Congratulations, young Themistokles. That's an unusual style you have!'

'Thank you,' said Themis.

They were now near the top of the north side of the stadium, looking down at the judges in the enclosure on the opposite side and the busy slaves and marshals on the floor. The sun was so hot it looked as though there was water shimmering over the sand.

Pantarkes said, 'I bet this match won't be as … unusual.'

'There's Diodotos,' said Themis and he waved and shouted, 'Up here, brother!'

He left Pantarkes and started down to meet Diodotos, who seemed very excited about something as he battled up through the crowd.

'What is it?' Themis called as he got nearer. 'What's happened? Did they find – '

Diodotos put a finger to his lips and came up close so that he could speak quietly. They sat down.

'No. The priestess is still missing. But they got the horse out of the river,' he said. 'It was deep and swirling just there, but they managed to move a rock and release the body. And … ' he paused.

'Well?' prompted Themis, his voice doing its uncontrolled tone change.

'Under the rock they found a casket.'

'What!?' Themis exclaimed. 'Is it – '

'Phidias says it's the missing pieces,' Diodotos was being careful of his words in the crowd.

'Truly?' Themis shook Diodotos arm.

'Truly. Real proof,' affirmed his brother.

The crowd suddenly all stood up and began to clap and cheer.

The herald called for quiet. The two finalist boxers were strutting and posing round the edge of the sand-filled square.

'I should go to the river.' Themis said.

'No, you shouldn't. It's all official and swarming with guards. You want to see this, don't you?' said his brother. 'It could be you in a few years.'

'The Kydonian will win, anyway,' said a man behind them. 'I've put money on him. And you won me twenty drachmas yesterday, young Themistokles! Bravo!'

'So the Kydonian did win,' said Diodotos as they left the stadium. 'I wish I'd bet on him myself now.'

'I just want to drop in at the workshop,' Themis said. 'Say goodbye to Tilemachos.'

'Fine. I'll wait for you out here,' said Diodotos, leaning against the wall in the shade.

Tilemachos was in the back yard. He ran over when he saw Themis. 'I didn't know where to find you,' he said. 'I wanted to thank you.'

'What for?' asked Themis.

'I made a lot of money yesterday because of you. No one really believed you could win once they saw you weren't taking punches. So the men around me in the crowd were prepared to bet against you.'

Themis shook his head. 'I'd forgotten all about the betting side of things until this morning,' he said. 'Look, I just came to say goodbye and thanks for what you taught me.'

'Well, it's me who has to thank you. Now I'm out of debt and soon I'll be finished here, so I'll probably see you back in Athens. Phidias said he'd keep me on there as long as I behave myself!'

'If I get back before you, I'll give your greetings to Straton and his family,' said Themis with a wry smile.

'You do that,' laughed Tilemachos. 'See you there,' and he went back to work.

Outside, Diodotos had a companion. The yellow dog was lying at his feet. When Themis appeared it came and sat to attention in front of him.

'What's this?' asked Diodotos. 'Friend of yours?'

'I think this is the dog that was with the man who was hunting me,' said Themis. 'Shall we take him to the guards and see if they can find his master? They haven't had much luck so far.'

'Better than leaving him here or having him follow us all day,' agreed Diodotos.

'Athena has paid her dues,' said Phidias as he ushered them into his andron. Three richly-dressed men, an official scribe, two soldiers, and the Commander of the Altis Guard, were with Panainos.

And on a table in their midst stood the casket. Its lid was open and the treasure sparkled with gold, sapphires and rubies in the sunlight from the window.

Two more armed guards stood by the door, while the scribe sat at the table, listing the contents of the casket on a scroll.

Themis and Diodotos went over and looked at the moulded pieces of gold and the gleaming gems among their linen and leather wrappings.

'We've only just opened it,' said Phidias. 'The pieces are clearly from the statue of Athena.' He picked one up. The guards stepped forward and were waved back by the Commander in his red tunic and dark leather cuirass.

Phidias went on, 'This is from the inner rim of the shield. Can you see the moulding?'

Everyone leaned forward a little.

'And these sapphires are from the straps over the insteps. I replaced them with stones of equal size and colour. We can demonstrate this back in Athens.'

The men nodded and mumbled.

'We'll re-wrap everything now,' the Commandant said. 'Are you done with the list?' he asked the scribe, who nodded.

As the official party of witnesses filed out, the Commandant and the scribe prepared a receipt in two copies for the casket and its contents. Phidias and the Commandant signed these.

Phidias and Panainos, Themis and Diodotos stood in the courtyard as the officials, the soldiers and the scribe finally left with the casket.

'They'll take it to be verified in Elis and bring it to the port for me to take back to Athens,' explained Phidias as the outer door closed on them.

'Are you sure?' said Panainos with a raised eyebrow.

'I have great faith in the Elian legal system,' Phidias said. 'They are the guardians of the essence of our humanity.'

He swung round and spread his arms.

'And now for our own private celebration,' he cried. 'The only sad thing on this wonderful day is that Kallistos is not here to enjoy it with us. But we do have his newly crowned champion son. So … '

He took a goblet from the slave at his elbow, and his voice rang around the walls of the courtyard. 'Has Hermes brought you the news, dear friend, there in the Underworld, that the oracle has been fulfilled? My innocence is proven, your family is now free from the machinations of a sorceress, and your son is champion of the Hellenic world's boy boxers. We offer our truest and most humble thanks to Mighty Father Zeus and wise and glorious Apollo. In Athens we will make a worthy sacrifice, but for the present …' He poured a full cup of dark red wine into the basin of the shrine of Zeus of the House, and handed the cup back to the slave.

They returned to the andron. Frog and other slaves hovered round tables now covered with platters and bowls of tiny eggs and pies and buns, fruits and sweet pastries.

'One thing still confuses me,' said Themis as they took their places. 'What did I, the "boy in two minds", win without a fight?'

'I asked the high priest who took you into the oracle about that and he says it must have been the chase on the mountain.' Phidias' hand hovered while he chose a small roasted bird. 'You didn't even know it was a fight at the time, but it was presumably a life and death contest,' he said as he delicately dismembered the bird.

'Makes me shiver just to think of it,' said Panainos.

'It doesn't … I can't get it out of my mind – or my dreams,' said Themis.

'You need to get home!' laughed Diodotos. 'Will Zeus let you go without your second "meeting"?'

Themis blushed. 'Actually, I did … dream of him again. I didn't say I had, because I wanted Mama to let me stay in Olympia.'

'You crafty conniver!' exclaimed Diodotos. 'She's been quite concerned about what that meeting would entail.'

'So was I!' said Themis. 'But it turned out to be, well … awe-inspiring,' He'd rehearsed what he would say at this moment many times as he felt no one would believe the presence of his 'visitor'. He had begun to doubt it himself sometimes. 'The dream was similar to the first one, but afterwards I had my memory back! I'm sorry I didn't tell anyone. I wanted to, because it was so good to know who I am, but I also needed to stay here.'

'Well, now you need to get home,' said Panainos sternly, 'and back to your studies or some work to keep you occupied. Otherwise, your success will go to your head!'

Themis bowed in apology.

Phidias said, 'The victory ceremonies are tomorrow. I shall leave for Athens as soon as possible after that. Come with me and we'll find you something to do in the city. I'll make it right with the foundry owner, and, if you remember, I promised your mother I'd bring you back on my ship.'

The door opened and Gulkishar appeared. 'The Priestess Asterodia has sent word that she wishes to speak with you when you have eaten,' he intoned.

The late afternoon sunlight emphasised the lines in the priestess's face when they joined her in the courtyard..

'Welcome, dear Asterodia,' said Phidias holding out both hands. 'You knew?'

'I … felt it five days ago. I was at Athena's precinct on the border of Attika and Megara,' answered the old lady. Themis looked across at Diodotos. Asterodia nodded her head. 'Yes. Where your father was overwhelmed and killed.'

Phidias said, 'I have no words sufficient to express my sympathy.'

'But you know I have long suspected Xenovia was a thief, and thus was inviting punishment of some kind,' said Asterodia. 'There was no proof, of course, and she always denied it. But it is better to know.' She sighed deeply. 'And now I know everything.'

'They are searching still,' Panainos reminded them.

'They will not find her.' Asterodia turned her steady gaze on Themis. 'You have been in my mind a great deal lately, Themistokles. I knew you were connected to Xenovia by death, but not how, or whose death.'

Themis couldn't speak. His eyes pricked with tears so he looked away.

Asterodia went on. 'And in our sorrow and confusion, we must not forget your great achievement in spite of such numerous obstacles, most of them placed in your way by Xenovia herself.'

Phidias saved Themis from having to answer by gesturing to the shady side of the courtyard. A fountain played there in a marble basin. 'Let us be cool,' he said. They all moved to cushioned stools out of the sun. They sat in silent respect for the pain etched on the old priestess' face.

Asterodia's hands were completely still in her lap. She ignored the cup of cordial set beside her. 'She has no father of course,' she said quietly. 'When I conceived her during the madness of the Dionysian festival, I was already considered too old to give birth. And I had never conceived before, so she was … god-given.'

'The lack of a father drove her to become attached to your cousin, Thukydides?' suggested Phidias.

'I believe he treated her with affection, unlike most men who saw her only as a thing – a beautiful thing, too beautiful to be a real person.' Themis was glad no one was looking at him as a deep blush rose up his neck. 'And later he helped her gain her position,' Asterodia added.

'Surely that was due to you,' Panainos said.

'No.' The priestess shook her head. 'No … I never felt she was suited to a religious life. Humility is essential if you wish to hear the true voices of the gods. And she lacked humility … to the point that she believed she had the right to kill.'

Chapter 49: inheritance

In the shocked silence, Asterodia looked slowly round at her four listeners. 'I have a story to tell you that will bring you pain,' she said. 'But it must be told.'

Diodotos straightened his back. 'To do with our father?'

Asterodia nodded slightly. 'As you know,' she said, 'Kallistos died at the precinct of Athena that I was visiting five days ago. I questioned an acolyte there, just a girl still, who was witness to the ambush. She climbed up into a space in the roof of the precinct temple, and so survived.'

'Surely the Megarans would not have killed an innocent acolyte?' said Phidias.

'It was not the Megarans who ambushed Kallistos and his men. They were dressed as Megarans, but the girl I spoke to heard them talking. They were mainly foreign mercenaries, about ten of them. As soon as they had slaughtered the two priestesses, the other acolyte, and the four guards – including your father – there was an argument as to their payment.'

Asterodia took a deep breath. 'No,' she went on, 'they were not Megarans. When the acolyte first looked me in the face she fainted with fear. When she recovered, I asked her why, and she said that the man who had killed Kallistos had thrown back his head and laughed, even as he shook drops of blood from his hands. He was slim and with little muscle and no beard. The girl saw his eyes clearly and has dreamt of them ever since … The one thing Xenovia and I have in common is the shape and colour of our eyes.'

Themis covered his face and shrank into himself in horror and shame, his head on his knees. He could hear the chatter and flutter of sparrows gathering to roost, and the cries of vendors in the street.

Diodotos' shocked voice said, 'Xenovia dressed as a man to attack the precinct? Why?! Why would she hate Father enough to kill him like that? And the temple staff? I don't believe it,' he declared. 'She always was so … friendly to him – to all of us.'

'A long time ago,' said Asterodia, 'before he married, your father came to the attention of Xenovia. Scores of men surrounded her, ready to please her in any way she dictated, but he, though always polite, hardly seemed to notice her. And he was the only one she ever told me she was attracted to. But he married your mother, a widow – a worse blow to her than if he'd chosen a virgin. And later, when

Xenovia was stealing from Athena's statue – which it was Kallistos' responsibility to guard – she was exhilerated. I now see that this was because she was paying him back for the insult.'

'It took more than a year for him to find out who was stealing,' said Phidias. 'She must have enjoyed that.'

'Until she learned from Thukydides that Kallistos had traced that last installment of treasure. Then she knew she would be exposed if he ever found proof.'

Diodotos leapt up. 'So she murdered him and his men!' he shouted. 'And then came after Myrto and Themis.' He strode up and down, his voice harsh and loud. 'Why wasn't Melanas with him? He brought his armour back home. He must know more than he has said.'

'I don't think so,' said Asterodia calmly. 'The girl said no one appeared at the precinct for some time. They had just changed the guard. She was too frightened to come down and raise the alarm. No, Diodotos, I don't think anyone believed it was not the Megarans, and that they had done their work and melted back into their mountains. Kallistos and his men had been billeted in the village on the Attican side of the border. It is well out of earshot of the precinct, so Melanas knew nothing until he finished his domestic duties and went up to join the guards.'

Diodotos stood rigid with his back to them, grabbing and pulling handfuls of hair. He roared wordlessly at the sky. Panainos rose and put an awkward arm round his shoulders. Diodotos turned. 'I didn't know,' he said, tears of anger on his cheeks. 'She stood so close, touched my face. I could have killed her so easily.'

'You look like your father,' said Phidias. 'She was playing a dangerous game.'

There was a knocking on the street door and Gulkishar appeared with an Elian guard. He was carrying a damp black bundle.

'This was found in the river, a hundred feet from where it emerges again,' said the guard. He shook the bundle open.

Themis gasped. 'Xenovia's cloak!' he exclaimed, his voice cracking.

'Are you sure?' asked Phidias.

'It was black, with a hood.' Themis turned to Asterodia. 'I can't swear to it, there must be hundreds of black cloaks, but it looks the same.' He wiped the tears off his chin.

Asterodia stood and went to examine the cloak. She found and unpinned a small silver brooch from the edge of the hood. 'It is hers. I gave her this when she was a child.' The brooch lying on Asterodia's wrinkled palm was the shape of a leaf with a central vein and three others crossing it at right angles. It was twisted a bit out of shape, perhaps from its tumbling in the river.

Themis stared at it. It was the design on the seal used on Molon's tablets. So *Xenovia* had sent Molon with the instructions to the Tainaron oracle. *And* the tablet to Judge Iasos! She wanted him to compete in the Games so that he would be hit again and die, not because she cared about him! And, even if he was only knocked stupid, as Phidias suggested, she'd make sure he wasn't believed if he said he'd seen her with the jewels …

Asterodia was still talking. 'If she has gone,' she said without expression, 'Hades will give her a warm welcome. She won't need this in his kingdom.'

>>>

From Suzanne's secret diary
August 6th, 2010, Friday

Still at Dad's.

My God! It was Xenovia! Bloody bitchface kleptomaniac!!!!! If someone had killed my dad … daren't even think about it …Themis is gutted. Been biting my lips till they bleed …
And he did win without a fight. Those oracle mediums or whatever they were, must have had real powers. I did some research. So many of the oracles actually came true, though usually not exactly as predicted, just like this one. P'raps *that* should be my project …
Our astrologers could learn a lesson or two. My horoscope says, 'this is the month to take control of your life. Be kind, but be insistent.' That's good advice for anyone at any time, not just me, now.
I was reading my horoscope cos I want to know whether my dad is going to give me an iPad for my birthday on the 18th.
Oh, and whether I'll have enough brain to go to school full time in September. And whether Ron and I will stay together. And if I'll be strong enough to compete again before I need to start training for the Olympics.
Life does seem empty without the training.

Later

And just then Cassie phoned! She asked how my arm is. I told her it's fine now. Then she asked if I'd been signed off by my GP as out of danger of epilepsy or other 'encephalic incident'. I told her ninety-nine per cent. She asked me to go to Carlisle and do a pole vault demonstration

on Sunday, 15th! She said I could practise this Sunday and next Saturday,
when she'll be at the stadium.
Amazing! Of course, I'm scared stiff. But I agreed. As Themis says, life
could be over any time. Give it a go!ß
Bernie's coming over tonight.

<<<

When Asterodia had gone, Phidias turned to his brother. 'I think it's time for the tablet,' he said.

Panainos led them into the andron. He reached to the top shelf and handed Diodotos a sealed tablet. 'Your father left this in Phidias' care in the Athens house,' he said. 'Phidias asked me to bring it when I came for the Games. It is to be opened by Kallistos' sons if the prophecy is fulfilled, as it says on the front.'

Diodotos took the tablet and read the writing on the outside. He looked up. 'That's what it says. And it is sealed with Father's seal.' He slit the seals with his knife and laid the tablet on the small table where the evening light from the window was strongest.

A piece of papyrus, dirty and folded, lay between the two halves. Diodotos opened it. It was a list of the contents of the casket, written in Kallistos' hand. There was a series of brown drops and a smear across it. Diodotos dropped it when he realised that this was his father's blood.

He turned to Phidias. 'Would you read the tablet, Uncle?' he whispered.

Phidias leaned closer and read aloud: 'To my sons, Diodotos and Themistokles. For you to be reading this, I am now with the shades in the Underworld. But even death cannot cut the ties of love that I have for you both. There is an oracle that says that the items listed here will be found. If they are, half their value belongs to me, the other half to Phidias, son of Harmides, cousin of your mother Eirini. When the time comes to receive their worth, my portion should be divided between you equally, even though Diodotos is my heir in other things. This is because Themistokles will have paid in some way for the prophecy to be fulfilled. I pray that this will come to pass and that you will both prosper and bring honour to our family and my name.'

Themis' feelings were so confused that he sobbed aloud. He moved to a couch and sat staring at his scarred and reddened hands. Frog stood beside him.

Diodotos wiped tears from his face with the hem of his tunic. 'I suppose we had better keep this tablet safe,' he said. 'Nothing is ever going to compensate for losing Father, but … ' he gritted his teeth and walked out of the andron.

Phidias sat on the couch beside Themis. He lifted the boy's chin up with a finger so he could see his face. 'There's something else I've been planning,' he said, wiping away tears from Themis' cheek. 'I have the right to set up a statue in the Altis, so I've been working on a free-standing athlete. It's in the final stages. Shall we have a look?'

Themis stood up. He felt as bewildered as he had in those early days after his accident. There seemed to be no pattern, no recognizable shape to his world.

And the two pairs of brothers walked to the foundry in silence. There, they passed through courtyards until they came to a closed door. The guards gave them a lantern. Phidias opened the door and, in the centre of a small, cool room, they saw a tall shape swathed in linen.

Phidias carefully pulled the cloths off and revealed a young man tying a ribbon round his head. He was worked in wax over a base of clay. He was quite clearly a boy victor.

'To commemorate your victory in the eighty-seventh Olympiad,' said Phidias with a subdued flourish.

'How did you know?' Themis was astonished.

'Kadmos told me it was a foregone conclusion,' said Phidias.

'But the cost … ' Themis said, with a wondering shake of his head.

' … is not as much as "Athena's dues",' finished Phidias.

'However,' said Panainos, stepping up to the statue and taking the lantern from his brother. 'The face at present is not yours.' He pointed to the features. 'We are … in negotiation with the Elian Council that you should have a likeness and not just the standard head, as usual for boy victors.'

'My original design was for a portrait,' said Phidias 'with your wide-apart eyes and your crooked smile.'

'Maybe we should pay a poet to write you an ode. You could have it inscribed on the plinth,' suggested Diodotos, only partly in jest.

Themis could not help smiling. His confusion and shame forgotten for the moment, he felt his chest would explode with pride as he walked round the statue, looking carefully at the legs, the hands, the hair.

'But you have already made it partly a portrait, Uncle,' he said to Phidias. 'The toes are like mine, and the shape of the legs …' He tried to gather his thoughts. 'You said once it can be difficult being famous. I am looking forward to being famous in Athens, but I know there may be times when I will wish I wasn't. So it's better that we stick to the rules and keep the standard face. It's better looking than I am, anyway.'

Phidias sighed. 'So be it. Alkamenes will deal with it now, and a mason will add your name and achievement on the stone plinth, ode or no ode.'

'Do you have your drawings?' Themis asked.

'Of course.' Phidias said.

'May I have them?'

'They have your own face,' warned Panainos. 'I did some of them myself.'

'I'll send them to your room so you can pack them,' said Phidias as he and a slave re-covered the statue. 'We leave in three days.'

From Bernie's private diary. Friday August 6th 2010

Home

Suzanne actually asked me what Ibiza was like. That must be the first time since the accident she's asked about what I've been doing. Anyway, when I'd told her all about the music and the dolphins and the paella and so on, I asked her how she'd been, and forced myself to say, 'What's happening with Themis?'

She looked at me a bit strangely, but said, 'It's been amazing. He boxed and won in the Games. Then the priestess chased him and fell over a cliff on her horse. And then they found all the stuff she'd stolen – the gold and jewels from the statue of Athena in your project.'

My face must have shown I thought she was making it all up, because the next thing she said was, 'It does sound a bit over the top, doesn't it?'

'*Well, duh,*' I thought but I didn't say anything. She went on, 'But then again, it's all complete in my mind, with sounds and smells and the feel of the clothes and the sweat and the pain and so on.' She went over to her computer. 'And there's nothing I can find that makes any of it impossible.'

'What are you going to do about Gordon and the tests?' I asked.

'What do *you* think?' she said, really interested. 'Am I mental?'

I said I used to think she was and that was what's been frightening me, but now I'm not so sure. 'Why not just email and say you don't want to take part. He can't force you,' I said.

She looked so relieved! Maybe she cares what I think after all, like before.

She said, 'Right. I'll do that.'

'I asked you,' I said, 'because … well, I was talking to my dad about your – what do you call them, visions?'

'Your dad!' She was furious again. 'What's he got to do with anything?'

'He gave me the money to come and see you in Athens, that's what he's got to do with things!' I was pretty angry myself. 'He asked how you were getting on, and I told him.'

She looked a bit ashamed and said, 'I didn't know about that.'

'Whatever,' I said. 'He seems to think there must be some explanation for such clear visions. He asked if we'd heard of "genetic" or "adaptive" memory and was anyone investigating you. I told him about the Edinburgh people. He thought they might just confuse you and even start a file on you that you might have trouble with later. P'raps you should do some research on line and see what explanation seems to fit. There seem to be a few possible ones.'

She ran her fingers up into her hair like her head was aching, and moved it from side to side. 'What *is* that genetic stuff anyway?'

'It's not proved, Dad said, but it's like you remember stuff your ancestors did in your dreams or whatever.' She was terribly tensed up. I was trying to think of how to calm her down. I said, 'It comes through your genes, not your brain.'

She suddenly relaxed and looked at me with her old jokey smile and said, 'There's nothing that's not me in my jeans.'

I just said, 'Well thank god for that,' and started putting CDs and pens and stuff off her desk down my jeans (still too big). 'Not like mine … '

We got the giggles and Granola came up and joined in.

<<<

Next day, Themis was walking behind Lykinos and beside Kadmos in the victory procession. The whole of the crowd in the Altis was singing the hymn of gratitude to Zeus as they walked between the trees. Their voices rose into the morning air to fill the valley and echo from the hills.

When the hymn finished they waited their turn at the Table of the Wreaths near the Temple of Zeus. The judges and councillors stood in their purple robes behind it. The table, like the god's statue, shone with gold and ivory, where it wasn't covered by the wild olive wreaths each victor would receive. On either end, incense burned in crucibles on gilded tripods.

One by one, the victors' names and events were called out. The judges took it in turns to present the wreaths. The crowd behind and around the temple cheered and sang verses of odes to former victors. The diagonal morning sun lit the newly gilded carvings of Herakles' labours above the doors of the temple. It glanced off the great shield and the golden flying Nike on the roof. Themis tried to mark all these things in his mind so that he would never forget this moment.

Lykinos was announced. His crown of olive leaves was laid over his red victor's headband by Judge Perilaos. His trainer sang a verse of thanks, and they were ushered aside.

'Themistokles, son of Kallistos, of the Deme of Diomea in the city of Athens, victor in the boys' boxing, greetings,' called the herald. The scribe of the Official Lists of Victors sat at a smaller table under a slim cypress tree. He wrote Themis' name onto his scroll.

Themis stepped forward and bowed his head as Judge Iasos fitted the olive crown on it.

Looking up, Themis was surprised to see how exhausted the judge seemed. His usually wise, goat-like eyes were now dull, lifeless pebbles. Wasn't he angry at how Xenovia had used him in her plans to get rid of Themis? There was no expression in his voice when he said quietly, 'You could have given up twenty times. It is to your immeasurable credit that you did not.'

Themis murmured, 'My thanks are due to many people for that, including yourself.'

The judge nodded wearily once, inclining his head.

Fortunately, Kadmos showed no signs of breaking into song, so they moved away to cheers from the crowd.

Diodotos joined them.

'Can we get into the temple now?' he asked. 'It's closed to the general public, but I heard the victors could go in with offerings and prayers.'

Kadmos turned to Themis. 'I won't come with you. You have made me the proudest I have been for years. Not just because you won, but because you overcame difficulties most other people cannot even imagine. I salute you, Themistokles of Diomea, and look forward to seeing you back in four years to take another victory.' He pulled Themis towards him in a brief embrace, turned on his heel and left them.

'Wow,' whispered Diodotos.

Themis stared after Kadmos in wonder.

'Themistokles!'

Themis turned and found Efthimios at his elbow.

'I want to congratulate you,' said the weaver's apprentice. 'And to wish you an easy journey to Athens.'

Themis put his arms around Efthimios and gave him a strong hug. This was the only time he had ever touched him as a friend. 'Thank you for that, Efthimios,' he said, standing back. 'You helped me more than you can know.'

'I can guess,' said Efthimios. 'But you have also done me a favour. My boss is a gambler, like so many others. And he believed me when I told him to put money on you. So he is happy and I have a new position. I am no longer an apprentice, but a junior weaver. And I'll never have to go back to Uncle Thukydides!' His long face was actually smiling.

'I hope you're a senior weaver within the year,' said Themis.

'Give it two,' said Efthimios. 'And come back in four years. Maybe we will meet in the square pit.'

Themis laughed. 'I'd be honoured,' he said.

Efthimios left them and Themis turned to his brother. 'Come on,' he said with a grin, 'let's go and have one last look at all the work I did on the statue.'

But as always, his mood changed as they entered the temple and looked up, and up … past the golden robes and the gleaming chest to that calm, serious face. They stood in the doorway, silent and awestruck.

When they were pushed from behind, they stepped forward and followed the slow flow of worshippers round the reflecting pool in the floor and the statue base, to the offering table behind it. There, Themis left the wrappings from his hands and the scraper he had used to take the oil and sand off after his winning bout. He and Diodotos chanted together the daily thanksgiving prayer to Zeus, and joined the throng to move along the other side of the statue on their way out of the temple.

As they passed the staircase up to the gallery, Themis noticed it was closed with a heavy rope. He looked around. There were no priests or officials looking at them. He grabbed Diodotos' arm and stepped over the rope. They ran up the stairs to the gallery.

'You have to draw this to show your children,' said Diodotos, shaking his head in wonder.

'Hush,' warned Themis. 'You can hear everything we say from below.' He leaned over the rail and threw a slim purple ribbon over the arm of the Nike on Zeus' right hand. 'Thank you again,' he whispered.

He raised his eyes to the glowing amber of Zeus' gaze. 'See you in my dreams,' he murmured. 'Tell my saviour thank you, and I hope she prospers.'

'Your saviour?' whispered Diodotos. 'You mean Asterodia?'

Themis took a breath to deny this, but then thought better of it. 'Yes, of course, Asterodia,' he said out loud.

As he took one last look at Zeus' face he added silently, '*And my friend with the inadequate clothes.*' He grinned at his brother, and ran down the stairs.

'There's someone to see you,' said Frog.

Themis finished rolling up his parcel of paints and brushes. 'What sort of someone?'

'A guard someone,' said Frog. 'I don't think you should keep him waiting.'

Themis went to the door. A guard from the Altis command stood to attention by the road.

'You wanted me?' asked Themis.

'Yes, young master,' said the guard sternly. 'I have to tell you that we think we have found the man who was hunting you. We want you to come and identify him if you can.'

'That is … wonderful,' said Themis. 'I doubt I can identify *him*, but I'm pretty sure about his dog.'

'It was the dog that led us to him,' said the guard.

At the command post, Themis was shown into the prison. He saw a middle-aged man sitting on the floor in a cell by himself. He was the right height and strong enough to have been the man with the whip, but Themis had never seen that man's face.

The guards asked Themis to put this in writing. His hands were still clumsy, so a guard wrote and he signed.

Then they brought the dog to him. He took its face between his hands and looked at it carefully. The intelligent brown eyes looked back. 'Yes, this is the right dog,' he said.

'The man has admitted his guilt in the hope of lenience,' said the guard. 'He says he was paid a lot of money by a young man in a black cloak who never showed his face. The trial will be tomorrow. Will you be available?'

'Of course,' said Themis. 'What will happen to the dog?'

'Once the trial is over, it will be released.'

'Could I take him then? I owe him a bone or two.'

'If you want it, it's yours,' said the guard. Then he added with a grin, 'and congratulations on your victory!'

>>>

Chapter 50: going back

Themis sent me a thank you message! That gives me a buzz every time I think of it.

And Bernie made me laugh so much yesterday. It felt really good. I think I haven't been laughing much lately. I made a new resolution this morning: as well as being nice to people, lighten up and have fun. With reference to which … Ron and I had a pizza and then we walked in the park by the river. We sat on a bench, discussing trainers – shoes, not people. The sun came out and reminded him of what I'd said about competing without clothes. He asked me why I'd said that, had I ever tried it? He was teasing me and I thought, 'This could be fun.' So I made like it was a lie and said, 'Well, yes, I have. But in another life, when I was a boy.'

He just laughed and said, 'I think I'd rather not know about that.'

'Oh it was great,' I said. 'No one had any hang-ups about being naked. It was just the way things were, no shame.'

'In this part of the world,' he said, standing up, 'it's not shame that would be the problem. It's the cold, and the resulting shrinkage.' He was smiling down at me. I jumped up and punched his shoulder.

'Behave,' I said, and we ran most of the way to the station.

Now I need to get myself ready to practise tomorrow. Haven't done a vault for … nearly nine months. OMG!!!

What did Asterodia say? Name your fear.

I'm afraid my arms won't be strong enough and/or that I'll break my collarbone again. Really afraid.

And Granddad? He said 'courage is fear that has said its prayers'. I certainly know how to pray now, but who do I thank for getting well – and who do I ask to help me now? It's not that easy to have courage.

<<<

Themis was on a tall white horse. It was restless in the crush of village children. A girl pressed a small straw doll against his thigh. It wore a scarlet tunic and a victor's wreath. Her eyes glowed with adoration as she held it up to him.

'Thank you, thank you,' he kept saying, as all the children tried to make him take the ribbons and tiny dolls they had made. He chose a long green ribbon and the doll with the scarlet tunic. Their shouts changed from pleading to naming the price, as it had done in all the villages they had passed through on that long, slow journey to the port.

Themis reached into his purse and dropped a small coin into each of the two relevant hands. The adoring eyes smiled and turned away. The way opened and the horse could proceed.

Themis' own tunic was covered in previous offerings. 'No room to pin that one on you,' said Frog from beside Themis' knee. He was leading the pale yellow dog and a mule whose panniers had got heavier as they progressed. Villagers had presented them with food and wine for the voyage, and gifts to remind him to come back and win again at the next Olympiad.

Now they were approaching the port in the estuary of the Alpheios where they had left the Pelican all those months before. Themis could see Phidias' ship from five stades away. She seemed half the width and twice the length of the Pelican. She stood proud of the other craft tied up beside her.

There was still a lot of traffic on the road, but most of it was commercial. The visitors had left Olympia by land and sea immediately the Games finished. Tents had disappeared overnight, leaving the riverbanks bare and filthy, with piles of rotting rubbish and lines of fetid latrines.

The trial of the whipman had been short and he'd been found guilty. He'd been offered slavery or death and chose slavery. He was taken away to work in the copper mine. From the look of him, more scheming than malicious, Themis guessed he would find a way to escape.

Phidias' party had left at dawn that morning. At last they were passing along the causeway between the river and the wide lagoon.

The lagoon was utterly still, milky blue, reflecting the afternoon sky and the causeway's tattered edge of wispy trees. Beyond the heat-shimmer of the dunes, the sea stretched indigo to the horizon.

Asterodia, Agorakritos and Anthoussa were travelling with them. Anthoussa and the baby were in a covered litter. Judge Iasos had come to see his daughter off to her new life in Athens. He and Agorakritos were riding side by side, deep in discussion. Themis pressed his horse to come level with Anthoussa.

'I never thanked you for the dancing lessons,' he said quietly.

'I'm glad they were useful,' said Anthoussa, gesturing to the crown of olive leaves he wore.

'I shall dedicate it to Zeus when I get to Athens,' he said, 'at the precinct on Mount Hymetos.'

'You must tell me all about Athens on the ship. We will have plenty of time,' said Anthoussa.

'Would you let me draw your portrait on the ship?' he asked.

'You'd have to ask Agorakritos that,' she said with a smile. 'I'd rather you drew the baby, so I can remember what she looks like when she's grown.'

'I'd love to draw both!' said Themis with a grin.

The sound of cantering horses from behind them made them look round. The Commander of the Altis Guard and three soldiers slowed to a walk and took up an escorting position.

As they got nearer to the quays, Themis could see now that Phidias' ship was half-decked with scrubbed oak, pale against the weathered wickerwork gunnels. She was called the Dolphin. Her vertical stem-post at the bow was carved into a dolphin leaping up and laughing at the skies.

They all arrived on the dock. Loaded donkeys, handcarts and mules milled around. Stevedores called to each other and to sailors on the boats alongside. Smells of cooking and spices wafted from the taverns. A small stone altar stood near the Dolphin. A priest was tending the fire on it, its flames almost invisible in the westering sunshine. Asterodia went and stood near him.

A ladder led to the bow, while a gangplank was set amidships. The captain of the Dolphin stood to attention at its foot.

'Don't run!' called Ismini to her daughters as she followed them up, and they bounced onto the deck. Panainos nodded to the captain.

'Welcome aboard, sir,' said the captain with a twinkle in his eye.

Panainos climbed gingerly up the plank, and stepped on board. From the deck, he turned and took a long look at the crowded dock, the mirror of the lagoon and the hills beyond. Themis guessed he was going to make a painting – 'Farewell to Alpheios' perhaps.

The Commander spoke to Phidias. 'This is Yron,' he said, indicating one of his soldiers. 'He will carry the casket, and deliver it to the authorities in Athens. He'll have these two hoplite guards with him.'

'Thank you, Commander,' said Phidias.

Agorakritos was helping Anthoussa up the gangplank. The nurse followed with the baby. Themis ran up behind them, overtaking Diodotos, and jumped on board.

'Hey, take it easy,' cautioned Agorakritos with a laugh as the ship swayed. 'Save your enthusiasm for my workshop!'

'Why your workshop?' questioned Themis as Diodotos pushed him jokingly out of the way.

'I thought I might persuade you to desert Phidias and work for me once the commissions start coming in.' Agorakritos was moving with Anthoussa towards the cabins in the stern. 'It won't be for a month or two,' he called over his shoulder.

'Does that mean I might not have to support you, little brother?' asked Diodotos.

Frog handed the dog's rope to Themis, put down two heavy bags and went back for more. Themis shrugged his shoulders. 'I suppose it does. Just now it feels as though I don't have much control over what I'll be doing back in Athens.'

'Well that's as it should be,' said Diodotos seriously. 'You're far too young to make your own decisions!'

Themis dropped the rope, grabbed his brother round the waist and lifted him towards the gunnel away from the quay. 'Would you like to rephrase that?' he asked breathlessly, threatening to heave him over the side.

Diodotos could hardly speak for laughing and having the breath squeezed out of him. 'P'raps not too *weak*, though,' he managed to say.

Themis put him down.

'I promise,' Diodotos declared, 'I'll stop teasing you when you are older than me.'

'Huh!' Themis handed him the dog's rope and turned away to watch the stowing of all their boxes, bags and bundles. One slave dropped a bundle as he was going into the cabins. It unrolled slowly across the deck. Themis ran to gather it up.

He found himself looking at a drawing of the face of a young man with turbulent curls caught in a narrow ribbon. He had wide apart almond-shaped eyes, a rather short nose, and a mole on his full upper lip. The expression in the eyes was enquiring.

'Not a bad likeness,' mused Panainos over his shoulder.

'The chin's too square,' said Themis, looking up at his uncle.

'On the contrary,' Panainos said. 'Your chin will be even stronger in a year or two. Your voice is already breaking. You are no push-over, young Themis.'

At which Diodotos made a long face and said, 'Sadly.'

Down on the quay, Alkamenes had ridden up. He dismounted and went over to Phidias. Themis ran down the plank again to wish him farewell.

'This came for you after you left,' Alkamenes was saying to Phidias. 'Overland from Tainaron. The ship it was on was sunk in the harbour during a brawl over money. The messenger managed to save it.'

Phidias took the tablet. 'Ah,' he said. 'From Egypt,' and he broke open the seals. He was quiet for a few moments, then he nodded his head with a thoughtful smile. 'So, Alkamenes, I have a commission in the Nile Delta for the municipal buildings of a small town. Would you be able to help if it gets beyond the planning stage?'

'Keep me informed,' grunted Alkamenes without enthusiasm. 'Those Egyptians can be tricky customers.' He turned to Themis. 'Now I'm going to oversee the casting of your statue,' he said. 'When you come back in four years to defend your title, you'll find it somewhere in the Altis.'

Themis bowed to Alkamenes. 'Thank you. And for all I've learned from you. Farewell.'

'Farewell, young Themis. But I dare say I'll see you again. I have commissions in Evia and Egina soon.' He turned to Phidias. 'Pantarkes and Gulkishar will be on the next ship.'

Phidias smiled and hugged Alkamenes to his chest for a moment. 'You have been an outstanding colleague,' he said.

The calls of the stevedores were quieter now. The priest and Asterodia raised their voices and exhorted Poseidon to protect the Dolphin and all on board. The passengers and crew lined up at the rail, looking down at the little ceremony on the quay. After the hymn, the priest threw powder on the fire. Smoke billowed from the altar, first white, then turquoise, then green. Phidias handed the priest a purse. The priest bowed his head and murmured, 'The sacrifice to Poseidon will be on the third day.'

The Row Master came marching past the tavern at the end of the quay, followed by twenty strong men. They had been at the distant temple to the god of the sea, visible against the bright sky at the summit of the isthmus above Pheia.

'We'd better get on board,' said Phidias. 'The rowers don't like to be kept waiting.' He clapped Alkamenes on the shoulder and took Asterodia's arm to help her up the plank.

Themis followed. As the rowers stepped on to the crew's ladder, the ship wallowed. They took their places in the open part of the hold, their master facing them, under the tall stern. An order rang out. A sail unfurled and began to flap.

Judge Iasos hurried down the gangplank. On the quay he turned and looked towards his daughter. Anthoussa had the baby in her arms and waved. Agorakritos stood behind them. 'Come and see us soon,' he called. The judge nodded, but his words were lost as the cry went up to cast off.

The Dolphin moved slowly away from the quay as the sailors pulled in the plank and pushed her back. The sails caught the breeze and filled. As she freed herself from the land, the oars came out on both sides and the Row master's mallet began its rhythm.

A cheer came from the quay as the stevedores watched her pick up speed and the mallet began to demand full power. Themis stood near the stern with Phidias and Ismini, his hand on the yellow dog's head and Frog beside him. He could feel the sea breathing under him.

The line of the quay and the smoke of the town gradually faded to a trembling mirage in the heat of the sun's afternoon passage. Themis watched the wake turn white as they moved out into the deep blue sea. He remembered the crippling fears he'd been feeling the last time he was on a ship, and his heart lifted with thanks. '*Now I know what I can do, who I am,*' he thought. '*It'll be good to arrive as a champion in Athens.*'

And he lifted his face to the wind.

EPILOGUE – Now

It's Sunday August 15th 2010, and it's warm and sunny for once. Bernie walks into Sheepmount Stadium in Carlisle and looks around for Suzanne. There are groups of children of all ages running and throwing and exercising.

Bernie sees Suzanne sitting on the grass bank with sports bags and towels heaped near her. She's watching the marshals preparing the pole-vault pit on the other side of the track near the cherry trees.

'Hey, Suzz, you going to show us how it's done?' asks Bernie, sitting down beside her.

'Hope so.' Suzanne mimes biting her nails. 'What are *you* doing here? Don't tell me you're going to train for something.'

'Came to see you,' says Bernie. 'Oh, and Ron, of course. Is he here?'

'Over there, by the throwing cage,' says Suzanne.

'You texted things are good. Doing proper dancing again as well as training?'

'Yup.' Suzanne turns to Bernie. 'And Cassie's been working with me this last week. She says I'll be as good as I was in a month or two if I carry on.'

'Is that what you want? Not for your dad, or for Ron or whoever. Just for you,' asks Bernie.

'Yes. This is for me. I want to work at it like Themis did. Feel strong. Give it all I've got.' Suzanne takes a deep breath. 'When I'm jumping I feel like I'm flying. Nothing's quite as good as that.' Her face is alight and Bernie hugs her. 'Except,' she goes on, 'perhaps winning.'

'So you'll try out for the Olympics in 2012?'

'I'm not sure there'll be time,' says Suzanne.

'You've got two years,' urges Bernie.

'Less until I'd have to qualify. And you know how much a pole costs and I'll need five or six.' Suzanne's eyes are shining in spite of what she is saying. 'And there are other costs.'

'We could do a fund-raiser at school,' says Bernie. 'I bet you could beat the junior record within a couple of months.'

'Cassie says not to be in a hurry. There's the Commonwealth Games in 2014. And then Brazil in 2016.' Suzanne runs her hands down her legs, rolling the tops of her socks down as far as they'll go. 'She says not to push myself too hard too soon and burn out. And to keep working for my GCSE's, of course.'

'Ah ha,' says Bernie with a laugh. 'But what does she know?'

'She's only the best trainer in Cumbria,' says Suzanne, laughing too.

They sit and watch a group of younger kids doing push-ups on the grass in the middle of the stadium.

Suzanne says, looking straight ahead, 'Another thing I learned from Themis is to be grateful. I ... I have to thank you, Bernie. Without you, I'd probably be dead or a permanent vegetable.' She turns to Bernie, who has tears in her eyes.

'You're welcome,' says Bernie. 'Lots of other people were involved, too.'

Neither of them knows what to say next, so they stare at the children, who are now doing sit-ups.

After a few seconds, Suzanne stirs. 'Been thinking about that thing in my genes,' she says, dead serious.

'Hmm,' nods Bernie, keeping a straight face. 'And?'

'He's both-handed, you know. Ambidextrous,' says Suzanne. 'And so am I. I can use either hand for most things. I usually use my right because that's "normal", but when I'm on my own, I often use my left.'

'When you vault, I noticed. And in hospital, you wrote with your left.'

'And there's another thing,' Suzanne goes on. 'Saw a drawing of Themis. He had a mole exactly where mine is.'

'Really? On his lip?'

Suzanne nods. 'But it must be eighty generations ago. Could a mole survive in the genes that long? Wouldn't it get diluted or something?'

'It might get stronger. Survival of the fittest, remember?'

'Moles are not exactly fit.' Suzanne wrinkles her nose.

Ron throws himself down beside them with a grunt. 'Some moles, in some places, are extremely fit,' he says.

Suzanne laughs. 'Trust you,' she says.

'Talking of fit,' says Bernie to Suzanne, 'how often do you have to train?'

'Sprints most days. Weights and core strength three times a week.'

'Are these the signs of obsession,' Ron asks, looking up at the sky wth a slight smile. 'Or just the statement of a personal goal?' and he looks at Suzanne.

'Well,' says Suzanne with a conspiratorial smile at Bernie, 'when one obsession fades away, there's room for another, isn't there?'

Dear Reader

Thank you for reading this book!

The story is imagined, of course. Long ago, when I began writing about Themistokles son of Kallistos, it seemed to me that fiction writers were writing only about the Greek Gods and Heroes that we've all read about in the ancient myths. I wanted to write a story that could possibly happen to you or me at any time, a story that would answer the question, 'What was it *really* like to live in Athens in the 5th century BCE?' This was partly because I had spent more than 20 years of my own life in Athens, 25 centuries later!

The majority of my characters never lived (as far as I know!), and the personalities of those who did are imagined. However, I have tried to keep the story within the factual framework of what we know about 5th century BCE Greece (or Hellas as it was known then, and still is by Greek speakers), as well as the realities of life for a secondary school pupil in Cumbria in 2010CE.

However, I found that scholars through the ages have researched and disputed almost every facet of life in Classical Greece. In the words of Tom Holland, in the Preface to his book *Persian Fire*, 'Readers should certainly be warned that many of the details out of which this book's narrative has been constructed are ambiguous and ferociously disputed'. I have kept to what I found that was relevant to my story from primary sources like Herodotus, Pausanias, Thucydides and others, as well as painted vases and carved inscriptions. But none of these specifiy, for instance, the exact order of events at the Olympic Games. It must have changed many times during the twelve centuries or so that they were held. And I have used modern pronunciation to spell most of the names, as explained on page x.

After *The Boy with Two Heads* was published in 2012, the year of the London Olympics, 30th in the modern era, the main characters remained in my mind, insisting on growing up. Eventually, after many years of resistance, I began to record parts of their adult lives. This was before the Covid-19 pandemic that arrived in the UK in 2020.

The resulting Connection Trilogy is made up of *The Boy in Two Minds* (the revised version of the above title) as Book 1, *The Girl in Two Worlds* as Book 2, and *An Ancient Connection* as Book 3, which is planned for publication in 2022.

Author's Acknowledgements

Firstly, thank you to all those who reviewed *The Boy with Two Heads* (the earlier version of this story). The reviews encouraged and/or enlightened me and influenced this revised version and its sequels.

Many people helped and supported me while I wrote the original version and prepared this new edition. The following are among them.

Andrew Petch inspired me to begin and encouraged me throughout. Sally Brown, Vicki, Beth and Emily Richardson, Christina Steele, Tasia Vasilatou, and Gill Whittaker all had various drafts of the manuscript inflicted on them for comment. Alexandra Petch not only read the manuscript with minute care, but also took one of the photographs on the cover. Philippa Harrison and Marion Clarke read the final draft and Caroline Lawrence took an enthusiastic and helpful interest. David and Catherine Landsman gave me the opportunity for on-site research, which Costas Ioakimides and his family and students took part in. Helen Steele and the pupils of Thornhill School gave time and thought to the project. The sports staff and students of Queen Elizabeth's Grammar School, as well as Jean Cook and her Netherhall students, were patient with my questions. Brian Donnelly was my mainstay and support at all times, while Katy Donnelly and family kept me in touch with reality. Fliss Watts ironed out some important details and created the original artwork for the cover. Finally, Connie, Mike, Kate, Anna and Ted of Trifolium Books transformed my manuscript into a very fine book, now revised and transferred to Birkby Books.

Thank you all.

Twitter: @JuliaMNewsome, FaceBook: J M Newsome, author
Blog: www.kneadtowrite.blogspot.com

Birkby Books